England Manchester

The Constables' Accounts of the Manor of Manchester

from the year 1612 to the year 1647, and from the year 1743 to the year 1776.

Printed under the superintendence of a committee appointed by the municipal

council of the city of Manchester - Vol. 3

England Manchester

The Constables' Accounts of the Manor of Manchester
from the year 1612 to the year 1647, and from the year 1743 to the year 1776. Printed under the superintendence of a committee appointed by the municipal council of the city of Manchester - Vol. 3

ISBN/EAN: 9783337301781

Printed in Europe, USA, Canada, Australia, Japan

Cover: Foto ©Andreas Hilbeck / pixelio.de

More available books at **www.hansebooks.com**

THE

Constables' Accounts

OF THE

MANOR OF MANCHESTER

FROM THE

Year 1612 to the Year 1647, and from the
Year 1743 to the Year 1776.

PRINTED UNDER THE SUPERINTENDENCE OF A COMMITTEE
APPOINTED BY THE MUNICIPAL COUNCIL OF THE CITY
OF MANCHESTER, FROM THE ORIGINAL BOOKS OF
ACCOUNTS IN THEIR POSSESSION.

EDITED BY

J. P. EARWAKER, M.A., F.S.A.,

Editor of the "Manchester Court Leet Records,"

&c., &c., &c.

VOL. III.

FROM THE YEAR 1743 TO 1776,

WITH SEVERAL APPENDICES.

MANCHESTER:
J. E. CORNISH, 16, ST. ANN'S SQUARE.
—
1892.

HIS volume contains the Constables' Accounts for the Township of Manchester from October, 1743, to October, 1776—a period of 33 years—in which, however, there are several unfortunate breaks, many pages having been removed from the original book of Accounts before it was re-bound. The history of this book is somewhat curious. It was presumably kept in the custody of the Constables— most probably in the Boroughreeve's chest, in which the old records of the town were preserved—but some years after the sale of the manor of Manchester to the Corporation in 1845, it would appear to have been sold as waste paper, and in 1851 it came into the possession of the late James Crossley, Esq., F.S.A., who has left this memorandum in it :—" I purchased this volume from Phythian, a Bookseller in Shudehill, to whom it had been sold for Waste Paper, in Nov. 1851, and have since had it re-bound. Jas, Crossley, Dec. 1865." At the sale of Mr. Crossley's library a few years ago, it was bought by the Corporation, and is now kept in the muniment room at the Town Hall.

The contents of the only other earlier volume of the Constables' Accounts, now known, ended in 1647, and, with the exception of a portion of the Accounts for 1662 (printed in vol. ij., pp. 145-154), there is nothing to break this long period of nearly 100 years until the present volume commences in October, 1743. Many changes had taken place in this interval. The town of Manchester had greatly increased in size and importance, many new streets had been made, and new manufactures had been started—the increase of population having been very rapid. It was, however, still governed by a Boroughreeve and two Constables, and the duties of the latter officers remained pretty much as they had been previously, and as described at some length in the Introductions to the first and second volumes of these Accounts.

They still had to see to the punishment of all persons convicted of misdemeanours, who were either imprisoned in the DUNGEON, sent to the HOUSE OF CORRECTION, made to stand in the PILLORY, or tied to the ROGUES' POST and there whipped; or who were punished by being put in the STOCKS, ducked in the CUCKING STOOL (or DUCKING STOOL), or led through the town wearing the SCOLDS' BRIDLE. All these punishments will be found duly mentioned in this volume (see Index), and it was not till the beginning of the present century that they fell into disuse. Poor persons travelling from one place to another were still sent on by means of "passes," the want of which subjected them to arrest and to the punishment of whipping. But the number of these "whippings" was much less than in the previous century, even although we find an entry of no less than six women whipped on one occasion, one after the other, for immorality, so late as 1776 (see p. 343). The two Constables were assisted in their duties by a Deputy-Constable and a Beadle, the former of whom received £30 and the latter £10 per annum, as well as certain fees, &c. The Beadle was somewhat gorgeously arrayed in a "cap and gown," the cap being adorned "with gold lace and a tassel," and was provided with "scarlet stockings" (see p. 88), whilst both the Boroughreeve and the two Constables had "truncheons," mounted with silver and adorned with the arms of the town, as symbols of their official rank (see pp. 13, 62, 132, 244, 344).

We also find from these Accounts that it had by that time become customary to commemorate certain days in the year—such as the anniversaries of the King's Birthday, of the Gunpowder Plot (November 5th), of the Restoration of Charles II. (May 29th)—by bonfires and by banquets in the town, on which comparatively large sums of money were spent. The most important of the various battles on the Continent and in North America, which took place during the period covered by this volume (1743 to 1776) were occasions of great rejoicings in the town, which took the form of ringing the bells, bonfires, and banquets, with occasional balls and illuminations. Thus, in 1743 there were rejoicings for the battle of Dettingen (see. p. 1), in 1757 for the capture of Prague (see p. 91), in 1759 for the capture of Quebec (see p. 115), and so on.

There are many curious and interesting entries in this volume such as a payment for the relief, in 1753, of "two vagrants from Turkie" (see p. 60), whilst shortly afterwards there are entries for "relieving a passenger to Bengal" and one "from Bengal to Ireland" (see pp. 63 and 69). Such old customs as "throwing at cocks" at Shrovetide (see pp. 66, 178, &c.) and "lifting" on Easter Monday and Tuesday (see pp. 68, 163, 178, &c.) were prohibited, and in 1764 a woman was punished for the latter offence (see p. 164). There are several references to the "Shakers" (see pp. 227, 241, 256, &c.)—a body of religious fanatics led by John Lees and his daughter Ann Lees, or Lee—which came into notoriety at this time (1772-3). Combinations amongst workmen, or "unions" as we should now call them, were illegal, and were put down with a firm hand (see pp. 65, 106). The names of the more active of the local magistrates occur frequently, and there are many references to the various inns in the town, where Coroner's inquests, public meetings, &c., were held. The burials of suicides are once or twice mentioned (see pp. 14, 32), and the "window tax" is frequently alluded to; whilst those who were appointed to ascertain the number of windows in the various houses were designated "window peepers" (see pp. 82, 83, 134, 178).

The town during this period could boast of its Exchange, on the top of which Syddall's and Deacon's heads were put up in 1746 (see p. 33), its Infirmary, and, later on, its Lunatic Asylum. There are frequent references to the Fire Engines which the town possessed, and which were regularly exercised. There would appear to have been only two lamps in the town—one at the Dungeon, on Salford Bridge, and the other at the Cross, in the Market Place; but during the night the safety of the town was in the hands of "the watch," armed with "bills" (see p. 31). "Players" were occasionally "suppressed" (see pp. 12, 13), "ballad singers" were driven out of the town (see pp. 274, 278), and almost every year a new "cat o' nine tails" had to be supplied to the Beadle for the purpose of whipping the unfortunate men and women sentenced to that punishment by the magistrates. Two places in or near Manchester, one called "Poplar Temple" (see p. 8) and the other "Sodom" (see p. 83), merit attention, and have not yet been identified.

Manchester seems to have had bodies of soldiers quartered in it subsequently to 1757, generally Dragoons or Dragoon Guards, but occasionally a militia regiment, like the Lincolnshire Militia in 1760 (see pp. 117, 124), or a foot regiment, like the Welsh Fusiliers in 1771 (see p. 194), or a cavalry regiment, like the Royal Foresters in 1763 (see p. 147). These troops were always at hand in case of any riots or other disturbances, the magistrates profitting by the experience they had acquired in 1757.

Owing to the fortunate preservation of the unique set of Harrop's *Manchester Mercury*, now in the Chetham Library, I have been enabled to annotate a number of entries in and after the year 1757, by quotations from the columns of that old Manchester newspaper, and much curious information has been thus brought to light. The rejoicings at the Coronation of George III. in 1761 (see p. 127) and the visit of the King of Denmark to the town in 1768 (see p. 182) are events of some interest, very quaintly described, in addition to which many entries in the Accounts will be found more fully explained by the extracts from this newspaper given in the notes.

The most important entries in this volume, however, are the Accounts for the months of November and December, 1745, when the Young Pretender and his army were in England—during which time they visited Manchester twice. I have fortunately been able to illustrate the entries relating to these visits, which are historically interesting and important, by quotations from the *Journal* of Miss Elizabeth Byrom (Beppy Byrom as she was familiarly called), printed by the Chetham Society in 1857, and also from the *Diary* of Mr. Thomas Walley, one of the two Constables in that eventful year, which I discovered and published a year or two ago (see pp. 20 to 25). His brother Constable (Mr. William Fowden) was tried at Lancaster, for High Treason, in 1747, and although the Accounts for that year are unfortunately missing, I have been enabled to print in Appendix No. I. a very curious broadside, describing that trial and Mr. Fowden's return to Manchester, after he had been acquitted on the ground that he had acted from compulsion and not of his own free will (see pp. 354-5).

Second only to these entries of so much historical interest are the references to the riots in the town in 1757 and 1762. Of these, that of the 15th November, 1757, long known as "the Shude-hill Fight," was the most serious—many lives being lost, and much property destroyed. Full descriptions of these riots, taken from *Whitworth's Manchester Advertiser* and Harrop's *Manchester Mercury*, are printed in Appendices Nos. III., IV., and V., and will now be preserved to posterity, should the unique copies of these old newspapers, from which they are taken, ever be destroyed.

As in case of the previous volumes, every care has been taken to make the following pages an *exact* reproduction of the original, the proofs being compared line for line with the MS. Any necessary explanatory words or letters have been added in square brackets to make the meaning quite clear, but, as a rule, the Accounts in this volume have been carefully entered and are in an excellent state of preservation. The usual list of the curious dialect and obsolete words, which have been met with, will be found at the end of the volume in Appendix No. VI.

J. P. EARWAKER.

PENSARN, ABERGELE, NORTH WALES,
   APRIL, 1892.

[Constables' Accounts.][1]

••••••••••••

An acco^t of cash disburs'd by MILES BOWER and ROBERT HIBBERT,[2] *Constables of Manchestr*, elected Oct 12th, 1743.

[Disbursements]

1743.		£	s	d
October 15.	to two soldiers wives with passes to Scotland	0 ,,	1 ,,	,,
15.	p^d for conducting John Foster, a Coiner to Lancaster	1 ,,	10 ,,	,,
17.	to ffran: McCarroll disbanded from Dettingen[3] very lame	,, ,,	1 ,,	,,
22	to Patrick Ward disbanded from Port Mahon[4]	,, ,,	,, ,,	6
30	to a Boonfire, his Majesty's Birthday[5]	,,	6 ,,	,,

[1] As already pointed out in note 2 on p. 144 of volume ij., although the earliest volume of the *Constables' Accounts* ends in 1647, the next volume does not begin till 1743—an interval of nearly 100 years. With the exception of the accounts for the year 1662-3—already printed in volume ij., pp. 145 to 154—no records of any kind during that long period are at present forthcoming. Many changes had happened in that time. Manchester had very considerably increased in size, population, and importance, and, as will be seen by a perusal of the Accounts, there is a marked change in the character of the various entries.

[2] These two Constables were elected at the Court Leet held on the 12th October, 1743. (See *Court Leet Records*, vol. vij., p. 123.)

[3] The celebrated battle of Dettingen, between the English, Hanoverian, and Hessian troops against the French, was fought in the summer of this year, 1743, and resulted in a great victory for the allied forces. King George II. commanded in person, together with his son the Duke of Cumberland.

[4] Port Mahon is a seaport in the Island of Minorca, one of the Balearic Islands, off the coast of Spain.

[5] The birthday of His Majesty King George II. appears to have been annually celebrated by a large bonfire for the edification of the townspeople, and by a dinner given to the chief persons in the town.

		£	s	d
	to Mrs Dickanson[1] for Wine and broken Glasses...	4 „	3 „	2
	to sundrys for Ale to the soldiers[2] Ld Mark Kerr's Drag^s	1 „	1 „	„
Nov 5.	to a Boonfire as usual[3]	„	6 „	„
5	to Jos: Wrigley for repairing great Engine[4] p Bill	„ „	12 „	3
6	to Porters for playing att the Engines[5]	„	10 „	„
17	p^d for a general Warrant to search for Strollers[6] &c.	„	2 „	„
22	to Wm Dawson disbanded from Cottrells Marines	„	„	6
24	to Beadle for cleaning Dungeon[7] 6^d fresh Straw 8^d	„	1 „	2
Decr 7.	p^d high Constable for repairing Burden Bridge...	7 „	9 „	„
	Warrants to the Hamlets for their proportion of d°...	„	1 „	„
10	to Eliz: Price with two small children p pass...	„	1 „	6
11	Mittimus for 3 whores cau't this Sunday by Ch: wardens...	„	2 „	„
	to Cottrell and Ashton for tending them and Expenses	„	1 „	6
13	p^d Porters for playing the Engines[5]...	„	10 „	„
21	to James Smith disbanded from Otway's..	„	1 „	„

[1] Mrs. Dickanson kept one of the principal inns in the town, and the result of the feasting is shown by the amount paid for wine and broken glasses.

[2] These soldiers—Lord Mark Kerr's Dragoons—were probably stationed in Manchester at this time. This entry of the payment of £1 1s. to these men was subsequently referred to at the meeting of the Court Leet held on the 10th October, 1750, when it was decided that it should not be a precedent for future years. (See *Court Leet Records*, vol. vij., p. 195.)

[3] The anniversary of the Gunpowder Plot was also celebrated by a bonfire.

[4] There would appear to have been two fire engines belonging to the town at this time, the larger of the two is here referred to.

[5] There are frequent entries relating to the practice with the fire engines.

[6] Strollers might here simply mean strolling persons, or all kinds of travellers who had not "passes," as well as the large class of "rogues and vagabonds"; but, taken in connection with later entries, where "players" are mentioned, it probably means "strolling players."

[7] The Dungeon was, I think, the same as that mentioned in the earlier Accounts, and was situated on the bridge over the Irwell connecting Manchester and Salford.

		£	s	d
24	to Mark Pritchard and wife p pass ...	,,	1	,,
26	to Bellman for Crying a Towns meetings this day	.,	1	,,
	p^d Expenses of d° meeting, to fix new Surveyors of highways	,,	3	,,
26	writing Warrants to Hamlets to pay their Land tax	,,	2	,,
	D° to D° for new Surveyors 2/- a Quire paper 9^d	.,	2	9
	p^d Mr Jos. Birch for Beadles Cap and Gown[1]...	2	9	11
	to Bennet for making 'em[1]	,,	8	
	to two pair shoes 9/- two pair Stockens /6 dying 'em 4/- to painting and Gilding his Staff[1]	,,	19	
27	p^d for meat and lodging a strange Boy found in Garret lane			
31.	p^d half the Expence of fixing a Lamp at Dungeon...			
[1743-4]				
Jan 3.	to a disbanded soldier with 2 children to Wrexham	. .	.	
6.	to Manch^r jurors at Saml Jackson's Mosside. Tho. Hulbert Shot	. . .	.	
14	to Tho: Grimes and Jam: Douglass disbanded Scotsmen	.		
	to jurors a 2^d time on Acc^t of Hulbert's being shot, Casualty	. .		
21	to Goater Conduct money[2] with Jam^s: Barlow p ord^r of Sessions	. . .	.	
23	playing Engines and Oyl...	. .	.	
28.	to two disbanded soldiers with 4 children p passes	. .	.	
31.	Cleaning Dungeon and fresh straw...	. .	.	
Feb. 6	p^d high Constable for Ribble Bridge Walt. Cop [Walton Cop.][3] & Gov^n [wages][4]	. . . . .		

[Torn off]

[1] The Beadle's yearly outfit cost £3 16s. 11d. As appears from other entries, his two pairs of stockings were scarlet in colour.

[2] "Conduct money" was the money paid for forwarding soldiers or other persons, or the pressed men who had to serve on behalf of the town.

[3] "Cop," a word still in use in Lancashire for an embankment.

[4] That is, the wages of the Governor of the House of Correction in Manchester.

		£	s	d
	Warrants to the Hamlets for their proportion	.	.	.
	p^d Healey's Bill for Iron work about Engines[1]	.		
Feb. 17.	p^d Justicis Ctks for two press warr^{ts} for 2 Troops Kerrs Drag^s[2]	00 ,, 04 ,, 00		
	Messenger with them to Stretford and ffixton	00 ,, 00 ,, 08		
March 7.	Warrants to Hamlets for presentments to the Assises	00 ,, 02 ,, 00		
	parchm^t and writing Manch^r presentm^t 1/-	00 ,, 01 ,, 00		
	horsehire and expences to Oldham to deliver it	00 ,, 02 ,, 00		
7	Warrants to the Hamlets to return all papists &c[3]	00 ,, 02 ,, 00		
	Expences and trouble being out 3 days collecting their names and delivering above 60 Sumons's &c[3] ...	00 ,, 07 .. 06		
8	p^d porters for playing the Engines ...	00 ,, 10 ,, 00		
10	Warrants to the Hamlets for new overseers of the poor...	00 ,, 02 ,, 00		
10	Warrants to D^o to pay their Land tax	00 ,, 02 ,, 00		
	Warrants to D^o to pay window mony[e][4]	00 ,, 02 ,, 00		
12	Warrants to D^o for Militia to appear and produce their Arms, the Nation threatn'd with an Invasion[5]	00 : 02 : 00		
	p^d forCouncel's opinon howto Conduct ourselves[6]	01 : 01 : 00		

---

[1] See p. 2, note 4.

[2] See p. 2, note 2.

[3] A list had to be sent in, each year, to the Magistrates, of all the papists living in the various parishes, towns, hamlets, &c.

[4] The "window tax" was one which every householder had to pay, according to the number of windows in his house.

[5] The "threatened invasion" here referred to, was probably the threatened expedition of the French on behalf of Prince Charles Edward, the Young Pretender, as he is generally called. In February of this year, a French fleet, guarding transports carrying 15,000 French soldiers under Marshall Saxe, had set out from Dunkirk, but they were all dispersed by a very violent storm, which caused the loss of many of the transports, with all on board. A declaration of war on the part of the French was daily expected, and was in fact deliveerd on March 20th.

[6] The authorities of the town took Counsel's opinion as to the best course of procedure.

		£	s	d
16	Expences attending Dep: Lievten[u] all day at [Dangerous] Corner [1] ...	00	02	00
16	to John Johnson an old Serj[t] with a pass	00	01	00
18	horsehire and Expences to Lancaster being bound by Recognizance to prosecute ffoster the Coiner	01	11	06
	to John and James Ashton Evidences by Justices order	01	05	00
22	to Porters to keep off Crowd when Militia[2] appeard yesterday at Dangerous Corner with their old Arms ...	00	03	06
24	to Charles Dalton a sick old Soldier...	00	01	00
24	to Ringers this day the Judge in Town returning from Assises[3]	00	17	00
	p[d] Expences of treating him at Bull's head by Towns Consent[4]...	06	01	00
1744 [March] 26.	p[d] John Wroe for cleaning Dungeon Lamp 5 weeks	00	02	06
	p[d] M[rs] Robinson for 3 Gallons Oyl for D[o]	00	06	09
28	p[d] Porters for tending again at [Dangerous] Corner on Acc[t] of Militia[5] ...	00	05	00
30	to Manch[r] jurors when Betty Shawcross hang[d] herself in the house of Correction, Lunacy	00	01	04
	p[d] Beadle for going with Coroners Warrants &c	00	01	00
[April] 4.	to James Ritchie p pass to Portsmouth	00	01	00
. . .	to Geo: Parrot, his wife and 4 children from Scotland	00	03	00
. . .	p[d] Porters for playing Engines... ...	00	10	00
. . . . .	. . to some shipwreckt Sailors ...	00	01	06

[1] Dangerous Corner was a narrow entry leading out of St. Ann's Square, and in a room near there the Magistrates and Deputy-Lieutenants met for the transaction of public business.

[2] The militia assembled this day in the town in pursuance of the warrants issued on the 12th inst.

[3] The Assizes at this time were always held at Lancaster.

[4] The expenses of "treating" the Judge show that an entertainment on a somewhat large scale must have taken place at the Bull's Head Inn.

[5] See notes 1 and 2.

		£	s	d
. . . . two passengers with two Children		00	02	00
. . . [Warrants] to the Hamlets to impress men into his Majesty's service		00	02	00
. . . [Sp]ecial Messengers with d° by special ord' of Justices		00	02	06
. . . [Exp]ences this day warr being declar'd ag' ffrance [1]		02	11	00
. . . [precep]ts for new assessors		00	02	00
. [Mar]ket Lookers for Kidds [2] &c first half year		02	14	04
. . [Six] passengers to Dublin 3 sick ...		00	06	00
. . . . ing Jn° Thorp ats Smoot John and 3 others		00	01	00
[Mitti] mus for Mal Raynow, all cau't by Ch. Wardens...		00	02	00
. . . several Cries ag' Milk Kans standing in Streets [3]		00	01	06
May 13. to Pet. Pass with his wife and 3 children to Durham...		00	02	00
p^d M' Hodges for new Mutiney Act...		00	01	00

[Torn off]

[1] The declaration of war against England, which was delivered by the French to the English on the 20th March, 1744, was this day publicly proclaimed in the town, no doubt with considerable ceremony, the amount expended being large, judged by other entries.

[2] "Kids," an old word for bundles of faggots. From an entry in the *Court Leet Records*, 5th May, 1732, it is probable that special officers were appointed to look after the stacks of "kids" used by the bakers, to see that they were not left in any places dangerous to the town, should they get on fire. This entry is as follows (see *Court Leet Records*, vol. vij. p. 11) :—

"We the Jury of this Court do revise the order made Michaelmass 1723 concerning the Bakers Stacks of Kids of Gorse and Wood and that all the Bakers in Town have notice thereof."

[3] At the Court Leet held on the 19th April, 1744, the following order was made by the Jury (see *Court Leet Records*, vol. vij., p. 131) :—

"Whereas severall good Orders (to witt) one for five Shillings for every Offence in the Year 1731 and another for ten Shillings for every Offence in the Year 1733 have been heretofore made by Jurors of this Court for preventing the Milk people suffering their horses to stand Loaden with Milk-kans at Smithey door and other places in this Town to the great Hinderance and Danger of the Inhabitants thereof passing and repassing about their Lawfull Occasions Notwithstanding which the said Orders are still neglected, therefore we the Jurors aforenamed do hereby amerce every person who shall after the first day of May next offend against any of the said Orders in Thirty nine Shillings each for every such Offence and do order the Constables to give Notice hereof by the Towns Cryer three severall days at least."

It is the notice given by the "Towns Cryer" which is referred to in the text.

		£	s	d
	p^d D° for new Press Act with the amendment...	00	01	06
[May] 13	to Beadle for going with Coroners Warr^t Mary Kirkman a Girl killd with a Cart in Acres Gates	00	01	00
	to Manch^r jurors who attended 1 4 Coroners ffee 15 4	00	16	08
25	to wid: Bold with 3 children to South-wales	00	02	00
	Warr^{ts} to Hamlets for new Window Duplicates [1]	00	02	00
29	Boonfire K. Cha. 2 Restoration [2] ...	00	06	00
30	to Beadle with Coroner's Warr^{ts} John Jackson a Strang^r drownd at Bolton wheel with bathing	00	01	00
	to 4 men for carrying him to the Lodge [3] and Ale...	00	01	06
	to Manch^r jurors 1 4 Cororers ffee 15 4	00	16	08
	p^d for his Coffin 4 – Church dues 22^d	00	05	10
31	to Cha: Smith. John Jones. and 6 more shipwreckt Sailors	00	04	00
June 1.	Warrants for Surveyors to appear at [Dangerous] Corner	00	02	00
1.	Warrants for Constables to appear with their prest men	00	02	00
2.	Straw. 8^d cleaning Dungeon 8^d... ...	00	01	04
2.	to Cha: Dutton from Cottrell's Marines sick	00	01	00
4.	playing Engines 10 – new ropes 4 –	00	14	00
5.	to John Dickanson p pass to London	00	00	08
8.	p^d high Const for conveying Vag^s [vagrants] and relief of prisoners ...	06	10	07
	Warr^{ts} to the Hamlets for their pro-portion...	00	01	00
9.	p^d Mrs Dickanson expences of privy Watch this night [4]	00	18	02

---

[1] This relates to the window tax. (See p. 4, note 4.)

[2] This is the third occasion, which was yearly celebrated by a bonfire, of the anniversary of the restoration of King Charles II.—May the 29th.

[3] The "lodge" here referred to was probably a small building standing in the churchyard, used as a mortuary. (See *Constables' Accounts*, vol. ij., p. 5, note 4.)

[4] This was the "privy watch," or "special watch," held at Whitsuntide to clear the town of all suspicious characters.

		£	s	d
10.	Warrant to impress 2 Baggage horses to Chester	00	02	00
	Messenger to fetch em back 6/- keeping all night 2/6...	00	08	06
11.	to a Boonfire his Majesty's Inauguration [1]	00	06	00
16.	to Dan¹ Bewith his wife and one child	00	01	06
24.	Warrants to pay Land tax...	00	02	00
28.	to John Douglass and wife p pass to Chelsea	00	01	00
July 8.	to Alex: Le Brun with his wife and child	00	01	06
8	to Ann Nichols and Mary Wood 2 Soldiers wifes & 1 child	00	01	06
9	to Beadle with Coroners warrⁿ Sam¹ Wright a Soldiers Boy drownd near Roch-house in Parsonage	00	01	00
	Manchʳ jurors 1/4 Coroners ffee 15/4	00	16	08
10	pᵈ Porters for playing Engines... ...	00	10	00
17	Beadle with Coroners warrants Eliz Thorp in Miln gate poisond herself by drinking a Decoction of ffox Glove leaves	00	01	.
	Manchester jurors 1/4 Coroners ffee 15 4	00	16	.
22.	Manchʳ jurors at Poplar Temple,[2] Walsh's child drownd in Mʳ Chetham's Kannal at Smedley	00	01	[Torn off]
Aug 3.	to two scots women with 3 Children to Perth	00	02	.
3.	Warrants for presentments to the Assises...	00	02	.
	Writing presentment and parchment 1/- Expences 1/-	00	02	.
	Warrⁿ for Lycencing day on 13 ...	00	0:	.
Aug 3.	pᵈ high Constable for Governors wages[3]...	01	04	06

---

[1] Yet another occasion to be commemorated by an annual bonfire—the anniversary of the "inauguration" of his Majesty King George II.

[2] I cannot at present identify this place ("Poplar Temple") in the neighbourhood of Manchester.

[3] That is, the Governor of the House of Correction.

		£	s	d
	warrants to the Hamlets for their proportion	00	01	00
6	p^d Beadle with Coroners warr^t Sara ffurnival a child drownd in Mr Edge's Brick Croft at Sudehill	00	01	00
	to Manch^r jurors 1 4 Coroners ffee 15 4	00	16	08
9.	to Sam: Lightboun for mending 15 Buckets	00	10	00
17.	to Ringers, Judge Burnet passing thro' Town [1]	00	17	00
18.	Mittimus for W. Beckwith with a. forgd pass & tending him...	00	03	02
18	Expences of apprehending and tending Partington by Mr Dukinfield's [2] special Warrant...	00	03	06
19	3 passengers	00	01	09
20	p^d high Constable for repair of Irk & Windy bank Bridges	18	09	04
	Warrants to Hamlets for their proportion	00	01	00
20	playing Engines p^d Porters	00	10	00
	Oyling Leathern pipes 3 6 Oyl 3 8...	00	07	02
21.	new Ley Book 20 - Expences Leying Ley, 3 – 5 – 3.	04	05	03
Sept 25.	playing Engines...	00	10	00
29	Warrants to pay Land tax 2 - D^o window mony 2 -	00	04	00
29	to Mr Croxton 2 years rent for Engine house to this day	04	00	00
	Sweeping Steps at Miln Brow and Salf^d [Salford] whole year	00	08	00
	p^d Market Lookers for Kids [3] latter half year	02	17	00
	to sundry passengers by Mr Bower [4]	00	06	06

[1] On this occasion the Judge does not seem to have been "treated" anywhere by the town, as on a previous occasion. (See p. 5, note 4.)

[2] This would be Robert Dukinfield, Esq., an active magistrate, resident in Manchester.

[3] See p. 6, note 2.

[4] Mr. Miles Bower and Mr. Robert Hibbert were the two Constables of Manchester at this time.

	£	s	d
to sundry passengers by Mr Hibbert [1]	00 : 06 : 00
to Deputy's [2] Sallary 10^l Beadles D^o 7^l	17 : 00 : 00
p^d for this Book to Mr Newton... ...	00 : 10 : 06

paid in all ...	117 :	11 :	6
Balł due to the Town ...	4 :	17 :	8¾

122 :	9 :	2¾

An acco^t of cash reced by MILES BOWER and ROBERT HIBBERT, *Constables of Manchester.*

[Receipts]

1743-4.

		l . s . d
	By Cash from the late Constab' Balł in their hands	12 : 07 : 5¼
	By Cash from ·Sun ffire Office for use of the Engines	00 : 10 : 0
	By Sale of John Jackson's Cloths, a Stranger drownd	00 : 09 : 06
Decr 7.	By Cash from the Hamlets their two thirds of 7-9-0 for repairing Burden Bridge...	04 : 19 : 4
Feb 6. 1744	By Cash from the Hamlets their two thirds of 2-1-9 for repairing Ribble Bridge Walton Cop [3] & Gov^n wages...	01 : 07 : 10
June 8.	By Cash from the Hamlets their two thirds of 6-10-7 for Conveying Vagrants and relief of poor prisoners	04 : 07 : 00½
Aug. 3.	By Cash from the Hamlets their two thirds of 1-4-6 for Governors wages	00 : 16 : 04
20.	By Cash from the Hamlets their two thirds of 18-9-4 for repairing Irk and Windy bank Bridges...	12 : 06 : 5½
	By Cash from the Misegatherers ...	85 : 05 : 3½

rec^d in all	122 : 09 : 2¾

---

[1] See p. 9, note 4.

[2] That is, the Deputy-Constable, who received £10 a year, whilst the Beadle had £7.

[3] See p. 3, note 3.

Nov 22ᵈ 1744. We the Jurors of this Court Leet have perus'd the Accounts of Mᴿ MILES BOWER and Mᴿ ROBᵀ HIBBERT, late Constables, and do find in their hands four pounds seventeen shillings and Eight pence three farthings which we order them to pay into the hands of Mᴿ JOHN UPTON and Mᴿ THOMAS TIPPING, and do allow the same.

(*Signed*) THOˢ CLOWES[1]
JOSEPH ALLEN
ROBᵀ AYRTON
JOHN CLOWES
JOHN CLOUGH
JOS. BANCROFT
RA. WOOLMER.

---

[1] These were some of the Court Leet Jury at the Michaelmas Leet held on the 4th October, 1744 (see *Court Leet Records*, vol. vij., p. 133), and afterwards adjourned.

[Constables' Accounts.]

[4th Oct., 1744, to 18th Oct., 1745.]

••••••••••••

An acc^t of cash disbursd by JOHN UPTON & THO:
TIPPING,[1] *Const[ables of Manchester]*, chosen Oct 4.
1744.

[Disbursements]

1744		l	s	d
[Oct] 4	To a woman with a pass	00 :	00 :	06
11	to a Boonfire[2]	„ „	6 „	„
23	Expences at [Dangerous] Corner[3] with the Justices &c	„ „	1 „	3
24	to Patrick Coyney p pass to London..	„ „	1 „	„
	to sundry Expences in Suppressing Players[4]	„ „	2 „	2
30	Boonfire his Majestys birth day[5] ...	„ „	6 „	
30	Wine to Mr Bartholomew[6] p rec^t ...	2 „	9 „	„
30	Warr^{ts} for Militia to appear and produce their Arms...	„ „	2 „	„
Nov. 1.	to John Macnabb and wife dischargd from St Clairs	„ „	1 „	„
3.	to Joseph Mucklewain a Sick Passenger	„ „	1 „	„
5.	Boonfire as usual	„	6 „	
5.	p^d porters for playing Engines... ...	„ „	10 „	
8.	Mary Clapham with a pass	„	„	6

---

[1] These two Constables were elected at the Court Leet held on the 4th October,
1744. (See *Court Leet Records*, vol. vij., p. 133.)

[2] The object for which this bonfire was provided is not stated.

[3] See p. 5, note 1.

[4] There are other entries as to "players" being suppressed. (See also p. 2, note 6.)

[5] The birthday of the King, George II., was an annual festival in the town. (See
p. 1, note 5.)

[6] This year the entertainment to the gentry of the town was held at Mr. Bartholomew's, and cost only £2 9s., as compared with the £4 3s. 2d. paid at Mrs. Dickanson's
last year "for wine and broken glasses." (See p. 2, note 1.)

		l	s	d
9.	further Expences in Suppressing Players [1]	,,	1	,,
12.	to Geo: Atkinson p pass to Clitheroe	,,	,,	6
17.	to a disbanded Soldier and wife with a pass to London	,,	1	,,
21.	to Manchester jurors. Fra: Baxters child drown'd in Salford	,,	1	4
21.	to a Passenger	,,	1	,,
21.	Warrants to Hamlets for Militia to receive new Arms	,,	2	,,
Dec' 3.	to Henry Burton with 3 children passing to Durham	,,	2	,,
5.	p^d high Constable for repairing Ribchester Bridge & Walt[on] Cop. [2]	2	0	6
	Warrants to the Hamlets for their proportion	,,	2	,,
11.	Sara Humphreys and two children to Wrexham	,,	1	6
15.	p^d porters for playing Engines	,,	10	,,
25.	Warrants to pay Land tax	,,	2	,,
	Lighting Cross & Dungeon Lamps 4 weeks 4'- p^d for Wake[?wick] 1^d	,,	4	1
	to Mr Jos: Birch for Cloth for Beadles Cap & Gown	2	9	,,
	p^d Bennet for making and Trimming.	,,	8	,,
	p^d Mr Byrom for Gold ffringe and Lace	,,	10	,,
	p^d Mr Blinkhorn for his hose 6'- dying em 3 6 his shoes 9/-	,,	18	6
	painting his Staff [3]	,,	2	6
	to Mr Coppock for new Painting Deputy's Truncheon [3]	,,	6	,,
26.	to Bellman for a Towns meeting about new Surveyors &c	,,	1	,,
[1744-5]	p^d Expences at D^o meeting to Mrs Dickanson	,,	5	,,
Jan. 5.	to two soldiers wives and children with passes	,,	3	,,
14	to Manch^r jurors on view of Matthew Crompton a Boy	,,	1	4

[1] See p. 12, note 4.   [2] See p. 3, note 3.

[3] It appears from these entries that the Deputy-Constable had an official staff (here called a " truncheon "), as well as the Beadle.

		l	s	d
	to Coroner for the Inquisition hangd himself ith Parsonage	„	„ 15 „	4
16.	to Manch^r jurors at Phil. Antrobus's in Newton Lane when John Leigh his Apprentice had also hangd himself	„	„ 1 „	4
	to Cottrell for going with both the Coroners Warr^{ts} &c	„	„ 2 „	„
17.	p^d for hire of a Sledge to draw Leigh[1] upon making his Grave &c he being found ffelo dese, & buryed in the highway at Barlow Cross[2] 5/- several persons for Assistants 4/6	„	„ 9 „	6
19	to Manch^r jurors at a 2^d meeting ab^t Matthew Crompton	„	„ 1 „	„
	to P. Cottrell[3] for attending and fetching in Witnesses both days	„	„ 1 „	„
Jan 24.	to Joseph Ellis and Robt Jagger with passes	00	02	00
Feb. 5.	Jane Johnson & Jane Smith 2 Soldiers wives with Children	00	03	00
10	to Sara Hughs a big bellyd passenger to Namptwich	00	01	00
18	rep^d Mr Tipping w^t he had given to several Passengers	00	06	00
22.	p^d high Const: for repairing public Bridges, Conveying Vagrants and Governors[4] wages	37	09	03
	Warrants to the Hamlets for their proportion	00	02	00
23.	p^d for Lighting Lamps this moon ...	00	03	10
26.	to John Bennet a sick passenger ...	00	01	00
March 6.	to Alice Worsley for lodging and dieting a Sick Stranger	00	05	00
	p^d Mr Dickin for Physic for D^o ...	00	01	06
6	to Peter ffury a disbanded Soldier ...	00	00	06

[1] This is an interesting entry, showing how the body of a suicide, on whom the Jury had brought in a verdict of *felo-de-se*, was dragged on an open "sledge" to Barlow Cross, where he was buried at the point where four roads met, with a stake, most probably, driven through his body, as was then customary.

[2] Barlow Cross was somewhere near Ancoats. (See *Court Leet Records*, vol. i., p. 34, and vol. ij., pp. 11 and 300.)

[3] Peter Cottrell, whose name frequently occurs in these Accounts, was the Bailiff.

[4] That is, the Governor of the House of Correction.

		l	s	d
6	Warrants to Hamlets for presentments to the Assises	00	02	00
	parchment and writing Manchester presentment..	00	01	00
	horsehire to Bolton to deliver it 1/8. Expences 2/-	00	03	08
15.	p^d high Constable for repairing Ribchester new Bridge	02	00	06
	Warrants to the Hamlets for their proportion	00	02	00
	playing Engines and Oyl, after fire at Spread Eagle¹ Salford	00	10	06
	to a disbanded Soldier with his wife and 3 children	00	02	06
	Warrants to pay Land tax 5 April 2/- D^o for window mony 2/-	00	04	00
16	to James Oldham for meat and lodging Jane Carter & child a sick passenger nine days and nights...	00	09	00
1745. April 5.	to S. Lightboun for Oyling and cleaning Engine Leathers & Buckets ...	00	14	10
	Warrants for Surveyors of the highways to appear &c.	00	02	00
8.	Mary Crawford and 4 children with a pass	00	02	06
8.	p^d John Smith Grocer for Oyl p rec^t	00	02	04
9.	Warrants for new Overseers of the poor	00	02	00
11.	to Mr Newton for new Mutiney Act...	00	01	06
15.	p^d for new Press Act...	00	00	09
20.	p^d Market Lookers first half year p rec^t	02	18	00
22.	p^d porters for playing Engines... ...	00	10	00
	Warrants for new Assessors of Land tax	00	02	00
25.	to John Cummins a disbanded soldier very lame	00	01	00
May 1.	to James Ritchie a disbanded Serj^t going to Chelsea...	00	01	00
2.	Expences at Sessions about Cornbrook Bridge, & transporting Ellen Clay ...	00	13	00
6.	p^d for a warrant to press a horse for a lame Serj^t...	00	02	00

¹ This entry gives us the name of one of the public houses in Salford at this time.

		l	s	d
7.	to Jane Jeffrys and 4 children p pass to Wales	00	02	00
16	press Warrants to the Hamlets... ...	00	02	00
18	five Passengers	00	02	06
26	Mittimus for a whore cau't this Sunday morn in the Exchange	00	02	00
	to Ashton for tending her...	00	00	06
29.	a Boonfire [1]...	00	06	00
	press Warr'ᵗˢ a second time to the Hamlets	00	02	00
	pᵈ Sundry Expences of privy Watch going about...	00	12	06
[June] 8	playing Engines...	00	10	00
11	a Boonfire his Majesty's Inaugura-tion [2]	00	06	00
June 13.	Warrants for new window Duplicates	00	02	00
15.	Warrants for Surveyors to appear &c.	00	02	00
15.	Sundry Expences about a Dumb-man	00	03	10
24.	Warrants to pay Land tax...	00	02	00
27.	to Matthew Matthews and wife p pass	00	01	00
July 1.	to a Soldiers widow going to Preston	00	01	00
8.	pᵈ high Const. for repairing Radcliff, Ringley & other Bridges	09	05	09
	Warrants to the Hamlets for their proportion	00	02	00
13.	to Margret Pratt and children with a pass	00	01	00
16	playing Engines...	00	10	00
18.	Alex. McKie and wife from Royal Irish Dragoons	00	01	00
	new Ley Book 20/- Expences at Laying Constable Ley 50'-	03	10	00
	pᵈ Mr Battersbee for a Lock for Stocks [3]	00	01	00
25.	pᵈ Belman for sundry Cryes	00	02	02
Augᵗ 6.	pᵈ Jos: Wrigley for repairing Engines	00	02	01
15.	jurors at Broughton, Geo: Hollands child killd by a Cart wheel	00	01	04

---

[1] In commemoration of the 29th May, the anniversary of the restoration of Charles II. (See p. 7, note 2.)

[2] This was an annual celebration. (See p. 8, note 1.)

[3] The stocks have been referred to in previous accounts. (See *Constables' Accounts*, vol. ij., p. 42, note 2.)

		l s d
23.	p^d high Const. for conveying Vagr^{ts}, poor prison^{rs} & Gov^{rs} wages	05 : 03 : 08
	Warr^{ts} to the Hamlets for their proportion...	00 : 02 : 00
	Expences privy Watch	00 : 16 : 00
23.	Warrants for presentments to the Assises...	00 : 02 : 00
	writing presentment 1/- Expences with high Const. 1/-	00 : 02 : 00
24.	p^d John Healey Smith for repairs at Engines	00 : 07 : 09
26.	p^d porters for playing Engines... ...	00 : 10 : 00
	p^d Ringers on his Majesty's safe Arrival to England [1]	00 : 15 : 06
Sep^t 12.	Warrants for Lycencing day	00 : 02 : 00
27.	D^o to pay Land tax 2/- D^o to pay Window mony 2/-	00 : 04 : 00
29	Sweeping Steps at Milnbrow & Salford Bridge whole year	00 : 08 : 00
Oct 3.	Warr^{ts} to return Lists of ffreeholders.	00 : 02 : 00
	paper and writing 7 lists	00 : 07 : 00
	p^d Ringers when News came of the Emperor being chosen [2]	01 : 01 : 00
6	p^d Ringers this day Genl Cholmondeley being march'd into town with 1,700 soldiers going ag^t the Rebellion in the North [3]	00 : 10 : 00
	p^d for a warrant to keep a Strict Watch	00 : 02 : 00
10.	p^d at Bull's Head and other Expences on the Officers and soldiers and for Guard rooms &c whilst Gener^l was here	02 : 14 : 10
	p^d for 3 press warr^{ts} for their Carriages	00 : 06 : 00
	p^d Mr John Kenworthy on Acc^t of the Militia...	00 : 13 : 00
	p^d Marketlookers latter half year ...	02 : 15 : 00

---

[1] The King had been abroad this year in Hanover, but returned in haste to London on hearing of the landing of the "Young Pretender" in Scotland.

[2] This news seems to have excited the enthusiasm of the Manchester people, and the Constables paid the ringers £1 1s—much more than on any other occasion in these Accounts.

[3] This is the first reference in these Accounts to the invasion of the Prince Charles Edward, the "Young Pretender" as he was generally called. He had landed in Scotland in July of this year, 1745, and had succeeded in capturing Perth on the 3rd September, and Edinburgh on 17th September.

	l	s	d
p^d Mr Robinson for Oyl for Dungeon & Cross Lamps	00 : 15 : 02		
p^d Messenger with an Express to Lord Derby's	01 : 01 : 00		
14. playing Engines 10/- rent for D° to Mr Croxton 2^l	02 : 10 : 00		
to passengers &c paid by Mr Upton and Mr Tipping...	00 : 19 : 06		
to Mr Wright Brasier for repairing Engines	01 : 10 : 10		
Deputy's Sallary 10^l Beadles wages 7^l	17 : 00 : 00		
tot p^d ...	120 : 7 : 3		

An acco^t of Cash rec^d by JOHN UPTON & THO^s TIPPING.

[Receipts]

1744.

Oct 4.	By Ballance from the late Constables	4 – 17 – 8¾
	By Cash at sundry times from the Hamlets being their two thirds of the five mony Warr^{ts} p^d as p our Acco^t ...	37 – 6 – 5½
	By Cash from the Mise Gatherers ...	82 – 18 – 1
	tot rec^d ...	125 – 2 – 3¼
	p^d as on the other side ...	120 – 7 – 3
	Batt due to the Town ...	4 – 15 – 0¼

Novr 7. 1745. We the Jurors of this Court Leet have perus'd the Acco^t of MR JOHN UPTON and MR THOMAS TIPPING late Constables & do find in their hands four pounds fifteen shill^{gs} and one farthing wth we order them to pay into the hands of THO^s WALLEY Esqre & MR WILL^m FOWDEN present Constables and do allow the Same.

(Signed)   JA. MARSDEN [1]
RA. WOOLMER
JA^s LIPTROTT
CHA^s NEWDIGATE
JAMES EDGE
JOHN CLOUGH.

---

[1] These were some of the Jury at the Court Leet held on the 16th October, 1745 (see *Court Leet Records*, vol. vij., p. 142), and afterwards adjourned to 7th November, at the Bull's Head.—(*Ibid.*, p. 146.)

[Constables' Accounts.][1]

[18th Oct., 1745, to 6th Oct., 1746.]

• • • • • • • • • • • •

An acco[t] of cash disburs'd by THOMAS WALLEY Esq[r] and WILLIAM FOWDEN,[2] *Constables of Manchester.*

[Disbursements]

		l	s	d
1745				
Octob[r] 19.	p[d] ffrancis Read for lighting Dungeon and Cross Lamps	00	00	10
19	writing Warr[ts] to the Hamlets for Militia to appear on 1st Nov[r] ...	00	02	00
25.	to Margret Hand and child p pass from Battereans Reg[t]	00	01	00
25.	p[d] for a pass for Rose M[c] Cloud, an Irish woman very big[3]	00	02	00
	gave her when she went away ...	00	00	06
30.	to a Boonfire his Majesty's birth day[4]	00	06	00
30.	p[d] M[rs] Bartholomew for wine this day to drink the healths p Bill ...	05	09	08
Nov[r] 1.	Expences tending Deputy Lievtenants this day, Militia muster'd ...	00	01	09
5.	Boonfire as usual	00	06	00
7.	to a disbanded soldier, with his wife and two Children p pass[5]	00	02	00
8.	p[d] 8 hired watchmen last night, by an especial order of the Justices ...	00	05	04

---

[1] This year's Accounts have already been printed, but with little or no annotation, as an Appendix to Volume vij. of the *Court Leet Records*, 1731 to 1756, pp. 250 to 260.

[2] These two Constables were elected at the Court Leet held on the 16th October, 1745. (See *Court Leet Records*, vol. vij., p. 142.)

[3] That is "big with child." Pauper women who were *enceinte* were sent on from parish to parish till they reached the place of their birth, so as to avoid burdening any other parish with the cost of the maintenance of the child.

[4] This was an annual festival in the town (see p. 1, note 5.)

[5] Poor people, travelling from one part of the country to another, were passed on from parish to parish by the respective Constables and other officers by means of "passes" signed by one or more magistrates. If they travelled on foot without these "passes" they were liable to arrest and imprisonment as "rogues and vagabonds."

		l	s	d
9.	p^d 4 D^o last night p D^o orders 8^d p..	00	02	08
10.	p^d 4 D^o last night p D^o orders ...	00	02	08
11.	p^d for Straw for Dungeon to John Stringer	00	00	06
12.	writing warrants to Hamlets to raise Militia, on 14 instant	00	02	00
12	p^d special Messengers with D^o by order of Dep. Lievtenants	00	02	03
12.	p^d for a Grate for Watchhouse 10^d seting it 8^d a Load Coal 9^d	00	02	03
12.	fform, Tonges, and ffire shovel for d^o	00	01	10
14.	tending Dep. L^{tt} [Deputy Lieutenants] all this day[1] 3 Co^t ffoot and one Troop of Horse Militia[2] came in, and to Cottrel and Ashton for Errands &c	00	04	03
15.	tending Dep. L^{tt} all this day, 2 Co^t more of Blackburn Militia[2] came in	00	02	00
15	Coal & Candle for Guard house 11½^d d^o for Watch house 9^d Quire paper 9^d	00	02	05½
16.	to Ann Walker a soldiers wife p pass	00	00	06
17.	Coal to the Guard house	00	01	00
18.	playing Engines 10/- Lighting Lamps 1/-	00	11	00

[1] On this day it is recorded in Miss Beppy Byrom's *Journal* (Chetham Society), "the 14th [Nov.] my Lord Derby is come to town to have the militia put in readiness, they are all quartered in town." So, too, in the *Diary* of Mr. Thomas Walley, one of the Constables of Manchester for this year, recently printed by me in the *Transactions of the Lancashire and Cheshire Antiquarian Society*, 1889, there is a long memorandum dated November 14, 1745, beginning as follows : " My Lord Derby being come to Manchester with several officers of the militia, as a great number of the militia was in town his Lordship as Lord Lievetenant of the County sent for Mr. Fowden my brother Constable and I to the Bulls Head. At which meeting it was proposed by Mr. Edward Chetham that the gentlemen had been considering upon the large quantity of gunpowder that was in several persons hands in town, that care should be taken that it should not fall into the hands of the Rebells should they come to Manchester. Mr. Chetham proposed that we as Constables should take care of it and thought if we paid for the same powder we might be repaid by the town. I was desired to go and consult with my brother Constable [Mr. William Fowden] and the gentlemen of the town which we did at the Old Coffee House . . . . . . I then said to my Lord Derby that if they came to any resolution of removing the said powder out of town, if they would send the powder to the Governour of Chester Castle or to His Royal Highness the Duke of Cumberland, who was then with the army in Staffordshire, we would send it at the expense of the town His Lordship and the gentlemen came to no resolution upon the affair."

[2] These troops came in to guard the town, owing to the advance of the rebel army from Scotland under the command of the " Young Pretender," Prince Charles Edward.

		l s d
19	Expences this day, two Companies more Militia[1] came in	00 : 01 : 00
21.	p^d Ann Clegg for Cockades for Manchester Militia p rec^t	00 : 04 : 00
22.	p^d for 3 Loads Coal for Guard house p Pet. Cottrel[2]	00 : 02 : 03
25.	p^d Bellman for crying ag^t Beding being remov'd out of Town	00 : 01 : 00
25.	Warrants to Hamlets to bring in 14 days pay for Militia	00 : 02 : 00
25.	tending Dep : L^n all this day ...	00 : 02 : 02
26.	Load Coal to the Watch house p P. Cottrel	00 : 09 : 00
26.	rep^d Mr Walley sundry Expences at Old Coffee house Bul's head & Angel[3]	01 : 06 : 00
26.	rep^d Mr Fowden d^o at meetings to Consider w^t was best to be done[4]...	01 : 06 : 00
*30.	p^d sundry Labourers fforc'd this day by the Rebels[5] into their Artillery Park[6]	01 : 13 : 02

* The entries to which an asterisk is affixed have a special mark in red ink made against them, and this note is written in the margin " for the sums thus markt thro' out this Acct see Const. Acc^t 1748." There is, however, unfortunately a gap in this volume of Accounts from 1746 to 1752, the intervening accounts having been taken out or lost. These entries all relate to payments made on behalf of the Rebels, and no doubt were referred to at the trial of Mr. Fowden, one of the two Constables, at Lancaster in 1747.

[1] See p. 20, note 2.

[2] Peter Cottrell was the Beadle.

[3] These were the three chief inns in the town, to which the Court Leet frequently adjourned, and where the principal inhabitants met one another and consulted on the affairs of the town.

[4] Mr. Thomas Walley records in his *Diary*: "Upon *Tuesday the 26th of November* Mr. Walley one of the Constables of Manchester waited upon James Chetham Esqr and Robert Booth, Esqr two of his Majesties Justices of the Peace, for the County of Lancashire at the House of John Rawsthorne at the sign of the Griffin at Dangerous Corner [in Manchester] being the house that the Justices meet at. And their took the directions from James Chetham Esqr aforesaid, in what manner he the said Thomas Walley and his brother Constable and there Debity [Deputy] should act and behave if the rebels should send for them, when they came to the said town. The said James Chetham by his directions said whatever they forced the Constables to do we must be obliged to observe, which directions from him, we strictly perform'd and by force obeyed." It is evident from the entries in the text that, as well as this conference with the local magistrates at Dangerous Corner, other meetings of the principal inhabitants of the town were held at the other three inns mentioned, where they were entertained at the expense of the town.

[5] The Rebels had entered Manchester on Thursday, November 28th, when, at three o'clock in the afternoon, "two men in Highland dress and a woman behind one of them, with a drum on her knee," reached Manchester, and began beating up for recruits, not meeting with the slightest opposition. About eight o'clock that evening a body of the

		l s d
*30.	to sundry Labourers fforc'd by the Rebels to Crosford Bridge [1]	02 : 09 : 00
*30.	to Drink for them at Stretford ...	01 : 08 : 05
*30.	to wid Lightboun for Ropes &c taken to Crosford Bridge [1]	01 : 02 : 06
*30.	to M[r] Battersbee for Chains &c taken thither [1]...	02 : 15 : 06
*30.	to sundrys for Nails and hold fasts taken thither [1]...	02 : 07 : 03
*30.	to Mess[rs] Hulme and Hardman for Torches taken thither &c [1]	02 : 12 : 00
Dec 2	to John Shaw[2] for going to Leeds, Bradford &c with an Express to inform Gen[l] Wade of the time the Rebels left this place, their Number &c	01 : 11 : 06
	p[d] Isaac Grantham for horse hire, & Sons riding with several Expresses	00 : 08 : [Torn]

rebel horse came in, and on the next day, Friday, the 29th November, at three o'clock in the afternoon, the Prince marched in with the rest of the rebel army, and at four o'clock King James III., his father, was proclaimed at the Cross. They remained in the town all Saturday, November 30th, when the various bridges in the neighbourhood which had been broken down were repaired, as mentioned in the text, and on Sunday, December 1st, the Prince and his troops left Manchester and marched by various routes to Macclesfield and Congleton, where they stayed that night.

⁶ As appears from Miss Beppy Byrom's *Journal*, the "artillery Park" where the rebels put their guns was in Camp Field. She writes under date Saturday 30th, "then the officer went with us all to the Camp Field to see the artillery."

* See p. 21, note *.

¹ Mr. Walley has a reference to this in his *Diary*. "*Saturday* [*Nov.*] 30*th* I was sent for by an officer to go to the Prince, as they call'd him but first I must go to know if the timber planks &c was gone to Crossford. Upon which I went up to the Timber yard and with another officer, where I found Mr. Bowker [the other Constable] two carts with timber and some men with planks was going. The officer commanded me to send for a number of links which I must have for them, which I did [These are the "torches" referred to in the text] Then I was to go with an officer up to the Prince, as they call'd him and make a report. I was at the door of the Parler where the officer asked me 'Did you see the Timber, Planks, Nails, Ropes &c go towards Crossford Bridge.' I made answer 'several carts was gone and others agoeing.'" Prince Charles issued the following proclamation to the inhabitants of Manchester (Chambers's *History of the Rebellion*, vol. i., p. 271).

"Manchester. Nov. 30. 1745. His Royal Highness being informed that several bridges had been pulled down in this county, he has given orders to repair them forthwith, particularly that at Crossford, which is to be done this night by his own troops though his Royal Highness does not purpose to make use of it for his own army, but believes it will be of service to the country; and if any forces that were with General Wade be coming this road they may have the benefit of it.—C. P. R."

² Query, was this the founder of the well-known John Shaw's Club. ?

		l	s	d
Decr 2.	p^d Josiah Hibbert for hire of horses that carry'd Expresses	00	10	06
	p^d at Angel for Corn for imprest horses standing ready for Expresses	00	02	06
3.	p^d wid Jackson for Ale for several men that went Errands &c	00	03	09
4.	to two soldiers wives and children p pass	00	02	00
4.	Mittimus for Harry-go-loose¹ 2/- D° for Matth : Townson 2/-... ...	00	04	00
5.	Coal and Candle for Watch house 11½^d Jack Brooks 1/-	00	01	11½
5.	to William Martin a lame disbanded soldier	00	00	06
5.	to Josia Hibbert for a horse to Knotsford with an Express	00	02	06
6	to John Ashton for assistance and Errands two days	00	01	06
7.	to Berry Senr and his son for the like	00	01	04
7.	p^d Mr Smith sundry charges of pulling up Crosford Bridge² to retard the Retreat of the Rebels p order of Jam^t Chetham³ Esqr ...	01	14 .	00
	*to Samuel Molesdale and other Labourers	01	11	11½
	to Timo: Eaton for horse and himself going tow^{ds} Macclesfeld⁴ &c to reconnoitre the Rebels on their retreat	00	04	00
	to William Bowers for horses that carryd Expresses	00	05	09
9.	p^d James Ashworths Bill for Coals	00	08	06

---

* See p. 21, note *.

¹ This curious nickname is worth notice.

² This was the bridge referred to before as having been hastily repaired by the Rebels, and over which many of them marched on their way to Macclesfield and Congleton. There was now "great talk of the Highlanders coming again," and so James Chetham, Esq., one of the magistrates, ordered the bridge to be destroyed.

³ This was James Chetham, of Smedley, near Manchester, Esq., one of the most active Magistrates at this time.

⁴ The Rebels had nearly reached Macclesfield once more in their retreat, and it was feared would come on to Manchester.

		l	s	d
9.	p[d] Watchmen at Redbank & Newton Lane set to prevent Mob[1] coming into Town...	00	05	00
11.	p[d] John Hulme at 7 Starrs[2] for Horses with Expresses	00	05	06
12.	p[d] James Ashton for going with sundry Expresses to inform his Royal highness the Duke [of] Cumberland of the Rebels retreat[3] ...	01	03	06
12.	p[d] sundry Watchmen set on Salford Bridge, and all other ends of the Town for 36 hours to prevent any	03	17	08

[1] With reference to the "mob" here mentioned, Miss Beppy Byrom, in her *Journal*, has the following entries :—" Saturday 7th [December] great talk of the Highlanders coming again . . . they are for raising a mob to stop them, they are ringing the firebell as hard as they can, great hurries [*i.e.*, commotions] in the street. Sunday 8th [Dec.] . . . The bellman is going by order of D[r] Mainwaring and Justice Bradshaw, ' This is to give notice to all the inhabitants of this town that they are desired to rise and arm themselves with guns, swords pickaxes, shovels or any other weapons they can get, and go stop all the ends of the town to prevent the rebels from coming in for two hours and the King's forces will be up with them ' and I met the D[r] on horseback in the midst of the mob encouraging them much and promising them to send all the country in as he went (for he ran his way as soon as he had done) and accordingly he did, for all the country folks came armed with scythes, sickles &c at the ends of mop sticks, and all other kind of weapons and made a very great hurry [*i.e.*, commotion] all day. M[r] Walley went to Smedley, but M[r] Chetham was gone, so M[r] [Robert] Booth and he sent the bellman to quell the mob again ' Whereas a tumultuous mob has been raised &c. This is to desire that all the country folks will go to their own homes and that everybody will lay down their arms and be quiet ' and so a great many did . . . A paper was read in several churches the same as the bellman said."

Mr. Thomas Walley in his *Diary* generally confirms what Miss Beppy Byrom has stated, his account being as follows :—" [*Sunday*] *Dec[br] the* 8th We received an account from Macclesfield that the Rebells was near that town in their retreat. Upon which I was inform'd that notice had been given in several churches as Oldham, Sadellworth and other Parish Churches, to desire all persons who had arms or any weapons to appear at Manchester the next day, which was thought by several in the town of Manchester, that it would be the ruin of the town if those persons came in. Upon which we was advised to set persons towards Ashton and Oldham in the road, to desire they would return home. There was about three or four hundred gathered together, part of which number was the Militia. M[r] Bradshaigh one of his Majesties Justices of the Peace and D[r] Manwaring had sent the Bellman of the town to desire all persons in town to rise, which the Bellman, as I sent for to know who gave him [such] orders, acquainted me. I desired him to go to the same place where I call'd him off and do as the Justice and D[r] Manwaring ordered. I then went to wait of M[r] Booth, who is in the Commission of the [Peace] to advise, being the only Justice in town, to see if we could not prevail with this mob, as was gathered together to disperse, which we did . . ."

[2] This is the first time this well known inn has been mentioned either in the *Court Leet Records* or in any document printed with them.

[3] It was on Tuesday, the tenth of December, that the Rebels finally quitted the town, after levying a fine of £2,500 on account of the rough behaviour of the mob.

		l	s	d
	intelligence following the Rebels of his Royal Higheness's army being in Close pursuit			
13.	Load Coal for the Guard 10^d Straw for d^o 3/–...	00	03	10
13.	p^d a man for sumoning the Gent of the Town to meet his Royal Highness, being expected from Macclesfield this day[1]...	00	00	03
14.	to John Cowper p pass to the Duke [of] Kingston's[2] Regiment	00	02	06
14.	p^d sundrys for imprest horses for his Royal Highness's Army to Wigan	02	05	04
	to Geo: Cook for his horse wch was also imprest to Wigan and from thence taken forward, cost him 7/– following it besides hire	00	10	00
	p^d Hen. Walwork for his horse wch was also 'prest to Wigan & from thence taken forward to Carlisl &c and detain'd near 7 weeks &c	02	07	02
	to Mr Ibitson for a Second hand Saddle, wch was rode away with ...	00	06	00
	to Hu: Shakeshaft for a new Mail pillion was taken forward	00	05	06
	p^d Miles Sandiford for going to wigan to bring back prest horses &c	00	05	00

---

[1] Miss Beppy Byrom, in her *Journal*, says that on Tuesday, the 10th December, an express reached the town that the Duke of Cumberland would be there on the next day with his army. Accordingly on the 11th December she writes: " the bells are ringing for they expect the Duke every minute . . . . now the bellman is going again to tell folks they must not illuminate for the Duke will not be here to night, and desired the folks to go to their own homes for all the country is come in to see." Then, again, on the 12th, "my brother came and fetched me to see the Duke . . . . . saw nothing but the light horse and hussars which went straight through the town." And finally on the 13th " the Duke goes by Warrington another way"—following the rebels. So, in spite of the entry in the text, the Duke never came to Manchester after all. Her father in a letter to a friend writes, "the Duke of Cumberland was expected here for three nights and a vast mob from all parts to receive him but he went another way."

[2] The Duke of Kingston was in or near Manchester on the 12th December, for Miss Byrom states that on that night he lodged at the house of her uncle Houghton, probably at Baguley Hall, near Northenden, "with his chaplain and nine more of his attendants."

		l	s	d
	p^d P. Cottrell's son and another man for the like	00	06	00
21.	to Wm Smith with his wife and Child p pass to Limeric	00	01	00
	p^d Mr Joseph Birch for Beadles Cap and Gown	02	09	00
	p^d Bennet for making them	00	08	00
	p^d for 2 pair hose and dying 9/– two pair Shoes 9/–...	00	18	00
	p^d for new painting his Staff... ...	00	02	06
21.	to Kat. Best a Soldiers wife with Mr Dukinfields[1] pass	00	01	00
23.	to six other soldiers wives following Kerrs & Blands[2] Dragoons	00	02	00
	to another soldiers wife...	00	00	06
Decr 23.	p^d Wm Oakes Bill for Oats the Rebels took from him...	02	12	00
	p^d for two pound Candles	00	00	09
24.	to Mary Birmingham and two children p pass from R. D.[3] Esqr..	00	01	00
24.	to Ellen Spratt another Soldiers wife and two Children	00	01	00
24.	to 6 other Soldiers wives and Children p passes from Genl Wade's Army...	00	06	00
24.	Coal and Candle for Guard house yesterday and to day	00	02	01 ½
24.	to two press warr^{ts} for 5 wagons, 3 of 'em out of Stretford	00	04	00
24.	Messengers with D^o	00	00	06
25.	to Isabel Stathom a sick soldiers wife	00	01	00
25.	to Phil : Hyde for going to wigan to fetch back a prest horse...	00	02	06
25.	to Kat. Ormrod and Child p pass to Blackburn	00	01	00
25.	to subsisting 19 Soldiers wives & 21 Children bro^t in Carts from Stockport	00	13	04
25.	to Taylor & Warburton for Carting them forward to wigan	01	16	00
25.	Warrants to Hamlets to pay Land tax	00	02	00

[1] For a short account of Robert Dukinfield, Esq., see page 9, note 2.
[2] So called after Major General Humphrey Bland.
[3] That is, Robert Dukinfield, Esq., referred to in note 1.

		l	s	d
26.	to a soldiers wife with a broken arm, and two Children	00	01	06
26.	to Cuthbert Williams a disbanded Soldier	00	00	06
26.	p^d Bellman for notice about new Surveyors this day...	00	01	00
26.	p^d Expences at D^o meeting as usual	00	07	06
27.	subsist^d 28 women & Children bro' in two other Carts from Stockport 4^d p...	00	09	04
28.	to Fisher and Blaykling for Carting them to wigan	01	16	00
29.	to two soldiers wives and 4 children went on Roylands wagon to wigan	00	03	00
29.	p^d John Haworth for an imprest horse for Lord Boyd's Servt... ...	00	02	00
29.	p^d to a watchman that tended Duke Kingston's Carriage in the Street...	00	00	06
[1745-6] Jan 1.	to Betty Craig a soldiers wife & 2 Children sent p Mr R^t Birch Danes g^{s1}	00	01	00
1.	Coal to Guard house Marquis Grandby's^2 Reg^t came in	00	00	09
1.	playing Engines	00	10	00
1.	p^d for 4 press warrants for 21 Carts	00	08	00
1.	Messengers with D^o to Chorlton Roe, Crumpsal &c....	00	01	06
2. 2	p^d Carters to make up their wages £7 - 16 - 0 the Act of Parliament price, Col. Stanwicks who commanded refusing to pay more than 6^d	01	16	00
2	to Hen: Hesford for an imprest horse for an Officers Servant... ...	00	02	06
3.	Boonfire Carlisl^3 taken 6'- p^d Mr Bartholomew for wine p Bill 3 - 0 - 6	03	06	06

---

[1] That is, sent by Mr. Robert Birch, of Deansgate.

[2] The Marquis of Granby was a famous commander at this time and later, and many inns were called after him. Miss Byrom writes under January 1, 1746, "the Marquis of Granby's [misread Grenville's] regiment came in to day, some of them were so rude at Dr. Deacon's that he went out of town again."

[3] Carlisle, which had been garrisoned by the Rebels on their retreat into Scotland, was besieged by the Duke of Cumberland for some weeks, but finally surrendered to him on the 30th December, 1745. The dates in the text are a day wrong, the payments there mentioned being probably made on the day after the bonfires, &c., took

		l	s	d
3	p^d John Fisher for a Cart Load women and Children to Bolton ...	00	12	00
3	subsisting them at 4^d p being 17 in number	00	05	08
4	another Boonfire for Carlisl,[1] & Town illuminated, Marq^r Grandby[2] here...	00	06	00
4	p^d Pat M^{c}quoid &c for Rent and Coal for Guard house	04	09	00
8.	to 5 soldiers wives and children bro^t by Betty Bordman from R. D. Esq [Robert Dukinfield Esq]...	00	05	00
9.	Warrants to Hamlets for new Surveyors of the Highways...	00	02	00
12.	p^d Fisher for Carting 15 Soldiers wives and Children to Rochdale ...	00	12	00
12	p^d him for their Subsistance at 4^d p	00	05	00
13	to 5 women & Children returning from Marq^r Grandby's Regiment...	00	03	00
13.	Load Coal for the Watch house ...	00	00	09
13.	Kat. Ormrod and Child p pass from Rigby Mollencux Esq '...	00	00	0. [Tom]
14	to John Radcliff for horses and going with Sundry Expresses &c.	01	04	0

place. Miss Beppy Byrom, in her *Journal*, writes on Thursday, January 2nd, 1746: "this morning we were waked with ringing for the taking of Carlisle again, but we hear no particulars . . . . the bellman is going to-night to order every body to illuminate tomorrow night; there has been a great bonfire all day and the bells have scarce ever ceased."

[1] On the next day Miss Byrom gives the following graphic account of the illuminations and the riotous behaviour of the mob :—" Friday 3rd: the bells again and illuminations in every house in the town except Mr Cattells. . . . . The Presbyterians have made two effigies of the Prince one in his Scotch and one in his English dress and carried them up and down the town and raised a great mob, which was headed by some of the young Presbyterian gentlemen, and went to all the houses in town where any were gone from and broke their windows although lighted, and a great many more besides that were not thick enough ; they were very rude and they carried their bunch of rags down to M^r [Robert] Dukenfields and the Justice out of his great courage got a gun and shot at it, and then it was brought into the house and he wrung it by the nose and then his wife and daughter were introduced and had the honour to slap it in the face, and so on till they all were tired and drunk, for all the heads of the Presbyterians were at the Angel and gave the mob drink ; then they hung it upon the signpost, and quartered it, and then threw it into the fire ; somebody threw a piece of it into the drink, which put them into a violent passion. The next day several gentlemen went down to the [Dangerous] Corner to make complaint but the justices would hear none."

[2] See p. 27, note 2.

		l	s	d
16.	to two soldiers wives sent p R. Dukinfield Esq'r	00	00	08
16.	to Jeñy Thomas for lodging 7 Soldiers wives and Child	00	00	08
16.	to Saml Green, Wm Claridge, Stephen Holmes, Solomon Price & Thomas Village, soldrs of the Duke Bedfords Regt p order of R. D. Esqre	00	02	06
16.	pd for a pair Shoes for said Green. p Do orders	00	04	06
16.	to Tho. Wilson of Ld Hallifax's Regt p Do orders	00	00	06
17.	pd for a pair Shoes for said Claridge p Do orders	00	04	06
17.	pd him 2 days subsistance more p Do orders	00	01	00
17.	to Bridget Wilson a soldiers wife with a Child p pass..	00	01	00
18.	pd Francis Read for lighting Lamps	00	01	10
20.	pd Conduct money with Alex: Campbel, a Rebel, to Lancr... ...	02	05	00
20.	pd Claridge 2 days more 1/- Holmes 4 days 2'- p R. D. Esqr...	00	03	00
26.	repd H. Leyland more for Claridge and Holmes p Do ordr	00	06	00
	pd for a double horse[1] to carry them to Wigan p Do ordr	00	04	00
	pd James Oldham for going with 'em, & to bring horse back, 2 days out	00	04	00
31.	two press warrts for Brigadr Bligh's Baggage, 5 Carts	00	04	00
Feb. 2.	pd Taylor for Carting Soldiers wives and Children to Rochdale	00	12	00
2.	pd John Fisher for the like	00	12	00
	pd their Subsistances at 4d p... ...	00	11	04
6.	to Ra. Clayton and wife disbanded from Cholmondley's	00	01	00
	to Mr Gibbons Apo: for tending a Sick Soldr p ordr of R. D. Esqr ...	00	18	00
13.	pd Read for lighting Lamps... ...	00	00	08

[1] That is, a horse with a saddle large enough to carry two people.

		l	s	d
13.	p^d John Stringer for Straw for Guard house p rec^t..	00	02	06
17	playing Engines p rec^t	00	10	00
24.	to Wm Edmundton with a wife big, [1] and one child to Devonshire.. ...	00	02	00
25.	· Conveying Serj^t Greens wife & Children on horseback to Rochdale	00	04	02
	gave her when she went p ord^r of R. Dukinfield Esqr...	00	01	00
27	p^d for a General warrant to apprehend Strollers &c²...	00	02	00
28.	rep^d Mr Fowden what he had given sundry Passengers &c p Bill... ...	00	14	04
[March] 3.	p^d high Constable for repairing Lanc^r Bridge, conveying Vagrants and Kings fforces, repairing Lanc^r Castle and public Bridges, and Governor of the house of Correction in Manchester's wages	36	16	04
	Warrants to the Hamlets for their proportion of d°	00	02	00
3.	p^d Martha Sheperd for lodging 3 passengers	00	00	03
4.	to a Boy, was a Drummer, with a pass...	00	00	04
6.	to 3 soldiers wives and children, sent p R. D. Esqr	00	02	00
13.	to 3 soldiers wives, two had two children each...	00	02	06
14.	Warrants for presentments to the assises	00	02	00
14.	Parchm^t & writing Presentm^t 1/- horse hire to Rochdale 1/4. Expences 1/-	00	03	04
14.	to Mr Beswick rent for watch house 16 weeks at 2/6 p week...	02	00	00
15.	to a disbanded Serj^t and wife, sent by R. D. Esquire	00	01	00
18.	to two soldiers wives with passes from Edenburgh, sick	00	02	00

[1] That is, big with child. (See page 19, note 3).
[2] See page 2, note 6.

		l	s	d
20.	pᵈ Samˡ Goodier for Candles for Watch house & Guard house.. ...	00	09	03½
24	playing Engines	00	10	00
[1746]				
25.	Warrants to pay Land tax 2'- Dᵒ to pay Window mony 2'- ...	00	04	00
25.	Warrants for new Overseers of the poor 2/- Quire paper 8ᵈ..	00	02	08
25.	pᵈ P. Cottrell & Son for searching out & tending Ann Morris aˡs Tomlinson suspected to have murder'd a Bastard Child found in Benjᵃ Costerdine's pit	00	03	09
30.	to two Soldiers wives from New Castle	00	01	06
31.	Messⁿ with Coroners Warrⁿ old Rᵈ Dickanson found dead in Garret field	00	01	00
	to Dep: [Deputy]¹ as Coroner for taking the Inquisition	00	15	04
	to Manchester jurors who attended the Enquiry	00	01	04
April 5.	to two soldiers wives and Children p pass	00	02	00
7.	to John Brown with his wife and 2 children p pass from R. D. Esqʳ ...	00	02	06
8.	to Ann Sutherland and 4 Children p pass and for Lodging them ...	00	03	00
8.	repᵈ Mʳ Walley what he had given sundry Passengers	01	05	03
14.	to Tho: Ovington with his wife and 4 Children p pass	00	02	00
16.	pᵈ Mʳ Green Grocer for Oyl for Cross & Dungeon Lamps²	00	18	00
17.	pᵈ Market Lookers their half years Bill³...	02	10	00
18.	pᵈ John Healey for two pair handcuffs & repairing Watch Bills⁴ ...	00	14	05

¹ Probably the Deputy-Steward, not the Deputy-Constable, acted as Coroner on this occasion.

² It would appear that there were only two lamps in the town at this time, one at the Market Cross at the bottom of Marketsted lane, and the other at the Dungeon.

³ See page 6, note 2.

⁴ The "bills," or "bill hooks," carried by the town watchmen, were formidable weapons, having sharp curved blades fixed at the end of a long staff.

		l	s	d
19.	p^d Conduct mony with John Briggs to Lanc^r for seditious words... ...	01	11	06
20.	to a soldiers wife and a Soldiers widow each 6^d	00	01	00
21.	to two soldiers wives and one Child	00	01	00
21.	Messeng^r wth Coroners warr^{ts} about Jo. Rowbothom, poison'd himself..	00	01	00
*was dragg^d & bury^d [in] the highway at Barlow Cross.^{2}	to Dep:^{1} as Coroner for the Inquisition, found Self Murder *	00	15	04
	to Manchester jurors each 4^d ...	00	01	04
	p^d sundry Expences of burying him in the highway at Barlow Cross^2...	00	06	06
25.	Boonfire for Defeat of the Rebels at Culloden^3	00	06	06
August 16.	rep^d Mr Smith sundry Expences on Towns Acc^t to this day p Bill ...	10	07	08
20.	p^d the high Constable for Conveying Vagr^{ts} relief of Prisoners &c ...	06	09	04
	warrants to Hamlets for their proportion of D^o	00	02	00
	D^o for proportion of another mony warr^t of £6-10-7 included in Mr Smith's above Bill of £10 . 7 . 8	00	02	00
20.	to Jane McKartie, sick & big, p pass to Edinburgh...	00	01	06
20.	to Marg^t Doughtie p pass to Dublin	00	00	06
	p^d Conduct mony with Jam^s Smethurst to Lanc^r suspicōn [of] Treason	01	10	00
	p^d sundrys on Ac^t of Militias viz. Mr Kenworthy^4	01	05	03
	Mr Danl Bayley	03	01	00
	Mr Abram Hawarth	01	11	00
	Mr Richd Taylor	02	00	10
	Mr Tho: Touchet	02	14	06
	Mr James Marsden	01	11	00
	Mr Joshua Marriot	02	02	02½
	Mr John Lees, ith' Square ...	03	00	06
	Mr James Hilton	01	04	00

---

^{1} See p. 31, note 1.

^{2} See page 14, note 1, where there is an entry of another unfortunate suicide buried at Barlow Cross.

^{3} The battle of Culloden was fought between the Young Pretender, with about 5,000 men, against the Duke of Cumberland, who had 8,000 men and 900 horse. It resulted in the total defeat of the Rebels, and put an end to all further opposition on their part.

^{4} These were some of the chief inhabitants of the town at this time.

		l	s	d
30.	p^d Mr Bartholomew[1] sundry Expences p Bill	04	16	07
Sep^t 1.	to John Bromley and wife to Armaugh p R. D. Esqr	00	01	00
6.	rep^d Mr Walley w^t he had given 2 soldiers wives & Children	00	01	06
8.	to Mary Murray and Dau^r p pass...	00	01	00
9.	p^d Porters for playing Engines 4 times to this day	02	00	00
9.	p^d John Healey Smith for repairing them whole year	02	06	09
9.	to Mary wife of Nicholas Myers and 2 small children	00	02	00
10.	p^d Expences at Leying Constable Ley...	02	16	00
	p^d for new Ley Book	01	00	00
11.	warrants to the Hamlets for Lycencing day	00	02	00
12.	to Nicholas Grimes, with Mr Chetham's pass to Chelsea... ...	00	00	06
15.	to Alex. Mordough p pass from York to Liverpool...	00	00	06
16.	rep^d Mr Walley what he had given 3 other Passengers...	00	01	06
18.	Expences tending the Sherriff this morn. Syddall's & Deacon's heads put up[2]	00	01	06
18.	to Jane Buckley and Child p pass...	00	01	00
21.	to Wm Stephens p pass to Pattin in Wiltshire...	00	00	06

---

[1] Mr. Bartholomew, whose name has frequently occurred in these Accounts, kept the Bull's Head Inn in the town, which was the place of resort of the Tory party at this time.

[2] This is a very noteworthy entry: " Syddall's & Deacon's heads put up " in the presence and by the orders of the Sheriff of Lancashire, Daniel Willis, Esq. Thomas Theodorus Deacon was one of the three sons of Dr. Deacon (a non-juring minister in Manchester) who joined the Rebel army and became officers in "the Manchester Regiment " as it was called. Thomas Syddall was the son of Thomas Syddall, a peruke maker, who had been executed in 1716 for taking part in the rebellion of 1715. He joined the Rebels in Manchester, and acted as adjutant of the Manchester Regiment. They, and other officers of this regiment who were taken prisoners at Carlisle, were tried for high treason in London, and were executed at Kennington Common on the 30th July. Their heads were ordered to be sent to various places, and were preserved in spirits for that purpose. Those of Deacon and Syddall were sent to Manchester and put upon the Exchange there, but not till seven weeks after the execution.

		l	s	d
29.	Warrants to pay Land tax 2/- D^o to pay window mony 2/-	00	04	00
29.	p^d for a Grate for Guard 1/- seting it 1/- two Troops Blands Drag^s came in	00	02	00
29.	Sweeping Steps at Milnbrow and Salford Bridge whole year	00	08	00
29.	p^d Mr Croxton a years rent for Engine house due this day... ...	02	00	00
	p^d Mr Parker for Cotton-wake [wick] for Lamps at Cross & Dungeon ...	00	03	02
Oct 3.	p^d for Coal for Guardhouses p Bill	00	06	02
7.	p^d Hugh Shakeshaft rent for Guard-houses to this day	00	15	00
7.	p^d Market Lookers latter half year p Bill	03	01	00
	to Deputies Sallarie whole year, by order of Court Leet [1]	20	00	00
	to Beadles D^o wch with £1 . 15 . 0 p^d him by Mr Smith, & included in his aforegoing acc^t of £10 . 7 . 8, makes up his wages £7 - 0 - 0 [2] ...	05	05	00
7.	p^d for Candles to the Guard houses to this day p Rec^t	00	05	00½
		217	09	04½
	*p^d Sundry Expences of spoiling Cheadle fford [3] &c. when Rebels were retreating p Bill and Rec^t ...	3	—	—
		220	09	04½

---

* See p. 21, note *.

[1] At the Court Leet held on the 16th October, 1745, the Jury ordered that the Constables for the year ensuing should appoint a Deputy "with a Sallary of Twenty Pounds" and "a Beadle with a Sallary of seven pounds for the Year." (See *Court Leet Records*, vol. vij., p. 145.) Previously the Deputy-Constable had only £10 and the Beadle £5 a year.

[2] See previous note.

[3] Miss Beppy Byrom records, in her *Journal*, that, after the dispersion of the mob on Sunday the 8th December (as already noted, see p. 24, note 1), "one part [of the mob] went to Cheadle ford headed by old Mr Hilton with a design to cut it up as the D^r [Manwaring] desired, but by nine o'clock they returned from their fruitless expedition and Mr H. gat out of the way." Mr. Thomas Walley also refers to this in his *Diary*: "then they [the mob] went out of town to Cheadel fiord. One Hilton who they call'd Captain desired them to goe with him in order to destroy the Ford in hopes of preventing the Rebells returning that way."

An acco': of cash reced by THO: WALLEY Esq' & WILLIAM FOWDEN, Constables of Manchester.

[Receipts]

1745.

Nov 7. [1745-6]	By Cash being Ballance of last years Acc'¹	04 : 15 : 00¼
March 3.	By Cash from the Hamlets their ⅔ᵈ of £36 – 16 – 4...	24 : 10 : 09¼
1746. Aug' 20.	By Cash from D° their 2⅓ᵈ of £6 – 9 – 4...	04 : 06 : 03
20.	By D° from D° their 2⅓ᵈˢ of £6 – 10 – 7	04 : 07 : 00½
Nov. 3.	By Cash for the fire Grate, was in the Watch house	00 : 00 : 10
	By Cash at sundry times from the Misegatherers...	165 : 12 : 4½
		203 : 12 : 03½
1746[-7].	January 8. Reced more from the Misegatherers...	1 : 6 : 7½
		204 : 18 : 11
	D° Ballance due to the late Constables	15 : 10 : 05½
		220 : 9 : 4½

January 15. 1746[-7]. We the Jurors of this Court Leet have perused and examined the Accounts of MR WALLEY and MR FFOWDEN late Constables and do find the Sum of ffifteen pounds ten Shillings and five pence half peny to be due to them upon Ballance which we do order them to be reimbursed by the present Constables MR RICHARD WALMSLEY and MR THOMAS BIRCH² and we do allow the Same.

(Signed) SAMˡ BIRCH
THOˢ CLOWES
JOHN TAYLOR
ROBERT HIBBERT Jun'
JOHN UPTON
JOSEPH BULLOCK
Wᴹ ETHELSTONE
JOSEPH ALLEN.

¹ See p. 18.
² These were the two Constables elected on the 7th October, 1746. (See *Court Leet Records*, vol. vij., p. 150).

[Constables' Accounts.]

[7th Oct., 1746, to 13th Oct., 1747.]

✦✦✦✦✦✦✦✦✦✦✦

An accot of cash disburs'd by RICH^D WALMSLEY and THOMAS BIRCH,[1] *Constables of Manchester.*

[Disbursements]

1746.

Oct 7.	p^d late Constables Batt of their Acco^{ts} [2]	15 :	10 :	5½
9.	to two Boonfires being the General Thanksgiving Day [3]	„ :	13 :	3
10.	to Marg^t Coffee a soldiers wid: with one child p pass	„ :	1 :	„
11.	to a Boonfire, his Majesty's Coronation day	„ :	6 :	6
13.	p^d for lighting Lamps at Dungeon and Cross p rec^t	„ :	1 :	6
18.	p^d for Coals for Guard houses p rec^t	„ :	5 :	4
19.	to Tim. McCartie a sick sailor with a pass	„ :	1 :	„
22.	to Marg^t Reed p pass	„ :	0 :	6
25.	p^d Porters for playing the Engines p rec^t.	„ :	10 :	„
30.	Boonfire his Majesty's birth day ...	„ :	6 :	„
	p^d for wine and musick at drinking the healths ith' Square [4]	4 „	3 „	3
Novr 1.	p^d for Coals for the Guard to this day p rec^t..	„ :	12 :	9

[1] These two Constables were elected at the Court Leet held on the 7th October, 1746. (See *Court Leet Records*, vol. vij., p. 150).

[2] See page 35.

[3] This General Thanksgiving Day was probably in recognition of the defeat of the Rebels and the Young Pretender.

[4] This is an interesting entry, showing what festivities were indulged in on the occasion of His Majesty's birthday. The "square" in which this "wine and musick at drinking the healths " was provided, was St. Ann's Square.

		£	s	d
5.	to Boonfire as usual..	„ :	6 :	„
8.	pᵈ Lamp Lighter	„ :	0 :	10
	pᵈ for two Tin Sconces for Guard house p recᵗ	„ :	1 :	„
9.	to James Woods with a pass to Chester	„ :	0 :	6
9.	pᵈ for a warrᵗ to press a Carriage for Capᵗ Debuts Baggage	„ :	2 :	„
12.	to Johnson and Leak two passengers with 2 Children	„ :	1 :	6
17.	pᵈ for Coal for the Guard to this day p recᵗ..	„ :	10 :	6
20.	pᵈ for Collinge's Comitmᵗ to Lancʳ for seditious words...	„ :	4 :	„
29.	to Pet: Ashton and Jane Owens two Passengers..	„ :	1 :	„
29.	pᵈ for Coal for the Guard to this day	„ :	9 :	9
Decʳ 15.	warrᵗ to Hamlets to pay their Land tax, on 3ᵈ Janʸ..	„ :	2 :	„
15.	Expences of privy watch this night at Dog & partridge ¹	„ :	11 :	9
19.	to Samˡ Blackley disbanded from Pulteny's...	„ :	.„ :	6
19.	pᵈ Messengʳ with Coroners warrᵗˢ to Ardwick, Chorlton Roe &c. ...	„ :	1 :	„
	pᵈ Coroners ffee on view of Tho: Ogden, kill'd in Mʳ Townley's Kalender ²	„ :	15 :	4
	pᵈ Manchester jurors according to custom	„ :	1 :	4
20.	pᵈ for the Comitmᵗ of Evelyn Franks³ Esqʳ to Lancaster	„ :	4 :	„
	pᵈ Bernard Shaw & Son for Conducting him thither..	2 :	2 :	„
23.	pᵈ Beadle for going with Coroner's warrᵗ to Pendleton Hulm &c.. ...	„ :	1 :	„

---

¹ The "Dog and Partridge," one of the Manchester inns, was, I believe, in Fennel Street.

² A "Kalender," or "Calender" as now generally written, was a machine, then recently come into use, for pressing cloth smooth and glossy between two rollers.

³ Who "Evelyn Franks Esq." was, and on what grounds he was committed to Lancaster, is nowhere stated. It is possible, however, that he was responsible for the death of "Ann Plat casually shot in Danesgᵗ," on whom an inquest was held, as recorded in the text (see top of next page).

		£	s	d
	pᵈ Manchʳ jurors on view of Ann Plat casually shot in Danes gᵗ ...	„	1	4
	pᵈ John Beckwith a Dragoon, one of the witnesses	„	0	6
24	pᵈ for Coal for the Guards	„	12	„
24.	playing Engines p recᵗ	„	10	„
24.	pᵈ Mʳ Birch for Beadles Cap and Gown & Triming	2	9	„
	pᵈ Bennet for making them	„	7	11
	pᵈ Hugh Halliwell for his Shoes 9/- Mʳ Blinkhorn for hose 9/-	„	18	„
	new painting his Staff	„	1	„
26.	Warrᵗˢ to Hamlets for new Surveyors of the highways	„	2	„
26.	pᵈ Belman to cry meeting as usual 1/- wine at Dᵒ 3/-.¹	„	4	–
27.	pᵈ Manchʳ jurors a second time about Ann Plat	„	1	4
[1746-7] Jan 8.	John Emotson and Alice Pwendenter [sic] passengers...	„	1	„
8.	pᵈ Lamp Lighter to 4ᵗʰ instant ...	„	„	9
Jan 16.	to Edmund Lees disbanded from Cholmondely's	0	00	06
16.	pᵈ Coroner on view of Mary Howard, a Lunatic, hangd herself	0	15	0
	Beadle for going with warrᵗˢ 1/- Manchʳ jurors 16ᵈ	0	02	04
17.	pᵈ jurors on view of Mary Creswel, a lunatic, cut her throat	0	01	04
	Beadle for going with Coroner's warrᵗˢ	00	01	00
	repᵈ Mʳ Walmsley wᵗ he had given two Passengers	0	02	00
19.	pᵈ for Candles for Guard to this day. p Bill	1	11	07
21.	playing Engines p recᵗ	0	10	00
30.	pᵈ for Coals for Guards to this day.	0	14	03
Feb. 2.	pᵈ Lamp Lighter	0	00	09
11.	to sundry Passengers with wives and Children	0	05	00

¹ This "meeting as usual" on the day after Christmas-day has not, I think, been referred to before.

11.	p^d Hu: Shakeshaft in p^t [in part] for rent of Guard houses p rec^t ...	5 : 18 : 08
13.	p^d for Coals for Guard to this day p rec^t	0 : 04 : 06
	p^d for Straw for D^o and for Dungeon p rec^t	0 : 03 : 06
March 2	p^d sundry passengers to this day ...	0 : 03 : 00
7.	playing Engines p rec^t	0 : 10 : 00
9.	p^d Lamp Lighter	0 : 00 : 09
10.	to a big bellyd passenger with one Child p Ord^r of J. C. Esqr [James Chetham, Esq.]	0 : 02 : 04
14.	p^d sundry Expences of repairing Great Engine p rect^t	4 : 04 : 10½
16.	p^d Healey the Smith for repairing watch = Bills^1 p rec^t	0 : 04 : 00
17.	warr^u to the Hamlets for present-ments to the Assises	0 : 02 : 00
	writing presentm^t 1/- horse & Ex-pences to Bolton to return it 2/4...	0 : 03 : 04
1747. [March] 25.	warr^u to the Hamlets to pay Land tax 2/- D^o for window mony 2/- ...	0 : 04 : 00
	sundry passengers 2/4. a Quire paper 9^d...	0 : 03 : 01
26.	p^d for Coals for Guards to this day p rec^t	0 : 15 : 00
27.	p^d Belman for crying some stoln yarn found in Sutley's house ...	0 : 01 : 00
27.	rep^d Mr Birch for sundry Passengers	0 : 04 : 11
27.	p^d high Const. for Conveying Vagrants & his Maj^{ties} fforces re-pairing house of Correction & Governor's wages p rec^t	10 : 09 : 04
	warrants to the Hamlets for their proportion	0 : 02 : 00
April 1st	playing Engines and Oyl p rec^t ...	0 : 10 : 06
16.	p^d Ringers yesterday, for the defeat of the Rebels at Culloden,^{2} & to day for this Royal Highness's birth Day^3	1 : 06 : 00

^{1} The "watch-bills" were the "bills" or "bill-hooks" carried at night by the "watch." (See p. 31, note 4.)

^{2} The battle of Culloden was fought in April, 1746 (see p. 32, note 3), so that this celebration was on the anniversary of that decisive victory.

^{3} This was the birthday of His Royal Highness the Duke of Cumberland, the victor of Culloden.

[April] 16.	Boonfire 5/4, wine in the Square [1] 2-9-0	2 : 14 : 04
	p[d] Manch[r] jurors, Rich[d] Radcliff cut his throat, in Salford	0 : 01 : 08
22.	p[d] jurors on view of Edw. Whitaker, kill'd in M[r] Townley's Kalender [2]...	0 : 01 : 04
	Coroners ffee 15/4, Beadle for going with Warr[ts] 1/-	0 : 16 : 04
23.	warr[ts] for new Overseers of the poor	0 : 02 : 00
24.	p[d] Coroners ffee on view of W[m] Crawley an Irishman kill'd by Pet. Penkstone by Stabing him into the Eye with a Stick	0 : 15 : 00
	jurors 1/4. Beadle for going with warr[ts] 1'-...	0 : 02 : 04
28.	jurors a 2[d] time, Verdict Manslaughter...	0 : 01 : 04
	p[d] Expences of Comiting Penkstone to Lanc[r] Castle	1 : 15 : 06
30.	warr[ts] to Hamlets for new Presentors or Assessors of the new Duties on houses and windows ...	0 : 02 : 00
	to sundry Passengers to this day...	0 : 04 : 06

[These Accounts end here abruptly, the remaining portion being missing.]

---

[1] Here we have more wine drinking, &c., in St. Ann's Square. (See p. 36, note 4.)

[2] A previous death of a man "kill'd in M[r] Townleys Kalender" has already been reported this year. (See p. 37, note 2.)

[Constables' Accounts.][1]

[22nd Oct., 1751, to 11th Oct., 1752.]

♦♦♦♦♦♦♦♦♦♦♦♦

[Accounts of Mr. JOSEPH ALEXANDER and Mr. THOMAS PARKER[2], *Constables of Manchester.*]

[Previous portion missing.]

[Disbursements]

1752.			
	[Brought forward]...	105 :	9 : 11 ½
June 3.	pᵈ Porters at twice	1 :	:
6.	pᵈ Boonfire for 29ᵗʰ of May[3]		: 6 :
6.	pᵈ James Byer and family to Pensance		: 1 :
6.	pᵈ Peter Hutchingson for mending } Engine Pipes ... ... }		5 : 5 :
6.	pᵈ for Paving Stones & paving about } the Cross[4] ... ... }		: 16 : 10
12.	pᵈ sundry passengers...		: 3 : 8
17.	pᵈ a passenger into Scotland		: : 6
18.	pᵈ Warᵗˢ to Hamlets for proportion...		: 2 :
18.	pᵈ Dᵒ for Ale Lycences 2 :- for } Surveyors 2 - ... ... }		: 4 :
20.	repᵈ Mʳ Alexander Charges of Privy } watch[5]... ... ... }		: 12 :
	pᵈ two Coroner's Fees	1 :	10 : 8

[1] Unfortunately there is a break in the sequence of the Accounts at this point, those for the four years between Oct., 1747, and Oct., 1751, being unfortunately missing. They would seem to have been removed for some reason or other and never replaced, the volume being bound up without them. As will be noticed, the first portion of this year's Accounts is also missing, the first entries being in June, 1752.

[2] These two Constables were elected at the Court Leet held on 22nd October, 1751. (See *Court Leet Records*, vol. vij., p. 200.)

[3] This was an annual celebration. The anniversary of the restoration of Charles II.

[4] The Cross was situated at the bottom of Market Stead Lane, now Market Street, in what is now called Market Place. See next page, note 2.

[5] This would be the "privy watch" or "privy search" at Whitsuntide, in order to clear the town of all suspicious characters.

24.	p[d] Arthur Dunlap to Bristol	:	:	6
24.	p[d] John Thorp's bill for Iron-work ...	:	2 :	9
24.	p[d] Belman twice decrying firing of Chimneys	:	2 :	
29.	p[d] W[m] Fenley to Berwick upon Tweed	:	:	6
30.	p[d] Thomas Nadin to Cambridge ...	:	2 :	
July. 2.	p[d] Thomas Johnson & his two Sons to Cambridge	:	1 :	
4.	p[d] John Healey's bill for Iron-work...	:	4 :	8
	p[d] Committing four Whores	:	4 :	
	p[d] M[r] Alexander for three vagrants...	:	1 :	6
	rep[d] D[o] more on the Watch Account.	:	:	6
	rep[d] him for three other vagrants ...	:	1 :	6
11.	p[d] for a New Watch-bill[1]	:	2 :	
	p[d] the Engine-men	:	10 :	
	p[d] War[ts] for Land Tax 2/– D[o] for Window Duty 2/–	:	4 :	
	p[d] Boardman for Iron-Work about y[e] Cross	1 :	7 :	7
	p[d] sundry passengers...	:	4 :	6
	p[d] Oliver Nabb for Massons Work at the Cross[2]	18 :	5 :	9
	p[d] Thomas Wild's Bill for Scaffolding[2]	2 :	15 :	9
	p[d] James Green for Oil	:	13 :	6
	p[d] Peter Brooks for Lead had to the Cross[3]	3 :	8 :	10
18.	p[d] a passenger	:	:	6
25.	p[d] War[ts] for Presentments to the Assizes	:	2 :	
25.	p[d] parchm[t] & writing that for Manchester...	:	1 :	
	p[d] High Constables Clerk for these & last presentm[ts]	:	2 :	
July 27.	p[d] Belman to decry Sky-Rockets[3] ...	:	1 :	
31.	p[d] Eliz. Horsop to Leighgo	:	1 :	
	p[d] two other passengers	:	1 :	

---

[1] See page 31, note 4.

[2] Some important repairs seem to have been done at the Cross this year, if, indeed, an entirely new Cross was not erected.

[3] This is a curious entry, the bellman having to proclaim against the letting off of "sky-rockets."

Augt 3.	p^d Ale for Engine-men		: 2 :	
3.	p^d Expences ab^t Evidences abusing the Watch		: 3 :	3
10.	p^d Paper writing & laying the Ley ...	1 :	1 :	
	p^d two of Mr Birch's permits with passengers		:	: 10
11.	p^d three passengers into Scotland ...		: 1 :	
15.	p^d Porters playing Engines		: 10 :	
24.	p^d for a Lamp at the Cross		: 7 :	
24.	p^d Warⁿ for Lists of Freeholder's to be Jurors		: 2 :	
	p^d writing fair Copy and Duplicate for Manch^r...		: 3 :	
25.	p^d Mary Harrop to Chapel le Firth ...		:	: 10
27.	p^d Warⁿ to Hamlets to take Lycences		: 2 :	
29.	p^d Joseph Lightboun mending Buckets		: 14 :	8
Septr 18.	p^d Warⁿ to Hamlets for Land Tax 2/- D° Windows		: 4 :	
18.	p^d Sundry passengers		: 1 :	7
20.	p^d Charges apprehending three whores...		: 1 :	6
22.	p^d a discharged Soldier to Harwich...		: :	6
23.	p^d taking a List of Alehouses for Lycences		: 1 :	6
23.	p^d Porters playing Engines		: 10 :	
30.	p^d deliniating the Sun Dyal upon the Cross[1]	1 :	1 :	
30.	p^d John Healey's Bill mending Engines		: 7 :	8
30.	p^d John Bayley		:	6
30.	p^t a passenger ordered by Justice Birch		: :	6
30.	p^d a passenger from London with two Children		: 1 :	
Octob 9.	p^d to give notice to Alehouses to provide Quarters		: 1 :	
	p^d Expences wth Officers billeting Soldiers		: 2 :	6
10.	p^d for paper		: 1 :	6
11.	p^d sundry passengers & Expences ab^t 'em...		: 10 :	6

---

[1] This Sundial on the top of the Cross is shown on some of the views of the Cross.

11.	p^d cleaning Steps	: 2 :	0
12.	p^d porters in full	1 : :	
	rep^d Mr. Parker advanced to passengers	: 4 :	6
1752.	p^d Mr Ambler for five County Passes	: 12 :	6
Octob^r 12.	p^d Mr Ambler for two Com^{ts} to Lancaster	: 8 :	
	p^d on Sepr 2^d Marketlookers bill ...	5 : 5 :	
	p^d Expences when the Ley was laid	4 : 10 :	
	p^d Beadles Salary[1]	7 : :	
	p^d Deputy's Salary[1]	20 : :	
	p^d for Beadles Gown to Mr Moss ...	2 : 15 :	6
	p^d Soldiers on the 30th of October last	2 : 2 :	

Total disbursed ... ... 195 : 5 : 3½

Cash received by the Constables.

1751.			
Decem^r 30.	received from the County for conveying Baggage[2]	12 : 5 :	
	received from the Hamlets their proportion	19 : 14 :	9
	received from the Ley-book	119 : : 10½	

151 : 0 : 7½

Balance owing to the Constables ... £44 : 4 : 8

We the Jurors of the Court Leet have examined & do allow the Accounts of Mr Joseph Alexander & Mr Thomas Parker late Constables of Manchester & finding a Ballance of forty four pounds four shillings & eight pence due to them, We order the same to be

---

[1] For many years the salary of the Deputy Constable was £10 a year, and that of the Beadle £5, raised to £7 in 1734. (See *Court Leet Records*, vol. vij., p. 33.) But at the Court Leet held on the 16th October, 1745 (see *Court Leet Records*, vol. vij., pp. 145-6), the following order was made fixing the salaries at £20 and £7 respectively:—

"We the Jurors aforenamed do Order and appoint the Constables for the Year ensueing a Deputy with a Sallary of Twenty Pounds and a Beadle with a Sallary of seven pounds for the Year and for defraying their Charges to have a Towns Ley assessed by the Miseleyers and Liberty and Power is hereby given to the said Constables to remove either of the said Officers for Default."

[2] That is, soldiers' baggage.

paid by the present Constables & that they charge the same in their Accounts, and do also order the said Constables to pay James Smith five shillings for taking a fair copy of the Verdicts of the Court Leet to be kept by the Borroughreeve for the time being & to charge the same in their Accounts.

(Signed)

THOS CLOWES	THOS: JOHNSON
JOHN CLOWES	THO: BATTERSBEE.
SAMLL CLOWES Junr	ROBERT GARTSIDE
EDWD BYROM Junr	WM STARKIE
JOHN FEILDEN	JAS LIPTROTT
ROBT AYRTON	CHARLES FORD
JOHN BROOME	JOSEPH BANCROFT

[Constables' Accounts.]

[11th Oct., 1752, to 10th Oct., 1753.]

••••••••••••

Cash disbursed by WILLIAM EDGE and JAMES HULME,[1] *Constables of Manchester*, elected Michaelmas Court Leet 1752.

[Disbursements]

1752.	Paid last year's Balance as p Order of Court[2]	44 : 4 : 8	
	pd James Smith fair copying the Verdict[s][2]	: 5 :	
Octob. 16.	Margaret Johnson to Kingston upon Hull	: 6	
16.	pd Enginemen cleansing and playing Engines	: 10 : 6	
19.	Margaret Thompson for London ...	: : 6	
20.	John Wild an old lame Passenger ...	: 1 : 6	
20.	A Soldiers Wife and two Children to Scotland	: 1 :	
23.	pd Warrts to Hamlets for Surveyor's presentments	: 2 :	
25.	pd Horsehire 2/- Expences 1/6 Wart 2/- pressing Carts for conveying the Kings Baggage	: 5 : 6	
Novr 6.	pd porters playing Engines	: 10 :	
9.	pd John Hollingworth a Passenger ...	: : 6	
9.	pd for a Quarter of Coal on the 22d last	: 6 :	
	for another ... ... 5th Instant	: 6 :	
	for another for tomorrow	: 6 :	
	& for Fewel for the three Fires ...	: 1 : 6	

[1] These two Constables were elected at the Court Leet held on the 11th October, 1752. (See *Court Leet Records*, vol. vij., p. 210.)

[2] See pp. 44 and 45

10.	p^d Expences drinking his Majesty's Health...	2 : 15 : 6
15.	Bernard Smith, Wife and two Children	: : 6
16.	Mary Lowry a passenger	: : 6
18.	p^d Sundry persons carting Baggage...	3 : 6 :
18.	p^d Jurors of two Inquisitions	: 2 : 8
18.	p^d lighting the Lamps at Cross & Dungeon	: 2 : 6
19.	p^d Charges carrying Hind and others under War^t before Sr Ral. Asheton[1] Baronet	: 3 : 8
19.	Danl Farguson to Stockport	: 8
19.	Mich^l Wade and Family to Cumberland	: 10
21.	Ann Hill and Family to Newcastle...	: : 6
21.	John Heys and family to Scotland ...	: 1 :
21.	p^d sundry Messengers to serve Coroners War^ts having but short Notice...	: 2 :
24.	Ann Sampleton to Whitehaven ...	: : 6
Novr 28th	Seven Sailors in Company with a pass	: 2 :
Decr 8.	p^d the Engine men	: 10 :
8.	p^d Elianor Jones...	: : 6
8.	p^d James Crompton's Expences in Custody waiting for a Justice of Peace	: 2 : 6
8.	p^d Commitment and his Conveyance	: 2 : 6
8.	p^d War^ts to Hamlets Land Tax 2.- D^o Window Duty 2'-	: 4 :
8.	p^d D^o Notice of Appeal 2'- and for new Surveyors 2 -	: 4 :
12.	p^d lighting Lamps last Dark	: 1 : 10
12.	p^d Deputy[2] and Beadle collecting a very considerable part of the Constable Ley, the Misegatherers either neglecting to do it, or not knowing where payers lived[3]	1 : 1 :
12.	p^d Joseph Lane and family to Newcastle	: : 9
12.	p^d more to three other passengers ...	: 1 : 6

---

[1] Sir Ralph Assheton, of Middleton, Bart., succeeded his uncle of the same names in 1716. He died 24th December, 1765, aged 73.

[2] That is, the Deputy Constable.

[3] This item was disallowed by the Jury. (See p. 56.)

12.	pd Ann Sampleton to Whitehaven ...	: 6
12.	pd John Heys and family to Libertine[1]	: : 6
13.	pd for a Privy Search War'	: 2 :
14.	Margaret Seaman to Stockport... ...	: : 6
15.	making Beadles Cap and Gown ...	: 7 : 6
15.	pd for a Quire of Paper	: : 9
15.	pd attending Slater a Vagrant	: : 6
15.	pd mending the Dungeon Lamp ...	: 2 :
15.	Tho' Sewell to Leverpool...	: : 6
23.	John Baddy a discharged Soldier ...	: : 6
26.	pd Belman 1/- Wine &c. 3/6 meeting at Coffeehouse to nominate Surveyors	: 4 : 6
30.	pd Sundry Vagrants this Week ...	: 3 : 7
30.	pd burying a Vagrant Child brought to the Deputy's Door dead upon its Mother's Back	: 8 : 6
1753. Jañry 2d	A disbanded Soldier	: : 6
5.	pd Porters playing Engines	: 10 :
5.	pd lighting Lamps	: 2 : 6
6.	pd a passenger to London...	: : 6
Jañry 13.	pd trouble and Expences taking a Survey of the Inhabitants of the Town when a Design was on foot to regulate the Watch & Lamps...	: 15 :
20.	pd an Assistant along with the Bead[l]e in the day and Watch in the night apprehending Vagrants and Nightwalkers a fortnight	: 8 :
	pd them sundry Expences during that time and conveying Vagrants to Justice...	: 5 : 7
	pd Expences commiting Isaac Chantler a Vagrant	: 3 : 6
29.	pd Eliz: Stephenson from Bedlam[2]...	: : 3
	pd lighting Lamps last Dark	: 2 : 8
	Isaac Mellor by pass...	: 1 : 6
	pd Enginemen's Bill	: 13 : 6
	pd John Mac Donald...	: : 6
Febry 12	pd sundry Articles as p Note	: 18 : 8
	pd Horsehire to Lancaster to Henry Walwork	: 12 :

[1] I cannot identify this place. [2] Probably meaning from an asylum.

20.	p^d lighting Lamps	: 2 :	2
	A Woman with two Children to Bristol...	: :	6
	A Woman and a Child to Wales ...	: :	6
	A Soldier's Wife very lame	: 1 :	
	A Stranger waiting for ye Infirmary[1]..	: 1 :	6
	p^d Isaac Clayton more	: :	6
	Joseph Lyon from Scotland	: 1 :	
22.	paid nine passengers	: 1 :	6
	p^d half Charges repairing Roof of Dunge"	: 8 :	10
	p^d an Assistant to Lancaster with Tildsley	: 5 :	6
	p^d Ben Oldham apprehending Vagrants	: 5 :	
	Committing two Vagrants 4 - Conveying 1/-	: 5 :	
23.	A Woman & three Children to Berwick	:	6
24	Two passengers	:	9
	Expences with Officers settleing Quarters	: 2 :	6
	Apprehending, relieving & Commit^g a Whore	: 3 :	4
	John Wolly to Newcastle...	: :	6
March 1st	Belman decrying ye Entertainm^t of Vagrants	: 2 :	
Mar. 1st	Mary Brooks by pass...	: :	6
3.	p^d John Healey's Bill	: 3 :	6
	p^d lighting Lamps at Cross and Dungeon	: 2 :	
5.	p^d Sarah Gosling out of Darbyshire	: 1 :	
	p^d War^{ts} to Hamlets for Land Tax 2/- Window Duty D^o	: 4 :	
	p^d War^{ts} to Hamlets for Surcharge of Window Duty[2]	: 2 :	
	p^d War^{ts} to Hamlets for proportion of 1^l. 4^s. 6^d	: 2 :	

---

[1] The Manchester Infirmary had been founded the previous year, having been opened on June 24th, 1752. It was originated by Mr. Joseph Bancroft and Mr. Charles White (a well-known surgeon at this time), and a house was taken in Garden Street, Shudehill. On December 4th, 1753, Sir Oswald Mosley conveyed the present site of the Infirmary for that purpose.

[2] See p. 4, note 4.

		£	s	d
	p⁴ for a War' ag' persons assaulting Beadle...		2	
8.	pᵈ High Constables War' for Governor's Wages¹	1	4	6
	Expences with the High Constable as usual			2
	John Hill a discharged Soldier ...			3
10.	pᵈ Enginemen		10	6
	pᵈ Attending Hollins and Mellor felony		2	6
	James Gordon and family to Sterling			6
	pᵈ for a Quire of Paper			9
12.	pᵈ a Woman & four Children from Newcastle		1	
	pᵈ lighting Lamps, and Wick		2	2
17.	pᵈ War" to Hamlets for Present-ments		2	
21.	Parchm' and writing that for Man-chester...		1	
	pᵈ High constables Clerk with yᵉ presentment		1	
	pᵈ Belman crying a Vagrant		1	
	pᵈ Mʳ Peter Touchet a Years Rᵗ [rent] Engine house	2		
	repaid Constable Holme advanced to passengers		6	
22.	pᵈ Messenger to Bolton wᵗʰ present^{mts} Horse & Expences		3	
23.	pᵈ Charges a second Journey, refused by a Messenger		3	
23.	Ellen Normon to London			6
	pᵈ Marg' Mallaburn to London ...			6
29.	pᵈ a Sick passenger			4
31.	pᵈ John Healy mending Watch bills² &c.		3	7
31.	pᵈ half year's cleansing Steps at Salford bridge and those at Milbrow near Dangerous Corner		2	
	pᵈ Thoˢ Wilson's bill concerning Hollins & Mellor		14	6

¹ That is, the Governor of the House of Correction.
² See p. 31, note 4.

	p^d a lame Woman and two Children to Leek		:	6
Ap^l 2^d	p^d Enginemen	: 10	:	6
2.	A Woman & Child from Wales to York		:	6
April 4.	p^d Jurors of an Inquisition	: 1	:	4
	p^d serving the Coroners War^{ts}	: 1	:	
5.	p^d seven passengers to Carlisle... ...	: 1	:	
7.	p^d War^{ts} to Hamlets for New Over-seers	: 2	:	
7.	p^d Belman giving Notice for Quarters	: 1	:	
9.	p^d Jurors about Shenton's Inquisition	: 1	:	4
	p^d serving Coroners Warrants	: 1	:	
10.	p^d Jurors, a second Inquisition... ...	: 1	:	4
10.	Attending Lydia Thompson in ye Stocks^1	: 1	:	
10.	Three passengers this day...	: 1	:	2
19.	Eliz: Lewis a Vagrant	:	:	6
	John Hornbey to Whitbey Yorkshire	:	:	3
21.	p^d for a Watch bill	: 1	:	
21.	p^d Belman to discover breaking Cross Steps	: 1	:	
22.	p^d Cordelia Barrell to Scarborough...	:	:	3
23.	Thos Carlton and another Sailor ...	:	:	6
28.	p^d conveying Healey for Burglary to Lanc^r	2 : 2	:	
May. 2.	p^d making Greave for a Felodese ...	: 1	:	2
2.	p^d commit^g Collyer assaulting Beadle	: 2	:	6
	Robert Jones to Plymouth	:	:	6
6.	p^d Belman crying Stolen Yarn found upon a Man by the Watch	: 1	:	
	p^d Examin^g commit^g and attending ye Thief	: 4	:	6
	Marth. Wilkinson & two Children ...	:	:	6
8.	Four Passengers...	: 1	:	
	John Garn discharged to Scotland ...	:	:	6
12.	p^d playing Engines	: 10	:	6
14.	p^d Wm Napper discharged to London	:	:	6
	Two other Sick Passengers	:	:	8
	p^d War^{ts} to Hamlets for Surveyors present^t [presentments]	: 2	:	

^{1} See p. 16, note 3.

	p^d D° Assessors Land tax 2/- D° Window Duty 2/-	: 4 :
16.	p^d a passenger from Leverpool Infirmary[1]	: : 3
	p^d farther Charges examining Ra: Latham	: 4: 6
	p^d an Irishwoman & Child	: : 9
	Bridget Leatherbarrow a Vagrant ...	: : 6
May 16.	p^d Belman & Expences a Town's Cry	: 1: 6
	p^d a Commitment to ye house o' Cor[r]ection[2]	: 2:
	and a Comm^t to Lancaster for Healey	: 4:
23.	and another Comm^t to Lanc^r for Wm Latham	: 4:
26.	p^d conveying Wm Ingham to Lancaster Castle dangerously striking Deputy's Eye	2: 2:
	p^d Beadle sundry Expences ab^t Dungeon	: 3: 6
29.	p^d John Kerly and Family to Edenburgh	: : 6
29.	Marg^t Forester and Child to Stafford	: 1 :
	Belman decrying Sabath-breakers ...	: 1 :
	Boonfire	: 6:
30.	Charles Wilson and family to Brenton	: : 5
June 9.	p^d for Oil for the Engines...	: 2: 6
	p^d cleansing & oiling the Leather Pipes	: 7: 6
	Luke Bentl[e]y to Ringly in Yorkshire	: : 3
	Eliz: Smith permitted to Leeds ...	: : 4
10.	Five Vagrants from Justice Birch ...	: 1 :
11.	Oliver Cotton from D°	: : 6
12.	Judith Phillips and two Children ...	: : 6
16.	p^d Commissioners Clerks for Assessors War^t	: 1 :
	and Expences attending ye Assessors of Window Duty	: 2: 6

[1] The Liverpool Infirmary had been opened for the reception of patients on the 25th March, 1749.

[2] It may here be mentioned that Mr. William Harrison printed an interesting account of the HOUSE OF CORRECTION, situate at Hunt's Bank, in the *Transactions of the Lancashire and Cheshire Antiquarian Society* for 1885.

21.	p^d charges attending 8^d and Commitm^{tt} 4 – two Whores...	: 4 : 8	
22.	p^d Beadle whipping John Wrigley a Vagrant [1]	: 1 :	
	p^d an Evidence attending some time ago upon Mr Banks the Attorney to discover the persons who broke the Lamps in Town...	: 2 : 6	
25.	p^d Paper and writing the Constable Ley	1 : 1 :	
30.	p^d Oliver Nabb's bill repairing Cross Steps	: 10 : 1½	
July 3^d	p^d eleven Sailors with a pass	: 6	
4.	p^d Wart^s [Warrants] for proportion of 28^l : 17^s : 6^d	: 2 :	
4.	p^d High Constables augment^t Treasurer's Stock [2]	28 : 17 : 6	
4.	p^d Mrs Chapman's [3] bill at privy Watch	1 : 3 :	
4.	p^d charges laying the Ley...	3 : 14 :	
5.	p^d War^{tt} for Land tax 2 - and for Window Duty 2 -	: 4 :	
5.	p^d John Healey repairing Engines ...	: 1 : 6	
July 10.	paid three Vagrants into Scotland ...	: 1 : 6	
14.	p^d a Stranger in the Exchange [4] ...	: : 6	
	Six Sailors in Company to Whitehaven	: : 6	
	p^d Jurors Inquisition, a man scalded to death	: 1 : 4	
21.	p^d two Vagrants...	: 6	
23.	p^d Charges apprehending & Conveying Maude	: 2 : 6	
	p^d a Vagrant from Shefield	: : 6	
	p^d Job West's Bill for Scaffolding at ye Cross	: 13 : 6	

[1] This is, I think, the first instance of any person being "whipped" that is recorded in this volume of Accounts. In previous volumes, especially the first, there are many entries in each year.

[2] This is the first reference to any "stock" in these Accounts.

[3] Mrs. Chapman was the landlady of the Bull's Head Inn, in the town, where she had apparently succeeded Mr. Bartholomew. (See *Court Leet Records*, vol. vij., pp. 195 and 204.)

[4] The EXCHANGE here mentioned was erected by Sir Oswald Mosley, Bart., lord of the Manor of Manchester, in 1729, an engraving of which is in existence. It was taken down in 1793, and is often spoken of as the "Old Exchange" to distinguish it from the one erected near the same site in 1806.

	p^d Thomas Fletcher for carting Baggage	:	6 :	
30.	p^d John Gland wife and four Children	:	1 :	6
31.	p^d James Blinkhorn's bill for Beadles Hose	1 :	2 :	6
	p^d repairing Pinfold	:	2 :	3
Augt 4.	p^d Beadle whipping a Vagrant... ...	:	1 :	
6.	p^d High Constables War^t for Governor's Wages	1 :	4 :	6
	p^d War^{ts} to Hamlets for their proportion...	:	2 :	
8.	p^d Eight Sailors in Company to Whitehaven	:	1 :	
11.	p^d War^{ts} for notice to appeal to Window Duty	:	2 :	
	p^d D^o for notice for Ale Licences ...	:	2 :	
	p^d the same for Presentments to ye Assize	:	2 :	
	p^d Enginemen laid out on ye Engines	:	2 :	2
13.	p^d a passenger	:	:	4
	p^d sundry others since 29th June last	:	2 :	6
	p^d for a Quire of Paper	:	:	9
18.	p^d relieving Richard Edge in the Dungeon		: 10	
25.	p^d mending the Dungeon door ...	:	1 :	8
30.	p^d Widow M.[ac] Donald & Daughter	:	:	6
31.	p^d Manchester Presentment to the Assizes	:	1 :	
	Parchment and writing it	:	1 :	
Sepr 8.	Archibald Boyde and Wife with family	:	1 :	
	p^d sundry Expences for the Enginemen	:	2 :	4
19.	p^d serving Coroners War^{ts} on Inquisition	:	1 :	
	p^d Jurors thereupon Child found dead	:	1 :	4
	p^d the same Jurors a Second time ...	:	1 :	4
	p^d War^{ts} for payment of Landtax ...	:	2 :	
	p^d D^o Window Duty 2/- and D^o Ale Lycences 2/-	:	4 :	
Octob^r 2^d	Michael M[ac] Auley and Wife to Scotland	:	:	6
3.	p^d Six passengers to Scarborough ...	:	1 :	

8.	p^d Engine men five times cleansing...	2 : 10 :
8.	p^d Jurors of an Inquisition. Child drown'd	: 1 : 4
8.	p^d serving Coroners Warrants... ...	: 1 :
8.	p^d Charges enquiring after the Mother of the Child found dead in the River.	: 2 : 6
	p^d Robert Taylor for Carting Baggage	: 6 :
	p^d him carting two lame Vagrants by War^t to Sale	: 5 :
	p^d three passengers	: : 6
	p^d Widow Green by permit to Exeter	: : 6
9.	p^d Belman giving Notice of Quarters	: 1 :
	p^d half year cleansing Steps	: 2 :
	repaid Constable Holme advanced to Vagrants	: 1 :
25.	p^d Marketlookers Bill	7 : 4 : 8
	p^d some time since attending a man under a War^t before Mr Percival at Middleton	: 2 : 4
26.	p^d Christopher Linch discharg'd ...	: 6
	p^d M^n Bowdler for new Glass for Lamp &c.	: 8 :
	p^d Horsehire to press a Cart early the morning the last Dragoons left Town & Exp...	: 1 : 6
	p^d Robert Edmundson for Assistance	: 2 :
	p^d Saml Smith's bill for Lamp-oil ...	: 15 : 2
	Mr Joseph Birch for D^o this Year ...	2 : 19 :
	p^d Beadles[1] Salary	7 : :
	p^d Deputy's[2] Salary	20 : :
		£165 : : 6½

Cash received by the Constables Wm Edge & Ja^s Holme.

	l	s	d
From the Treasurer for carrying Baggage	3 :	6 :	
From the Hamlets, proportion of 1^l. 4^s. 6^d ...		: 16 :	4
From D^o proportion of 28 . 17 . 6 ...	19 :	5 :	
From D^o proportion of 1 . 4 . 6 ...		: 16 :	4

[1] The Beadle was Mr. John Dutton, elected 11th October, 1752. (See *Court Leet Records*, vol. vij., p. 214.)

[2] The Deputy Constable was Mr. John Kay, elected at the same time. (*Ibid, ibid.*)

	l	s	d
From M' Hilton Misegatherer ... 74 : 4 : 3			
From M' Johnson D° ... 48 : 4 : 11½			
	122 :	9 :	2½
From Deputy, collected from old Ley	1 :	4 :	3
From Ashton Lever Esq		: 14 :	7
From present Constables yᵉ Balance	16 :	8 :	10

$$£165 : \quad : 6½$$

We the Jurors of the Court Leet have Examined the above
Accounts of the late Constables above named and finding one
Guinea charged for collecting a Remainder of the last Years
Constable Ley[1] do disallow the same, and then the Balance will be
only fifteen pounds seven Shillings and ten pence which we order
the present Constables M' James Gratrex and M' Thomas Chadwick
to pay to the abovemamed [sic] Wᵐ Edge & Jaˢ Holme and so allow
the above Accounts.

(Signed)	SAMᴸ RIDING	GEO. LLOYD
	THOˢ GARDNER	THOˢ CLOWES
	JAMES CLOUGH	EDWᴰ GREAVES
		JNᴼ MOSS
		ROBERT GARTSIDE
		JOHN BROOME.

[1] See p. 47, note 3.

[Constables' Accounts.]

[10th Oct., 1753, to 14th Oct., 1754.]

•••••••••••

Cash disbursed by JAMES GREATREX and THOMAS CHADWICK,[1] *Constables of Manchester,* elected Michaelmas Court Leet 1753.

[Disbursements]

1753		l	s	d
October 10.	paid last Constables their Balance ...	15 :	7 :	10[2]
16.	p^d Jurors of an Inquisition a Child drowned		1 :	4
16.	p^d serving the Coroner's Warrants upon the Hamlets		1 :	
16.	p^d Expences apprehending two Felons		1 :	
17.	p^d Expences maintaining them two Nights in the Dungeon		2 :	
17.	p^d D° on Ann Coe's Acc^t suspected of having murder'd a Child		1 :	3
17.	p^d Thomas Fletcher's Cart with Baggage to Rochdale		6 :	
18.	p^d Belman for Scavengers to do their Duty		1 :	
18.	p^d Mr Berwick[3] Coroner to produce an Inquisition before Esqr Birch ...		3 :	
22.	p^d Robert Hobson for a Cart along with Fletcher's to Rochdale Soldiers for Bradford &c to prevent Riots &c		6 :	
22.	p^d Boonfire on the King's Coronation Day		6 :	6

[1] These two Constables were elected at the Court Leet held on the 10th October, 1753. (See *Court Leet Records,* vol. vij., p. 221.)

[2] See p. 56.

[3] Mr. Berwick's name as Coroner has not, I think, occurred before.

			£	s	d
22.	pᵈ for Warrant to press Carriages 2 – Expences—Executing it 2 6		:	4 :	6
23.	pᵈ Expences setling Accounts with Misegatherers		:	2 :	4
23.	pᵈ Edward Under by Pass to Liverpool			:	6
23.	pᵈ Mary Barns to Preston...		:	:	6
23.	pᵈ George Gordan to Scotland... ...		:	:	6
23.	pᵈ Jaᵉ Cockburn, Wife and one Child to Whitehaven			:	6
23.	pᵈ Jane Smith with two Children to Glo[u]cester			:	6
23.	pᵈ Wᵐ Raddey to Edinburg in North Britain...		:	:	6
29.	pᵈ Porters playing Engines 10/- and for Ale /6		: 10 :	6
29.	pᵈ committing John Dewhurst for a Riot		:	2 :	6
29.	pᵈ Kath: Varnival a Soldier's Wife to Southampton			:	2
30.	pᵈ Mary Smith and five Children to Scotland		:	:	6
30.	pᵈ Mʳ Newton old Bill for Wine had in the yʳ 1748¹	1 : 16 :	
Nov. 2.	pᵈ an Assistant to serve Crouchley with a Warrant of Assault		:	:	6
3.	pᵈ Porters playing Engines		: 10 :	6
3.	pᵈ Ann Starling with one Child to Leverpool		:	:	4
3.	pᵈ Belman giving Alehouses Notice for Quarters		:	1 :	
3.	pᵈ him for two former Cries on the same Account		:	2 :	
3.	pᵈ Eliz: Booth and Child to Liverpool		:	:	6
5.	pᵈ for Boonfire this Day		:	6 :	6
Nov. 5.	paid Assistants with four Prisoners to Justice...		:	1 :	2
5.	pᵈ Thoᵉ Culbert and John Williams with their Wives and five Children to Irwin in Scotland		:	1 :	
5.	pᵈ Roger Charlton to York		:	1 :	

¹ This is one of the years for which the Accounts are now missing.

		l	s	d
5.	p^d lighting Lamps at Cross and Dungeon	:	1	3
	p^d sundry other Vagrants	:	2	:
10.	p^d Paper and writing Warr^{ts} to Hamlets requiring Surveyors of Highways to bring in their Presentments	:	2	:
10.	p^d Messenger to the Hamlets with 'em	:	1	:
10.	p^d for Boonfire this Day being the Birth of King George[1]	:	6	6
10.	Henry Kirk's Bill for Wine drinking Healths &c[1]	3	15	:
12.	p^d Mary Johnson to Whitby in Yorkshire	:	:	6
13.	p^d Charges to Governor Oldham[2] keeping William Tildsley ten Days after his Commitment to Lancaster...	:	10	6
15.	p^d Mrs Worral Sundry Expences for Prisoners by Dutton	:	2	6
15.	p^d Commitment 2 – Exam 1 – Expences in the Dungeon and conveying to the House of Correction & Ba[i]liffs 1/9 a notorious Nightwalker[3] from Stockport	:	4	9
16.	p^d Expences of Privy Watch at the Ax[e][4] in Toadlane	1	:	:
22.	p^d Ann Aldred and another to Kent	:	:	6
	p^d conveying Wm Tildsley for Horse stealling to Lancaster...	2	2	6
23	p^d Ishmael Jones and his Wife to Suffolk...	:	:	4
	p^d Bailiffs attending Matthew Prior under a Bench War^t...	:	1	:
24	p^d Bailiffs attending Ja^s Ogden to Justice and conveying him back to the House of Correction	:	1	:

[1] King George's birthday, 10th November, "new style." The celebration took place in previous years on October 30th, the date in the "old style," before the alteration in the calendar in 1752.

[2] This gives us the name of the then Governor of the House of Correction in Manchester.

[3] The use of this old word is noteworthy. It occurs again later on in this year's Accounts.

[4] The name of this Manchester Inn occurs here for the first time.

		l	s	d
24.	pᵈ Beadle relieving three Persons in the Dungeon	:	1 :	4
24.	pᵈ him whipping a Vagrant	:	1 :	
24.	pᵈ Tho' Sandiford's Bill two Carts to Rochdale		: 12 :	
24.	pᵈ to Ja' France Dᵒ		: 12 :	
24.	pᵈ three Persons all Night in quest of infamous Houses Whores and Night Walkers		: 3 :	6
26.	pᵈ Assistants with three Persons in the Dungeon	:	1 :	
26.	pᵈ Mary Morris		:	6
	pᵈ sundry Charges advanced by the Constables		: 2 :	6
	pᵈ Expences of Beadle and Deputy at Court Leet last		: 2 :	6
Nov 28.	pᵈ four Sailors with a Pass to Whitehaven		: :	6
30.	pᵈ Bailiffs attending four Prisoners to Ardwick Green		: 1 :	
30.	pᵈ Ann Radford by Pass to London		: :	6
30.	pᵈ Bailiffs attending John White charged with murder		: 1 :	6
Decʳ 1.	pᵈ Lighting Lamps		: 1 :	6
1.	pᵈ Ben Birket assisting the Watch &c		: 2 :	6
1.	pᵈ John Hanson by Pass to Bradford in Yorkshire		:	6
4.	pᵈ Cobler Oldham two Days assisting Deputy with twelve notorious Whores		: 2 :	6
4.	pˡ Mary Mac. Donald		: :	6
6.	pᵈ two Vagrants from Turkie[1]		: 2 :	
6.	pᵈ John Cooper carrying Baggage to Stockport		: 7 :	6
6.	pᵈ John Gilbert to Newcastle		: :	6
6.	pᵈ Expences at Bull's head about several persons before Justices apprehended by the privy Watch		: 3 :	6
6.	pᵈ Justice Clerks two Examinations 2 - two Commⁱⁱ 4 - and conveying two Vagrants to the House of Correction ⁻⁄6		: 6 :	6

[1] These men had come a long way, and it is difficult to understand what "two vagrants from Turkie" were doing in Manchester at this time.

		l	s	d
6.	p^d Robert Slater two Days and two Nights attending, apprehending and conveying the twelve Whores &c. ...		: 5 :	
7.	p^d seven Passengers		:	6
8.	p^d a Woman with three Children to Whitehaven		: :	6
8.	p^d John Healey's Bill...		: 10 :	6
8.	p^d Ja^s Royle a passenger		: :	6
8.	p^d Alex^r Mac Land to North Britain		: :	6
9.	p^d three Persons assisting Beadle Yesterday & Night		: 3 :	
10.	p^d Expences with Quartermasters Billeting &c		: 2 :	6
12.	p^d Thos Archer, Wife and Child to Parke Gate		:	6
15.	p^d making Beadles Cap and Gown ...		: 6 :	
18.	p^d Jane Smith and two Children to Kerbylansdale [Kirby Lonsdale] ...		:	6
19.	p^d attending Wm Whitaker under Warrant		: 1 :	
19.	p^d an Examination and Warrant against John White		: 3 :	
19.	p^d apprehending and attending Leonard Holden suspected of Robery ...		: 2 :	8
19.	p^d Warr^t & Carriages impressing for Stockport		: 2 :	6
Decr 19.	paid Expences maintaining and attending Ja^s Heap in Custody for dangerously striking his Wife 1,6 his Comm^t 2 : — and conveying him to the House of Correction		: 4 :	
20.	p^d a Vagrant		: :	6
23.	p^d a sick Stranger in the Streets ...		: :	6
23.	p^d at Thos Vaux's attending three Bailiffs under Warrant		: 1 :	7
23.	p^d at Ardwick Green 1 6 Commitment 2, — Assistants		: 3 :	6
24.	p^d Eliz : Royley into Staffordshire ...		: :	3
26.	p^d War^tt to Hamlets for Landtax 2 — Messenger sending 'em 1 :—		: 3 :	
26.	p^d D^o for Window Duty 2 — & Messenger with them		: 3 :	
26.	p^d D^o for new Surveyors of the Highway		: 3 :	

		l	s	d
26.	p^d Belman to give Notice of Meeting to name Surveyors		: 1 :	
26.	p^d for Wine at the meeting & Deputy a Pint		: 3 :	
26.	p^d George Plant's Bill		: 5 :	
29.	p^d lighting Lamps and for oil		: 3 :	1
29.	p^d Wm Lorax and Wife to Carlile ...		: 1 :	
2. [1754]	p^d John Morris a discharged Soldier to Ireland			: 4
Jañry 3.	p^d Marg^t Napper with two Children to Leeds		: 1 :	
5.	p^d Thos Fletcher with three Carts of Baggage to Rochdale		: 18 :	
7.	p^d Engine men playing Engines two Months	1 :	:	6
7.	p^d with Soldiers removing Billets ...		: 1 :	
7.	p^d Jurors of an Inquisition a Child drown'd		: 1 :	4
7.	p^d serving Coroner's Warrants... ...		: 1 :	
9.	p^d three Sailors with a Pass to Whitehaven		: :	6
11.	p^d John Dale to Newcastle		:	3
11.	p^d War^ts to Hamlets a second time for new Surveyors		: 2 :	
11.	p^d Messenger carrying them away ...		: 1 :	
14.	p^d Expences quartering Soldiers to day Hay very dear and Landlords extremely troublesom[e]		: 1 :	
14.	p^d Isaac Hazzlehurst repairing Engines	2 : 11 : 11		
14.	p^d painting Beadles Staff		: 1 :	
14.	p^d Mary Johnson and Child to Warrington...		: :	6
15.	p^d Expences attending Col. Forbes and Justice Birch[1] about Complaints of Soldiers Quarters		: 1 :	
	p^d John Shaw in Augt last for Ale had By Massons repair^g Cross[2]... ...		: 5 :	6
Janry. 17.	paid Roger Charlton a sick Passenger to York		: 1 :	

[1] This was Samuel Birch, of Ardwick, Esq., whose death occurred on December 18th, 1757. He is frequently mentioned in these Accounts.

[2] See p. 42. note 2.

		l	s	d
17.	p^d for a Press Warrant for Carrriages omitted 14th Augt last		: 2 :	
17.	p^d Persons assisting the Watch, Vilains breaking Windows		: 2 :	6
18.	p^d John Dunkardly Wife & Child to Cumberland		:	6
18.	p^d John Healey's Bill for Engines ...		: 6 :	7
21.	p^d Bailiffs attending three Prisoners to Ardwick & Expences		: 1 :	
24.	p^d Ben Berket assisting with a Prisoner		: 1 :	
	p^d Edward Coppock painting two new Truncheons[1]	1 :	1 :	
24.	p^d Danl Ashton turning Piston Leathers for Engines		: 4 :	6
24.	p^d preferring a Bill of Indictment ag^t Wm Mellor		: 3 :	4
24.	p^d Extraordinary Expences attending Sessions		: 2 :	6
30.	p^d Eliz: Leatherbarrow from Salsbury by Pass		: 1 :	
30.	p^d a poor Passenger last Sunday for Scotland		:	6
Feb. 2.	p^d lighting Lamps last Dark		:	: 10
2.	p^d Beadle sundry Expences ab^t Prisoners		: 3 :	2
2.	p^d Robt Hobson for carting Baggage	1 : 16 :		
4.	p^d Horse 1/- Mess. 1/- Expences 4/- [sic] returning War^t ag^t Ralph Shepherd from Sr Ralph Ashton[2]...		: 2 :	4
6.	p^d Ann Dale and two Children to Knarsborough		:	6
	p^d a Pass and relieving a Passenger to Bengal[3]		: 2 :	
11.	p^d Porters playing Engines		: 10 :	
13.	p^d drawing and correcting Advertisements ab^t John Hilton alias Wilson the Horsestealer &c		: 2 :	

[1] These "truncheons" must have been very elaborately painted for so much money to have been paid for the work.

[2] See p. 47, note 1.

[3] It would seem very improbable that a passenger to "Bengal" in India would be passing through Manchester, but I am not aware of any other place of that name. It occurs again later on. (See p. 69.)

		l	s	d
13.	p^d Dutton[1] whipping two Vagrants...	:	2 :	
13.	p^d him relieving Prisoners	:	2 :	4
13.	p^d him ab^t Indictment of Wm Mellors	:	1 :	4
13.	p^d for two Informations ag^t Aspinall & Lumb for Entertaining Rougus [sic] & Vagabonds	:	2 :	
13.	p^d Hugh Shakeshaft for two Cats with nine Tails[2]	:	4 :	11
13.	p^d him for a Leatherpeak for Beadle's Cap	:	1 :	
13.	p^d Wm Worrall's for Ale to Dutton & Prisoners from time to time attending there	:	6 :	6
13.	p^d Ed. Morgan to North Britain ...		:	6
13.	p^d for two Summonses and Summoning two Alehouse keepers, to shew Cause before Sr Ralph Ashton[3] why they do not provide sufficient Stabling	:	2 :	
Feb. 13.	paid Horsehire 1 6 Expences 11^d Messenger 1 obtaining the Summons at Middleton	:	2 :	11
14.	p^d Hos hire 1 6 Expences 6^d going to Middleton by the Summons with John Pickford & Jonath Worthington ...	:	2 :	
14.	p^d Bailiffs apprehending Charles Sutliff under Mr Percivall's[4] Warrant detaining Leather he had undertook to curry for Wages...	:	1 :	2
14.	p^d maintaining an Irish man's Wife and two Children one Night in a publick himself in the Dungeon ...	:	1 :	6
15.	p^d Expences overnight apprehending him and Messenger returning the Warrant agreed 1^s/-	:	1 :	6

---

[1] John Dutton was the Beadle, elected at the Court Leet held on the 11th October, 1752. (See *Court Leet Records*, vol. vij., p. 214.)

[2] This is the first reference in these Accounts to the "cat-o'-nine-tails," the well-known instrument with which the unfortunate persons who had to suffer corporal punishment were flogged.

[3] See p. 47, note 1.

[4] This was Thomas Percival, of Royton Hall, near Oldham, Esq., F.S.A., described as "an excellent magistrate, an intelligent antiquary, and a respectable churchman."

		l	s	d
15.	p^d horsehire to Royton[1] 2 – Assistants with two Prisoners 1 8 Expences Selves and Prisoners 2 1 one for detaining Leather the other for entering into the Weaver's Combination[2]..		: 5 :	9
16.	p^d Messenger returning a Warrant to Sr Ralph Ashton agreed. Smith ag^t Butterworth		: 1 :	3
16.	p^d for two Quire of Paper...		: 1 :	6
17.	p^d for two Copies of the Register of John Lees Marriage		: 1 :	
17.	p^d horsehire 1 6 Messenger 1 – Expences 9^d for a Cer^t of John Lees marriage at Ashton Underline 6^d ...		: 3 :	9
18.	p^d Deputy's Horse to Royton 2 – Exp. 8 – [sic] with John Lees		: 2 :	8
18.	p^d two Bailiffs assisting with him and his three Wives[3] to Royton 3 – ...		: 3 :	
18.	p^d Justice Clerks for their four Examinations...		: 4 :	
18.	p^d for his Commitment to Lancaster		: 4 :	
18.	p^d for four Recognizances...		: 8 :	
18.	p^d for three double Horses,[4] Women[3] not able to walk thither and he refusing to do so...		: 7 :	6
19.	p^d High Constables War^t for the Governor's Wages[5]	1 :	4 :	6
19.	p^d Messenger and Expences Yesterday to find out John Lees three Wives and getting 'em together[3]...		: 1 :	6
	p^d conveying John Lees to the Castle at Lancaster	2 :	2 :	
	p^d for a Receipt for him from the Keeper		: 1 :	

[1] This entry relates to the previous one, in which Mr. Percival, of Royton, is referred to as the acting magistrate.

[2] Here we have an early instance of a "strike," in which one of those who joined the "Weaver's Combination" was punished for so doing.

[3] All the entries at this point appear to relate to one John Lees, who had been too much married, his "three wives" having to be taken on horseback to Lancaster to give evidence against him.

[4] That is, horses with broad saddles capable of seating two people, the woman riding 'pillion' behind the man.

[5] That is, for the Governor of the House of Correction.

		l	s	d
25.	p^d Belman and writing Notice to decry Cock throwing[1]		1 :	6
	p^d writing War^{ts} to Hamlets for Presentments to the Assize		2 :	
Febry 25.	paid Messenger getting War^{ts} to the Hamlets		1 :	
25.	p^d returning a War^t agreed Unsworth ag^t Taylor to Royton		1 :	6
25.	p^d Parchment & writing Presentment for Manchester		1 :	
26.	p^d lighting the two Lamps last Dark...		2 :	1
26.	p^d with the Attorney consulting how to draw Briefs [a]gainst John White & John Lees both in Goal		1 :	2
26.	p^d Justice Birch's Clerk by Governor Oldham[2] for two Liberators[3] for Mary Birch & Susan Bowker two notorious Whores 4/- Fees 2/-...		6 :	
26.	p^d Dorothy Walker a Passenger ...		:	6
March 1.	p^d High Constables Clerks with Presentments for the Assize at Oldham 1/- horsehire thither and to Royton with a War^t 2/- Expences Horse & Self 1/2		4 :	2
1.	p^d Warr^{ts} to Hamlets requiring Surveyors to bring in their Presentments 2/- & Messenger 1/-...		3 :	
	p^d D^o to Constables to return their Search Warrant		2 :	
	p^d Eliz: Smith and her son to Plymouth		:	6
4.	p^d Ja^s Elidishaw by Justice Birch's Pass		:	2
5.	p^d Mary Fitton's loss of Time 1/- & her Information 1/-		2 :	
9.	p^d Ann Coe's Examination ag^t White 1/- Governor 1/- Liber^r 2/-		4 :	

[1] The old so-called sport of "cock throwing" took place on Shrove Tuesday, and was generally indulged in by boys and young men. The unfortunate cock was tied securely to a stake fixed in the ground, and sticks were thrown at it from a certain distance. In the foundation statutes of the Manchester Grammar School, in 1515, the "Schole Maister and Ussher" were to teach the children without any payment or fee such as "cokke peny" [cock penny], &c. This was money paid by the scholars to the Master for permission to throw at cocks at Shrovetide.

[2] Mr. Oldham was the Governor of the House of Correction.

[3] That is, two persons to give bail.

		l	s	d
p^d Dutton's Bill 24th February		:	9:	6
p^d Deputy's[1] Bill of Sundrys (see his Memorandums)		:	17:	6
11.	Expences of Six Persons to Lancaster, John Lees[2] to be tryed for Bigamy & John White suspected of murthering an Infant born on the Body of Ann Coe (viz)			
	p^d Ja^s an Evidence ag^t his Brother (on foot)	1:		
	p^d Martha Thorp's loss of Time and Expences	1:	11:	6
	p^d Ann Paulden's D^o	1:	11:	6
	p^d Ann Coe's D^o	1:	11:	6
	p^d John Duttons D^o in part ...	1:	1:	
	p^d Deputy Subpaena to Lancaster ...	2:	2:	
	Mr Berwick the attorney in part of his Bill 7 . 5 . 8	5:	5:	
17.	Deputy out of Pocket more than is charged above by paying for Meat & Drink at Lanc^r for the Women and upon the Road, Cash paid 'em to come home and his own Extraordinary Expences	1:	7:	6
	p^d Porters 10/– & for Oil for Engines 8^d		10:	8
March 17.	p^d Ringers Judge Clyve in Town[3] ...		10:	6
	p^d Renewing the Vagrant Warr^t ...	:	:	6
	p^d Belman giving Notice for Dragoons Quarters	:	1:	6
	p^d for Ja^s Crank & Slater attending Prisoners	:	:	4
19.	p^d High Constables Warr^t repairing Ribchester Bridge	2:	:	6
	p^d Warr^ts to Hamlets for their Proportion 2/– Messenger 1/–	:	3:	
	p^d D^o for Governor's Wages 12th Febry last	:	3:	
20 .	p^d Warr^ts to Hamlets for Landtax & Window duty	:	3:	

---

[1] That is, the Deputy Constable, Mr. John Kay.   [2] See p. 65, note 3.
[3] It was customary to entertain the Judges as they passed through the town. See p 5. note 4.

		l	s	d
24.	pᵈ a Vagᵗ Woman in Labour in the Streets...		: 2 :	
27.	pᵈ two Passengers into Suffolk... ...		: : 4	
30.	pᵈ cleansing Steps at Salford Bridge half a Year...		: 2 :	
30.	pⁱⁱ a discharged Soldier to Brampton		: : 3	
April 1.	pᵈ Porters playing Engines		: 10 :	
2.	pᵈ Extraordinary Watch after two naughty Women, at Mr. Higginson's Complaint in Hanging ditch		: 1 :	
4.	pᵈ Danˡ Barret his Wife and Child to Durham		: : 6	
13.	pᵈ Horse 1/6 & baiting at Middleton, returning a Warrᵗ agᵗ Solomon Dooly		: 2 :	
15.	pᵈ Warrˡˢ to Hamlets 2/- Messenger 1/- for Assessors Landtax		: 3 :	
17.	pᵈ Dᵒ &c. calling Overseers to Account		: 3 :	
17.	pᵈ Belman decrying Custom of Lifting [1]		: 1 :	
17.	pᵈ two poor Passengers unto Kent each 6ᵈ		: 1 :	
19.	pᵈ Henry Walwork for a Horse double [2] to Royton with John Lees and his Concubine		: 3 :	
20.	pᵈ Market lookers their former Bill...	2 : 11 :		6
20.	pᵈ Dᵒ their latter Bill in full	3 : 7 :		4
20.	pᵈ Expences at a meeting to go upon the Privy Watch		: 5 :	3
22.	pᵈ Ruth Hulme to Berwick upon tweed		: : 3	
22.	pᵈ Jane Welsh and two Infants to Bristol...		: : 4	
30.	pᵈ John Graham his Wife and two Children to Pearth		: : 6	
May. 2.	pⁱⁱ Jaˢ Blakeling's Bill carting Baggage	1 : 16 :		
4.	pᵈ Wᵐ Worrall's Bill...		: 4 :	6
5.	pᵈ Porters playing Engines		: 10 :	
7.	pᵈ Kath. Gordon with a sick Child ...		: : 6	

[1] "Lifting" was an old custom practised on Easter Monday and Tuesday, and had reference to the rising of our Lord from the tomb on Easter Sunday. The custom was for groups of women to catch hold of and to "lift" from the ground all the men they met, whilst the men did the same by the women. A small payment evaded this rough horse-play, which was apt to become indecent and annoying. Easter Monday this year was April 15th. There are many other references to this custom of "lifting" in the later Accounts.

[2] See p. 65, note 4.

		l	s	d
9.	p^d Esther Higson & her Child to Stafford	:	:	3
May 9.	p^d Bernerd Mac Manns a discharged Soldier	:	:	3
11.	p^d John Dutton sundry Expences with Prisoners	:	1 :	6
17.	p^d maintaining a Thief in the Dungeon	:	:	4
17.	p^d Tho' Eccleston to Garthstang ...	:	:	6
21.	p^d for Paper for Billets &c	:	1 :	8
21.	p^d Expences at sundry times with Prisoners 2^d 4^d 10^d 6^d 6^d	:	2 :	4
21.	p^d Expences with Officers setling Quarters for a Regiment	:	1 :	6
21.	p^d Hannah Hunter and one Child ...	:	1 :	
21.	p^d Eliz : Kennady to Carlile	:	:	4
23.	p^d Archibald Frazier to Edinburg ...	:	:	6
23.	p^d Charles Gibbons to Peterborough	:	:	4
25.	p^d Wm Sipio from Bengal[1] to Ireland	:	:	6
28.	p^d two Sailors	:	:	6
29.	p^d for a Boonfire	:	6 :	
	p^d Walter Wilson's Bill	:	1 :	5½
	p^d repairing Constable's Staff	:	:	8
	rep^d Mr Tho' Chadwick's Bill	3 :	9 :	6
	p^d Hugh Halliwell for Beadles shoes	:	4 :	6
30.	p^d Ja' Commins to Plymouth	:	:	6
30.	p^d committing two Vagrants and conveying them	:	4 :	6
	p^d Charges as p Memorandum, apprehending four Irish men followed by Warr^t out of Yorkshire	:	1 :	6
	p^d for a Darklanthorn to Wm Mostyn	:	1 :	6
June 2.	p^d Mrs Collins's Bill at Privy Watch ...	:	11 :	10
8.	p^d Ben. Birket assisting at the privy Watch...	:	1 :	6
8.	p^d Mary Anderson by Pass with an Infant		:	4
8.	p^d High Constables conveying Vagrants &c	12 :	19 :	5

[1] Here we have Bengal again referred to, but this time the traveller was coming from Bengal to Ireland. (See p. 63, note 3.)

		l	s	d
8.	p[d] Clerk of the Peace 1/4 & Dantĕs. Smith[1] 1/- getting an Order upon the Treasurer to repay 6 . 1 . 0 Baggage		: 2 :	4
	p[d] War[u] to Hamlets for their proportion &c		: 3 :	
	p[d] John Worrall discharg'd to Darfold		:	6
	p[d] Bangbegger[2] whipping five Vagrants		: 5 :	
18.	p[d] committing three notorious Whores		: 2 :	
24.	p[d] Jurors of an Inquisition at Bagshaw's in Salford...		: 1 :	4
	p[d] mending five Watch Bills[3]		: 1 :	2
June 24.	paid John M. Quien from Eagermouth to London		: :	6
July. 1.	p[d] Porters playing Engines	1 :	:	
	p[d] them for Ale by M[r] Chadwick's Order		: 1 :	
3.	p[d] Kath. Cranshaw into the Fild[4] ...		: :	6
	p[d] Tho' Radford's Bill for a new Engine Pipe	1 :	2 :	1
6.	p[d] Robert Edmunson for Assistance...		: 3 :	9
6.	p[d] Committing two Whores 4/- Charges attending 'em 1/-...		: 5 :	
6.	p[d] sundry Expences attending upon John Barret's Daughter a notorious Whore...		: 1 :	6
6.	p[d] John Ashton for his Assistance Yesterday		: 1 :	
6.	p[d] Committing and conveying Jane Massey a Whore		: 2 :	6
10.	p[d] Jane Hance and two Children to Cumberland		:	6
10.	p[d] Alex' M[ac] Clarend to Scotland...		: :	6
11.	p[d] to carry the lame Man away to Pointon		: :	6
15.	p[d] Expences upon the privy Watch at Ja' Warmbey's		: :	6

---

[1] That is, a contraction for Dauntesey Smith.

[2] "Bangbeggar" was a word at this time in common use for a beadle, or one who had authority to take up vagrants, &c., and to whip them when sentenced by the magistrates.

[3] See p. 31, note 4.

[4] That is, the Fylde country in the North of Lancashire.

		l	s	d
	p^d Warr^{ts} to Hamlets for Surveyors of the Highways to return their Presentments		: 2 :	
	p^d Messenger bringing them to the Hamlets		: 1 :	
18.	p^d Charges Enquiring ab^t Hulm's bastard murthered		: : 8	
19.	p^d serving Coroners Warrants		: 1 :	
19.	p^d Jurors of an Inquisition		: 1 : 4	
19.	p^d Expences at Cadman's on Evidences &c waiting till eleven o'Clock no verdict		: 2 : 1	
20.	p^d Bangbegger[1] whipping three Whores		: 3 :	
22.	p^d for Mr Greatrex's Information ag^t Wm Crompton 1/- Comm^t 4$^-$		: 5 :	
23.	p^d conveying him to Lancaster Castle	2 : 2 :	
23.	p^d Andrew Petty discharged to Edenburg[h]		: : 6	
24.	p^d for Paper ruling and writing the Leybook	1 : 1 :	
	p^d Information 1$^-$ Commitment 2/- ag^t John Banton		: 3 :	
	p^d Charges to Coachman She not able to go to Ardwick without... ...		: 2 :	
25.	p^d Bailiffs attending two Men to Esqr Birch[2] found in a Riot		: 1 : 3	
25.	p^d Clerk of the Peace for John Banton's Bill		: 3 : 6	
26.	p^d for Committing and conveying two Whores		: 2 : 6	
Augt 2.	p^d Bailiffs with Wm Paulden to Ardwick Green...		: : 6	
3.	p^d Robt Edmundson's Bill...		: 6 :	
Augt 4.	p^d Barnaby M[ac] Laughlin to Ireland		: : 6	
4.	p^d Porters playing Engines		: 10 :	
5.	p^d writing warr^{ts} to Hamlets for their Proportion &c		: 2 :	
	p^d Messenger carrying 'em thither ...		: 1 :	
10.	p^d D^o for return of Assize Presentments		: 3 :	

---

[1] See p. 70, note 2.   [2] See p. 62, note 1.

		l	s	d
	p⁴ John Cambel and two Children by Pass to Liverpool	:	:	6
	p⁴ M⁴ Byrom's Bill for Trimming for Beadle's Cloaths	1 :	1 :	6
	p⁴ Sam¹ Smith's Bill for Oil for Lamps	:	6 :	6
	p⁴ High Constables Warr⁴ for Governor's Wages	1 :	4 :	6
17.	p⁴ M⁴ Blinkhorn for Beadle's Stockings two Pair	:	9 :	
	p⁴ whipping and relieving a Vagrant	:	3 :	
18.	p⁴ Richard Prichard a discharged Pensioner	:	:	6
20.	p⁴ Adam Grundey's Bill for Wine on the 11ᵗʰ June last¹	1 :	4 :	
23.	p⁴ Parchm⁴ and writing Manchester Presentment	:	1 :	
	p⁴ High Constables Clerks with Assize Presentments	:	1 :	
	p⁴ Bailiffs with a Thief to Middleton...	:	1 :	6
	p⁴ Dⁿ returning a Warr⁴ to Royton...	:	1 :	6
	p⁴ Warrⁿ to Hamlets requiring Alehousekeepers to take Licences... ...	:	2 :	
	p⁴ Messenger with 'em to their respective Hamlets	:	1 :	
Sep⁴ 2.	p⁴ Wᵐ Fendon his Wife and Child discharged to Lincoln	:	:	6
	p⁴ writing Money Warⁿ to the Hamlets for Proportion of £100	:	2 :	
	p⁴ Messenger carrying 'em to the Hamlets	:	1 :	
9.	p⁴ Wᵐ Wright wife and four Children to Dalton	:	1 :	
	p⁴ Porters playing Engines	:	10 :	
12.	p⁴ an Information 1/- Comm⁴ and conveying four Whores 4/-	:	5 :	
	p⁴ Ja⁴ Holden repairing Cross Steps..	:	1 :	6
	p⁴ High Cons⁴ Warr⁴ for repairing Spotland Bridge &c	9 :	6 :	
14.	p⁴ mending seven Engine Buckets...	:	3 :	6
18.	p⁴ a Passenger to Liverpool	:	:	6

---

¹ There is nothing to show what special rejoicing had taken place on the 11th June, at which this amount of wine had been consumed, unless it was the King's birthday, usually kept on June 10th. (See page 59, note 1.)

		l	s	d
	p⁴ Warrᵗ to Hamlets for return of Persons Names qualified to serve as Jurors at the Assize &c	:	2	:
	pᵈ Messenger to the Hamlets	:	1	:
	pᵈ writing a List for Manchester & Duplicate 2/- and Justice Clerks for its allowance 1.-...	:	3	:
19.	pᵈ six Women & Children for Scotland	:	:	9
Sep' 21.	paid Passengers to Wigan	:	1	:
	pᵈ for cleansing Dungeon 1 6 & for Straw 1'-	:	2	6
	pᵈ John Chetham an old Soldier to Dublin...	:	:	3
28.	pᵈ serving Coroners Warᵗ...	:	1	:
	pᵈ Jurors of an Inquisition on Richard Kay's Child	:	1	4
Octob. 3.	Expenses upon privy Watch at the Tavern in Deansg'	1	:	9
7.	pᵈ seven Passenger[s] to Ireland ...		:	6
	pᵈ Jurors of an Inquisition at Pendlebury, Man kil'd by falling off his Horse	:	1	4
	pᵈ serving Coroner's Warrᵗ	:	1	:
8.	pᵈ Expences with Quartermasters billiting Soldiers	:	2	6
12.	pᵈ Mʳ Touchet a Year's Rent for the Engine House	2	:	
16.	pᵈ John Higginson to Plymouth ...	:	:	2
20.	pᵈ Coroner's Warrᵗ to Ardwick Salford & Pendleton	:	1	:
	pᵈ Jurors of an Inquisition Reed-maker's Wife at Salford Bridge kil'd...	:	1	4
	pᵈ Beadle Whipping a Thief 1'- & attending two Drunkard's in the Stocks¹ 2'-...	:	3	:
	pᵈ him attending privy Watch 1/- & his going to Stockport 1 6	:	2	6
	pᵈ him Relieving Prisoners	:	1	1
	pᵈ Joseph Harrop's² Bill for printing Advertisemᵗ	2	2	:

¹ See p. 16, note 3.

² Joseph Harrop was at this time the printer of the well-known Manchester newspaper, Harrop's *Manchester Mercury*, of which the first number appeared on March 3rd, 1752.

	l	s	d
p^d Ja' Smethurst to Lanc^r ag^t Wm Crompton	1 :	1 :	
p^d Ann Coe to Lancaster ag^t John White Butcher		: 18 :	
M^r. James Greatrex's Bill			
Mr Thomas Chadwick's Charges going to Lanc^r	1 :	5 :	6
p^d by D^o to four Passengers		: 2 :	
M^r Jo' Birch's Bill for Beadle's Cap & Gown	2 :	12 :	3
M^r Ja' Greatrex another Bill	2 :	18 :	6
Mr Walter Wilson's Bill for new Weights Measures	33 :	9 :	3
p^d Beadle his Year's Salary	7 :	:	
p^d Deputy his Year's Salary	20 :	:	

Total disbursed ... ...£206 : 4 : 4½

1753. An Acco^t of Cash received by Ja' Greatrex &c.
Thomas Chadwick Constables of Manchester.

Received from Mr Dickenson last Year's Ley ...		: 10 :	6
Received from the Hamlets ⅔ of the Warr^t 1' : 4' : 6^d		: 16 :	4
Received from the Hamlets ⅔ of the Warr^t 2 : 0 : 6	1 :	7 :	
Receiued from the Hamlets ⅔ of the Warr^t 12 : 19 : 5	8 :	12 :	11
Received from the Treasurer for carting Baggage [1]...	6 :	1 :	
Received from the Hamlets ⅔ of the Warr^t 9 : 6 : 0	6 :	5 :	
Received from the Hamlets ⅔ of the Warr^t 1 : 4 : 6		: 16 :	4
Received from the Collection of the Constable Ley	123 :	3 :	5½
Balance due to the said Constables	58 :	11 :	10

£206 : 4 : 4½

---

[1] That is, soldiers' baggage.

We the Jurors of the Court Leet have examined the above accounts of the late Constables and finding a Ballance of fifty eight pounds eleven shillings & ten pence due to them. We order the same to be paid by the present Constables & that they do charge the same in their Accounts.

(Signed)   Jno Moss
John Broome
John Todd
Thos Marriott
John Gatley
Robert Gartside
Wm Starkie
John Clowes
John Clough
Richd Walmsley
Edwd Byrom Junr

[Constables' Accounts.]

[14th Oct., 1754, to 8th Oct., 1755.]

•••••••••••

Cash disbursed by THOMAS TIPPING and ROBERT AYRTON,[1] *Constables of Manchester*, elected Michaelmas Court Leet, 1754.

[Disbursements]

1754

October.	paid last Year's Balance[2]	58 : 11 : 10
19.	p[d] for Beadle's Lanthorn	: 1 : 10
	p[d] Beadle whipping four Notorious Whores by Justice's Ord[er]	: 4 :
	p[d] Governor's[3] Fees for the same ...	: 4 :
	p[d] Thomas Crompton cleaning the Steps at Salford Bridge and Dangerous Corner	: 2 :
29.	p[d] Charges impressing Carriages 2/6 Warrant 2/-	: 4 : 6
	p[d] a Woman and a Child Passengers to Derby	: 6
	p[d] Expences last Night with the Watch...	: 1 :
31.	p[d] John Macqueen an old Man by Pass to Scotland...	: : 6
Nov. 2.	p[d] W[m] Worral a Publickhouse where Prisoners are usually detained Expences at Sundry Times in full ...	: 7 : 8
	p[d] Thomas Braithwait for Dutton's[4] Shoes two Pair omitted the last Year	: 10 :

---

[1] These two Constables were elected at the Court Leet held on the 14th October, 1754. (See *Court Leet Records*, vol. vij., p. 231.)

[2] See p. 74, where the Jury who examined the *Constables' Accounts* for the previous year found that this sum was due to them.

[3] That is, the Governor of the House of Correction.

[4] John Dutton was the Beadle.

	pᵈ committing and conveying two notorious Whores to the House of Correction	: 2 : 6
4.	pᵈ Porters playing Engines 10ˢ... ...	
4.	pᵈ Assistants and Expences four times to Ardwick with Prisoners this Day...	: 2 :
5.	pᵈ Expences with Quartermasters and Constables of Salford regulating four Troops of Soldiers	: 2 : 8
	pᵈ Samuel Craig a blind Passenger ...	: 1 :
	pᵈ for Parchment for Presentments ...	: 2 : 3
	pᵈ for Coals and Fuel for Boonfire this day	: 6 : 6
	pᵈ Dᵒ on the King's Accession	: 6 : 6
10.	pᵈ an Assistant with two Drunkards to Justice	: 6
11.	pᵈ for Boonfire on the King's Birth Day	: 6 : 6
	pᵈ a Passenger to Liverpool	: : 6
	pᵈ for Wine, Firing, drinking King's health &c.[1]	2 : 10 :
12.	pᵈ Horsehire 1 6 Clerks Fees 1′— Expences 1/4 carrying Geo. Timperley before Justice Richmond	: 3 : 4
Nov 14.	paid six Passengers to Dumbfrees ...	: 2 :
19.	pᵈ Warrants to Surveyors of Highways to return in their Presentments 2/- sending 'em to Eleven Hamlets 1′-	: 3 :
20.	pᵈ two Passengers to Sterling	: : 6
	pᵈ Lighting Lamps las[t] Dark... ...	: 1 : 8
	pᵈ John Mac Gland Wife and three Children to Edenburg	: 1 : 6
25.	pᵈ John Shatwell for Meat Drink &c for sundry Prisoners	: 11 :
	pᵈ sundry Passengers...	: 1 : 8
27.	pᵈ two Passengers into Wiltshire ...	: : 6
28.	pᵈ Beadle[2] attending Drunkards and Stocks,[3] viz...	
	John Thorp 1/6 John Wild 1 6 Fidd 1′- Holt 6ᵈ	: 4 : 6

[1] Great festivities would appear to have taken place on this occasion.

[2] A new Beadle (Mr. James Birch) had been elected this year. (See *Court Leet Records*, vol. vij. p. 235.)

[3] See p. 16. It would appear that women, as well as men, were set in the Stocks for drunkenness.

	Kitt Booth 1/- Nancy Bowers 1/- Bett Heys 1/-...	:	3	:
	Bett Knowles 1/- Abraham Walmsley 1/-	:	2	:
	Four other Women 2/- whipping Mary Smith[1] 1 -	:	3	:
	p⁴ Bailiffs and Beadle searching Lodging Houses...	:	3	: 6
Decʳ 2.	p⁴ two Passengers into Scotland ...	:	:	4
	p⁴ for Paper four Quire[s]...	:	3	:
	p⁴ Jurors over John Edge dead in Salford	:	1	: 4
	p⁴ Expences warning and attending them	:	1	:
9.	p⁴ Charles Edwards, Wife and two Children	:	1	:
10.	p⁴ lighting Lamps last Dark	:	1	: 10
	p⁴ Chaʳ Steward a Passenger to Aberdeen		:	4
20.	p⁴ John Shatwell Charges of Prisoners	:	8	: 6
	p⁴ Warrants to the Hamlets calling Surveyors to Accᵗ	:	2	:
	p⁴ Messenger as usual	:	1	:
	p⁴ James Clark a discharged Passenger	:	1	:
	p⁴ Eliz: Welsh a Passenger to Leverpool	:	:	6
	p⁴ Half the Expence repairing Dungeon Door	:	9	: 3
	p⁴ Beadle attending Stocks three times 3/- & for Errands 2/4	:	5	: 4
25.	p⁴ a Quarters Rent for a Cellar to set the Watch in	:	7	: 6
	p⁴ for two Pair of Shoes for James Birch the Beadle[2]	:	9	:
28.	p⁴ Bailiffs and Assistants with Deputy & Beadle searching for Vagabonds, Thieves & Strollers[3]	:	3	: 6
	p⁴ for Ale 1/2 whipping two 2/- Stocks one 1/2	:	4	: 4

[1] This is, I think, the first instance in this volume of a woman being whipped.
[2] See p. 77, note 2.
[3] See p. 2, note 6.

	p^d Hugh Halliwell for a pair of Shoes Beadle last Y^r	: 5 : 6
1755. Janŕy. 1.	paid Sundry Expences on Sunday last altering Quarters	: 1 : 7
	p^d Charges of an Extraordinary Watch Town all in an hurry with Drunkenness by Newyear's Gifts &c[1]	: 2 : 6
6.	p^d John Grey Wife and two Children by Pass to Liverpool...	: 6
7.	p^d Jurors of an Inquisition Man found drown'd in the River	: 1 : 4
11.	p^d Beadle's Bill for running Errands &c	: 5 : 6
	p^d serving Coroners Warrants	: 1 :
11	p^d Porters playing Engines	1 : :
	p^d Roger Royan discharged Soldier to Scotland...	: : 6
13.	p^d last Jurors a second Inquisition ...	: 1 : 4
	p^d Assistants and attentants [sic] apprehending a Man under Warrant from Chesterfield in Case of Bastardy	: 1 : 6
17.	p^d Lighting Cross Lamp	: : 10
18.	p^d John Healy's Bill mending Engine	: 1 : 2
	p^d Mary Wife of John Smith to Inverness	: 8
19.	p^d John Shaw's Bill at privy Watch...	: 10 :
20.	p^d sundry Expences maintaining and attending seven Vagabonds brought to Justice	: 2 :
25.	p^d Beadle his Expences with Prisoners &c	: 5 : 6
	p^d Robert Slater for Assistance a night & a Day	: 1 : 6
27.	p^d sundry Passengers...	: 1 : 7
	p^d Expences and attending James Seddon under Warrant last Night and this Morning	: 1 :
Febry 1.	p^d lighting Lamps at Cross and Dungeon	: 1 : 11

[1] This is an amusing entry. It shows that New Year's gifts were at this time more abundant than Christmas ones, and that their recipients put the town "all in a hurry" or commotion, by getting drunk.

3.	p^d Porters playing Engines	: 10 : 6
	p^d a Passenger	: : 8
8.	p^d Beadle's Bill for Errands	: 3 : 6
	p^d Sundry Expences regulating Quar- ters	: 2 : 11
	p^d Horsehire with three Vagrants by the Beadle	: 2 : 6
	p^d Mary Lucas & Mary Noble two poor Passengers...	: 8
10.	p^d committing Eliz: Haslam 2$'$- Ex- pences & Conveying 1$'$4	: 3 : 4
15.	p^d Beadle's Bill	: 2 :
	p^d Committing 2$'$ Conveying 6^d Expences 8^d Alice Husband a com- mon Whore	: 3 : 2
20.	p^d Mary Phillip with two Children to Ireland	: 1 : 8
Feb. 20.	p^d Bailiffs assisting to serve a Warrant at Thos Janney's Comp^t	: 1 :
22.	p^d Sundry Expences with the Prisoners at the Eight Bells[1]	: 3 : 11
	p^d Beadle relieving Persons in the Dungeon	: 2 :
March 1.	p^d Ann Greaves to Ireland Child dead	: 1 :
	p^d writing Warrants to the Hamlets for return of Assize Presentments 2$'$- Messenger with them thither 1$'$- ...	: 3 :
6.	p^d Jurors over Simpson's Daughter...	: 1 : 4
	p^d High Constables Warrant for the Governor's Wages	1 : 4 : 6
	p^d Parchment and writing Manchester Presentment	: 1 :
	p^d High Constables Clerk with the Presentments	: 1 :
	p^d Horsehire to Bolton with 'em 2$'$- Bating 6^d & Dep. Exp. 1/2	: 3 : 8
	p^d half the Charges mending Dungeon Door & Lock	: 9 : 3
15.	p^d mending the Dungeon Wall broke by Barlow	: 8 : 6

[1] The name of this public house—"the Eight Bells"—has not occurred in these Accounts nor in the *Court Leet Records* before.

	p^d James Smith to Oughton			: 6
17.	p^d Jurors of an Inquisition Child kil'd in Milgate	:	1 :	4
	p^d Expences serving & attending them	:	1 :	
	p^d Birch for Errands and Expences	:	5 :	
24.	p^d Mary Atkinson & an Infant to Lancaster	:	1 :	
	p^d Robert Edmundson assisting sundry times to Ardw[ic]k	:	2 :	6
25.	p^d a Quarter's Rent for a Cellar to set the Watch in	:	7 :	6
	p^d Wm Worral sundry Expences of Prisoners & Bailiffs	:	6 :	6
27.	p^d Mr Billinge mending the Dungeon Lamp	:	1 :	3
29.	p^d Beadle whipping and attending Persons in the Stocks	:	6 :	
	p^d Letitia Smith and Child [to] Ormeskirk	:		3
31.	p^d John Russell a Passenger to Scotland	:		6
	p^d Bellman decrying the Custom of Lifting[1]	:	1 :	
	p^d five Strollers[2] in distress to Nottingham	:	1 :	6
April 2.	p^d Ann Bristol with a small Child Passengers	:		6
	p^d Porters playing the Engines twice	1 :	:	
	p^d D^o repairing little Engine & for Oil	:	1 :	
	p^d Beadle's Bill	:	4 :	3
8.	p^d Expences with Quartermasters settling Quarters...	:	2 :	6
	p^d Bellman giving Notice Rem^r of the Regiment coming in	:	1 :	6
	p^d apprehending and attending John Cousins all Night	:	2 :	10
	p^d Messenger with him to Preston ...	:	5 :	
Ap^l 9.	p^d a Warr^t for Impressing Carriage 2/- Executing it three Days successively 3/-	:	5 :	

---

[1] See p. 68, note 1.　Easter Monday was on the 31st March this year.
[2] See p. 2, note 6.

	p^d cleansing the Steps due lady day last	: 2 :
	p^d Richard Shaw Wife and two Children to Stockport	: 1 : 2
	p^d Martha Sharp and two Children to Sheffield	: 1 :
23.	p^d Griffith Richard by Pass to Chester	: : 6
25.	p^d William Middleton's Bill for Lead	: 17 : 9
	p^d Thomas Fletcher for Carting Baggage to Stockport	2 :
	p^d Robt Hobson D^o to Wigan	: 18 :
	p^d Eliz : Gilbert with two Children to the City of Bristol	: 6
May 2.	p^d p^d [*sic*] Warrants to Hamlets for return of assessors of Land Tax 2/- D^o for assessors of Window Duty 2/-	: 4 :
	p^d Messenger with them to Eleven Hamlets	: 2 :
4.	p^d sundry Passengers	: 1 : 4
6.	p^d writing Return & Commissioners Clerks for Assessors of Land Tax 2/- Expences Deputy's attending at [Dangerous] Corner^1 8^d	: 2 : 8
	p^d Beadle sundry Expences on Prisoners	: 4 : 6
7.	p^d for three Quire of Paper for Billets Warr^{ts} &c	: 2 : 3
8.	p^d Warning or summoning 30 Window Peepers^2	: 2 : 6
	p^d Expences at [Dangerous] Corner^3 attending to get 'em swore 6^d War^t 1/-	: 1 : 6
	p^d for nine Blanks, one for each Couple of Assessors	: 4 : 6
	p^d Porters playing Engines	1 :
14.	p^d Mary Sess to Tanton Dane in Somersetshire	: 2 :
17.	p^d Jo' Lightboun's Bill mending 46 Buckets	1 : 10 : 8

---

^{1} See p. 5, note 1.

^{2} This was, I think, a slang term for the assessors who had to levy the "window tax," a tax made upon each householder according to the number of windows his house contained.

^{3} That is to say, attending before the local magistrates, who met at Dangerous Corner, and getting the warrants duly sworn.

	p^d Beadle relieving Prisoners, whipping 'em, and attending Stocks...	: 7 : 4
24.	p^d Repairing the Pinfold	: 8 : 3½
	p^d Beadle's Bill	: 3 : 10
26.	p^d Charges apprehending Ja' Lumb under Warrant	: 1 : 6
	p^d Information & Commitment ag^t him assaulting Hilton	: 3 :
	p^d Jurors attending James Hilton's Inquisition	: 1 : 4
29.	p^d for Boonfire this Day	: 6 : 6
	p^d Jurors attending Goolden's Son's Inquisition	: 1 : 4
	p^d Porters playing Engines 10 – & for Ale 6^d	: 10 : 6
	p^d Beadle whipping Prisoners, attending Stocks, for Errands &c	: 7 : 6
June 3.	paid drawing and Ingrossing Lamb's Recognizance to save Charges Conveying him to Lancaster	: 3 : 6
	p^d Justices Clerks returning same at Lancaster	: 4 :
	p^d Jurors attending Slater's Inquisition kil'd	: 1 : 4
	p^d serving the Coroner's Warrants & attending the Jury	: 1 :
	p^d Mary Lemmon a poor passenger...	: 1 :
	p^d Kath. Prichet & two Children by Pass to Liverpool	: 1 :
charg'd above	p^d Mr Smith for Blanks for use of Window Peepers[1]	
5.	p^d Charges apprehending and attending a Whore	: 1 : 6
	p^d for her Commitment 2 – conveying her to Justice & back 6^d	: 2 : 6
7.	p^d Jurors of an Inquisition Ogden's Child kill'd in Sodom[2]	: 1 : 4
	p^d an Especial Messenger to the Hamlets with Warr^{ts}	: 1 :

---

[1] See p. 82, note 2.
[2] The place here referred to under this designation is probably somewhere in or near Manchester, but I am not aware of any place of this name now.

	p^d whipping a Vagrant at the Rogues post[1]	: 1 :
	p^d a Passenger by Order of Justice Birch	: 2 :
7.	p^d at John Shaw's when met to go upon the privy Watch	: 3 :
	p^d Beadle whipping a Vagrant... ...	: 1 :
20.	p^d William Dean a Passenger to Leek	: : 6
21.	p^d Beadle's Bill going to Justice with Prisoners whipping 'em attending the Stocks &c	: 11 : 4
	p^d Ann Jackson to Liverpool	: 1 :
	p^d Expences with Miselayers consulting about the Ley	: 2 :
23.	p^d Charges laying the Ley	2 : 14 : 10
	p^d Jurors of an Inquisition Child dead	: 1 : 4
	p^d High Constables Warrant	38 : 11 :
	p^d a Quarter's Rent for a Cellar to set the Watch in	: 7 : 6
24.	p^d Paper ruling and writing the Ley Book	1 : 1 :
27.	p^d Eight Passengers	: 2 :
	p^d a Note for Mortar to the Pinfold	: 2 : 3
28.	p^d Beadle taking Drunkards to Justice & attending Stocks	: 6 : 6
	p^d for two Pair of Handcufts [sic] ...	: 10 : 6
30.	p^d Expences upon the Privy Watch...	: 10 : 4
	paid for four Quire of Paper for Billets &c.	: 3 :
	p^d four Persons assisting upon the Privy Watch	: 4 : 6
	p^d Committing three lewd Women taken last Night...	: 6 :
July 5.	p^d Noticing Collector of the Land tax to pay first quarterly Payment ...	: 1
	p^d for two pair of Handcufts more ...	: 9 :

---

[1] The ROGUES' POST has been referred to in previous Accounts (see vol. j., pp. 6 and 14, vol. ij., p. 43), but occurs here for the first time in this volume. It was the post to which the unfortunate persons, both male and female, were tied when they were whipped by the beadle.

8.	p^d Marg^t Mohun to Ireland	:	:	6
	p^d Porters playing Engines	: 10 :		
9.	p^d apprehending two Vagrants, sent away by Pass	: 2 :		6
	p^d Writing Money Warrants 2/– Messenger wth 'em to Eleven Hamlets 1/–	: 3 :		
12.	p^d Ja' Birch the Beadle running Extraordinary Errands	: 4 :		4
	p^d William Child repairing the Watch Bills[1]	: 5 :		
14.	p^d Bailiffs & Expences attending Partington a Gambler[2]	: 1 :		6
	p^d John Richard to Ireland	:		6
21.	p^d John Mac–Glan and Wife to Edenburgh...	:	:	6
	p^d writing Warrants for Proportion of 1^l. 4^s. 6^d for Governor's Wages 2/– Messenger with 'em to Hamlets 1/–...	: 3 :		
23.	p^d writing Warrants for Return of Assize Presentm^{ts} 2/– Especial Messenger to eleven Hamlets with 'em 1/–	: 3 :		
25.	p^d Writing to the Quarter Sessions Manch^r Presentm^t	: 1 :		
	p^d Birch's Bill whipping Vagrants & relieving them in the Dungeon ...	: 4 :		8
29.	p^d Marketlooker's Bill	6 : 3 :		
	p^d Expences at several Times with Prisoners at Wm Worral's	: 10 :		2
	p^d Charges enquiring after Rioters last Night a Man dangerously wounded...	: 1 :		
	p^d By Order of the Justice Robert Maxfield a Passenger	:	:	6
Augt 6.	p^d Charges and Extraordinary trouble going thro' the Town with the King's Surveyor of Window Duty[3]	: 5 :		
	p^d for two Informations against Scholfield rioting...	: 2 :		
	p^d Clerks for his Commitment	: 2 :		

---

[1] See p. 31, note 4.
[2] I suppose he had been arrested for gambling.
[3] See p. 4, note 4.

7.	p^d Information ag^t James Hulme, Samuel Kemp, Phillip Burnet, Robert Lees, & Robert Walker assaulting John Holt likely to die in the Infirmary [1] ...	: 2 :
	p^d Warrant 2/- & Bailiff's attendance 1/6	: 3 : 6
	p^d Parchment & Writing Manchester Presentment	: 1 :
	p^d Returning Presentm^{ts} to High Constables Clerk	: 1 :
Augst 9.	p^d Porters playing Engines due Monday last	: 10 :
	p^d Ja^s Birch's Bill	: 5 :
	p^d Information ag^t John Fenton swearing 1/- Expences going with him to Stockport 1/6...	: 2 : 6
	p^d Expences Deputy & Beadle taking a State of the Alehouses & regulating 'em for reception of Soldiers	: 1 :
13.	p^d Beadle's Trouble two Days with Deputy [2]	: 2 :
	p^d a Passenger	: 1 :
22.	p^d Sr Ralph's [3] Permit with Hannah Smedley a Soldiers Wife, Hannah Sara & Joannah her Children to Chester	: 1 :
23.	p^d Beadle whipping Vag^{ts} going to Justice with Drunkards and attending them 'ith Stocks	: 7 : 10
	p^d John Mather a Passenger to Hereford	: : 6
25.	p^d Writing a Notice upon the Engine Door to find the Key	: 2 :
	p^d Mr Ja^s Green's Bill for Oil	: 15 :
27.	p^d to decry the running of Swine in the Streets	: 1 :
	p^d James Palmer into Derbyshire ...	: : 6
Sepr 1.	p^d Engine Players	: 10 :

[1] This has probably to do with the rioting in the town referred to a few entries previously.

[2] That is, going about with the Deputy Constable.

[3] Sir Ralph Assheton or Ashton, of Middleton, Bart. (See p. 47, note 1.)

	p^d Horsehire 1 6 Expences 8^d Returning a Warr^t ag^t Thos Alwood before Sr Ralph Ashton	: 2: 2
4.	p^d Writing Warr^{ts} for Alehousekeepers to take Licences	: 2:
	p^d getting them to the Eleven Hamlets	: 1:
	p^d a Passenger to Curban in Cumberland	: : 6
	p^d Eliz: Sutliff to Heptonston in the West Riding of Yorks^r	: : 6
6.	p^d Coroner's Warr^{ts} to three Hamlets an old Man drown'd	: 1: 4
	p^d Manchester Jurors attending this Inquisition	: 1: 4
13.	p^d Ja^s Birch attending & relieving Pr[i]soners at several Times, his Expences & Extraordinary Trouble summoning Alehousekeepers to renew their Licences &c	: 10: 4
13.	p^d Thos Radford's Note mending Mean Engine[1] Pipe	1: 1:
20.	p^d Geo: Clayton's Bill mending the Engines	5: 10: 2
22.	p^d Jurors of an Inquisition a Child kill'd in the Churchy^d	: 1: 4
25.	p^d a Quarter's Rent for a Cellar to set the Watch in	: 7: 6
26.	p^d an Information 1/- Warr^t 2 - Messenger to Pendleton 1 -	: 4:
	p^d Expences ten Men all Night in quest of Thieves Rogues & Strollers in Pendlebury took six of 'em	: 5: 6
Sepr 26.	paid Horsehire to Pendlebury 1 6 keeping him 9^d	: 2: 3
	p^d Richard Dewhurst and two Persons attending Prisoners all Night 4 6 & Expences 6^d	: 5:
29.	p^d Warr^t 2 - Commitm^t 2 - Conveying Eliz: Winstandly	: 4:

[1] It would appear from this entry that there were at this time three fire engines in the town, "the great engine" and "the little engine" already referred to several times before, and the "mean engine" here mentioned for the first time.

	pᵈ Expences attending three Prisoners at Ardwick	: 8
	pᵈ Mⁿ Hobson sundry Expences by Deputy Beadle & Prisoners going to Justice Birch at sundry times	: 5 : 10
Octo 1.	pᵈ Jurors attending Thoˢ Row's Inquisition	: 1 : 4
	pᵈ Warning and attending 'em... ...	: 1 :
2.	pᵈ Rachel Stock passing to Edenburgh	: 6
	pᵈ Birch his Expences with Prisoners at sundry Times 4/- whipping them & attending Stocks 3/6	: 7 : 6
10.	pᵈ three Assistants this Night apprehending Danˡ Royle for breaking Glass Windows in the Night time ...	: 1 : 6
	pᵈ Mʳ James Smith for two Transcripts of the Court Leet Verdict¹ ...	: 10 :
	pᵈ for two Pair of Shoes for James Birch the Beadle	: 10 :
	pᵈ for two Pair of Scarlet Stockings for him²	: 9 :
	pᵈ Thoˢ Crompton cleaning Steps ...	: 2 :
	pᵈ Mʳ Birch's Bill for Beadle's Cap and Gown²...	2 : 10 : 7
	pᵈ Mʳ Byrom's Bill for Gold Lace & Tassel for Beadle's Cap²	1 : : 6
Octob 10.	paid Lighting Lamps at Cross & Dungeon	: [torn]
	pᵈ Beadle whipping two Persons 21ˢᵗ October last	: 2 : 2
	pᵈ Charges Conveying Sundry Vagabonds for which there is an Order upon the Treasurer of the County to repay	3 : 18 : 4
	pᵈ a Year's Rent for the Engine House...	2 :

---

¹ There is nothing in the *Court Leet Records* for this year (Oct. 1754 to Oct 1755) to show what "verdict" is here alluded to.

² These entries as to the Beadle's clothing—his "scarlet stockings," his "cap and gown," the cap being adorned "with gold lace and a tassel"—enable us, no doubt somewhat imperfectly, to picture to ourselves the gorgeous appearance of that functionary as he paraded the streets of Manchester nearly 150 years ago.

p⁴ Beadle's Salary	7 :	
p⁴ Deputy's Salary	20 :	
repaid Mr Thomas Tipping[1] advanced on sundry Occasions...	2 : 1 : 4	
repaid Mr Robt Ayrton[1] advanced to Passengers	: 2 :	
p⁴ part of Attorney Berwick's Bill contracted whilst Mr Greatrex and Mr Chadwick were Constbs[2]	16 : 12 : 2	
and Remainder of the same Bill contracted in the present Constables Time	3 : 7 : 10	
Omitted making Beadle's Cap and Gown	: :	
Omitted setting in the Column, see 4th Novemb. last...	: 10 :	

£222 : 14 : 5½

An Acco^t of Cash receiv'd by Thomas Tipping and Robert Ayrton Constables of Manchester.

1755.		li	s	d
Febr. 18.	Received from the Hamlets ⅔ of the Warr^t 1^{li}. 4^s. 6^d		: 16 :	4
June 6.	Received from the Hamlets ⅔ of the Warr^t 38 : 11 : 0	25 : 14 :	
July 12.	Received from the Hamlets ⅔ of the Warr^t 1 : 4 : 6		: 16 :	4
	Receiv'd for the old Weigh Scales and Beam[3]...		: 19 :	6
	Received from the Treasurer for conveying Vagabonds	3 : 18 :	4
	Received from the old Ley	2	1 :	4
	Received from Mr John Taylor Misegatherer	130 :	4 : 11

---

[1] These were the two Constables for this year.

[2] Mr. Greatorex and Mr. Chadwick were the Constables for the year Oct. 1753 to Oct. 1754, but there is nothing in these Accounts, or in the *Court Leet Records*, to show to what this charge related, or why it had been incurred.

[3] See p. 90, note 1.

	li	s	d
Received for an Old Pair of small Scales & Weights[1]	:	10 :	6
Received from Salford half mending Dungeon Lock and Door[2]	:	9 :	3
Received an Order upon the Treasurer for conveying Soldiers Baggage ...	2 :	18 :	
Received from High Constables apprehending Vagabonds in Pendlebury &c	:	11 :	9
Balance due to these Constables	53 :	14 :	2½

£222 : 14 : 5½

November 20. 1755. We the Jurors of the Court Leet held for the Manor of Manchester have perused the above Accounts of the late Constables & do allow the same.

(Signed) JOHN GATLIFF   THOS CLOWES
           JAS LIPTROTT   JAMES GREATREX
           JOHN CLOWES   ROBT LIVESEY
           JOHN BROOME   JAMES EDGE
                             WM STARKIE
                             GEO: JOHNSON
                             THOS GARDNER
                             SAML EDGLEY
                             SAM. GOODIER

[1] At the Court Leet held on the 2nd May, 1750, it was ordered that the "Weights Beams Scales and Measures" of the town be sent to London for examination, as follows (see *Court Leet Records*, vol. vij, p. 189):—

"Whereas Complaint has this day been made to us the said Jurors That the Weights Beams Scales and Measures of this Town are very much Defectife by long Use which tends much to the prejudice of many Traders Inhabitants and Shopkeepers thereof Therefore we the said Jurors do Order that all the said Weights Beams Scales and Measures be forthwith sent to London and be there forthwith regulated and tried by the proper Officers appointed for that purpose at the Expence and Cost of the Constables of this Town or other person or persons to whom the same shall properly belonge."

It is probable that these old articles had been condemned and that new ones had been provided in their place. The entries in the text record the sale of the old weights, &c.

[2] This shows that the Dungeon was still on the bridge between Manchester and Salford, each of which places had to contribute to its repair.

[Constables' Accounts.]

[12th Oct., 1757, to 11th Oct., 1758.][1]

●●●●●●●●●●●

D[r] Town of Manchester to WILL[M] STARKIE & ROB[T] GARTSIDE,[2] *Constables* [*of Manchester*, elected 12th Oct. 1757.]

[Disbursements]

		l	s	d
1757	To last Year's Balance	100 :	:11	
	omitted 5th November last conveying Baggage of Beauclerks Regiment to Nutsford [Knutsford]...		:18 :	
	omitted also paid to the Ringers on the 23[d] of May last. Prague said to be taken[3]	1 :	1 :	
	omitted last Year conveying Elizabeth Ogden to Justice Percival[4] at Royton for Felony with four Evidences ...		: 5 :	6
	To four Examinations 4[s] Comm[t] 2,-		: 6 :	
	p[d] Charges prosecuting two persons charged with stealing Box Wood from Hencock's Shop, Set at Liberty		: 4 :	6
Octo. 19.	To writing five long Warrants to the Hamlets about the Militia...		: 5 :	

---

[1] There is here, unfortunately, another break in the sequence of the Accounts—those for the years Oct., 1754, to Oct., 1757, being missing. By some means or other they have been lost, and the book has been bound up without them.

[2] These two Constables were elected at the Court Leet held on the 12th October, 1757. (See *Court Leet Records*, vol. viij., p. 11.)

[3] In Whitworth's *Manchester Advertiser and Weekly Magazine*, No. 3,152, "from Tuesday May 17 to Tuesday May 24, 1757," there is on the fourth page a long account from the *London Gazette Extraordinary* of May 20, giving a description of the victory obtained by the King of Prussia over the Austrian army near Prague on the 6th of that month. The prisoners taken were about 7,000 men, and 250 cannons were also captured. The Prussian troops entered Prague on May 8th.

[4] See p. 64, note 4.

		l	s	d
	To three Special Messengers to the Hamlets with the said Warrants ...		: 2 :	
20.	To writing forty three Notices for Inhabitants to appear before the Commissioners to be qualified for Militia Men		: 10 :	3
22.	To Boonfire, King's Coronation ...		: 5 :	6
25.	To Paper for Soldier's Billets		: 2 :	6
31.	to Belman a Cry about an Incendiary Letter. Both Towns		: 1 :	6
Nov'' 1.	To an Act of Parliament about Militia		: 1 :	6
1.	To Expences and Messeng[er]s fetching and attending the Militia to be swore		: 3 :	6
5.	To Boonfire, Gunpowderplot		: 6 :	
7.	To Porters playing and cleansing the Engines for one Month as usual ...		: 10 :	
8.	To writing nine Summons' for such Militia Men as are under Default ...		: 2 :	3
10.	To Boonfire, His Majesty's Birthday		: 6 :	6
	To James Crompton's Bill for Wine drinking the Royal Health's[1]	3	: 12 :	1
15.	To Joseph Harrop's[2] bill for printing		: 8 :	6
18.	To Juror's Fees. John Andrews Son shot by Accident		: 1 :	4
Dec'' 10.	To a Messenger for the Coroner at Rochdale a Man scalded to death at the Sugar house[3] in Manchester ...		: 2 :	
	To Serving the Warants on the hamlets		: 1 :	
	To Jurors Fees		: 1 :	4
12.	To Messenger again for Coroner ...		: 2 :	
	To Jurors fees another Man scalded in a Hatters Dyepan[4]		: 1 :	4

[1] Judging by this bill, there would seem to have been much jubilation in the town this year on the occasion of the anniversary of the King's (George II.'s) birthday, Oct. 30, "old style," but Nov. 10, "new style." (See also p. 59, note 1.)

[2] Joseph Harrop was the printer of Harrop's *Manchester Mercury*, one of the two papers then being published in the town. The other was Whitworth's *Manchester Advertiser*, referred to in p. 91, note 3.

[3] This is the first mention of any sugar refinery in Manchester either in these Accounts or in the *Court Leet Records.*

[4] The trade of hatting was at this time extensively practised in and near Manchester.

		l	s	d
	To repairing at the Hospital[1] for Kingsly's Soldiers, Windows &c ...		: 4 :	
	To Order for Vagabonds to sundry Countys by Justice Birch[2] (left un-signed at his Death	4	: 10 :	
12.	To thirty three Passengers since the nineteenth of October last		: 10 :	6
	To mony paid on the 16th of Novemb. last for and amongst Militiamen summoned to be swore there[3]...		: 5 :	
	To Deputy's Expences & horse ...		: 2 :	
15.	To lighting the Lamp at Cross two Darks 1 8 and Dungeon one 10d ...		: 2 :	6
19.	To three Quire of Paper for Billets...		: 2 :	
24.	To writing Warrants to the Eleven Hamlets for new Surveyors of High-ways		: 3 :	
25.	To Rent paid John Heys for Kingsly's Hospital[4]	2	:	
25.	To sundry Expences since Michalm' last in quartering Soldiers...		: 13 :	6
1758.				
Janry 1.	To writing 11 Preswarrants		: 5 :	6
	To three special Messengers		: 3 :	
5.	To Stephen Heys and Peter Pass for their Assistance in impressing Men...		: 3 :	6
10.	To the Governor of the House of Correction Fees and Expences ab' Prisoners		: 5 :	6
	To Expences impressing Soldiers on Saturday last		: 1 :	6
	To Thomas Tonge for Grate Shovel and Tongs for Guard Room &c ...		: 7 :	
Janry 16.	To lighting Lamps last Dark		: 1 :	8
16.	To Messenger for Coroner, all night...		: 2 :	6

[1] There are other references to this "Hospital for Kingsley's Soldiers" in this year's Accounts. It was probably a temporary building in the town used for the benefit of the soldiers in Col. Kingsley's regiment, which seems to have been raised in Manchester.

[2] See p. 62, note 1.

[3] These militia men were probably sworn in to aid the authorities of the town in quelling the food riots which took place there at that time. A full account of these riots from Whitworth's *Manchester Advertiser* will be found in the Appendix.

[4] See note 1.

		l	s	d
17.	To Jurors 1ˢ 4ᵈ serving Warrants 1ˢ a Man called Beewing dead of his Wounds received in the late Mob[1] ...		: 2 :	4
19.	To writing Constables Presentment for the Quarter Sessions		: 1 :	
	To Expences at Sessions prosecuting Rioters, Ingrossers &c[2]		: 7 :	6
23.	To Commitment 2. Informations &c 2ˢ 6ᵈ. agt Eliz: Hardman keeping a Bawdyhouse		: 4 :	6
24.	To Committing two other common Whores		: 4 :	
24.	To Walter Wilson nails for Engines...		: 1 :	10
24.	To Expences quartering Parties of Recruits coming to be view'd &c ...		: 2 :	6
25.	To Expences attending Commissioners of Press Act		: 1 :	6
27.	To Messenger for Coroner 2ˢ serving Warrants on yᵉ Hamlets 1ˢ/- Jurors 1ˢ4. Brown killed by a fall		: 4 :	4
Febry 1.	To writing Warrants for deficient Militia Men to appear at Ryton ...		: 4 :	6
8.	To Expences of nine Militia men 6ˢ 6ᵈ Deputy's Diner and Expences 1ˢ 8ᵈ and his horsehire 1ˢ 9ᵈ at Ryton ...		: 9 :	11
Febry 8.	To Hugh Haliwell for Beadles Shoes		: 9 :	6
10.	To Slaters Work at yᵉ Dungeon ...		: 6 :	6
	To twenty two passengers since 12ᵗʰ decʳ		: 11 :	5
20.	To summoning eight Militia to Ryton[3]		: 4 :	
21.	To Expences at Ryton[3] upon eight Militiamen now swore		: 5 :	
	To Deputys horse and Expences ...		3 :	7
25.	To Stephen Heys for serving a Warᵗ at Ashton and Assistance at Manchʳ...		: 3 :	
	To Warⁿ for Assize presentments ...		: 3 :	
Mar 1.	To High Constables Clerks with the Presentments at Rochdale 1ˢ. and Deputys Expences and Diner 2ˢ. 2ᵈ...		: 3 :	2

[1] See p. 93, note 3.

[2] Many of the persons arrested in connection with the riots in November, 1757, were tried at these Quarter Sessions.

[3] These men had to appear before Thomas Percival, Esq., of Royton, one of the Justices of the Peace. (See p. 64, note 4.)

		l	s	d
	To horsehire 2/- Manchester Presentm¹ 1/-		: 3 :	
	To War⁵ for the Hamlets proportion of 1¹. 4ˢ. 6ᵈ		: 3 :	
	To the High Constables War¹ for Governors Wages	1 :	4 :	6
3.	To a Special Messenger to Rochdale with Edmund Lees who had refused to be swore into the Militia		: 2 :	8
7.	To drawing the Invalids¹ Baggage to Altringham...		:12 :	
	To Oil Can and Lamp Glass for Cross		: 8 :	6
	To half Charges repairing Dungeon lamp		: 6 :	6
16.	To Mʳˢ Walker for puting the Baggage of Cornwallas's Regim¹ into her Cellar		: 5 :	
	To James Mills for conveying the Baggage of Stuarts² Regim¹ to Buxton	6 :	5 :	
	To Paper for Billets		: 3 :	4
17.	To expences making Quarters good		: 1 :	6
18.	To lighting Lamp at Cross		: 1 :	8
26.	To committing two Common Whores		: 3 :	
26.	To Bellman three Calls		: 3 :	
30.	To the Clerks for a Vagrant Warrant		: 2 :	
Apˡ 3.	To Charges of two Drunkards to the Dungeon and before the Justices ...		: 1 :	2
8.	To George Clayton repairing the Exchang done at the Justices Request...		: 6 :	2
	To fifty one Passengers since 10ᵗʰ Febry		':16 :	5
	To Thomas Fletcher conveying Kingsly's Baggage to Knutsford a Year ago	2 :	10 :	
	To Thomas Broughton assisting the Deputy all night last Mobb		: 1 :	6

---

¹ The "Invalids" were a body of troops mostly, I think, men who had served in war and had consequently had some experience, who were permanently stationed in various towns. The "Invalids" in Manchester defended the town against the rioters in November, 1757, as more fully narrated in the account in the Appendix.

² Col. Stewart's regiment is mentioned as arriving in Manchester on November 19th, and helping to protect the town against any further rioting.   (See Appendix.)

		l	s	d
11.	Summoning Deborah Jackson for refusing a Billet	:	:	6
12.	To John Tinsly repairing Seats in the Session's house,[1] broke by Soldiers...	:	3	:
13.	To removing Baggage of Riches[2] Dragoons to Rochdale	:	12	:
	To drawing a Presentment against two persons laying Muck as a Nu[i]sance in the Kings Highway	:	3	6
14.	To Robert Edmundson for Assistance	:	2	6
	To Bills of Indictmen[t] 4ˢ paid Clerk for Expidition 1ˢ– Bailifs fees 2ˢ. 4ᵈ. Evidences 2/6 Expences Deputys attending Sessions on this Accᵗ 2ˢ ...	:	11	10
24.	To a Pair of Figureight Handcuffs ...	:	5	:
29.	To Wᵐ Smalley with sundry passengers to Stockport	:	1	6
May 3.	To writing Return of the Assessors of Landtax	:	1	:
	To Bernard Shaw for sundry fees ...	:	6	:
4.	To John Townly setting a Grate in the Guard Room	:	2	:
	To summoning thirty Persons for Assessors of Window-duty[3] and attending the Commisioners when they were swore	:	2	6
9.	To Paper for Billets	:	2	3
	To Miss Houghton for Hulmes Baggage lying two months in the Theatre[4]	1	11	6
14.	To whipping and maintaining Sarah Jones a Vagrant...	:	1	8
14.	To twenty nine Passengers since 8ᵗʰ Apˡ	:	10	10
29.	To Boonfire King Charles's Restoration	:	6	:

[1] The "Sessions House" has not occurred before in these Accounts.

[2] A troop of Sir Robert Rich's dragoons is mentioned in the account of the riots as expected in Manchester on November 21st. (See Appendix.)

[3] These "assessors of window duty" are those who had to inspect the number of windows in every house, so that they could be taxed. They have been called by their slang name "window peepers" in these Accounts before. (See p. 82, note 2.)

[4] This is an interesting entry relating to "the Theatre" in Manchester, and is the first time that it has been mentioned in these Accounts. It would seem to refer to the building in Marsden Street, which was opened on December 3rd, 1753, and was the only theatre in the town until a new one was built in 1775.

		l	s	d
31.	To Bernard Shaw maintaining three prest Men sixteen days	1	: 4	:
	To Governor for Jane Edwards' fees		: 1	:
	To Charges apprehending Wm Bridge under Sr Henry Hoghton's Warrant		: 2	:
June 5.	To Thomas Crompton for cleansing the Steps at Salford bridge and Dangerous Corner		: 4	:
	To Jurors fees 1' 4^d Expences attending the Coroner 1'- a Child kill'd in Salford		: 2	4
	To Paper for Billets and Warrants ...		: 1	6
7.	To Isaac Dixon for removing King's Baggage to Knutsford		: 7	6
12.	To Expences with Soldiers billeting the Regiment over again		: 2	6
	To Bench Warrants against two persons laying Nusances in the Highway and Messenger to the Constable ...		: 5	:
14.	To Charges Committing Nell Holt a common Whore...		: 3	4
21.	To High Constables Warrant for repairing Penwortham and other public Bridges for Coroners Orders and Orders for prosecuting Felons	41	: 9	6½
21.	To writing Warrants to the Hamlets for their Proportion of the last Warrant		: 2	:
	To Messenger with 'em thither ...		: 1	:
July 3.	To drawing a fair Copy of the List of Assessors of Window-duty		: 1	:
	To Commissioners Clerk for Warrant		: 1	:
	To Expences attending when swore and regulating & dividing the Town..		: 2	6
10.	To Conveying a Party of Calvils Regim^t to Nutsford [Knutsford]		: 6	6
13.	To Jurors 1' 4^d serving Warrants 1'. a Man kill by a fall from a House ...		: 2	4
15.	To Messenger and Expences taking a Man to Stockport under Justice Richmonds[1] Warrant for Bastardy ...		: 2	6

[1] "Justice Richmond" was the Rev. Legh Richmond, rector of Stockport, one of the justices of the peace. His name has occurred before. (See p. 77.)

		l	s	d
17.	To Charges apprehending and keeping six Strollers[1] in the Dungeon ...	:	1 :	6
	To Beadle whipping them[1] and Expences at the House o' Correction ...	:	5 :	
	To Bailiffs Assistance...	:	1 :	9
	To thirty Passengers and Strollers[1] since 14th of May last...	:	10 :	1
27.	To writing Warrants to the Hamlets for Presentments to the Assize[s] ...	:	2 :	
	To Messenger to the Hamlets... ...	:	1 :	
17.	To Paper ruling binding and writing the Leybook	1 :	5 :	
28.	To James Birch's[2] Bill	3 :	18 :	
29.	To John Tinsly repairing Rogues post[3]	:	2 :	
Augt 1.	To Parchment and writing Presentmt	:	1 :	
1.	To High Constables delivering the Presentments for Town & Hamlets...	:	1 :	
	To Expences on this Occasion ...	:	1 :	6
2.	To Thomas Hanson painting the Engine	:	5 :	4
	To John Smith for Oil for the Lamps	1 :	1 :	4
20.	To Wine in drinking the healths Cape Breton taken[4]	3 :	4 :	
	To Ale for the Soldiers[4]	:	15 :	
Sepr 4.	To Warrants to the Hamlets for Alehouse keepers to take Lycences ...	:	3 :	
	To mending fourteen Engine buckets	:	3 :	6
	To Paper for Billets	:	1 :	6
	To John Dodd entertaining a parcel of Soldiers coming too late for Billets	:	4 :	7
7.	To Expences attending the Justices on the Ale licence day	:	1 :	6
8.	To Warrants for Lists of Jurors ...	:	3 :	
	To a Watch Bill	:	1 :	
	To thirty three Passengers since the 17th of July last	:	10 :	7

[1] In these instances the word "strollers" would appear to mean rogues and vagabonds rather than "strolling players." (See p. 2, note 6.)

[2] James Birch was the Beadle.

[3] See p. 84, note 1.

[4] A full account of the landing of "His Majestys Forces on the Island of Cape Breton and of the Siege of Louisberg" appeared in the *London Gazette* on August 19th, and the news seems to have reached Manchester very quickly. Cape Breton is an island near Nova Scotia, off the coast of Canada.

		l	s	d
16.	To Jurors fees twice over one of Grindrod's[1] Children in Salford ...	:	2 :	8
17.	To Jurors fees twice over another[1] ...	:	2 :	8
19.	To Jurors fees over his Wife all three poisoned by ye Father & husband[1] ...	:	1 :	4
19.	To drawing out and writing fair Copies of Jurors Lists	:	5 :	
	To Justices Clerks attesting d^o	:	2 :	
30.	To Warrants for Surveyors to present the State of ye Highways..	:	3 :	
	To Justice Clerks for Vagrant War[1] ...	:	2 :	
Octob 2.	To removing the Baggage of Calvils[2] [sic for Colville's] Regiment to Rochdale	3 :	16 :	6
7.	To Peter Cotrell taking Care of the Key of the Engine house a Year ...	:	4 :	
	To Marketlookers Bill	5 :	9 :	
	To Mr Touchet for the Enginehouse two Years Rent	4 :		
	To Mr Birch for Beadles Cloth[3] ...	2 :	15 :	
	To Mr Byrom for his Goldlace[3] ...	1 :	7 :	
	To making his Cap and Gown[3] ...	:	7 :	5
	To Mr Blinkhorns bill for Hose[3] ...	:	18 :	
	To Thomas Braithwaite for Shoes for two Years	1 :	1 :	6
	To Enginemen eleven Months ...	5 :	12 :	3
7.	To James Birch's Bill	2 :	1 :	6
	To his Years Salary	7 :	:	

---

[1] In Harrop's *Manchester Mercury* for September 19th, 1758, is the following paragraph:—

"*Manchester*, Sept. 18. On Friday last, one Grindret [sic for Grindrod] a Woolcomber in Salford, was apprehended on Suspicion of poisoning two of his Children. It appeared, by examining him, on the Coroner's Inquest, that he had bought Arsenick and administered it in Treacle mixed with Brimstone. The Children were both opened and large Quantities of Arsenick found in them. His Wife now lies a-dying, and it is fear'd to be from the same Cause that occasion'd his Children's Death. The Man is sent to Lancaster Castle, to take his Trial for the same the next Assizes."

He was tried and condemned to death at the Spring Assizes, and was executed at Lancaster on Saturday, March 25th, 1759, and his body was brought to Manchester to be hung in chains there.

[2] In the same paper for October 3rd is a note:—"On Wednesday next, the Regiment of Foot quarter'd here, commanded by the Hon. Col. Colville, marches from hence to Hull, in Yorkshire, in order to do Duty with the Garrison there."

[3] See p. 88, note 2.

	l	s	d
To Charges conveying John Dutton (assaulting Deputy Kay[1] in the Execution of his Office) to Lancaster omitted entering 11th June 1757[2]	2 :	2 :	
To the Ringers on two separate Occasions	1 :	11 :	6
To Deputys[1] Salary a Year	20 :	:	
To Straw for the Soldiers Hospital[3]...	:	3 :	
To two dozen of Candles for Guard...	:	13 :	

Total paid   ...   .£262 : 7 : 3½

[Receipts]

Town   ...   . Contra C^r

By Cash from last Years Ley... ...	62 : 16 : 3		
By proportion of 1 . 4 . 6	: 16 : 4		
By d° 41 : 9 : 6	28 : 9 : 4		
By Collection by Mr Bent[4]	96 : 3 : 11¼		
By Collection by Mr Worsly[4] ...	86 : 17 : 7¾	275 : 3 : 6

Subtracting the mony paid from the mony received there remains in the hands of the present Constables to be paid to their Successors the Sum of twelve pounds sixteen Shillings and two pence half peny.

Balance   ...   ... 12 . 16 . 2½

October the twenty fifth 1758.   We the Jurors of the Court Leet held for the Manor of Manchester have perused the forgoing Acc^{ts} of Mr William Starkie and Mr Robert Gartside late Constables and do allow the same.   Witness our hands.

(Signed)	JOHN MARKLAND	JA^s HORTON
	THO^s CHADWICK	JOHN LEVER
	THO^s CLOWES	HY. FEILDEN
	JOHN BROOME	JN^o HEYWOOD
	THOMAS TIPPING	OTHO. COOKE
	THO^s STOTT	WYANT MARRIOTT
	JOHN CLOWES	W^M JOHNSON

---

[1] Mr. John Kay was the Deputy-Constable, for the duties of which he received £20 per annum.

[2] There was very serious rioting in the town on Tuesday, Wednesday, and Thursday, June 7th, 8th, and 9th, 1757, an account of which will be found in the Appendix to this volume. The *Constables' Accounts* for that year are, unfortunately, missing.

[3] See p. 93, note 1.

[4] Mr. James Bent and Mr. Joseph Worsley were the two Misegatherers elected at the Court Leet held on the 12th Oct., 1757. (See *Court Leet Records*, vol. viij., p. 12.)

[SPECIAL DISBURSEMENTS][1]

1757.

Nov' 25.

By Lieu' Reed Commanding a Company of Invalids against the Mob[1]	31	: 10	: o
By Ensign Page	15	: 15	:
By Captain Lawrence for his Men ...	8	: 3	:
By the Invalids who routed ye Mob ...	26	:	:
By sundry small Articles		: 12	: 1
By M' Budworth's Note...	12	: 18	:
By Tho' Marsdens d° Ale &c	1	: 8	: 8
By Cavendish Bread & Cheese		: 13	: 3½
By Wares note for d°		: 7	: 3
By M' Clegg for Express	3	: 12	: 8
By Sundrys paid by Deputy...	12	: 16	: 1
By M' Owen for Gunpowder		: 4	: 2
By M' Dutton an Entertainm^t	30	: 7	: 4
By John Parkes' Notes Coals Cand &c...	15	: 1	: 2
By Dan' Ashton		: 4	: 2
By Parks in full		: 19	:
By Deputy Kay for Mony paid Expences and extraordinaries	5	: 5	:
By Balance in Constables hands	21	: 15	: 1½
	187	: 12	:

D' M' Wm Starkie & Rob' Gartside Constables of Manchester. Contra C'

1757.   l   s   d

To Cash from M' Edwd Byrom being the remainder of a former private Contribution[2]	107	: 16	:
To 76 Guineas new Contribution[2]	79	: 16	:
	187	: 12	:

---

[1] These special disbursements were all occasioned by the RIOT which took place in the town on Tuesday, the 15th November, 1757, a full account of which, taken from a unique copy of Whitworth's *Manchester Advertiser*, "from Tuesday Nov. 15 to Tuesday Nov. 27" will be found in the Appendix to this volume. The riot was a food riot; the mob, which had come into the town from Ashton-under-Lyne and other places demanded "oatmeal at 20 shillings, and potatoes 4s per load and flour 1½d. per lb." The "invalids" or troops in the town were stationed at Shude Hill, and after enduring for some time a shower of stones and brickbats, by which many of his men were bruised and hurt and a corporal was killed, the officer in charge gave the order to fire, whereby three people were killed and very many wounded, who were treated at the Infirmary. This was long known as "the Shudehill Fight," and an allegorical account of it by Tim Bobbin will be found in his *Works*.

[2] In the Appendix will be found a transcript of an interesting document, dated 1749, by which all the chief residents in the town agreed to contribute £10 10s. apiece in

1758. Octob 25ᵗʰ Examined this Account and Allowing the same do order the Balance twenty one pound fifteen Shillings and one peny half peny to be paid into the hands of Mʳ James Hodson and Mʳ Robert Hibbert present Constables.[1]

(*Signed*)　THOˢ CLOWES
　　　　　OTHO COOKE
　　　　　THOˢ CHADWICK
　　　　　THOMAS TIPPING Junʳ
　　　　　THOˢ BATTERSBEE
　　　　　JOHN LEES.

25ᵗʰ October 1758.

Received from Mʳ Wᵐ Starkie and Mʳ Robᵗ Gartside the above mentioned Balance of twenty one pounds fifteen Shillings and one peny half peny, and the farther Sum of three pounds thirteen Shillings and six pence to be paid on demand by me.

(*Signed*)　JOHN KAY, Deputy

```
        21 : 15 : 1½
         3 : 13 : 6
        ─────────────
       £25 :  8 : 7½
        ═════════════
```

1758.	Dʳ the Subscription accᵗ.	l	s	d
Octob. 25.	To Cash in the hands of John Kay deputy...	25 :	8 :	7½
1759.	Contra ... ... Cʳ			
Octob 31.	By a Guinea paid to Mʳ Hodson for a new Gun lost by the Soldiers last Mob	1 :	1 :	
1760.				
Novʳ 6.	By setting keeping and supporting a special extraordinary Watch a great part of the last Winter the remainder of this Account was expended and paid to Watchmen and others to preserve the Town against a Gang of Thieves and Robbers who almost every night attempted the breaking some House or other	24 :	7 :	7½

order to form a fund for the better protection of the town from riots and disturbances. It was from some such association as this that the "contributions" here referred to were derived, the money being spent in paying the soldiers who protected the town in the fight at Shudehill. (See p. 101, note 1.)

[1] These were the two Constables elected at the Court Leet held on Oct. 11, 1758. (See *Court Leet Records*, vol. viij., p. 22.)

[Constables' Accounts.]

[11th Oct., 1758, to 10th Oct., 1759.]

••••••••••••

Dr Town of Manchester to JAMES HODSON & ROBT HIBBERT [Junior], *Constables*[1] [*of Manchester*, elected 11th October, 1758].

[Disbursements]

1758

Octob' 15.	To M' Nangreave a fee attending the Examination of Evidences before Justice Bradshaw against Esther Partington for secreting and suspiciously murthering her own Infant[2]	1 : 1 :
	To Expences on Evidences same time[2]	: 2 : 4
	To Justices Clerk for examinations[2]	: 6 :
	To d° her Commitment to Lancaster[2]	: 4 :
17.	To sundry Vagrants	: 1 : 6
20.	To three other Vagrants	: 1 :
26.	To maintaining Ester Partington[2] in Childbed under Commitment	: 8 : 6
	To writing eleven Warrants to the eleven Hamlets for their proportion of 2. 9. 0 for Governors[3] Wages ...	: 2 :
	To Messenger with the Warrants ...	: 1 :
	To Governor Shaw[3] sundry fees ...	: 3 :

[1] These two Constables were elected at the Court Leet held on Oct. 11, 1758. (See *Court Leet Records*, vol. viij., p. 22.)

[2] In the *Manchester Mercury* for Oct. 17, 1758, is this note, " Last week, a woman at Shudehill, delivered herself of a Child in the Night time, which it is said she immediately destroyed. Proper care is taken of her." There are many entries in these Accounts about this unfortunate woman, Esther Partington, wife of Joseph Partington. She was ultimately taken to Lancaster and tried at the March Assizes there, when she was convicted of wilful murder, but she was subsequently reprieved from execution.

[3] That is, the Governor of the House of Correction in the town, whose name occurs here for the first time in that capacity.

	To James Crompton Charges laying last Years Constable Ley[1]...	3 : 16 : 6
	To a Vagrant to Tormordine	: 3
Nov' 5	To a Boonfire on the King's Coronation and another on Powder Plott ...	: 12 :
8.	To cleansing the Lamps at Cross and Dungeon	: 2 : 6
	To writing and returning a presentm' to the last Quarter sessions	: 1 :
	To Deputys Expences attending the same	: 2 :
Nov' 9	To three Vagrants to Kendale... ...	: 1 :
10.	To Boonfire, his Majesty's Birthday[2]	: 6 :
	To Musick and Wine drinking the Royal Healths[2]	2 : 16 :
11.	To playing and cleansing the Engines last month 10/- Ale 6[d]	: 10 : 6
	To sundry Vagrants and passengers	: 2 : 6
	To High Constables Warrant the Wages of the Governor of the House o' Correction	2 : 9 :
	To more maintenance for Esther Partington[3] kept till now in Custody	: 5 : 6
	To the Women keeping her in Custody a month and three days[3]	: 15 : 6
	To Messenger, horsehire and other incident Charges attending and conveying her to Lancaster Castle[3] ...	2 15 :
15.	To sundry Expences more on her Acc'[3]	: 3 : 6
	To apprehending, attending committing and conveying Bet Barret a notorious Whore to the House of Correction	: 4 :
	To Charges bringing James Batty to Justice dangerously abusing Jn° Dean	: 2 : 6
	To paper for Billets &c.	: 2 : 3

[1] That is, the "ley" or assessment to raise money to pay the £20 salary of the Deputy-Constable.

[2] See p. 59, note 1.

[3] See p. 103, note 2.

	To charge of an especial Watch twelve nights Justice Bayley[1] complaining of being abused in the Night time...	1 : 7 : 6
Nov' 30.	To expences punishing nine Strollers[2]	: 3 : 6
Dec' 1.	To Expences apprehending and whipping three Strollers[2] and one Fortuneteller	: 5 :
9.	To lighting Lamps last Dark	: 2 :
9.	To Expences with Officers of Light horse and setling their Quarters ...	: 5 :
20.	To sundry passengers...	: 3 : 6
	To Assistants visiting Lodging houses and bringing Mary Lees a common Whore to Justice	: 3 : 2
21.	To two Strollers...	: 1 :
21.	To Charges of a privy Watch	1 : 2 : 9
	To three Assistants on this Occasion	: 3 :
	To committing Su Taylor 3 - and for whipping Nan Farcet, two Whores 1 -	: 4 :
	To Expences and waiting all day at Justices	: 2 : 11
22.	To Birch and James Haworth serving Summonses upon disorderly persons	: 2 : 6
	To Warrants to Hamlets for Surveyors of Highways to account	: 3 :
23.	To making Beadles Cloaths	: 8 : 6
	To Stephen Heys for Assistance ...	: 2 :
	To three Summonses and Warrant against John Lees abusing Constables	: 3 : 6
26.	To Belman giving notice to meet and make a List of new Surveyors of the Highways of this Town	: 1 : 6
	To writing Nomination and duplicate	: 2 :
	To Expences of the meeting	: 4 :
28.	To sundry passengers	: 3 : 6
	To lighting Lamps last Dark	: 2 : 9
[1759] Janry 9.	To Paper 3 - to Strollers 4 6	: 7 : 6

[1] This was James Bayley, of Withington, Esq., who was the High Sheriff at the time of the riots in the town in June and November, 1757. (See Appendix.)

[2] Here again these "Strollers" seem to be the ordinary "Rogues and Vagabonds" punished by whipping, &c. (See also p. 98, note 1.)

[Jan.] 10.	To removing two sturdy Beggars to Failsworth in the Night 2 6. pass 3 -...	: 5 : 6	
	To repairing the Stocks[1]	: 5 :	
24.	To Ringers Prussia King's Birthday[2]	:10 : 6	
	To sundry passengers	: 3 : 6	
Feb. 5.	To playing Engines two months ...	1 : : 6	
8.	To nine foot Messengers to Lancaster with twenty one Worsted smallware Weavers to Lancaster for combining against the Manufactury[3]	6 :15 :	
	To maintaining them upon the Way[4]	2 : 2 :	
	To their Entrance Fees[4]	1 : 1 :	
	To one horse Messenger[4]...	2 : 2 :	
	To their maintenance all night in the House o' Correction[4]...	1 : 1 :	
	To more maintenance on the Road[4]	: 5 :	

---

[1] See page 16, note 3.

[2] The King of Prussia was at this time in alliance with England, so that his birth-day was made an occasion of rejoicing. How that rejoicing was carried out is best given in the words used in Harrop's *Manchester Mercury* for January 30th, 1759 :— "On Wednesday last [Jan. 24] (the Birth-Day of the illustrious King of Prussia) a very elegant Ball was given to the Gentlemen and Ladies of this Town, by the Officers quartered here. The whole was conducted with that Politeness for which the Gentlemen of the British Army have been universally celebrated. After the Ladies were withdrawn, the Evening was concluded with the Healths of his Majesty, the King of Prussia, the Beauties who had honour'd the Ball with their Presence, and an hearty wish that every succeeding year may be as prosperous to the Arms of Britain, as that we have just past over."

[3] Here is another instance of workmen being punished for entering into an illegal combination.

[4] These twenty-one "worsted small ware weavers" seem to have entailed many heavy charges on the Manchester ratepayers before they could be landed in Lancaster jail. In Harrop's *Manchester Mercury* for Jan. 9th, 1759, the following notice was printed, which reads very strange to us in these days of strikes and combinations of all kinds :—

"*Manchester, January 8th*, 1759. Whereas all Combinations and Meetings among Weavers, or other Handicraft Workmen or Servants, to consult how to raise Wages, or to make other Rules or Orders among themselves, that have a tendency to ruin and destroy the Trade in which they are employ'd, is contrary to the Laws of this Kingdom.

"And Whereas there is at this Time, in and about this Town, an unlawful Combination among the Worsted Small Ware Weavers, under the Name of being Members, or being concern'd with, or Payers to a Box.

"*This is to give Notice,*

"That all Persons who are any Ways concern'd in those unlawful Combinations, or are any Ways aiding or assisting thereto will be prosecuted to the utmost Rigour of the Law; and that no Weavers will be taken in to Work, that are any Ways concern'd in those unlawful Associations."

	To Expences of Assistance and Wages apprehending and attending them at Manchester[1]	1 : 1 : 6
[Feb.] 8.	To two Carts carrying the twenty one Weavers to Lancaster[1]	7 : 17 : 6
12.	To sundry passengers	: 3 : 6
17.	To Robert Brooks to Haslingden ...	: : 6
17.	To serving a Warrant on George Radford and carrying him to Stockport before Justice Richmond[2]... ...	: 2 : 6
	To Govenor Shaw[3] three Fees... ...	: 3 :
	To Expences at Peter Barrows attending the Justices there	: 3 : 6
19.	To Joseph Harrop[4] for printing bills and Advertisements about the late Mob,[5] and for blank Warrants touching the Militia	1 : 11 : 6
20.	To committing Ann Coppock a Whore	: 2 :
	To Expences of her and her Bully in the Dungeon and before Justice ...	: 1 : 6
	To Paper	: 1 : 6
Mar 3.	To lighting Lamps	: 2 : 9
	To Warrants to the Hamlets for the Assize Presentments	: 2 :
	To special Messengers thither having short Notice	: 2 :
	Paid Expences and Assistance about a parcel of Rioters[5] who had almost killed a Soldier in Newton Lane ...	: 3 :
3.	To porters playing Engines	: 10 :
6.	To parchment and writing two presentments to the Assizes one on a suspected murther on an Infant by its mother Esther Partington,[6] another on a Burglary unknown	: 2 : 6
7.	To Mark Jones into Darbyshire ...	: : 6

---

[1] See p. 106, note 4.
[2] See p. 97, note 1.
[3] See p. 103, note 3.
[4] See p. 73, note 2.
[5] The "mob" and "rioters" here mentioned seem to point to another outbreak in the town this year, but I do not find any account of it in the local newspapers.
[6] See p. 103, note 2.

7.	To Mony Warrant for repair of Eye plat Bridge and Governors Wages ...	7 : 17 : 2
	To Hamlets for their Proportion ...	: 3 :
	To horsehire to Bolton 2/- High Constables Clerk with Presentments 1/- Expe. 1/11	: 4 : 11
10.	To Ringers Martinaco said to be taken from the French [1]	: 10 : 6
	To a distressed Sailor to Leverpoole...	: 1 :
21.	To Robert Colling and Alice his Wife two Evidences against Esther Partington [2] Condemned for murthering and burning her own lawful Infant... ...	3 : 3 :
	To Expences of Betty Matthews another Evidence [2]	1 : 19 :
	To Prosecutors Expences and horse [2]	2 : 12 : 6
	To Crown Office and Bailiffs fees [2] ...	: 14 :
24.	To a Vagabond	: : 6
26.	To decrying sweeping Chimneys by Fire [3] 1/- d° lifting [4] 1/6	: 2 : 6
30.	To mending the Dungeon Lamp ...	: 1 :
Ap¹ 3.	To John Sampson a distressed passenger	: 1 :
3.	To decrying the galloping of Horses in the Streets twice	: 3 :
	To d° the Selling of Arsenic	: 1 : 6
6.	To Examination and Warrant agᵗ Pegg Higginson, bound over	: 3 :
	To d° against Richard Isherwood fighting naked in the Night	: 3 :
7.	To Pe[ter] Cotrell keeping the Engines	: 4 :
	To three persons driving away and apprehending Strollers	: 3 :
	To Warrants for new Overseers ...	: 3 :
9.	To sundry Vagabonds &c...	: 3 : 2
	To lighting Lamps	: 2 : 6

[1] In the *London Gazette* for March 7th, 1759, an account of the capture of Guadalupe and the action of the fleet off Port Royal Harbour, in the island of Martinico, is given, but this island was not taken after all.

[2] See p. 103, note 2.

[3] That is, what is now termed "firing" them, setting the soot on fire instead of sweeping it out.

[4] See p. 68, note 1.

17.	To Assistants to prevent Lifting[1] on Monday and Tuesday and some other small Articles	: 7 :
23.	To charges conveying three Whores to the House of Correction	: 4 :
28.	To High Constables Warrant for making good the damage done to George Bramall[2] by the late Mobb...	27 : 16 : 5
	To Warrants for their proportion ...	: 3 :
	To Warrant for Assors of Landtax...	: 1 :
	To d° for Assessors of Window duty	: 1 :
	To summoning thirty Window Assessors	: 2 : 6
28.	To John Parks for Guardroom and what he advanced last Year for Soldiers	1 : 9 : 3
May 3.	To writing presentm[t] for Sessions ...	: 1 :
	To Ann Beard to Shefield...	: : 6
7.	To porters playing Engines	1 : : 4
18.	To an old Soldier to London	: : 5
18.	To High Constables Warrant for Vagrants, Forces, Coroners Orders and prosecuting Felons	12 : 19 : 5
	To Warrants for their proportion ...	: 3 :
19.	To John Parks for Guardroom forty days	1 : 7 : 6
	To George Clayton repairing the Engines	1 : 8 : 2
22.	To two old Soldiers	: 1 :
29.	To Boonfire King Charles, Restoration	: 6 :
	To an old Sailor...	: : 3
	To James Birch his Years Wages[3] ...	7 : :
June 1.	To Enginemen 10/– and Ale 1/– ...	: 11 :
4.	To Soldiers firing 21/– Boonfire 6[d]...	1 : 7 :
	To Wine drinking Royal healths the Prince's birthday at his full Age[4] ...	3 : 16 : 6

---

[1] Active steps apparently were taken this year to stop the practice of "lifting" on Easter Monday and Tuesday, which this year fell on the 16th and 17th of April.

[2] Mr. George Bramall was, I believe, the miller who worked Travis Mill, which was greatly injured by the mob in the riot of Nov. 15th, 1757. (See Appendix.)

[3] As Beadle.

[4] These festivities were for the coming of age of the Prince of Wales, afterwards George III., who was born 4th June, 1738. He was the grandson of the then King.

	To High Constables Warrant repairing Penwortham bridge	6 : 11 : 1
	To Warrants for proportion	: 3 :
9.	To Warrants for Surveyors presentm"	: 3 :
	To paper 3/- Vagrants 3 6...	: 6 : 6
21.	To Clerks for a Vagrant Warrant ...	: 2 :
	To John Stephenson to Leeds... ...	: : 6
27.	To James Smith to Ormskirk	: : 6
July 29.	To two Jurors fees	: 2 : 8
	To serving Jurors War" on Townships	: 1 :
Aug' 1.	To Warrants to Hamlets for the Assize Presentments	: 3 :
	To Enginemen last month	: 10 :
	To Sam' Smith's bill for Oil	2 : : 6
13.	To High Constables for repairing publick bridges	9 : 6 : 3
	To Warrants for proportion	: 3 :
15.	To Parchment and writing the Manchester Presentm' to Lancaster ...	: 1 :
15.	To High Constables Clerks	: 1 :
	To decrying Fustian-dyers following their Busines on Sundays	: 1 : 6
15.	To John Brown's bill repairing and beautifying the Exchange[1]	16 : 19 : 2
	To John Tinsly repairing Dungeon...	: 12 : 8
15.	To High Constables for damage done to Joseph Hawthorn[2] by the late Mobb	11 : : 3
	To Warrants for proportion of dᵘ ...	: 3 :
24.	To John Barlow's bill for Law... ...	7 : 8 : 4
28.	To Warrants to the Hamlets for Alehouse keepers to appear and take Lycences	: 3 :

George II., and son of Frederick, Prince of Wales, and Augusta, Princess of Saxe Gotha. The festivities in the town are thus described in the *Mercury* of Tuesday, June 5th, 1759 :

"Yesterday being the Birth-Day of his Royal Highness George, Prince of Wales, who then enter'd into the 22ᵈ Year of his Age, the Morning was ushered in with ringing of Bells, at Noon a Bonfire was made in the Market Place, and at five in the Afternoon, the Light Horse, quartered here were drawn up near the Bull's Head Inn, attended by the Magistrates, and a great Number of Gentlemen of the Town, when after drinking several loyal Healths, the Soldiers fired four rounds of Powder. In the Evening, a Ball was given at the Assembly-Room, at which was provided a grand Desert, of most Sorts of Fruit, Sweatmeats, &c."

[1] As already pointed out (see p. 53, note 4), this was the Exchange erected by Sir Oswald Mosley in 1729. It stood at the bottom of Market Street Lane until it gave place to a larger building in 1793.   [2] See next page, note 2.

	To summoning Manchester houses...	: 2 :
Sep' 3.	To sundry Vagrants	: 5 :
	To Enginemen playing Engines &c	: 10 : 6
12.	To Ringers good News from America[1]	: 5 :
13.	To Expences apprehending 11 ⎫ Strollers bringing them to Justice ⎬ Assistance &c ... ... ⎭	: 3 : 6
17.	To Edmund Wrigly repairing En- ⎱ gines ... ... ⎰	1 : 5 :
	To John Thorp for Iron Work... ...	: 12 : 6
	To George Henshall repairing Stocks	: 3 : 9
20.	To High Constables for defending ⎫ the Action brought against the ⎬ Hundred by Joseph Hawthorn[2] ... ⎭	2 : 11 : 11
	To Warrants for proportion	: 3 :
28.	To Marketlookers bill for Kids[3] and ⎱ Expences this Year ... ... ⎰	5 : 7 : 6
Octob 1.	To Enginemen and Ale	: 10 : 6
1.	To Expences privy Watch	: 10 : 6
	To seven Assistants	: 7 :
3.	To repairing a Constable's Staff ...	: 1 :
4.	To Wages and Expences at Sundry ⎫ times upon a Special Watch to appre- ⎬ hend Robbers &c ... ... ⎭	: 12 : 6
8.	To Thomas Barrows bill beautifying ⎱ the Cross[4] ... ... ⎰	2 : 2 : 2
Octob. 8	To John Townlys bill for Scaffolding ⎱ and work beautifying the cross[4] ... ⎰	1 : 16 :
	To Expences of a meeting at Coffee ⎱ house making a List of Alehouses ... ⎰	: 5 :
	To Jonathan Shelmardine removing ⎫ Kings Baggage of a Troop of light ⎬ horse to Knutsford ... ... ⎭	: 8 : 4
	To Thomas Crompton keeping clean ⎫ the River Steps at Milbrow and Salford ⎬ bridge ... ... ⎭	: 4 :

[1] This probably had reference to the capture of Niagara in Canada. The *Mercury* of Sept. 18th, 1759, refers to it, and states that "as Niagara is a Place of such Conse-quence, and taken by Sir William Johnson, let it be remembered, that that Gentleman is nephew to the late brave Sir Peter Warren."

[2] This probably had to do with the recent riots—Mr. Hawthorn claiming compen-sation from the authorities of the Hundred of Salford. (See previous page.)

[3] "Kids," an old word for bundles of faggots.

[4] See p. 42, note 2.

To Timber and sawing the Dungeon Laddar	: 5 :	5
To painting the Ladder	: 1 :	
To sundry Expences by the Deputy attending the Justices with the Beadle Assistants and prisoners, upon Witnesses &c during this Year ...	1 : 6 :	
To paper ruling and writing the Constable Ley book...	1 : 5 :	
To Belman calling a meeting to consider of proper Steps for the preventing of Housebreaking &c	: 1 :	6
To M[r] Byroms bill Beadles Trimming[1]	1 : 18 :	
To M[r] Birch, for Beadles Cloth[1] ...	2 : 15 :	
To Beadles bill money advanced, and for Work	8 : 2 :	1
To Beadles Shoes this Year[1]	: 15 :	
To his Stockings[1]	: 9 :	
To Expences when the Ley [was] laid	3 : 18 :	
To Sam[l] Smith's bill for Oil Colour &c Cross[2] and Gibbet[3] beautified	2 : 5 :	4
To defending the Watch ag[t] Hobly who pretended they had robbed him...	: 4 :	
To committing Thomas Hulme for stabbing Barsly and Wife...	: 3 :	
To prosecuting Henry Royle, fees to the Justice Clerks for Examination &c	: 3 :	
To Justice Clerks for Vagrant passes...	: 9 :	
To Walter Wilson for Ironwork ...	1 : 17 :	3
To mony advanced by M[r] Hodson ...	: 7 :	9
To M[r] Nangreave[4] a Fee	: 10 :	6

(marginal: **8.**)

---

[1] See p. 88, note 2.

[2] See p. 111, note 4.

[3] The "Gibbet" was the customary name for the Pillory, which stood in the Market Place, near the Cross. (See *Constables' Accounts*, vol. ij., p. 42, note 3). There are occasional entries in the *Manchester Mercury* of persons having to stand in the Pillory for various offences. One such occurs in the Accounts for May, 1763. (See *postea*.)

[4] Mr. Nangreave was a lawyer in the town. In the next year's Accounts he is called "Lawyer Nangreave," when a fee of £1 1s. was paid him. He is also mentioned in subsequent Accounts.

31.   To money retained in the hands of ⎫
        William Newton[1] late Misegatherer ⎬ 42:12: 9½
        who is become insolvent ... ... ⎭
        To the Deputy's Salary ... ...   20: :

                Total paid £295: 4:10½
                Total received £274:15: 5

        Owing to the late Constables £21: 9: 5½

[Receipts]

Dr The late Constables.

1758.

To last Years Balance[2]	12:16: 2½
To Cash from the Old Ley book	7:18: 7
To Cash from Mr Henry Hesky[3] one of the Mise-gatherers	112: :
To Cash from Mr William Newton the other Misegatherer	19: 6: 9½

Note he keeps in his hands

to wit, One Sum 21:16: 0½		
Another Sum 7: 8: 1		
Another Sum 9:17:11		
And also the Sum 3:10: 9		
Making in the whole...	42:12: 9½
To Cash received since the Book was took out of Newton's hands	27:19: 2½
To Cash from the Hamlets two thirds of 6:11: 1	4: 7: 5	
two thirds of 12:19: 5	8:12:11	
two thirds of 27:16: 5	18:10:11	
two thirds of 9: 6: 3	6: 4: 2	
two thirds of 11: : 3	7: 6:10	
two thirds of 7:17: 2	5: 4:11	
two thirds of 2:11:11	1:14: 8	52: 1:10

                Total received £274:15: 5

[1] The two Misegatherers elected on the 11th October, 1758, were Mr. Henry Hesketh and Mr. William Newton, of Market Street Lane. (See *Court Leet Records* vol. viij., p. 23.)

[2] See p. 100.

[3] The local pronunciation of Hesketh. (See note 1.)

1759. October 31[st][1]   We the Jurors of the Court Leet have examined the foregoing Accounts of the late Constables and allowing the same do order the balance due to them namely twenty one pounds nine Shillings and five pence half peny to be paid by the succeeding Constables and that the same shall be allowed in their Accounts.

(Signed)   W[m] CLOWES
THO[s] CLOWES
OTIIO COOKE
THOS. BATTERSBEE
W[m] HARRISON
JAMES BORRON
SAMUEL GOODIER
JOHN HARDMAN
JOHN FEILDEN
EDM[d] HOLME
HENRY FEILDEN
PETER CROMPTON
JOHN ROBINSON
EDW[d] BYROM Jun[r]

---

[1] As shown by the *Court Leet Records* (vol. viij., p. 38), the adjourned meeting on this date was held "in the House of M[r] James Crompton, called Saint Ann's Coffee House," the first time that particular house had been mentioned.

[Constables' Accounts.]

[10th Oct., 1759, to 15th Oct., 1760.]

••••••••••••

An Acco^t of Cash disburs'd by MR JOHN FEILDEN & MR JOSHUA MARRIOTT,[1] *Constables of Manchester* [elected 10th October, 1759].

[Disbursements]

1759	p^d the Balance of last Year's Acco^t[2]...	21 : 9 : 5½
Octr 20.	p^d for Boonfire upon the News of Quebec[3] being took ... ... }	: 6 :
	p^d for Musick on the Coronation-day[4]	: 10 :
	p^d the Soldiers firing on this Occasion	1 : 1 :
22.	p^d for Wine drinking the Royal Healths at the taking of Quebec[3] ... }	8 : 11 : 9

---

[1] These two Constables were elected at the Court Leet held on October 10th, 1759. (See *Court Leet Records*, vol. viij., p. 33.)

[2] See p. 114.

[3] This was a very celebrated victory, although attended by the sad loss of General Wolfe. It took place on September 14th, 1759, and resulted in the conquest of Canada. It seems to have been celebrated with more than ordinary enthusiasm in the town, the sum spent on wine being unusually large. I do not find any account of these rejoicings in the *Manchester Mercury* for October 23rd; but in that for October 30th there is a reference to the words exhibited in six windows "during the late illumination." But in the same paper there is the following account of some special rejoicings on the 23rd October, as follows :—

"*Manchester, Oct.* 30*th.*—On Tuesday Evening last [Oct. 23] the Ancient and Honourable Society of Free and accepted Masons met at their Lodge Room, at the King's Head in Salford, to celebrate the Signal and Glorious Victory obtained over the French at Quebec; about Six o'clock the Room was grandly Illuminated, in which were several curious Paintings, in particular the Middle Window, (being taken out and replaced with a beautiful Transparent one) on which were painted several Emblems of Masonry, with their proper Mottos, the meaning of which are best known to that Society; also the English Arms and Garter, with the word QUEBEC in large capital letters.   On this occasion a grand Entertainment was provided, after which many Loyal Healths were Drank [all duly set out]. The Illumination lasted till Twelve and every thing was conducted with the greatest Decorum, and the Gentlemen broke up with that decency and regularity as become that Honourable Fraternity."

[4] Both the anniversary of the day of the King's (George II.'s) Coronation, October 20th, and his birthday, November 10th, were celebrated with bonfires and festivities in the town. (See previous Accounts.)

	p^d for a Boonfire the King's Coronation[1]	: 6 :
Novr 5	p^d for a Boonfire as usual	: 5 : 6
5.	p^d John Perry to Wrexham a Passenger	: : 6
	p^d Porters playing Engines	: :
	p^d lighting Lamps last Dark	: 2 : 6
10.	p^d for a Boonfire on the Kings birth day[1]	: 5 : 6
	p^d Ja^s Crompton for Wine[1]	2 : 18 : 6
	p^d for Ale for the Soldiers[1]	1 : 1 :
	p^d Musicians hereupon[1]	: 10 :
	p^a carting the Militia Baggage to Stockport	: 3 : 9
24.	p^d setling Bills and Bailiff's Fees, several Fortune Tellers and Bawdy housekeepers Indicted &c...	: 14 :
	p^d ten Witnesses attending Sessions on these Acco^{ts} and other Expences Relative thereto	1 : 5 :
Decr 4	p^d Porters playing Engines & for Oil	1 : 1 :
	p^d mending Eleven Buckets	: 5 : 6
	p^d Lawyer Nangrave advising in Roger Blomely's Case bringing Actions ag^t the Constables for puting him in the Dungeon for being drunk on Sunday in time of divine Service ...	1 : 1 :
	p^d Slater & John Clegg two assistants to detect Persons selling Drams to the Militia under Exercise	: 2 :
	p^d Warrants to the Hamlets for new Surveyers	: 3 :
25.	p^d making Beadles Cap and Gown ...	: 8 : 7½
	p^d Beadle a quarters Salary	1 : 15 :
	p^d Messengers & Expences summoning the Manch^r Militia to appear before the Lieutenants	: 7 : 6
30.	p^d for Boonfire French Fleet overcome by Admeral Hawk[2]	: 6 : 6
	p^d Musicians[2]	1 : 1 :
	p^d for Wine drunk upon this Occasion[2]	7 : 17 : 4

---

[1] See p. 115, note 4.

[2] This was the victory at Quiberon, on the French coast, in which Admiral Sir Edward Hawke was victorious over the French fleet. It took place on November 20th, 1759. I do not find any account of these festivities in the *Manchester Mercury*.

Dec' 30.   p^d a Post Messenger to Rolstone[1] for ⎫
liberty of the Exchange for a Guard ⎬ 1 : 7 :
Room ... ... ⎭

         p^d four Men taking a particular Acco^t ⎫
of all the Beds and Soldiers quartered ⎪
in publick houses to demonsterate the ⎬ : 10 : 6
Impossibility of a second Battalion of ⎪
Lincoln Militia[2] being quartered here ⎭

         p^d Charges from time to time prose- ⎫
cuting Landlords refusing to comply ⎬ 1 : :
with Billets... ... ... ⎭

         p^d a Messenger to Preston to examine ⎫
Thieves in the house of Correction ⎬ : 5 :
there ... ... ⎭

         p^d for Billet paper ... ... : 3 :

1760. Feb. 5. p^d Belman for nine publick Cries ... : 14 :

         p^d lighting Lamps 5 times ... ... : 10 : 10

         p^d Porters playing two Months... ... 1 : :

         p^d Warrant for the Governer's[3] Wages 1 : 4 : 6

         p^d Warrants to the Hamlets ... .. : 3 :

         p^d at Peter Barrows when Sharp and ⎫
other Felons were apprehended and ⎬ 1 : 9 : 6
kept in Custody... ... ... ⎭

---

[1] That is, Rolleston in Staffordshire, the residence of the Rev. Sir John Mosley, Bart., lord of the manor of Manchester, who was asked for permission to allow the Exchange to be used as a guardroom for the troops at this time quartered in the town.

[2] The Lincolnshire Militia were at this time quartered in the town. Their arrival is thus noticed in the *Manchester Mercury* of November 27th, 1759 :—

"On Wednesday last [Nov 21] four Companies of the Northern Battalion of the Lincolnshire Militia arrived here with Colours flying, Drums beating, and French Horns sounding, under the Command of the Right Hon. the Earl of Scarborough, who Headed them up on Foot, from Gainsborough to this Place, except about 12 Miles. On Friday [Nov 23rd] the other Division arrived here under the Command of Major Dashwood. They made a very handsome Appearance, and were all in high spirits. And this week the Southern Battalion is expected to arrive here."

Later on, in the issue of the same paper for March 18th, 1760, the arrival of the Southern Battalion is thus noticed :—

"On Tuesday and Wednesday last [March 11th and 12th] the whole South Battalion of the Lincolnshire Militia came in here from Liverpool, in the room of the North Battalion, which is quartered at the following Places, viz., Major Dashwood's and Capt. Wood's Companies at Stockport ;—Capt. Brackenbury's and Capt. Pilkington's at Macclesfield ; Capt. Dymoke Lister's and Capt Amcott's Companies at Knutsford ; the Earl of Scarborough's (Colonel) ; Lieutenant-Colonel Vinor's ; Capt. Matt. Lister's and Capt. Caldicott's Companies at Warrington."

[3] That is, the Governor of the House of Correction in Manchester.

7.	pᵈ Relief to Passengers Soldiers and Strolers during last three Months ...	1 : 17 :
	pᵈ Sundry Assistants apprehending ten Imbezellers upon John Sharp's Information	: 12 : 6
8.	pᵈ on their Accoᵗ at the house of Correction and attending the Justices, most of them Convicted	1 : 16 : 6
	pᵈ Expences abᵗ James Dean inform'd against for keeping a Bawdy-house ...	: 2 : 7
13.	pᵈ Bailiffs attending Sh[r]ew Taylor thro' the Streets with a Libel [sic for label] upon her Back for keeping a Bawdyhouse	: 5 : 4
	pᵈ Warrˡˢ to Hamlets for Presentments to the Assizes	: 3 :
25	pᵈ Sundry Persons assisting the Militia abᵗ removing and Impressing Carriages in the Night-Time commanded to Liverpool it being reported the French were come there to invade us	: 10 : 2
	pᵈ Carts Men and horses to Warrington with Baggage	1 : 18 : 9
	repᵈ Mʳ Feilden	: 2 : 3
	pᵈ for Summons's for seventeen Militia Men	: 8 : 6
28.	pᵈ Jurors Fees over an Infant brougᵗ dead into Town by its Parents... ...	: 1 : 4
March 2.	pᵈ a Post Messenger to Nottingham to stop by the King's Express Cavindish's Regimᵗ upon March hither ...	1 : 16 :
March 2.	pᵈ this Journey strain'd a Horse which had lately cost Eight Pounds to such a degree that at his return he was given away as worth nothing	5 : 5 :
3	pᵈ summoning and expences attending the enrolemᵗ of seventeen Militiamen	: 3 : 6
5.	pᵈ Manchester Presentmᵗ to the Assizes 1ˢ the High Constables Clerks therewith 1ˢ	: 2 :
28.	pᵈ Jurors a Child being drown'd in Chetham	: 1 : 4

	p^d John Clegg for a new whipping Stage at Rogues Post[1]	3 : 15 : 7
	p^d three Trampers[2] to Scotland ...	: 1 :
29.	p^d High Constables Warr^t repairing Ribchester Bridge &c	1 : 10 : 7
Ap^l 2.	p^d Warrants to Hamlets calling Overseers to Acco^t	: 3 :
7.	p^d Belman twice decrying Lifting[3] & 4 other Cries	: 7 : 6
	p^d Engine Men 2 Months...	1 : :
	p^d Sundry Passengers 5 6 & More Billet Paper 3^s	: 8 : 6
	p^d Goldsmith's for Dark Lanthorns and mending Lamps...	: 9 : 8
	p^d Barn^t Shaw's Bill	1 : 12 : 5
	p^d Thos Braithwaite's Bill for three Pair of Shoes for Beadle	: 15 :
	p^d Joseph Budworth's[4] Bills Left unpaid by the Constables from time to time ... ... one Bill	3 : 8 : 4
	another	3 : : 9
	another	3 : 14 : 6
	another	: 15 :
11.	p^d mending nine Buckets	: 4 : 6
	p^d Carter's Bill for Sundry Carriages	2 : 16 : 9
12.	p^d four Passengers	: 1 :
	p^d lighting Lamps	: 1 : 8
	p^d C[h]arges detaining a Man under Justice Bayley's[5] Warr^t ordered not to be put in the Dungeon	: 5 : 10
	p^d Wages to Assistants and Incidental Expences apprehending and Prosecuting Whores and Fortune tellers at James Deans and other Places... ...	1 : 12 : 6
	p^d for Bangbegger's[6] Whip	: 2 : 3
	repaid the Bangbegger[6] in advance...	: 7 : 8

[1] See p. 84, note 1. The "whipping stage" was the platform upon which the unfortunate person stood when fastened to the post and being whipped.

[2] This is the first time that this word "trampers," now contracted into the common word "tramps," has occurred in these Accounts.

[3] See p. 68, note 1.

[4] Mr. Joseph Budworth kept the Bull's Head Inn in Manchester, where meetings of the townspeople and of the Court Leet Jury were held.

[5] See p. 105, note 1.   [6] See p. 70, note 2.

	p^d Mr Blinkhorn's Bill for Beadles Stockings		: 13 :	6
	p^d John Smith for Assistance		: 2 :	
May 29.	p^d for a Boonfire		: 6 :	2
June 2.	p^d Porters Playing Engines	1 :	:	6
June 6.	p^d John Stephens to Carlisle very ill		: 1 :	
	p^d Oliver Nabb mending Dungeon Window		: 13 :	6
	p^d Richard Booth for Iron Bars for do.		: 10 :	3
	p^d John Smith for Lamp Oil	1 :	8 :	2
	p^d Richard Lightboun mending Buckets and for Oil...		: 7 :	
27.	p^d laying last Year's Constable Ley...	4 :	6 :	6
	p^d Ja^s Birch[1] a quarters Salary... ...	1 :	17 :	6
	p^d him at same time Remainder of his Salary	3 :	10 :	
	p^d Expences at Robt Shepherd's when Imbezellers [were] whipt		: 3 :	6
30.	p^d Ringers favourable News from Quebeck[2]	1 :	1 :	
July 7.	p^d Mr Budworth,[3] Charges laying Constable Ley	4 :	7 :	4
	p^d Charges burying two Twins found dead in a necessary house top of Deansgate		: 8 :	2
	p^d Thomas Baron for his Assistance by day and Night on Sundry Occasions		: 5 :	
	p^d 2 Women Passengers		: 1 :	
	p^d writing Sessions Presentm^t		: 1 :	
	p^d Law Expences Prosecuting a Soldier for assaulting the Watch and the Deputy Constable in the Night...		: 10 :	6
	p^d Warr^{ts} to the Hamlets for Presentm^{ts} to the Assizes		: 3 :	
	p^d three Passengers		: 1 :	6
Augt 4.	p^d Law Expences Prosecuting Ruth Hall a Fortune-teller who was whip[t]		: 5 :	6
	p^d Stephen Heys for assistance ...		: 5 :	

---

[1] James Birch was the Beadle.

[2] This probably relates to the arrival of some "favourable news" about the conquest of Canada. Quebec itself had surrendered on the 18th September, 1759. I do not find any account of these rejoicings in the *Manchester Mercury*.

[3] See p. 119, note 4.

	pᵈ off Mʳ Tomkinson¹ an old Accoᵗ for Law	17	8	
	pᵈ Manchester Presentmᵗ and High Constables therewith...		2	
	pᵈ four Strolers into Yorkshire ...		1	
	pᵈ for Paper for Billets		2	3
	pᵈ for a Book for the Militia List ...		2	
	pᵈ for another Book for the same Purpose		2	
	pᵈ writing 2 Duplicates of Manchester Militia	2	2	
29.	pᵈ Warrⁿ to Hamlets for Ale Licences		3	
	pᵈ B[e]llman crying Notice of a Gang of Pickpockets		1	6
	pᵈ Sundry Passengers and Strolers ...		1	6
Sepᵗ 15.	pᵈ a discharged Sailor to Whitehaven			6
	pᵈ Edmund Wrigley's Bill for Work at the Engine	1	1	
	pᵈ John Thorp's Bill for Ironwork do.		10	
	pᵈ Peter Cotrell for care of the Engines a Year...		4	
	pᵈ Thoˢ Crompton cleaning Steps at Millhill and Salford Bridge		4	
Octʳ 6.	pᵈ Porters playing Engines three Months	1	10	6
7.	pᵈ writing Warrⁿ summoning Surveyors		3	
	pᵈ for a Search Warrant		2	
	pᵈ Costs Charges Assistants and Evidences apprehending five Whores		2	4
	pᵈ Jurors in nine Coroners Inquisitions		12	
	pᵈ serving the nine Warrⁿ upon the Hamlets		9	
	pᵈ Ringers two several Times half a Guinea upon good News²...	1	1	
	pᵈ do. when Montreal was took from the French²	1	1	

---

¹ Mr. James Tomkinson was at this time a very celebrated lawyer at Nantwich, in Cheshire, where he had an extensive practice and acquired a large fortune.

² These celebrations were probably on account of victories in Canada, as is clearly shown by subsequent entries. A very full account of the capture of Montreal is contained in the *Manchester Mercury* for Oct. 14th, 1760, but there is no account of the rejoicings in the town.

p⁴ an High Constables Warrᵗ for Governor's Wages	1 : 6 : 7
pᵈ another conveying Vagrants and Forces, &c	6 : 10 : 7
pᵈ damage done to Mʳˢ Irlam's house by the Mob	: 8 : 4½
pᵈ Mʳ Barlow's Bill for Law	38 : 7 : 2
pᵈ Bernᵈ Shaw for Prison Fees and Expences	: 13 : 2
pᵈ Deputy's Salary	20 : ˙
pᵈ Coffee house Bill when Montreal was taken¹	3 : 6 :

	224 : 12 : 0½
Receiv'd from the Misegatherers in full	203 : 15 : 1½
The Balance of this Accoᵗ owing to the late Constbᵉ	. 20 : 16 : 11

1760
Novʳ 6ᵗʰ   We the Jurors of the Court Leet now holden for the Manor of Manchester in the County of Lancaster have examin'd the foregoing Accoᵗˢ of the late Constables of Manchester and do find a Balance of twenty Pounds sixteen Shillings and Eleven Pence due and owing to them and we allowing the same do order the said Balance to be paid to them by the succeeding Constables whom we allow to charge it in their Accounts.

(Signed)   THOˢ CHADWICK
THOˢ CLOWES
SAMˡˡ CLOWES Junʳ
DORNING RASBOTHAM
JNᵒ HEYWOOD
RICHARD BARTON
JOHN MOSLEY
GEO: JOHNSON
JOS: BUDWORTH
ARNᴰ BIRCH
RICHᴰ GRANTHAM
WALTER WILSON
FOLLIOTT POWELL
GEO: HILTON
JOHN WILSON

¹ See p. 121, note 2.

[Constables' Accounts.]

[15th Oct., 1760, to 7th Oct., 1761.]

• • • • • • • • • • • •

Cash disbursed by M[R] CHARLES FORD and M[R] EDWARD KENYON, *Constables of Manchester*[1] [elected 15th October, 1760].

[Disbursements]

1760

Octob 16.	Paid last Year's Balance[2]	20 : 16 : 11
	p[d] Beadles Bill for last Year	7 : 12 :
	p[d] for a Warrant of Peace ag[t] Jo[n] Swindels	: 3 :
	p[d] Information and Commitment ag[t] a lame Cobler	: 4 :
	p[d] for a Vagrants pass	: 3 :
	p[d] Committing a riotous Soldier ...	: 3 : 6
	p[d] Examination ag[t] Taylor abusing his Wife	: 1 :
	p[d] Information and order of Whipping Ruth Hall a Fortune teller	: 3 :
	p[d] sommoning a Coroners Jury and Juror's Fees, a Child burnt to Death	: 2 : 4
	p[d] drawing five presentments ag[t] persons keeping Mastifdogs unmuzled	: 5 :
	p[d] an old Woman tramping to Leeds	: 1 :
	p[d] Peter Clark to Sterling...	: 1 :
	repaid M[r] Marriott in Advance... ...	: 9 : 6
	p[d] for ten Indictments against keepers of Mastifdogs 22 6 Bailif's Fees 14 8, other Charges thereupon 10 6	2 : 7 : 8

---

[1] These two Constables were elected at the Court Leet held on the 15th October, 1760. (See *Court Leet Records*, vol. viij., p. 44.)

[2] See p. 122.

	p^d Evidences attending three days ...	: 12 : 6
	p^d Charges impressing Carriages for Lincolnshire Militia[1]	: 11 :
	p^d a Messenger and horse to Chapel in the Firth and others ab^t the Militia	: 18 : 3
	p^d Ringers on two public Rejoicings for good News[2]	2 : 2 :
Novr 4.	p^d Ringers his Majesty George the Third proclaimed King[3]	1 : 3 : 8
27.	Summoning twenty Militiamen to appear before the Commissioners ...	: 6 : 8
Decem 24.	p^d making Beadles Cap and Gown ...	: 8 : 6
26.	p^d at the meeting for making new Surveyors of the Highways	: 6 :
29.	p^d Charges prosecuting two Whores...	: 11 : 6
	Summoning eight Militia men... ...	: 2 : 8
	p^d Belman four Cries...	: 5 : 6
	p^d repairing the Stocks	: 6 : 2
	p^d Robt Smethurst assisting Deputy &c	: 10 : 6
[1761]		
Jan 22.	p^d writing presentment to the Sessions	: 1 :
	p^d Charges at Sessions prosecuting the Indictments about Mastif dogs ...	1 : 10 : 6
Febry 2.	p^d committing two Whores	: 4 :
	p^d summoning fourteen Militiamen[4]	: 4 : 8
	p^d Musicians at the King's Proclamation[5]	2 : 2 :

---

[1] The departure of the Lincolnshire Militia from the town is thus recorded in the *Manchester Mercury* of Oct. 21st, 1760 :—

"On Saturday [Oct. 18th] five Companies of the South Battalion of the Lincolnshire Militia, marched from hence, and on Monday the remaining five Companies marched for Lincoln to remain there till further Orders. The same Days the North Battalion marched from Chester for Lincolnshire."

[2] These rejoicings were probably for victories in Canada.

[3] The late King, George II., died very suddenly on the 25th October, 1760, aged 77. He was succeeded by his grandson, George III., then 22 years of age. In the *Manchester Mercury* of November 4th, 1760, it is stated—"This Day, between the Hours of ten and eleven o'Clock in the Forenoon, his Majesty King George the Third will be proclaimed at the Market Cross here."

[4] The *Manchester Mercury* of January 6th states that "Yesterday Major Patten, marched in here, at the Head of two Companies of the Lancashire Militia, all cloath'd and arm'd ; and on Friday next three Companies more are expected, to lie here till further orders."

[5] The King's Proclamation took place on November 4th. (See note 3.)

	p^d John Heywood Baggage to Knutsford	: 3 :	9
3.	p^d James Birchs[1] bill in full	2 : 11 :	
9.	p^d Charges of a private Watch... ...	: 10 :	6
14.	p^d Charges committing and otherwise punishing ten lewd Women	: 17 :	
14.	p^d High Constables for Governors Wages...	1 : 4 :	6
	p^d Beadles Hose and Shoes	: 7 :	6
21.	p^d Charges prosecuting Samuel Barret for Embezzelling	: 6 :	6
	Summoning eight Militiamen	: 2 :	8
22.	p^d Charges committing a riotous Man	: 4 :	
Febry 23.	p^d putting up a thousand Advertisements against Immorality...	: 10 :	
	p^d Thomas Braithwaite for Shoes had by the late Beadle James Birch ...	1 : 11 :	6
	p^d writing Warrants to the Hamlets 2 - for presentments to the Assizes, and Messenger with them 2 -	: 4 :	
28.	p^d Charges apprehending and conveying Six Pickpockets to Justice... ...	: 12 :	6
Mar 2.	p^d conveying a lame Soldier on his March to Warrington...	: 5 :	
11.	p^d parchment and writing the Assize presentment 2 - High Constables Clerks at Bolton 1 - horse 2, - Expences 2 4	: 7 :	4
12.	p^d for Straw and cleansing Dungeon	: 3 :	
	p^d noticing and Warrants for Collectors of Landtax and Window duty	: 3 :	
	p^d like for Overseers to account ...	: 3 :	
19.	p^d two Soldiers for Assistance	: 2 :	
	p^d mending Mean Pipe in the Engine	: 10 :	
	p^d Mr Byrom for Beadle's Trimming	2 : 9 :	
	p^d Jurors a Child drown'd in Salford &c	: 2 :	4
25.	p^d High Constables for Publick Bridges	11 : 3 :	4
31.	p^d for a Search Warrant	: 2 :	

[1] James Birch was the Beadle. Shortly after this date he is called, on February 23rd, "the late beadle James Birch."

Ap[l] 6.	p[d] George Holland repairing and plastering the Exchange[1] damaged by the Lincolnshire Militia[2]	2 : 18 :		
	p[d] for Billet Paper	: 3 :		
9.	p[d] writing presentment to Sessions ...	: 1 :		
Ap[l] 12.	p[d] Charges and Expences at Sessions	: 7 : 6		
17.	p[d] John Brown for carpentry Work at the Exchange[1] damaged by the Militia...	2 : 2 :		
	p[d] Luke Ashly repairing the Windows[1]	2 : 3 : 9		
23.	p[d] summoning four Militiamen, and attending with them at Middleton ...	: 4 : 6		
	p[d] Belman twice decrying lifting[3] ...	: 2 :		
May 2.	p[d] High Constables repairing Lancas[r] Cas[le]	12 : 19 : 5		
2.	p[d] Landtax and Window Warrants...	: 2 :		
9	p[d] Expences threeday summoning and attending the Assessors of Landtax and Window duty	: 4 : 6		
16.	p[d] High Constables repairing County Bridges &c...	34 : 9 : 9		
June 4.	p[d] Soldiers firing it being his Majestys Birthday[4]	2 : 12 : 6		
	p[d] Musicians same Occasion[4]	1 : 10 :		
	p[d] Committing John Smith a Drunkard	: 4 : 8		
	p[d] Thomas Tonge for Smithwork at the Fire Engines	2 : 5 : 4		
16.	p[d] Ringers, say Belisle taken[5]	1 : 1 :		
	paid for Ale[5]	: 2 :		
	p[d] for paper ruling and writing the Leybook	1 : 5 :		
17.	p[d] Assistants at sundry times	: 5 : 6		
	p[d] Goldsmith for Lanthorn's for the privy Watch and for Work at the Cross and Dungeon Lamps &c ...	1 : 16 :		
18.	p[d] Ringers Belisle News confirm'd[5] ...	1 : 5 :		

[1] See p. 53, note 4.   [2] See p. 117, note 2, and p. 124, note 1.
[3] See p. 68, note 1.
[4] The birthday of the King was on June 4th. (See an account of the celebration of his coming of age in Manchester, p. 109, note 4.)
[5] Belleisle was a small island off the coast of Brittany, which was very strongly fortified by the French. It was captured by Commodore Keppel and General Hodgson, and its fall was considered a great blow to the French.

[1] Octob 5.   p^d Cotrel keeping Keys of the Engine   : 4 :

p^d Expences of Evidences at Lancaster
last Assizes about trying the Action }   6 : 13 : 6
against Roger Blomely ... ...

p^d Deputys Salary ... ...   20 :

p^d James Crompton's bill on sundry } 18 :   : 10
publick Rejoicings this Year[2] ... ...

paid Joseph Budworth[3] on like Acc^{t2} 22 : 9 : 10

p^d Harrop[4] printing on Constables } 2 : 11 :
Acc^t this Year and last ... ...

paid John Heywood conveying the
Baggage of Lancashire Militia[5] to } 1 : 1 :
Knutsford in Cheshire ... ...

repaid Mr Kenyon in Advance... ...   : 10 : 6

p^d Beadle attending the Stocks ...   : 8 : 6

p^d Mr Barlows Bill for Law   ... ...   21 : 16 :

    Disbursed totally. ... ...£283 : 6 : 9

Rec^d from the Ley book 208 : 19 : 8 } 239 : 13 : 0
from the Hamlets ... 30 : 13 : 4 }

    Balance owing by the Town... £43 : 13 : 9

---

[1] There is a gap here in the Accounts, one leaf, containing the entries between June 18th and October 5th, being missing.

[2] The "public Rejoicings" here referred to were those at the coronation of the King (George III.) and his consort, Princess Charlotte of Mecklenburgh-Strelitz, of which I find the following account in Harrop's *Manchester Mercury* for September 29th, 1761 :—

"Last Tuesday [Sept. 22nd] being the day appointed for the Coronation of their Majesties, the same was ushered in with Firing of Cannon and Ringing of Bells, and about eleven o'Clock in the morning, the Workmen in the several Branches of Trade being formed into Companys, with their proper Emblems and Devices, went in Procession through the Town, amidst the greatest Concourse of People ever assembled here.

"About three in the Afternoon, all the principal Inhabitants, with Favours in their Hats, in Honour of the Day, attended on Horseback upon the Boroughreeve and Constables, and with them paraded through the Square and principal Streets of the Town. Several Oxen and Sheep were roasted whole in different parts of the Town and Salford. Three Stages were erected, one in St. Ann's Square, one at the Cross, and one in Within Grove, from which a number of Barrels of Beer and Wine were distributed amongst the Populace. An Entertainment was provided at the Old Coffee House and another at the Bull's Head Inn for the Repast of the Gentlemen, from whence they adjourned to the Exchange to conclude the Evening, by drinking the Healths of their most gracious Sovereign and the Queen.

"The whole Town was most splendidly illuminated; and notwithstanding so many Thousand People were assembled, there was not the least Disorder or Tumult, an undeniable Proof of their Affection for the best of Kings."

After reading the above one can only be surprised at the moderation of the two bills in the text. Later on, however, in the next year's Accounts, there are entries of further payments of over £40 in connection with this rejoicing.

[3] See p. 119, note 4.   [4] See p. 73, note 2.   [5] See p. 124, note 4.

1761.   Nov[r] 11th.   We the Jurors of the Court Leet, now holden
for the Manor of Manchester in the County of Lancaster, have
examined the foregoing Accounts of the late Constables of
Manchester and do find a Balance of Forty three pounds thirteen
Shillings and nine pence, and we allowing the same, do order the
said Balance to be paid to them by the succeeding Constables,
whom we allow to charge it in their Accounts.

(Signed)   THO[s] JOHNSON
THO[s] CHADWICK
WIL[M] KENNEDY
THO[s] GARDNER
MARSDEN KENYON
LUKE COTES
JAMES HODSON
ROB[T] BOARDMAN
ROB[T] STOTT
JONA[N] PATTEN Jun[r]
JOHN CLOWES
D[G] RASBOTHAM[1]
JOHN ROBINSON

[1] That is, Dorning Rasbotham.

[Constables' Accounts.]

[7th Oct., 1761, to 13th Oct., 1762.]

• • • • • • • • • • •

An Acc^t of Cash disburs'd by Mr JOHN TIPPING and Mr HENRY FEILDEN,[1] *Constables of Manchester* [elected 7th October, 1761].

[Disbursements]

1761		l	s	d
	Paid last years balance[2]	43	13	9
October 8.	p^d presentment to the Sessions... ...		1	
	p^d sundry passengers...		1	
Nov. 7.	p^d High Constables repairing for repairs of House o' Correction &c ...	1	18	4
	p^d writing Warrants to the eleven Hamlets for their proportion		3	
	p^d sundry passengers last Month ...		3	6
	p^d serving thirteen Alehouse keepers with summonses for selling Ale without Licences		6	6
15.	p^d four men searching bad houses ...		4	
	p^d attending John Townsend all night, a suspicious Rogue		4	1
16.	p^d five Assistants to day with him and seven or eight Whores		3	6
	p^d six Evidences against them &c ...		3	
	p^d Expences on this Account		3	5
	p^d Mrs Irlam damages done to her house and Windows by a Mobb at the last boonfire...		13	6

---

[1] These two Constables were elected at the Court Leet held on the 7th October, 1761. (See *Court Leet Records*, vol. viij., p. 54.)

[2] See p. 128.

		l	s	d
24.	pᵈ apprehending and attending in the Stocks Alice Kaynall[1]		: 2 :	
	pᵈ apprehending and detaining Thomas Hewit three days and three nights suspected of writing incendiary Letters		: 9 :	6
27.	pᵈ to find an itenerant Dancing Master[2] at the Justices Request		: 1 :	6
Nov 27.	pᵈ for a Lamp Ladder & oil Bottle		: 5 :	3
Decʳ 4.	pᵈ Lighting Lamps two Months ...		: 3 :	8
	pᵈ conveying and attending upon an apprentice boy committed		: 3 :	
	pᵈ Assistants about Strollers[3] &c ...		: 5 :	
14.	pᵈ sundry Strollers[3] since last Entry		: 7 :	6
	pᵈ for a Search Warrant		: 2 :	
	pᵈ passing Higginbotham's family to Ashton under line		: 4 :	8
24.	pᵈ four persons assisting to take and attend Strollers[3] 4 6 Expences 2 6 ...		: 7 :	
	Committing and conveying four of them to the house o' Correction ...		: 5 :	6
	pᵈ for Sustenance in the Dungeon ...		: 2 :	
26.	Attending Ellis Walwork two days in Custody for Felony 3/- whipping &c. 1/6		: 4 :	6
	pᵈ Belman noticing a meeting for new Surveyors of the Highway		: 1 :	
	Writing Return 1/- Charge of meeting 4/-		: 5 :	
	Warrants to yᵉ Hamlets for Surveyors		: 3 :	
29.	Going to Royton with Wᵐ Haworth under Justice Percivals Warrant ...		: 2 :	6
	pᵈ an Attendant...		: 1 :	6
1762.	pᵈ Lighting Lamps		: 1 :	10
Jan 3.	pᵈ mending Engine pipe and Ale ...		: 2 :	
	pᵈ Expences of five persons in Custody a night and a day for quarrelling ...		: 3 :	6
	for persons attending them		: 4 :	

---

[1] This is another instance of a woman being put in the stocks, probably for drunkenness. (See p. 77, note 3.)

[2] This is a curious entry, and it is not easy to understand why the Justices of the town should request the Constables to find "an itinerant Dancing Master."

[3] "Strollers" here seem to mean simply "vagabonds," or, as we should now call them, tramps. (See also p. 119, note 2.)

		l	s	d
11.	p[d] Musicians, War declaired ag[t] Spain[1]	2 :	7 :	6
	p[d] Pikemen in Cash 10 6 in Ale 5 6[1]...		: 16 :	
	p[d] other Expences same day[1]		: 7 :	6
	p[d] Belman 1 6 Messengers 5 -... ...		: 6 :	6
	p[d] Sundry Strollers by Memorandum		: 5 :	6
14	p[d] Expences billeting Soldiers &c ...		: 10 :	
Dec[r] 25.	paid making Beadles Cap and Gown		: 9 :	6
[1762]				
Janry.	p[d] for a Cat with nine Tails		: 3 :	
14.	gave three Invalids in distress to Liverpool		: 5 :	
15.	p[d] sunck another into the north ...		: 1 :	
	p[d] for a Search Warrant		: 2 :	
	p[d] Joseph Budworth[2] omitted Coronation[3]		: 13 :	8
19.	p[d] Expences of a privy watch last night		: 5 :	6
	Serving War[t] 1 - Jurors fees 1 4 a Lad killed by his Mistress		: 2 :	4
23.	p[d] abought two Sailors before Justices		: 3 :	8
	p[d] an Inquisition a Lad dead in y[e] Infirmary		: 2 :	4
	p[d] for Beadles Shoes		: 5 :	
25.	p[d] horsehire with a Soldier to Buxton		: 6 :	8
	p[d] Messengers Wages and Expences		: 6 :	8
	p[d] for Books for Survey of Militia ...		: 6 :	4
	p[d] Charles Davenport ruling, binding and preparing twenty one books d[o]...		: 10 :	6
	p[d] Expences getting forty two Assistants to survey the Windows		: 2 :	6
31.	p[d] Beadle attending Stocks with a drunken man		: 1 :	

[1] What took place on the declaration of war against Spain is thus narrated in the *Manchester Mercury* of January 12th, 1762 :—

"Yesterday [January 11th] War was proclaimed in this Town, when a grand Procession was made from the Bull's Head Inn, to the Market Cross; his Majesty's Justices of the Peace in and next to Manchester, the Boroughreeve, Constables and other Officers of the Town attended the Under-Sheriff of the County, and after a martial Salute by a Band of Music, consisting of Trumpets, &c., the Herald, by Order of the Sheriff, repeated aloud his Majesty's Declaration of War against the King of Spain; after which the Sheriff proceeded into Salford and proclaimed the same there, during all which Time the greatest Decency and Order was observed suitable to the Occasion."

[2] See p. 119, note 4.   [3] See p. 127, note 2.

		l	s	d
Feb. 1.	p^d Enginemen and Joseph Butter-worth attending at the Coronation[1]...		4	6
13.	p^d Jurors twice 2/8. Messenger twice 2/-		4	8
	p^d writing duplicates of Militia ...	2	2	
	p^d Expences and assistants to serve a Warrant from a Justice in Yorkshire		3	6
15.	p^d sundry Strollers		5	
	p^d for Billet paper		1	6
	p^d for two pair of Stockings to Mrs Blankhorn for Beadle		8	6
	p^d William Hardwick for repairing the Boroughreeves Staff[2]...		13	6
16.	p^d for Brick at the Coronation[1] ...		2	10
Febry 18.	paid four or five men assisting to take John Sutliff two several nights and days for felony the Constables threat-ned with an Indictment if negligent		12	6
22.	p^d Belman for four public Cries ...		4	6
	p^d four persons warding to prevent throwing at Cocks,[3] Shrove Monday...		6	
23.	p^d on same Occasion to day[3]		5	
24.	p^d Elizabeth Smith to Liverpool ...			6
	p^d Widow Barrow's bill arising upon Towns business attending the Justices there last Year and this		15	6
27.	p^d Warrants to the hamlets for pre-sentm^{ts} to the Assizes		3	
	p^d Lighting Lamps		1	10
	p^d two horses to Rochdale on Roger Blomely's Acc^t 4/- Expences two men and horses 3/-		7	
	p^d Goldsmith for a new Lamp at Cross		7	
	p^d for Ale for Soldiers till they could be billeted		5	
Mar 4.	p^d for parchment for presentments ...		1	9
	p^d sundry passengers...		3	6
5.	p^d writing Manchester presentment to the Assizes		1	

---

[1] See p. 127, note 2.

[2] This is the first time there has been any reference to the Boroughreeve's staff of office.

[3] See p. 66, note 1.

		l	s	d
	pᵈ Journey to Rochdale with presentmᵗ	:	1 :	7
	pᵈ horsehire thither	:	2 :	
	pᵈ High Constables Clerk with pre- sentmᵗ...	:	1 :	
	pᵈ Dⁿ a Warᵗ repairing Lancᵗ Bridge	1 :	7 :	7
	pᵈ Warrants for proportion of this ...	:	3 :	
	pᵈ James Oldham going to Rochdale to serve Blomely with a Rule of Court, & attending the Affidavit by him made	:	3 :	
	pᵈ his horsehire	:	2 :	
20.	pᵈ sundry persons watching in Saint mary's Churchyard three nights on Mᵗ Down's Complaint	:	4 :	6
	pᵈ Beadle twice attending Stocks ...	:	2 :	
	pᵈ Expences attending and pro- secuting four Drunkards this Week...	:	2 :	4
	pᵈ Jurors fees upon Mᵗ Mather[1] killd by a fall from his horse 1 4 Warⁿ 1 '–	:	2 :	4
Mar 20.	pᵈ for paper...	:	1 :	6
	pᵈ repairing Boroughreeve's Staff[2] ...	:	1 :	
27.	pᵈ cleansing Steps at Salford bridge and at Dangerous Corner...	:	2 :	6
	pᵈ Jurors fees &c a Woman killed ...	:	2 :	4
	pᵈ cleansing and lighting Lamps ...	:	2 :	9
	pᵈ sundry passengers...	:	3 :	4
	pᵈ Harrop[3] printing sundry Articles for the Constables during the two last Years	2 :	11 :	
	pᵈ Ringers upon news of our having taken Martinico[4]	1 :	11 :	6
	pᵈ Committing &c two drunkards ...	:	8 :	
	pᵈ Committing Townsend a Rogue and Hawksworth his Whore	:	6 :	

---

[1] Mr. Mather's unfortunate death is thus noticed in the *Manchester Mercury* of the 23rd March, 1762 :—

"On Wednesday last [March 17th] as Mr. Benjamin Mather was taking an airing in Trafford Meadows, his Horse suddenly ran away with him, and flung him off, by which Accident he was so much bruised as to expire in a short Time after, notwithstanding all possible Assistance was got."

[2] See p. 132, note 2.   [3] See p. 73, note 2.

[4] A false report of the taking of the island of Martinico was celebrated in the previous year. (See p. 108, note 1.) Its subsequent capture, however, took place in January of this year.

		l	s	d
	p^d for a Vagrant Warrant		: 2 :	
	p^d Examining and Committing Leonard and others Vagabonds ...		: 3 :	
30.	p^d Expences attending and conveying John Worsly		: 2 :	8
Ap^l 2.	p^d summoning three Militia		: 1 :	6
	p^d sundry passengers		: 4 :	8
3.	p^d Expences of a privy Watch	1 :	1 :	6
	p^d five men assisting		: 5 :	
12.	p^d sundry passengers		: 3 :	6
	p^d summoning two more Militia ...		: 1 :	
	p^d Apprehending and prosecuting Loiterers and Drunkards last Week ...		: 2 :	
13.	p^d attending four drunkards in Stocks		: 4 :	
15.	p^d three passengers		: 1 :	6
	p^d Expences on sundry Occasions at Charles Wagstaffs attending prisoners		: 7 :	4
26.	p^d sundry Strollers		: 2 :	
	p^d Warrants to ye hamlets for new Overseers of the poor		: 3 :	
May 2.	Summon[in]g Window peepers[1] and Expences at the [Dangerous] Corner		: 3 :	6
May 6.	p^d for Lan[d]tax Warrant 1/- Windows 1/-		: 2 :	
	p^d for Blank Instructions to Window-men[1]		: 2 :	2
	p^d for eleven Books for Window duty		: 5 :	6
	p^d Writing ruling d^o &c		: 5 :	
	p^d Thomas Bancroft assisting Assessors		: 5 :	
9.	p^d with Officers of Pendleton meeting to apprehend Whores infesting both Townships		: 2 :	
10.	Committing three Whores 4^s conveying 1^s		: 5 :	
14.	paid sundry passengers		: 3 :	6
22.	paid Bailifs apprehending Roger Blomely at Rochdale for refusing to obey a Rule of Court obtained ag^t him at the Sute of the Constables of Manch^r	1 :	10 :	
	p^d conveying him to Lancaster	2 :	2 :	

[1] See p. 82, note 2, and also p. 96, note 3.

		l	s	d
	p⁴ High Constables Warrant for the repairing of Lancaster Castle, Relief of prisoners and support of the families of Militia Soldiers	14	2	5
	p⁴ Warrants to the Hamlets		3	
	p⁴ Conveying Thomas Thorp to Lanc' refusing to be distrained upon his Goods for the King's Window duty	2	10	6
	p⁴ Thomas Baron and John Brocklehurst a night and a day after James Taylor suspected of murder		2	6
	p⁴ apprehending and committing Rothwel on the same Account ...		6	
	p⁴ for paper			9
	p⁴ Expences several days distraining for the Window duty		3	
25.	p⁴ Arnold Birch Beadles Clothing ...	2	19	3
31.	p⁴ Beadle advanced to the keeping of persons in the Dungeon		3	
	p⁴ sundry passengers...		3	6
June 7.	p⁴ paper ruling and writing the Constable Ley Book	1	7	
	p⁴ sundry small Articles by Memdᵐ...		3	6
24.	p⁴ Smith for Enginework...	1	1	
	p⁴ Edmund Wrigly for Enginework	1	6	
30.	p⁴ High Constables Warrant for the repair of Public Bridges	20	7	2
July 3.	p⁴ summoning hamlets for Landtax		3	
	p⁴ Mʳ Edwᵈ Kenyon advanced for the Town at the King's Coronation[1] ...	29	19	4
	p⁴ Mʳ Charles Ford on same Acct[1] ...	11	17	0½
	p⁴ apprehending Mary Clegg and whipping her		3	6
6.	p⁴ sundry passengers		5	6
10.	p⁴ three Messengers to know the Intention of the Mob[2] at Stockport, Ashton, Oldham, Saddleworth &c ...		7	6

[1] See p. 127, note 2.

[2] Another violent riot occurred in the town on Monday, July 12th, in this year, of which the account which is given in the *Manchester Mercury* for July 20th will be found in the Appendix. Like the previous ones it was a food riot, and the mob attacked the shops and warehouses of several of the corn dealers and destroyed all the

		l	s	d
12.	The Mob[1] entered Manchester ...			
19.	p[d] Jurors fees James Taylor killed in the Mob[1]	:	1 :	4
	p[d] horsehire 8[s] Expences 7 . 6 Wages 3[s] to Liverpool about buying Corn ...	:	18 :	6
	p[d] five men running and enquiring after Rioters the Country round ...	:	17 :	6
	p[d] or expended on dragoons[2] sallying out into Blackly amongst Rioters ...	:	3 :	2
	p[d] four foot Assistants on like Acc[t] ...	:	4 :	
	p[d] horsehire on same Occasion ...	:	1 :	6
	p[d] James Oldham 1 6 other Charges 2.-	:	3 :	6
	p[d] sundry passengers...	:	3 :	6
	Gave Thomas Gadman for Support...	:	1 :	
21.	p[d] Assistants all last night and this day about Rioters	1 :	7 :	6
	retaining Lawyer Nangreave[3]	1 :	1 :	
July 26.	p[d] James Oldhams bill into Cheshire and Yorkshire getting Search Warrants indorsed by the Justices there...	1 :	19 :	2
	p[d] Jurors fees four Inquisitions and mesengers to the hamlets...	:	9 :	4
	p[d] horsehire seven short Journeys ...	:	10 :	6
21.	p[d] James Oldham going to Lancaster with Fleetwood Hill[4] a Rioter... ...	2 :	2 :	
	p[d] John Dutton on same Account ...	2 :	2 :	
	p[d] for paper	:	:	9
	p[d] Justice Clerks in Cheshire for War[t]	:	6 :	
	p[d] d[o] in Yorkshire	:	12 :	
	p[d] Jurors fees over Robinsons Wife &c	:	2 :	4

stock-in-trade, as well as the furniture in their houses. The damage was estimated at quite £1,000. A corps of the Flintshire Militia was sent for, and they arrived on the Tuesday afternoon, July 13th, whilst a corps of the Cheshire Militia came in the same night.

In the Liverpool Corporation Accounts there is the following entry :—

"1762, 10 Aug. Ordered that M[r] Mayor [John Williamson, merchant] and M[r] Blackburne be paid the Money they were out of Pocket in going with and sending the filintshire Militia to Manchester to quell a Riot there."

[1] See p. 135, note 2.

[2] Probably some of Sir Robert Rich's dragoons, which seem to have been stationed in the town at this time. (See p. 96, note 2.)

[3] See p. 112, note 4.

[4] There are several references to this Fleetwood Hill, who seems to have been one of the ringleaders in the late riot.

		l	s	d
	pᵈ Soldiers to drink at Oldham ...	:	10 :	6
	Treating the Officers there wᵗʰ Constables...	:	5 :	6
	pᵈ other Expences at and about Ryton	:	3 :	6
	pᵈ Evidences Charges and Expences at Sessions four Rioters prosecuted...	2 :	5 :	6
Augᵗ 2.	pᵈ Porters for Watching & Messages	1 :	2 :	
6.	pᵈ Thomas Bayron for Assistance ...	:	9 :	
	pᵈ Robert Smethurst	:	9 :	
	pᵈ Expences to apprehend two Colliers at Lees behind Oldham three persons all night	:	5 :	6
	pᵈ Deputy Kay's horse 2 - Expences 2 6	:	4 :	6
7.	pᵈ James Oldham's horse to Oldham	:	1 :	6
	pᵈ him and three other men	:	8 :	
	pᵈ James Cooper three Weeks Assistance...	1 :	1 :	
	pᵈ committing James Ogden	:	3 :	
	pᵈ other Charges about him	:	2 :	6
	pᵈ Charges when four Women taken	:	4 :	
	maintaining them a night and day ...	:	3 :	
8.	pᵈ three persons all day before the Justices six Rioters committed ...	:	6 :	6
Augᵗ 8.	pᵈ High Constables for Governor's Wages...	1 :	3 :	2
	pᵈ Warrants for proportion	:	3 :	
	pᵈ two Jurors fees	:	2 :	8
	pᵈ sundry passengers...	:	5 :	6
	pᵈ horsehire to Lancaster for two to Henry Work one double	1 :	6 :	
	pᵈ for turning thirty Truncheons [1] ...	:	6 :	
14.	pᵈ Expences going in the night and day after, with thirty Soldiers to Oldham, and with five or six special Constables from Ryton searching Shover and Saddleworth for Rioters, horsehire 5 - Soldiers 5 - Assistants 12 Expences in Crompton 5 6 at Ryton 3 6 at Oldham 7 6 & more ...	2 :	7 :	6

[1] These 30 "truncheons" would be for the special constables who were no doubt sworn in for the protection of the town.

		l	s	d
16.	p^d Expences quartering Soldiers ...	:	2 :	6
	p^d other small Articles	':	9 :	
	p^d Richard Byrn an Express	:	13 :	
	p^d Bernard Shaw maintenance of Rioters and Evidences	1 :	11 :	6
17.	Fetching James Lees a Rioter... ...	:	3 :	6
18.	p^d High Constables with presentments	:	1 :	
	p^d horsehire to Bolton 2'– Expences 1'10½...	:	3 :	10½
19.	p^d four trampers[1]	:	2 :	
	p^d a Messenger after fine Jim[2]... ...	:	1 :	6
20.	p^d horsehire ten Journeys...	:	15 :	
	p^d Warrants for new Jurors	:	3 :	
	p^d same for Ale Licences	:	3 :	
21.	p^d fetching an Evidence from Hayfield	:	7 :	6
	p^d James Cooper assisting Deputy a fortnight	:	10 :	
	p^d Utensels for the Lamp...	:	1 :	7
	p^d two Jurors fees	:	2 :	8
	p^d Deputys memorandum'd disbursem^{ts}	1 :	7 :	6
Augt 22.	p^d to Mr Percival[3] for persons to watch the Neighbourhood and for assisting Constables from time to time	1 :	1 :	
	p^d sundry Expences same time ...	:	10 :	6
16.	p^d Musicians at rejoicing for good news from Germany,[4] and on the birth of the Prince of Wales[5]	2 :	7 :	
	p^d two passengers	:	1 :	
Sepr 3.	p^d James Upton an Evidence at Lanc^r ag^t Fleetwood Hill[6]	2 :	12 :	6
	p^d Deputy Kay the same	2 :	12 :	6
	p^d William Whitehead d^o	2 :	2 :	

[1] See p. 119, note 2.

[2] This was probably a local nickname.

[3] See p. 64, note 4.

[4] This was probably the news of some victory by the allied forces, the English and the Prussians against the French, but I cannot trace any particular victory becoming known just at this time.

[5] George, Prince of Wales, was born on August 12th, 1762.

[6] In the account of the Assizes held at Lancaster in August, it is stated that "Fleetwood Hill, an Indictment of High Treason being found against him by the Grand Jury, for being concern'd in the Riot at Manchester was order'd to remain in Goal and to take his Trial at the next Assizes."

		l	s	d
	p^d Thomas Sefton d°...	2 :	2 :	
	p^d Betty Wyat d°	2 :	2 :	
	p^d William Booth	2 :	2 :	
	p^d Peter Finney d°	2 :	2 :	
	p^d Bailiff's fees, Extraordinaries, and other Expences there by the Deputy	1 :	5 :	6
	p^d Mr Barlow the Attorney in part of his Law Bill[1]	30 :		
	p^d him since	1 :	1 :	
	p^d for Coals to the Guard Denbyshire Militia being sent for to quell the mob[2]		: 1 :	6
	p^d at Swan attending David Robinson suspected of killing his Wife		: 3 :	8
	p^d two men attending him		: 5 :	
	p^d three persons three days getting Informations against, and endevour[in]g to apprehend Rioters in several parts of the Country, Baron, Smethurst, Cooper		:13 :	6
	p^d Joseph Butterworth for Errands ...		: 3 :	
	p^d sundry Vagabonds...		: 5 :	6
4.	p^d John Heywood removing the Baggage to Oldham...		: 3 :	9
6.	Gave a Tramper[3]		: :	6
7.	p^d Robert Smethurst Assistance ...		:10 :	6
Sep' 9.	paid for a Grate for the Guardhouse...		: 6 :	6
	Tongs and Shovel 3^s Wiskets[4] 6^d ...		: 3 :	6
	p^d setting the Grate and Brick... ...		: 2 :	
	p^d for Coals 4 6 Sundry Strollers 3 6		: 8 :	
	p^d two other passengers		: 1 :	
20.	p^d Belman five Cries		: 6 :	
	p^d paper and writing three duplicates for Jurors to the Assize		: 4 :	6
22.	p^d for a Load of Coals to ye Guard ...		: 4 :	6

---

[1] That is, for prosecuting Fleetwood Hill, one of the rioters, at the recent Lancaster Assizes.

[2] This has reference to the riot of July 12th. The Denbighshire Militia would appear to have come as well as the Flintshire Militia, which were sent for from Liverpool to quell the riot. (See p. 135, note 2.)

[3] See p. 119, note 2.

[4] A "wisket" is an old word for a large basket. It has occurred before in these Accounts. (See vol. 1, pp. 111 and 275.)

		l	s	d
24.	p^d Expences seeking fine Jim[1] twice	:	4 :	1
	p^d Cooper and Baron for Assistance...	:	4 :	
25.	p^d committing Thomas Chapman insulting the Constables	:	3 :	
26.	p^d taking up and detaining two men suspected of carrying incendiary Letters about the Mob[2]	:	3 :	6
30.	paid for Beadles Shoes	:	5 :	
Octob 3.	p^d James Wrigly repairing Engine ...	:	3 :	
	p^d horsehire 3/- to Ashton Expences 2/8 after John Townsend a Mobber[3]...	:	5 :	8
4.	p^d a Load of Coals for the Guard ...	:	6 :	
	p^d horsehire 3/- Expences & Turnpike 1/5 four Mobbers[3] from prestwich	:	4 :	5
	p^d Market Lookers their Bill	4 :	15 :	6
	p^d sundry passengers...	:	6 :	4
	p^d Peter Cotrell keeping Engine Key	:	4 :	
6.	p^d detaining four Mobbers[3] from Monday till Wednesday	:	10 :	6
	p^d Expences at the going away of two of them to Lancaster...	:	2 :	4
	p^d Soldiers assisting, in Cash	:	5 :	6
	gave one of the prisoners	:	2 :	6
	p^d Jurors fees and Messenger a Child killed by a Cart	:	2 :	4
	gave Nancy Mackeen a Stroller ...	:	:	6
Octob 10.	p^d three persons to take Joseph Makin	:	4 :	
	p^d conveying John Lees and Wm Morris two Rioters to Lancaster ...	5 :	7 :	
11.	p^d Thomas Baron six nights to apprehend Rioters	:	9 :	
	and his Expences	:	2 :	6
12.	a Load of Coals for the Guard ...	:	5 :	
	p^d Expences three Messengers for Evidences into Moston 1/- Wages 3^s	:	4 :	
	p^d a Messenger to Ryton on like Acc^t	:	1 :	6

[1] See p. 138, note 2.

[2] An "incendiary letter" which had been left on the doorstep of Mr. James Bayley. one of the local magistrates, is printed in the *Manchester Mercury* for September 21st, 1762, and fifty pounds reward was offered by the Constables for the conviction of the offender.

[3] This word has fortunately not come into general use. The word "rioter" is much preferable to "mobber."

	l	s	d
p^d serving six Summonses	:	3	:
p^d Carter with Kings Baggage... ...	:	4	6
p^d John Oldham going to Lancaster	:	6	:
p^d Music when Havannah taken[1] ...	1	:	:
p^d Mary Brown attending Sessions as a Evidence	:	3	:
p^d five other Evidences there	:	15	:
p^d James Kay for Assistance	:	6	6
p^d Bernard Shaw's bill	1	10	:
p^d at Sevenstars[2] a bill on Mobbing Acc^t	1	:	8
p^d Belman for five Cries	:	6	:
p^d James Dales bill on like Accou[n]t	1	14	3
p^d at John Gomersals in Mobbing time	:	3	:
p^d porters playing Engines and Ale	6	2	:
p^d Beadles Salary a Year	7	:	:
p^d Deputy's Salary a Year	20	:	:

D^r or total of money paid   ... ... £319 : 16 : 8

Cash received or ... ... C^r

1762.		l	s	d			
Octob 16.	By proportion from the hamlets two thirds of the War^t 1 : 18 : 4	1	5	7			
March 5.	By d° of the War^t 1 : 7 : 7	:	18	5			
May 22.	By d° of the War^t 14 : 2 : 5	9	12	11			
June 30.	By d° of the War^t 20 : 7 : 2	13	11	6			
Augt 7.	By d° of the War^t 1 : 3 : 2	:	15	5½	26	3	10½
	By Cash from the Ley				213	1	5½
	By Balance owing				80	11	4

£319 : 16 : 8

---

[1] Havannah was taken on the 12th August, but the news did not reach Manchester till some time afterwards.

[2] This well-known inn in Manchester, the "Seven Stars," is here, I think, mentioned in these Accounts for the first time.

1762. Novr 9. We the Jurors of the Court Leet, now holden for the Manor of Manchester in the County of Lancaster, have examined the foregoing Accounts of the late Constables of Manchester, and do find a balance of eighty pounds eleven Shillings and four pence; and we allowing the same, do order it to be paid to them, by the succeeding Constables, whom we do likewise allow to charge it in their Accounts.

(Signed) THOMAS TIPPING
JOHN PARKER MOSLEY
JOSHUA MARRIOTT
JAMES GREATREX
JAMES HODSON
JOHN HARDMAN
EDW^D MARKLAND
RICHARD CLOWES
MARSDEN KENYON
BENJA. BOWER
JOHN CLOWES
SAMUEL SMITH
W^M NEWTON
CHARLES FORD

[Constables' Accounts.]

[13th Oct., 1762, to 12th Oct., 1763.]

••••••••••••

An Accot of Cash disburs'd by Mʀ JAMES BORRON & Mʀ ROBT HAMILTON[1] *Constables of Manchester* [elected 13th Oct. 1762.]

[Disbursements]

1762

October 19.	paid last year's Balance[2]	80 : 11 : 4
19.	pᵈ for one Load of Coals to the Guardhouse	: 6 :
28.	pᵈ for one Load of Coals to the Guardhouse	: 5 : 6
	pᵈ nine Passengers	: 2 : 6
	pᵈ Sundry other Passengers	: 1 : 6
30.	pᵈ Robert Nabb ½ repairing the Dungeon	: 11 : 11
Nov. 5.	pᵈ for a Load of Coals for Guardhouse	: 5 : 6
7.	pᵈ Jurors Fees a Man kill'd by a fall...	: 1 : 4
	pᵈ serving Warrants upon the Hamlets	: 1 :
	pᵈ two Soldiers passengers	: 1 :
	pᵈ five Trampers[3]	: 1 : 7
9.	pᵈ Lampman lighting Lamps	: 2 : 6
	pᵈ whipping two Whores	: 2 :
	pᵈ a Messenger to Hollinwood for Henry Booth	: 1 :
	pᵈ him for coming on Secret Business	: 1 : 6
	pᵈ an old Soldier, going home... ...	: : 6
11.	pᵈ several attendants many Mobbers[4] took at Oldham	: 3 :

---

[1] These two Constables were elected at the Court Leet held on the 13th October, 1762. (See *Court Leet Records*, vol. viij., p. 64.)

[2] See p. 142.   [3] See p. 119, note 2.   [4] See p. 140, note 3.

	p^d conveying two of 'em to the house of Correction	:	1 :	
15.	p^d Luke Asley's bill repairing the Windows of the Exchange broak by the Militia[1]...	:	15 :	
	p^d John Brown Carpenter repairing the Exchange[1]	:	11 :	4
	p^d a Tramper[2]		:	6
Nov 18.	p^d Expences getting horses attending Matthew Barns[3] a Mobber,[2] ordered to Lancaster	:	1 :	4
19.	p^d serving Jurors With Coroners Warrants 1^s Fees for the Jury 1^s 4^d a Child killed by a Cartwheel	:	2 :	4
	p^d three Men and two horses with Matthew Barns[3] to Lancaster	3 :	1 :	2½
	p^d a Messenger to Ribble Bridge 2^s 6^d horse 5^s 3^d Expences 5 11 ... ... with a Commitment for Matthew Barns,[3] which the Messeng^r had lost...	:	13 :	8
26.	p^d John Coppock a Vagabond... ...		:	6
	p^d for twelve days Coal and Candle for Lancashire Militia[4]	:	6 :	
	p^d hire of two horses to Darwen for Richard Smith Rioter	:	7 :	
	p^d Thomas Baron's Wages thither ...	:	3 :	
	p^d Turnpike and bating 2 6 Messenger 1 6	:	4 :	
	p^d Expences all Night	:	7 :	6
	p^d bating comming home...	:	2 :	5
27.	p^d Ellen Yong a Vagrant...	:	:	3

[1] The Flintshire and Cheshire Militia, called in to protect the town against the mob (see p. 135, note 2), were probably quartered in the Exchange.

[2] See p. 119, note 2.

[3] There are several entries referring to Matthew Barns, who seems to have been one of the ringleaders of the rioters in July last. He was put up at the March Assizes at Lancaster, and an indictment for High Treason being found against him, he was ordered to be kept in prison and tried at the next Assizes. In the following August "the prosecution was withdrawn at the earnest request of the prisoner on his acknowledging the heinousness of his Crime, and entering into a Recognizance for his good Behaviour for two years."

[4] The Lancashire Militia were at this time quartered in the town, but on Dec. 18th, two companies marched thence for Rochdale and Bury, and they were shortly afterwards disbanded.

	p^d Messenger into Yorkshire 4 6 Clerks 3 - Expences 12 1 horsehire 7^s to get Warr^{ts} indors'd against Rioters in Saddleworth	1 :	6 :	7
29.	p^d attending James Heginbotham 1^s and conveying him for a Breach of the Peace 6^d	:	1 :	6
	p^d two Messengers to Lancaster with Barns (one went Gratis)		: 12 :	
	p^d the hire of two horses thither ...	1 :	1 :	
30.	p^d Sundry Passengers		: 2 :	6
Nov. 30.	p^d impressing Carriages in this Town, Rusholme, & Gorton for the Militia[1]		: 1 :	6
Decem^r 4.	p^d for eight days Coals for 'em... ...		: 4 :	
	p^d two Soldiers going to Scotland ...		: 1 :	
	p^d mending Dungeon Door		: 1 :	2
	p^d Widow Critchlow's Bill for Prisoners Expences in the Dungeon		: 10 :	3
11.	p^d for Coals for the Guard house ...		: 3 :	6
13.	p^d Sundry Passengers		: 3 :	4
	p^d high Constables Warr^{ts} to the Hamlets for numbering Militia ...		: 3 :	4
	p^d Jurors Fees a Man killd by a fall into a Cellarhole...		: 1 :	4
	p^d serving the Eleven hamlets with Warrants		: 1 :	
	p^d Bellman for two Cries		: 2 :	
	p^d Charles Pilling a Passenger to Colne		: :	6
	p^d John Ingham do. to Halifax... ...		: :	6
17.	p^d Warr^{ts} to the hamlets for new Surveyors of the highway...		: 3 :	
	p^d John Butterworth after Rioters to Chorley Preston Crompton and other Places		: 8 :	
	p^d Ralph Fletcher an Evidence against Morris of Blackworth Brough a Rioter		: 2 :	6
18	p^d Sundry Vagrants this Week ...		: 5 :	6
	p^d for a new Book to be a Transcript of the Militia		: 2 :	6
	p^d Lighting Lamps 2 9 and at another time 1 10		: 4 :	7

[1] See p. 144, note 4.

20.	p^d three Strollers[1] going towards y^r Settlement	: 1 :
Decem^r 20.	p^d Landlord at the seven Stars[2] maintainance of horses and their hire in apprehending Mobbers[3]	: 18 : 3
	repaid the Constables of Royton what they Advanc'd relative to the Mob by direction of Justice Percival[4] ...	3 : 3 :
24.	p^d Mending the Dungeon Lock ...	: 5 : 4
24.	p^d three weeks Coal and Candle for the Guardhouse	: 10 : 6
	p^d clearing Rubbish from the Theatre[5] to make room for the Baggage... ...	: 2 :
	p^d Making the Beadle's Cap and Gown	: 9 : 6
	p^d Thomas Baron's Bill for his Wages, Expences and extraordinary Trouble about the Rioters[6]	1 : 4 : 6
	p^d Margaret Sephton and her Child to Ormskirk	: 1 :
	p^d James Cooper for his assistance since the 12th day of July last running after and apprehending Rioters[6] ...	2 : 12 : 6
31.	p^d Sundry Passengers	: 7 : 6
1763. Jany 4.	p^d the Beadle a quarter's Salary ...	2 : 10 :
	p^d John Butterworth and Son Evidences against Rioters[6] and for Enquiries about Mobbers	: 9 :
	p^d writing Return of new Surveyors...	: 1 :
	p^d Expences of Meeting on the same Acco^t	: 7 :
	p^d a Stroler by Joshua Farrer	: : 6
5.	p^d John Butterworth for Errands ...	: 10 : 6
	p^d Betty Holmes to Ashton	: : 6
8.	p^d for Coals and Candles to the Guard	: 3 : 6

---

[1] This entry confirms the belief that "strollers" were merely vagabonds.
[2] See p. 141, note 2.
[3] See p. 140, note 3.
[4] The death of Thomas Percival, Esq., "many years in the Commission of the Peace for this County," at Royton, after a tedious illness, took place on Dec. 7th, 1762.
[5] See p. 96, note 4. The "Baggage" here referred to was that of the soldiers newly quartered in the town.
[6] These rioters were those engaged in the riot of the 12th July last.

	p^d committing and attending two Whores	: 6 :	
	p^d Charges committing Nell Oldham a Whore	: 3 :	
Janu^y 10.	p^d John Butterworth again for Errands	: 2 :	6
	p^d attending Bill Andrew apprehended as a Mober upon the oath of Midgley	: 2 :	9
14.	p^d Light^g Lamps the last Dark ...	: 2 :	6
	and for extraordinary Wick	: 1 :	
15.	p^d Jurors 14 Messenger 1' a Man kill'd in a Coalpit	: 2 :	4
	p^d for Coal and Candle for the Guard	: 3 :	6
22.	p^d James Oldham's bill into Staffordshire and Darbyshire for Ann Makin an Evidence against Cason	1 : 11 :	1
	p^d him for Errands and attending Sessions	: 2 :	
	p^d making and drawing List and Duplicate of the Militia very troublesom and long	2 : 2 :	
	p^d Evidences at Sessions, Bailiffs Fees for Indictm^{tt} and other Incidents by Deputy	2 : 7 :	
	p^d Mr Oliver for the Guard and Storerooms at Theatre[1]	2 : 12 :	6
	p^d for Coal and Candle used by the Guard	: 3 :	6
	p^d Charges committing Snaffleing Peg[2]	: 3 :	6
	p^d John Oldham advanced to Prisoners	: 1 :	
	p^d Sundry Assistants about Bill Andrew	: 3 :	
25.	p^d five Strolers	: 2 :	6
	p^d Charges biliting Royal Foresters[3] over and over again	: 10 :	
29.	p^d four Watchmen last Night Whores very troublesom in the Streets	: 4 :	

[1] See p. 146, note 5.

[2] This is another instance of the use of nicknames at this time.

[3] When the Lancashire Militia marched out of the town on Dec. 18th last (see p. 144, note 4) their places were taken by the Royal Forresters, as thus noticed in the *Manchester Mercury*:—

"Also on Saturday [Dec. 18th] two Troops of Royal Forresters commanded by the Marquis of Granby, came in here from Northampton, and are to be quartered in this Town till further Orders. The remaining four Companies marched for York."

Feby 2.	p^d four Watchmen for their Trouble 2 Nights more	: 8 :
3.	p^d when Constables of Oldham were swore at the Bull's head	: 7 :
Febr^y 3.	p^d Robert Peers for watching one Night	: 1 :
	p^d Ann Ashley to her Place of Nativity, the Divises [Devizes]	: 1 :
6.	p^d Porters playing the water Engines four Months at 10/-	2 : :
	p^d Mending thirteen Engine Buckets	: 3 : 3
	p^d for a pair of Shoes for the Beadle...	: 5 :
	p^d for his Stockings	: :
	p^d Thomas Baron's bill for Errands, Expences, and assistance about the Rioters	: 12 : 6
	p^d taking up two Women, gui[l]ty of Whoredom & Theft	: 2 :
	p^d George Henshall Blacksmith repairing Dungeon door	: 5 : 4
	p^d for Lamp Glass at Cross	: 7 :
	p^d John Buckly's Bill of Royton about the Rioters	: 14 :
	p^d Mr Thackeray for ½ Year's Rent for a Guardhouse & Store Room ...	3 : 15 :
11.	p^d for Fire and Candlelight in the Guardroom	: 3 : 6
12.	p^d conveying Abram Beswick to Lancaster with two Messengers, their Expences 1. 17. 3 five days Wages 15/-	2 : 12 : 3
	p^d Lighting the Lamp 1/10, and Mending the Lamp Ladder 16^d ...	: 3 : 2
17.	p^d for Coals and Candles this day Sr Robt Rich's Dragoons came in [1] ...	: 3 : 6

---

[1] In the *Mercury* for Feb. 15th, 1763, there is the following paragraph :—

"This Day three Troops of Sir Robert Rich's Dragoons arrived from the South in order to be quartered here in the room of the two Troops of Royal Forresters, commanded by Lord Robert Sutton, who, as soon as the Roads are passable, will march from hence for Nottingham, where they are to be disbanded."

The remainder of this regiment, consisting of three troops, marched into the town on March 14th, and on the 23rd two troops left Manchester for Warrington.

20.	p^d the Royal Foresters[1] for qui[e]tness sake, on Acco^t of some pretended [loss] to them, for staying some days after their Rout, till Sr Robert Rich's Dragoons[2] could come	20 :	:	
	p^d Sundry Passengers	:	5 :	6
	p^d Expences biliting Sr Robert Riches Dragoons[2]	:	10 :	
	p^d serving Coroner's Warr^{ts} 1^s Jurors 1 $\cdot$4	:	2 :	4
Febr^y 23.	p^d a distressed Sailor...	:	1 :	
	p^d high Constables Warrant for Governors Wages	1 :	3 :	2
24.	p^d Mr Chippindall at the Bull's head examining six Evidences about Rioters	:	2 :	4
	p^d same Evening on like Acco^t at the Boarshead[3]...	:	4 :	8
	p^d Lighting the Lamp at Cross ...	:	2 :	
	p^d for Fortnight's Fire and Candles at the Guardroom	:	7 :	
	p^d Mary Holland a Vagrant to Cumberland	:	:	6
	p^d John Midgley Relief being a Witness against Rioters	:	5 :	
March 10.	p^d John Oldham and Thomas Baron's bill conveying Jonathan Jackson, Mary Scholfield and Robert o' Jack's[4] to Lancaster Castle	3 :	10 :	7
	p^d for the hire of one horse to Lancaster	:	10 :	6
	p^d for a Table for the Guardroom ...	:	4 :	
	p^d for a Beesom for . . do...	:	:	2
	p^d writing Manchester Presentm^t to the Assizes	:	1 :	
	p^d the high Constables Clerks with it	:	1 :	
	p^d Warr^{ts} to the hamlets for their Presentm^{ts}	:	3 :	

[1] There had been a very heavy fall of snow at this time, and the Royal Forresters did not leave until Feb. 21st.

[2] See p. 148, note 1.   [3] This Inn has not occurred before.

[4] In the report of the Assizes at Lancaster, on March 23rd, it is stated that "Robert o' th' Jacks, Abraham Berwick, John Leigh, and William Morris, charged with Rioting at Manchester and Fleetwood Hill, charged with High Treason, were all acquitted."

p^d Bellman's Bill...	: 7 : 6
11. p^d for Coals and Candles for the Guardroom...	:3 : 6
p^d Sundry Trampers[1] towards their homes...	: 7 : 6
p^d John Butterworth a Mob Inteligencer[2]	: 1 :
p^d 17 of Sr Robert's Dragoons[3] to Oldham to apprehend Rioters and also 12 other assistants their Breakfasts &c	:18: 6
p^d at the Shears[4] at Newtonheath coming back	: 3 :
p^d four more assistants thither and back with Prisoners	:10:
March 11. p^d towards maintaining sundry Evidences in the house of Correction ...	: 7 : 6
p^d Lighting Lamps	: 3 :
p^d Subpeneaing John Lees against Rioters	: 2 :
25. p^d for Fire and Candles consumed in the Guardroom	: 7 :
p^d for Forms for the do.	:10:
p^d Peter Winstanley a passenger to Hull	: : 6
p^d Peter Cotrell keeping the Enginehouse Key	: 2 :
p^d Lamp Lighter in full for this Winter	: 1 : 8
p^d George Clayton for handcufts ...	: 9 : 8
p^d a Jurors Fee at Prossers 1/4 & Messenger to the hamlets 1^s	: 2 : 4
p^d Baggage Carters extraordinari-expences	: 5 :
p^d other Furnature for the Guardroom	:10: 6
p^d a Bill at Seven Stars[5] on Acc^t of the Rioters, for maintainance of horses...	1 :10: 3
p^d Joseph Smithson for Maintainace of Evidences at Sessions...	:10:11

---

[1] See p. 119, note 2.
[2] I suppose a spy or some one giving information as to the late riot.
[3] See p. 148, note 1.
[4] This Inn on Newton Heath has not occurred before.
[5] See p. 141, note 2.

	p^d Jacob Taylor's, advance, on the Rioters Acco^t	: 11 :
	p^d Thomas Baron two Journeys to Lancaster and other business and expences	1 : 7 :
	p^d Bernard Shaw[1] for expence of Prisoners one bill	1 : 17 : 6
	p^d him another Bill on the like Acco^t...	2 : 5 :
	p^d James Oldham one Journey to Lancaster	: 6 :
	p^d him for extraordinary attendance at the Assizes	: 10 : 6
	p^d Richard Holt for two Journeys to Lancaster	: 12 :
	p^d himself and others Expences ...	: 12 : 7
Ap^l 9.	p^d Warrants to the hamlets for new Overseers	: 3 :
Ap^l 9.	p^d serving Eleven Summonses on Militiamen	: 2 :
	p^d Thomas Walker's Bill for Horschire	2 : 11 :
	p^d Jurors Fees 1/4 Warrants 1^s for Coroners Inquest over the Body of Woman hang'd[2]...	: 2 : 4
	p^d Summoning 7 or 8 Witnesses to Sessions	: 8 : 2
	p^d Carpentry Work repairing the Exchange[3]	3 : 18 : 6
May 3.	p^d Mr Thackeray ½ a Year's Rent for the Guard room	3 : 15 :
	p^d Plasterers Work at the Exchange[3]	1 : 12 : 6
	p^d Presentments to the Quarter Sessions	: 1 :
	p^d Expences getting the Money for carting the King's Baggage	: 7 : 6
	p^d to Council on the Same Acco^t ...	1 : 1 :

---

[1] Mr. Bernard Shaw was the Governor of the House of Correction in Manchester. His death, "after a lingering illness," took place on April 9th in this year. On April 20th, "Mr. Thomas Whitlow was chosen Governor of the House of Correction here, in the room of Mr. Bernard Shaw, deceas'd."

[2] The *Mercury* states that "on Friday last [April 21st] Johanna Collier hanged herself at the Poor-house in this Town. The Coroner's Inquest brought in their Verdict, Lunacy."

[3] See p. 53, note 4.

p^d a Messenger to the Treasurer for the Cash	1: 1:
p^d many Evidences for loss of Time and Expences attending the Quarter Sessions against Rioters	1: 15: 6
p^d two Evidences ag^t Ralph Harrison [1] condemed to the Pilory for Buggary	: 5:
p^d three Several Messengers to Crumpsal and Blakely for Evidences ag^t Thomas Nadin	: 4: 6
p^d Lawyer Nangreave for pleading ag^t him	1: 1:
p^d Ralph Fletcher attending several times as an Evidence and going to Lancaster	1: 10: 6
p^d three Persons all Night in quest of Thomas Nadin	: 5: 6
p^d High Constables Warrant repairing Lancaster Castle	12: 19: 5
June 2. p^d do. repairing Publick Bridges ...	19: 1: 7
p^d for Warrants to the Hamlets for their Proportion of these two Warrants	: 6:
p^d Expences &c committing three Whores	: 3: 6
p^d Belman for four public Calls ...	: 4: 6
p^d Mr Byrom an old Bill for Beadle's Trimming	1: 7: 6
p^d Jurors Fees a Child drown'd ...	: 1: 4
p^d for a Cart assistants and Expences apprehending Nancy Hill and committing her...	: 7: 6
June 2. p^d cleansing Steps at Salford Bridge...	: 2:
p^d noticing Surveyors of the Highway	: 3:
p^d Jurors Fees and Coroners Warrants to the hamlets	: 2: 4
20. p^d two Jurors Fees a Child kild and a man drown'd	: 2: 8

---

[1] In the *Manchester Mercury* for April 26th, in giving the results of the Quarter Sessions in the town, there is a reference to this man, who "was order'd to stand in the Pillory the three next Saturdays for the space of one Hour each Day, betwixt the Hours of twelve and two, and to be confined in the Castle of Lancaster for three months."

p⁴ Messenger Serving the Warrᵗˢ on the Hamlets	: 2 :	
pᵈ John Upton for a Horse to Lancaster with a Rioter	: 10 : 6	
pᵈ Horse hire to Middleton last Sessions for an Evidence against Rioters...	: 1 : 6	
pᵈ Expences and attending Wᵐ Kenyon a furious Madman	: 5 :	
pᵈ Warrᵗˢ to the Hamlets for Land Tax and Window duty	: 3 :	
pᵈ Governess¹ of the House of Correction advanced for Prisoners	: 3 : 6	
July 4. pᵈ Attorneys Business to Allen Vigor one Bill	6 : 11 : 1	
pᵈ him another Bill	10 : 1 : 4	
pᵈ Belman two Calls	: 2 :	
23. pᵈ Presentments to the Sessions... ...	: 1 :	
pᵈ Warrents to the Hamlets for Presentmᵗ to the Assize	: 3 :	
Augᵗ 3. pᵈ apprehending and attending John Chetham a Rioter, three Men two days and two Nights and Expences... ...	: 8 : 6	
5. pᵈ Parchment and writing Manchester Presentmᵗ	: 1 :	
pᵈ High Constables at Rochdale with the Presentmᵗ	: 1 :	
pᵈ Horse hire thither 2 – Dinner and Expences 2/–	: 4 :	
pᵈ James Crompton the Coffeehouse Bill²	18 : 10 :	
pᵈ Council's Opinion about Nancy Hills Goods detain'd by Thomas Feilding	: 10 : 6	
pᵈ two Messengers to Crompton to summon two Butterworths as Evidences agᵗ the Rioters	3 :	

¹ So in the original. From the next year's Accounts it appears that Mrs. Shaw, the widow of the late Mr. Bernard Shaw, late Governor of the House of Correction, bore this title. She probably had to look after the female prisoners.

² Probably for the expenses of meetings, &c., held at the St. Ann's Coffee House, now called Crompton's Coffee House. (See *Court Leet Records*, vol. viij., pp. 38 and 68.)

p^d Horsehire thither twice...	4 :	
p^d Thomas Ogden repairing and cleansing the Guardhouse...	: 2 : 4	
p^d Beadle half a Year's Salary	5 : :	
Augt 13. p^d James Dale, Meat, Drink and Expences ab^t Rioters and other Constables Business	2 : 12 : 6	
p^d John Howard conveying Capt Chadwick's Baggage of the Militia[1] to Camp at Preston	: 12 :	
p^d Nathl Bolton with Baggage to Preston when the Militia[1] were disbanded	: 9 :	
p^d Simeon Newton with Baggage at same time	1 : 16 :	
p^d Horsehire for four Evidences to Lancaster ag^t Rioters...	2 : 2 :	
Sep 10. p^d Engine Men for four Months ...	2 : :	
p^d High Constables Warr^{ts} repairing Ribchester Bridge	1 : 7 : 10	
p^d do. for Bramhall's[2] Loss by the late Rioters	37 : 18 : 6	
p^d Mr Henry Feilden[3] in part of Balance due to him	30 : :	
p^d John Whitacar for Assistance ...	: 3 :	
22. p^d Expences at the Swan[4] three Persons all Night suspected of Felony 4^s the day after 3/6	: 7 : 6	
p^d for Coals to the Guardhouse 26 Weeks at 3/6	4 : 11 :	
p^d to 192 Trampers[5] since the 25th of March last	3 : 17 : 11	
30. p^d two Weeks Coal for the Guardhouse	: 7 :	
p^d cleaning Steps at Salford Bridge...	: 1 :	
p^d for Paper for Billets &c	: 2 : 3	
p^d Expences . . . . noticing the Alehousekeepers to take Licences ...	: 3 :	

[1] This probably relates to the Lancashire Militia, which left Manchester in December last. (See p. 147, note 3.)

[2] Mr. George Bramhall was, I think, the person whose shop and house were so violently attacked by the mob in July last. (See Appendix.)

[3] This payment was probably for money advanced to the town by Mr. Henry Fielden. (See the Receipts on p. 159.)

[4] This Inn has not, I think, occurred before.

[5] See p. 119, note 2.

Oct. 1.	p^d Charges and Assistants sundry Persons brought before the Justice for Rioting in the Night [1]	:	3 :	6
3.	p^d Engine Men for one Month	:	10 :	
	p^d Edmund Wrigley for mending the Great Engine	4 :	:	
	p^d Peter Cotrell keeping the Key of the Engine-house	:	2 :	
4.	p^d Assistants and maintainance Thomas Mort Thomas Timperly, Isaac Dicken, Thomas Pierpoint and William Heys under Justices Warr" [2]	:	5 :	6
	p^d for a Weeks Coal for Guard-house	:	3 :	6
Octr 4.	p^d James Sutton for assistance several Times	:	2 :	6
	p^d John Dodd conveying the King's Baggage to Buxton	:	12 :	
	p^d him Horsehire twice to Lancaster	1 :	1 :	
	p^d Music the fourth day of June last [3]	:	15 :	
	p^d William Bennet for Smithwork at the Engines	:	11 :	8
	p^d Mrs Blinkhorn for Beadle's Stockings	:	13 :	6
11.	p^d for a Week's Coal for the Guard-house	:	3 :	6
	p^d 17 more Trampers	:	6 :	9
	p^d Beadle a quarters Salary [4]	2 :	10 :	
	p^d Deputy a year's Salary [4]	30 :	:	
	Expences at Lent Assizes 1763 [5]			

[1] I do not find any reference to this rioting in the *Manchester Mercury* for September and October.

[2] These were probably the men arrested for the rioting referred to in the last note.

[3] The anniversary of the birthday of the King, George III. Later on in this year's Accounts there is an item of £13 13s. spent at the Bull's Head on this occasion.

[4] At the Court Leet held on the 13th October, 1762, Mr. John Kay was appointed Deputy Constable at the yearly salary of £30, and John Oldham was appointed Beadle at the yearly salary of £10. (See *Court Leet Records*, vol. viij., p. 68.) Previous to this the salaries had been £20 and £7 respectively.

[5] These were the Assizes at which the rioters had been tried, and the persons to whom payment is here made had been called upon to give evidence against them. They were acquitted. (See p. 149, note 4.)

p^d the following Evidences and
Assistants in Cash viz.   ...   .

	l	s	
Thomas Sefton	2 .	2 .	
Betty Whyatt...	2 .	2	4 : 4 :
John Moss	2 :	2	
Tho' Haworth...	2 .	2	4 : 4 :
Abraham Heywood ...	1 . 13	.6	
Ra^l Fletcher	1 . 13	.6	3 : 7 :
Richd Jones	1 . 13	.6	
Young Butterworth ...	1 . 13	.6	3 : 7 :
John Midgley	1 . 13	.6	
John Butterworth	2 . 15	.	4 : 8 : 6
Rosey Mills	1 . 13	.6	
Saml Bentley	2 . 3		3 : 16 : 6
John Wild	1 . 18	.6	
John Buckly	1 .	1	2 : 19 : 6
William Kay	2 .	2 .	
John Duncuff...	2 .	2 .	4 : 4 :
Jos. Hankinson	2 . 12	.6	
William Booth	2 .	2	4 : 14 : 6
James Upton	2 . 12	.6	
Peter Finney	2 .	2 .	4 : 14 : 6
Henry Gartside	2 . 12	.6	
Wm Whitehead	2 .	2 .	4 : 14 : 6
John Ashton	2 .	2 .	
Jona. Winterbottom ...	2 .	2 .	4 : 4 :
Elizab. Bates	2 .	2 .	
John Lee	2 .	2 .	4 : 4 :
John Wright	2 .	2 .	
Thomas Baron	2 .	2 .	4 : 4 :
John Oldham...	1 . 8	.6	
Ja' Oldham	1 . 19	.	3 : 7 : 6
William Marsden	1 . 7	.	
John Kay	3 . 3	.	4 : 10 :

p^d Sundry small Expences amongst
many of the above Evidences attended
in custody upon the Road and at   6 : 10 : 10
Lancaster during the time of the
whole Assize   ...   .

p^d Betty Whyatt for Loss she sustained
by the Rioters order'd at Lancaster   2 : 2 :
before she wou'd give her Testimony

Charges at August Assizes 1763.[1]

p[d] the following Evidences and Assistants in Cash viz.

	l	s	d	l	s	d
John Butterworth	1 . 11 . 6			3 . 3 .		
young Butterworth ...	1 . 11 . 6					
Thomas Baron	1 . 11 . 6			3 . 3 .		
Thomas Gadman	1 . 11 . 6					
Rosey Mills	1 . 11 . 6			3 . : . :		
John Oldham...	1 . 8 . 6					
John Moss	2 . 2 . :			4 . 14 . 6		
John Buckly	2 . 12 . 6					
James Upton...	2 . 12 . 6			4 . 14 . 6		
William Booth	2 . 2 . :					
William Kay	2 . 2 . :			4 . 14 . 6		
Henry Gartside	2 . 12 . 6					
Samuel Bentley	2 . 2 . :			4 . 4 . :		
John Duncuff...	2 . 2 . :					
John Kay	3 . 3 . :			3 . 3 .		
Jonathan Winterbottom				2 . 2 . :		

p[d] Expences of six of the above Persons and their horses going to Lancaster ... ... } 3 : 12 :

p[d] the Maintainance of seven of the said Persons and their horses a long Assize ... ... } 5 : 6 : 4

p[d] keeping them coming home ... 2 : 5 : 10

p[d] Charges, horsehire and Messengers summoning some of the above Evidences before the Assize ... ... } 1 : 11 : 6

p[d] sundry unavoidable Expences amongst the Evidences at Lancaster and coming back with the Oldham People... ... ... } 2 : 1 : 10

p[d] Mr Samuel Smith's Note for Dungeon and Cross Lamp oil... ... } 2 : 9 : 9¾

p[d] for four pair of handcufts ... ... : 9 : 8

p[d] Mr Dutton's Bill at the old Coffeehouse[2]... ... ... } 4 : 1 : 6

---

[1] At these Assizes Matthew Barns was to have been tried, but was released on giving security for good behaviour. (See p. 144, note 3.)

[2] Probably for meetings which had been held there at various times.

	l	s	d
p⁴ John Shaw some Expences there	:	5 :	10
p⁴ Paper ruling and writing the Ley Book	1 :	7 :	
p⁴ James Hilton Extraordinary collecting the Ley	1 :	1 :	
p⁴ at Bull'shead on the King's Birthday &c[1]	13 :	13 :	
p⁴ Mʳ Hindly his Bill for Beadle's Cloathing[2]	4 :	8 :	8
p⁴ Thomas Fielding for Beadle's Trimming[2]	:	3 :	4
p⁴ Mʳ Dutton for Wine proclaiming Peace[3]	1 :	4 :	
p⁴ two Constables Expences to Lancaster Assizes	4 :	4 :	
p⁴ Mʳ Henry Feilden late Constable[4] in advance	10 :	5 :	10
p⁴ Mʳ Tipping late Constable[4] in advance	9 :	13 :	4
p⁴ Attorney Barlow his Bill for Law	5 :	9 :	6
p⁴ Attorney Chippindall[5] his Bill for Law	294 :	18 :	6
p⁴ Expences Horsehire and Assistants serving Warrants and apprehending Rioters in various Parts of the Country and in bringing and attending them before the Justices	2 :	15 :	

[Total] ... ... £884 : 3 : 6¼

---

[1] The King's birthday was on June 4th (see p. 155, note 3), and evidently this year it had been kept with very special rejoicings.

[2] See p. 88, note 2.

[3] The General Peace between France, Spain, Great Britain, and Portugal was concluded at Paris on February 10th, 1763, and it was formally proclaimed in London on March 22nd. The *Manchester Mercury* of April 5th states that "on Saturday last [April 2nd] the General Peace was proclaimed here by the Under Sheriff at the usual Places."

[4] These were the two Constables for the year October, 1761, to October, 1762. (See p. 129.)

[5] The riots in the town cost the Authorities large sums of money, this one lawyer's bill alone being a very heavy one.

[Receipts]

	Contra	Cr			
1763.			l	s	d
By Cash received from the Ley Book			419	7	:
By Cash received of Mr Henry Feilden...			30	:	:
By Cash receiv'd of James Crompton			6	6	:
By Cash receiv'd from the Hamlets being ⅔'s of the High Constables Warrants...			48	7	:
Balance owing to the Constables			380	2	6¼

[Total]... ... ... £884 : 3 : 6¼

1763. Novr 9th We the Jurors of the Court Leet, now holden for the Manor of Manchester in the County of Lancaster, have examin'd the foregoing Accounts of the late Constables of Manchester, and do find a Balance of three hundred and eighty pounds two Shillings and six pence farthing, and we allowing the same, do order it to be paid to them by the succeeding Constables, whom we do likewise allow to charge the same in their Accounts.

(Signed) EDWD BYROM
RICHD CLOWES
JOHN PARKER MOSLEY
MARSDEN KENYON
WYANT MARRIOTT
DANL WHITTAKER
MATTW NORTH
ROB: HYDE
SAMUEL HIBBERT
JOHN HARDMAN
ARCHD BELL
JOHN TIPPING
PETER CROMPTON
EDWARD KENYON

[Constables' Accounts.]

••••••••••••

An Acc[t] of Cash disburs'd by M[r] HENRY HINDLEY and M[r] JOSIAH BIRCH[1] *Constables of Manchester* [Elected 12th October, 1763].

[Disbursements]

	Last Year's balance[2]	380 : 2 : 6¼
1763		
Octob[r] 13.	paid writing presentment to the Sessions	: 2 :
14.	paid Expences attending the Sessions	: 5 : 6
15.	paid lighting Lamps this Dark... ...	: 2 : 10
	paid for Cotton for the Lamps... ...	: 1 :
17.	paid Ringers on the fourth of June last[3]	: 15 :
18.	paid Widow Shaw Governess[4] of the House o'Correction for Damage done to her Bedding by the Rioters... ...	1 : 5 :
20.	paid Marketlooker's bill for 1762 ...	5 : 3 :
25.	paid Baggage conveyed by Seddon	: 15 : 9
31.	paid Expences of a Privy Watch and three men to assist	: 7 : 6
Nov[r] 7.	paid High Constables Warrant for the Wages of the Governor of the House of Correction at Manchester	1 : 3 :
	paid writing eleven Warrants to the Hamlets for their proportion of the above money 2[s] and Messenger 1[s] ...	: 3 :

---

[1] These two Constables were elected at the Court Leet held on the 12th October, 1763. (See *Court Leet Records*, vol. viij., p. 73.)

[2] See p. 159.

[3] This was the Anniversary of the King's Birthday. (See p. 158, note 1.)

[4] This entry explains the previous one, in which "the Governess of the House of Correction" is mentioned. (See p. 153, note 1.)

12.	paid lighting Lamps this dark	: 1 : 10
15	paid Expences of another privy Watch	: 15 : 10
23.	paid John Heywood with King's Baggage to Warrington	: 9 :
	paid another Carter at same time ...	: 9 :
Dec' 12.	paid lighting Lamps this Dark	: 2 : 10
13.	paid Warrants to the Hamlets for the Return of Militia Men	: 3 :
	The same for Landtax & Window duty	: 3 :
	paid writing the Duplicates of the Militia very long	2 : 2 :
25.	paid Warrants to the Hamlets for new Surveyors of the Highway	: 3 :
Dec' 26.	paid the Return of Surveyors	: 1 :
28.	paid Constables of Blackley apprehending Thomas Nadin a Rioter[1] ...	: 7 : 4
29.	Warrants to the Hamlets for appealing to the Window Duty	: 3 :
30.	Conveying Thomas Nadin[1] to Lancaster	2 : 10 :
31.	Attending Justices three persons under Warrants Clerks Expences &c	: 4 : 6
	paid one hundred and forty passengers since the 13th of October last ...	3 : 10 :
	paid for paper for Billets &c	: 5 : 6
	paid for Coal and Candle for the Guardhouse 12 Weeks at 5 3	3 : 3 :
1764.	paid half a Years Rent for the Guard House due at Martinmas	3 : 15 :
Janry 1.	A man two nights in Custody for felony, who was committed at last ...	: 3 : 6
2.	Two men under Warrants to the Justices at Stockport, horses 3ˢ Expences 2 6 and two Messengers 3ˢ ...	: 8 : 6

---

[1] Thomas Nadin appears to have been a prominent rioter, who had for a long time evaded capture. He was ultimately tried and convicted at Lancaster, at the Spring Assizes in 1764, " for feloniously pulling down and destroying Heaton Mill, the property of Mr. George Bramall," and was sentenced to death. " John Chetham was to have been tried for being concern'd in the Riot at Manchester, but Naden being found guilty, the Prosecution against Chetham was withdrawn." Nadin was, however, respited and sentenced to 14 years' transportation.

3.	paid Belman for four public Cries ...	: 4 :
	paid three month's cleansing and play-ing the Engines 30ˢ and Oil 2ˢ 6ᵈ ...	1 : 12 : 6
5.	paid John Smith cleansing Steps at Salfordbridge and Milbrow	: 1 : 6
	paid sundry Expences attending the Justices and by paying Evidences and Assistants	1 : 19 : 2
7.	paid horse and Expences returning a Warrant at Stockport...	: 3 :
10.	paid lighting Lamps this dark	: 2 : 10
19.	paid presentment to the Sessions ...	: 2 :
21.	paid Bills of Indictment, Bailiffs Fees and Expences prosecuting Felons Whores &c	1 : 9 : 6
Febry.	paid for Straw 2ˢ cleansing Dungeon 2ˢ	: 4 :
28.	Warrants to the Hamlets for Constables presentments to the Assizes	: 3 :
Febry 28.	paid one hundred and twenty six passengers these last two months ...	3 : 3 :
	paid Beadle four times attending the Stocks with Drunkards	: 4 :
	paid him for meat and subsisting Prisoners &c	: 9 :
March.	paid Mʳ Barlow for Warᵗˢ and other fees	8 : 19 : 6
7.	paid High Constables repairing Lan-caster Castle and other things	7 : 18 : 9
	Warrants to the Hamlets for pro-portion	: 3 :
	Manchester presentment and High Constables with it	: 2 :
10.	paid mending Dungeon Roof	: 4 :
11.	repairing Guardhouse	. 6 : 1
13.	Warrants to the Hamlets for Militia...	: 3 :
14.	Conveying to Justice three Notorious Affrayers[1] Expences and Assistants...	: 4 : 6
16.	paid for an Assistant in nightly Watch and summoning thirty six militia men	: 6 :
17.	pᵈ Mʳ Touchet's Rent for the Engine House in King street	6 : :

---

[1] This word, which occurs again later on, is used, I think, simply as meaning a rioter—one who joins in an affray or riot.

21.	Summoning eight Evidences to Lancaster by Subpœanea	1 :	:	
23.	paid Thomas Radford repairing the Engines	1 : 17 :		
24.	paid Joseph Scholfield an Evidence ag' Thomas Nadin[1] condemned for rioting...	2 : 2 :		
	Four other Evidences on same Account	6 : 6 :		
26.	Thomas Cadman another Evidence cost	2 : 2 :		
27.	Robert Smethurst another	2 : 2 :		
28.	paid two horses hired to Lancaster...	1 : 1 :		
29.	paid Deputy Kay[2] bound to prosecute	2 : 12 :	6	
30.	Joseph Hankinson out six days ...	3 : 3 :		
31.	paid Lighting Lamps two darks ...	: 3 :	6	
April.	paid removing Baggage[3]	1 : 1 :		
1.	paid Belman a public Cry...	: 1 :		
	paid cleansing Steps at Salford bridge	: 1 :		
Ap' 2.	paid for Coal and Candle to the Guard	3 : 8 :	6	
3.	paid Engine men three months ...	1 : 10 :		
4.	paid Vagrants last month	1 : 7 :	6	
5.	Warrants for New Overseers of the poor	: 3 :		
	The same for Surveyors to appear ...	: 3 :		
	paid M' Clegg an Express for Soldiers	2 : 10 :		
	paid Jo. Budworth[4] as by Receit ...	7 : 17 :	6	
	paid Baggage to Rochdale 8 Carts[3] ...	2 : 11 :		
25.	paid keeping and apprehending seventeen Vagrants, most of them in Custody five days	1 : 7 :		
	paid whipping two of them	: 2 :		
	paid three persons three days assist[6]...	: 9 :		
	paid serving Jurors Warrants and their fees, a man killed	: 2 :	4	
26.	paid Belman decrying Lifting[6]... ...	: 2 :		

---

[1] See p. 161, note 1.

[2] Mr. John Kay was the Deputy-Constable.

[3] This was the baggage of Sir Robert Rich's Dragoons, for on the 27th March it is reported in the *Manchester Mercury* that "the Scots Grey Dragoons are on their march from Scotland for this Town, where they are to be quartered in the room of Sir Robert Rich's Dragoons, who are to march for Scotland on their Arrival here."

[4] See p. 119, note 4.   [5] See p. 68, note 1.

		£	s	d
	paid apprehending Ann White and committing her for lifting[1]...		3	
	paid for a Dungeon Lamp...		12	
	paid presentment to the Sessions ...		1	
	Indicting Bett Leyland a Whore ...		6	
	paid a Lawyer's fee	1	1	
	paid John Haworth a bill by privy Watch meeting at his house		19	2
	paid three Assistants		3	
	paid two Inquisitions...		4	8
	paid Expences this Sessions upon Evidences &c		5	
30.	paid Edmund Wrigly for Work at the Great Engine[2]	3	3	
	paid half a Year Guardhouse Rent ...	3	15	
	paid Musick on King's Birthday[3] ...		15	
	paid William Bennet for Ironwork about the Great Engine[2]		18	6
May 30.	paid Henry Booth repairing the Guardhouse		7	8
July 3.	paid High Constables repairing Lancaster Castle	14	3	5
	Warrants to the Hamlets for proportion		3	
July 21.	paid presentment to the Sessions ...		1	
	prosecuting Affrayers[4]		5	
	paid attending Moll Grestock a Vag[t] ·		4	6
	sending her away on horseback to Ribchester		15	
	Committing another Whore		3	
	paid conveying James Smith to Lancaster 50[s] and an extraordinary Messenger as far as Chorley 7[s] 6[d] ...	2	17	6
	Paid Beadle expences of prisoners in the Dungeon 6[s] 8[d] and whipping 3[s]...		9	8
	Attending Stocks three times		3	
	Cleansing Dungeon and Straw... ...		4	
	Apprehending William Kenyon a Madman 4[s] and a Cart for him and conducting him to the poorhouse 2 . 6		6	6

[1] This is the first instance of anyone being arrested and punished for "lifting."
[2] See p. 87, note 1.
[3] The King's birthday, June 4th, was annually celebrated in the town.
[4] See p. 162, note 1.

	paid Black Tom for Assistance... ...	: 1 :		
	paid decrying Mad Dogs	: 2 :	6	
26.	last night three men upon privy Watch disturbances in the Streets ...	: 3 :		
	paid last Sessions to sixteen Evidences against Ralph Hindly	1 :	: 11½	
Aug' 10.	paid High Constables repairing public Bridges	37 : 14 :	2	
	Warrants to the Hamlets for proportion	: 3 :		
	paid three nights privy Watch... ...	: 9 :		
	paid Enginemen	3 : :		
	paid Governor of the House o' Correction his bill for prisoners &c ...	: 15 :		
	paid Belman four Cries	: 4 :	6	
Aug' 27.	paid Robert Smethurst for Errands and Assistance Messages about Vagarants and the like	: 15 :	6	
28.	paid one hundred and twenty passengers	2 : 15 :	8	
	Warrants three times to the hamlets for Landtax and Window duty... ...	: 9 :		
	paid for Landtax Warrant this year	: 1 :		
	The same for Window duty	: 1 :		
	paid John Townly for brickwork about the Guardhouse	: 6 :	6	
	Apprehending maintaining whipping and conveying Moll Grestock a Second time	: 8 :	6	
	paid two Jurors fees	: 4 :	8	
Sep' 1.	paid Belman three Cries	: 3 :	5	
	detaining five Whores and Evidences conveying and committing them	: 4 : 10		
	Warrants for Surveyors of the Highway	: 3 :		
	Serving a Bench Warrant at Rochdale upon a militia man	: 3 :	6	
	paid Carting Kings Baggage to Wigan two Carts	: 18 :		
	paid eleven passengers	: 5 :		
	paid for Coal and Candle	: 1 :	4	

	paid Deputy's Journey to Lancaster Evidence against Henry Booth[1] for Perjury	2 : 12 : 6
	paid Luke Ashly for Glaziers Work at the Exchange[2]	1 : 12 : 1
14.	paid Attorney Barlow Clerks fees ...	1 : 19 :
Sep[r] 14.	paid Sam. Smith for Oil	2 : 17 : 7
	paid Jo. Harrop[3] for printing work and Acts of Parliament	2 : 18 :
	paid Marketlookers bill	3 : 10 :
	paid Beadle maintaining Vag[n]... ...	: 3 :
Octob[r] 1.	paid Enginemen	1 : 10 :
	paid Coals to the Guardhouse	: 4 : 6
	paid Belman crying Scavenging ...	: 1 :
	paid Guardhouse Rent in full	1 : 17 : 6
	paid John Barlow in part of his bill for Law during the rioting time[4] ...	35 : :
	paid Buckly Bower for Interest ...	4 : 6 : 6
	paid Lawyer Nangreave a fee ab[t] the prosecution of Henry Booth[1] for perjury	: 10 : 6
	paid Expences Kings Birthday[3] ...	7 : 14 : 8
	paid sundry small articles by M[r] Birch	: 3 : 4
	paid for the Beadles Cloaths[6]	5 : 12 : 11
	paid Buckley Bower a Years In[t] of two hundred pounds...	10 : :
	paid Joseph Budworth[7] an old bill ...	35 : 17 : 7
	paid Pe[ter] Cotrell keeping Engines	: 4 :
	Paid Beadle his Salary[8]	10 : :
	paid Deputy his Salary[8]	30 : :
	paid M[r] Barlow in full for Law ...	31 : 17 :
	p[d] Expences Laying Constable Ley	5 : 3 : 11

[Total] ... ... £768 : 4 : 7½

---

[1] At the autumn Assizes this year " Henry Booth, of Hollinwood, near this County, a Man of considerable Property, convicted of wilful and corrupt Perjury, on an Information, which he gave concerning the Riot at Manchester in 1762, was ordered to be transported for seven years."

[2] See p. 53, note 4.   [3] See p. 73, note 2.   [4] See p. 158, note 5.
[5] See p. 164, note 3.   [6] See p. 88, note 2.   [7] See p. 119, note 4.
[8] See p. 155, note 4.

Dr By Disbursements   ... ...   768 : 4 : 7¾

It may be noted, That the last Year's
balance stands ...   380 . 2 . 6¼
And that other bills came in afterwards tho' contracted before this Year
amounting to the Sum of

131 . 9 . 1

Making in the whole 511 : 11 : 7¼
The money owing }
now   ... ... } 295 . 3 . 11¾

The Debt is lessened 216 : 7 : 7½

[Total] ... ... £768 : 4 : 7¾

[Receipts]

Contra... ... ... Cr

By Cash received from the Ley   ... ... 421 : 3 : 10½
By two thirds of the money Warrants from the }
eleven Hamlets ... ... } 40 : 13 : 0½
By Cash in the hands of the Treasurer of the County }
Stock for Baggage &c   ... ... } 11 : 3 : 9
By Balance owing to the Old Constables and Joseph }
Chippendall[1] ... ... } 180 : 2 : 6¼
By Cash owing late Constable Hindley ... ... 47 : 1 : 4
By do to Luke Ashly... ... ... 1 : 12 : 1
By do to Jo : Budworth   ... ... 35 : 17 : 7
By do to Deputy Kay   ... ... 30 : 10 : 5½

[Total] ... ... £768 : 4 : 7¾

1764. November 28th We the Jurors of the Court Leet, now
holden for the manor of Manchester in the County of Lancaster,
have examined the foregoing Accounts of Mr Henry Hindley and
Mr Josiah Birch late Constables of Manchester aforesaid and finding

---

[1] Mr. Joseph Chippendall was a well-known lawyer in the town, who would appear
to have advanced money to the authorities of the town. His bill for prosecuting the
rioters of 1762 was paid last year. (See p. 158, note 5.)

a balance of Two Hundred ninety five pounds three Shillings and elevenpence three farthings owing to the several persons as above mentioned, And We allowing the same do order it to be paid to them by the succeeding Constables, whom we also allow to charge the same in their Accounts.

(Signed)   THO: BATTERSBEE
SAML ROBINSON
WILM KENNEDY
LAWCE GARDNER
JAMES BORRON
DANL WHITTAKER
RICHARD BARTON
JAMES HODSON
WILLIAM EDGE
EDWARD HOLME
ROBT HAMILTON
THOS CHESSHYRE

[Constables' Accounts.]

[15th Oct., 1766, to 14th Oct., 1767.][1]

••••••••••••

[An Account of Cash Disbursed by MR PETER CROMPTON and MR LAWRENCE GARDNER,[2] *Constables of Manchester*, elected 15th October, 1766.]

[Previous pages Missing.]

[Disbursements]

1767

Octor 12.	Brought forward ... ... £400 :	: 1
	paid James Sutton, William Barkley, Thomas Barron and Samuel Newton the remainder of a Bill for Watch and Ward in Manchester	7 : 7 :
	paid Justices Clerks for Business about the assize of Bread[3]	4 : 13 :
	paid two Men watching 130 Nights a[t] 0s 6d each Man Pr Night at the Exchange in King street[4] the Road being rendered dangerous and the Steps pul'd up by Persons claiming a right thereto	6 : 10 :

---

[1] Here again there is an unfortunate break in the continuity of these Accounts, those for the two years Oct., 1764, to Oct., 1766, being missing. The first portion of the present year's Accounts is also missing.

[2] These two Constables were elected at the Court Leet held on the 15th October, 1766. (See *Court Leet Records*, vol. viij , page 98.)

[3] The Assize of Bread was the list of regulations and prices which governed the sale and price of bread, and which depended upon the price of corn, &c. In the *Manchester Mercury* for Jan. 6th and Jan. 13th "the Assize of Bread" is printed. It begins "The Penny Loaf Wheaten is to weigh 9oz., the Penny Loaf Household is to weigh 12oz. 1dr.," and so on.

[4] The Exchange in King Street here referred to is a somewhat mysterious building, the origin of which does not appear to be known. The building generally known as the Exchange, situate near the bottom of Market Street, has been frequently mentioned in these Accounts. (See p. 53, note 4.) This King Street Exchange is mentioned in the

paid in part to M[r] Vigor for Law by the Hands of M[r] Bradley...	4 : 10 :
paid William Jenkinson and Daniel Thornally by Justices Order inspecting the Markets	4 : 4 :
paid Thomas Barron for runing Errands Assisting in serving Warrants and the like...	: 10 :
paid M[r] Henry Pullon's Bill of Expences at leying the Constable Ley	8 : : 9
paid remainder of Beadle's Salary ...	7 : 10 :
paid Deputy three quarter's Salary ...	22 : 10 :
paid for a Substitute for James Blackling a Quaker, into the Militia	1 : 11 : 6
paid for a Militia Substitute for Benjamin Busby Bynion a Quaker ...	1 : 11 : 6
October 12th paid sundry disbursments by M[r] Crompton Constable...	1 : 3 : 6
paid Joseph Harrop for an Advertisement by M[r] Gardner...	: 3 : 6
p[d] M[r] Chippindall[1] a year's Interest of £200 borrowed on this Account ...	9 : :
paid M[r] Walter Wilson's Bill for Iron Work about the Dungeon and Engine House	4 : 1 :
paid Bill at Crompton's Coffeehouse when the Royal Healths were drank[2]	3 : 7 : 6
paid Engine Men 7 Months Wages ...	4 : 7 : 6
paid for Oil to the Engines	: : 6
paid M[r] Chippindall[1] an error under casting his Account about the Rioters	2 : :
paid M[r] Richard Oliver one Year's Rent for the Engine House	3 : 3 :

[Total] ... ... £496 : 4 : 4

will of Henry Booth, of Houghton, gent., dated 23rd January, 1741-2, in which he states that he is seised in fee simple of "one moiety of a building in King-street, called the Exchange, which lies open and is used as a footway or passage for all persons passing and repassing for King Street and the new Church in Manchester [St. Ann's] with a chamber or room over the said way or passage now used for an assembly room and a cellar under the same." I believe the building over the entry in King Street is still called "the Old Exchange."

[1] See p. 167, note 1.

[2] Probably on the occasion of the King's Birthday, June 4th.

[Receipts]

Contra ... ... C^r

Rec^d from the Hamlets $\frac{2}{3}$ parts of £12 : 18 : 1 ...	8 : 12 :
Rec^d from the Hamlets $\frac{2}{3}$ parts of £16 : 18 : 9 ...	11 : 5 : 10
Rec^d from the Hamlets $\frac{2}{3}$ parts of £24 : 10 : 8 ...	16 : 7 : 1
Rec^d from the Hamlets $\frac{2}{3}$ parts of £18 : 9 : 9 ...	12 : 6 : 6
Rec^d from Mr Axon one of the Misegatherors ...	70 : :
Rec^d from Mr Bancroft one of the Misegatherors ...	70 : :
By Cash borrowed on bond at Interest from Mr Joseph Chippindall[1]	129 : 16 : 6
By Cash Received remainder of Mr Axon's Collection	80 : 7 : 10
By Cash Received remainder of Mr Bancroft's Collection	68 : 9 : 2
By Balance owing to the Constables	28 : 19 : 5
[Total]	496 : 4 : 4

We the Jurors of the Court Leet now holden for the Manor of Manchester in the County of Lancaster have examined the foregoing Accounts of Mr Peter Crompton and Mr Lawrence Gardner and do allow the same.

(Signed)   THOS STOTT
WILM KENNEDY
SAML. ROBINSON
JOHN HARGREAVE
THOS STARKIE
JOHN HAGUE
WM HURST
JOSIAH KEARSLEY
EDWD HUDSON

[1] See p. 167, note 1.

[Constables' Accounts.]

[14th Oct., 1767, to 12th Oct., 1768.]

•••••••••••

Dr Town of Manchester to Mʀ JOHN WHITTAKER and
Mʀ EDWᴰ PLACE *Constables.*[1] [Elected 14th October,
1767.]

[Disbursements]

1767.

October 13ᵗʰ To Mʳ Chippindall Money borrow'd at Interest[2]	129 : 16 : 6
To last Year's Balance advanced by Mʳ Peter Crompton and Mʳ Lawrence Gardnor late Constables[3]	28 : 19 : 5
To Presentment to Sessions	: 1 :
To Clerk of the Peace for Business done for the Constables about a Publick Riot in Milgate[3]	2 : 7 : 4
To returning a Warrant of Justice Whitehead's[4] at Bolton	: 2 :
To Charges of detaining a Woman all-night found in the Streets...	: 1 :
Novʳ 1ˢᵗ To attending two Drunkards in the Stocks...	: 2 :
2ᵈ To Enginemen for Ale	: 2 :
4ᵗʰ To Straw for the Dungeon	: 3 :
To Coal for the Guardhouse	: 6 : 7
To Thomas Geldor, Oil for the Lamp at the old Exchange[5] in Kingstreet 13 9 lighting 6 6 the Steps being pul'd down there by Persons claiming a right thereto	1 : : 3

---

[1] These two Constables were elected at the Court Leet held on the 14th October, 1767. (See *Court Leet Records*, vol. viij., p. 105.)

[2] See p. 171.

[3] I cannot find any account of this riot in the *Manchester Mercury.*

[4] This was probably the Rev. Edward Whitehead, Vicar of Bolton.

[5] See p. 169, note 4.

Nov' 9th	To Expences of a Privy Watch ...	: 7 : 3	
	To Belman two Cries about the High-ways	: 2 :	
	To Passengers since the 13th of October	: 12 :	
	To John Stock Brown's Bill of Work done at the Exchange in Kingstreet[1]	2 : 17 : 4	
18th	To apprehending a Gang of Young fellows disturbing the Streets in the Night with Sticks and Clubs, detaining and conveying one of them to [the] Justice the Day after	: 2 : 6	
	To Coal for the Guard	: 5 :	
19th	To Expences at Dale's Tavern[2] upon a Privy Watch	: 3 : 6	
20th	To Commiting and conveying Jane Williamson to the House of Correction for Felony, whom the Deputy Constable was bound over to prosecute	: 3 :	
	To Meat and Drink at Sun[3] in Milgate attending sundry Prisoners at various Times...	: 6 : 3	
21st	To Meat Drink and other Expences at the House of Correction since the 13th of October	: 7 :	
Nov' 21st	To attending committing and conveying two Street-Walkors to the House of Correction...	: 6 :	
	To attending George Sloan a Prisoner at the Eight Bells[4] in Highstreet ...	: : 8	
25th	To Warrants to the Hamlets for New Lists of Jurors of the Assizes and Quarter-Sessions	: 3 :	
	To Expences of quartering foot Soldiers since the 13th of October ...	1 : 1 :	
27.	To Coal for the Guard	: 5 : 3½	
Dec' 5th	To Coal for the Guard	: 7 : 4½	

[1] See p. 169, note 4.

[2] This was the inn kept by Mr. James Dale, and known as Dale's Tavern, to which the Court Leet Jury sometimes adjourned. (See *Court Leet Records*, vol. viij., p. 94.)

[3] This inn has not, I think, been mentioned before in these Accounts.

[4] This inn has been previously mentioned (see p. 80, note 1).

8th	To Charges conveying three Men charged with committing a Rape upon Ann Scholes of Blackley to Mr Harbord at Middleton, conveying back, and keeping them in Custody till next Day, who were all committed to Lancaster	: 7 : 6
15th	To Coronor's Warrants and Juror's Fees	: 2 : 4
	To Coal for the Guard	: 9 : 7
20th	To Passengers &c since the 9th Day of November	1 : 1 :
Decr 20th	To Lawyer Nangreave, for business heretofore done for the Constables of Manchester...	5 : 5 :
25.	To attending George Purtus two Days in Manchester, waiting of Justice Booth 4 - conveying to Middleton from whence he was committed and attending him all Night 5/- charged with Bastardy	: 9 :
	To Coal for the Guard	: 6 : 2
26th	To Coronor's Warrants and Jurors Fees on the Death of John Price a double Jury...	: 4 : 8
29th	To Coronors Warrants and Jurors Fees on the Death of Benjamin Taylor's Child a double Jury	: 4 : 8
	To making Beadle's Cap & Gown ...	: 9 :
	To Coal for the Guardhouse	: 2 : 2
	To cleansing Salford Steps half a year	: 2 :
1768		
Jany 3.	To Coal for the Guardhouse	: 8 : 6
14th	To Warrants to the Hamlets for Proportion of 36^l : 18^s : 8^d	: 3 :
18th	To maintaining and keeping Wm Pass a Felon two Nights and a Day... ...	: 2 :
Jany 20th	To Coronors Warrants and Jurors Fees Joseph Wood kil'd by a Cart ...	: 2 : 4
	To Coal to the Guard House	: 9 : 6
21st	To a pair of Shoes for John Oldham Beadle...	: 5 : 3

To attending James Gimney two Days and two Nights under a Warrant, runing away from his apprentiship ...	:	2	:
To Thomas Barron for attendance ...	:	1	:
To apprehending Ashton Hind under a Bench Warrant and attending him a Day and a Night	:	2	6
To two Men three Days in quest of two Simpsons for a violent assault ...	:	3	6
To a Warrant against Isaac Dicken for striking a Soldier	:	3	:
To Expences amongst the Soldiers settleing the matter by Justice Booth's Directions	:	1	6
To the Sessions Presentment as usual	:	1	:
To Indictment against Jane Williamson for Felony 2/- Witnesses attending the Court and Jury 3/- swearing Witnesses 1 6 Bailiffs Fees 1 6	:	8	:

Jany 21st — To an Indictment against Persons suffering a Wagon to stand in Deansgate 4/- five Witnesses and Expences 7/6 swearing Witnesses 2/6 Bailiffs Fees 1 6 ... ...   : 15 : 6

To Deputys Expences and other Evidences attending the Sessions three Days ... ...   : 5 :

To maintaining Strollers[2], and Passenger since the 20th Decr last, and Cash given to Trampers,[1] during the last Month, it being a severe Storm, and a very great Snow so that they could not Travel ... ...   1 : 7 : 6

To Clerk of the Peace for Orders and Allowance of Certificates for conveying Vagabonds ... ...   : 9 :

28. — To Expences apprehending attending and conveying to Prison Thomas Timperley Committed as a Cheat ...   : 5 :

To two Messengers in Cheshire 2 - Meat and Drink for six Persons in Ashton 3/- in Stretford 1 - Wages of

---

[1] See p. 119, note 2.   [2] See p. 130, note 3.

	three Persons all Day and Night 4 6 when four of a Gang of Theeves were apprehended and afterwards committed to the House of Correction ...	: 10 : 6
	To an Atty at Law and the Constables of Saddleworth for Business done in the last Riot[1] at the request of the then Constables of Manchester... ...	2 : 9 : 10
Jan[y] 29	To a load of Coal to the Guard ...	: 6 : 1
Feb[y] 4th	To attending and conveying to Justice three Persons Feloniously carrying away Goods which were found in the House of John Moors in Tib Lane...	: 3 :
	To Maintenance & Expences quartering Soldiers at sundry Times they being very numerous and very Troublesome	1 : 1 :
	To three Men searching for stolen Cloth in Manchester 1 6 Ale 0 10 a Man & Horse in to Burnage for Evidences on the same account 2 6	: 4 : 10
	To one Load of Coal	: 6 : 9
	To the Constables Expences on sundry occasions at Dale's Tavern[2]...	1 : : 6
16.	To Coal to the Guard	: 5 : 9
	To M[r] Barlow's Bill for Clerkship on the Constables Account	2 : 2 : 6
	To Matthew Pickford carrying Water Buckets from London	1 : 3 : 4
March 3[d]	To a Money Warrant	: 18 : 4
	To conveying two old Vagrants in the late Storm to Burton in Kendal cost more than the County allowance ...	1 : 2 : 6
	To John Haslingden for Paper ruling and binding Books for the Assessors of Window Duty	: 5 : 4
	To Coal to the Guard	: 6 : 6
	To Coronors Warrants and Jurors Fees on the death of John Penny ...	: 2 : 4

[1] This is probably the rioting referred to in October last, of which I do not find any account in the local paper.

[2] See p. 173, note 2.

To Wages of People attending him till his Burial	: 5 :	
To Warrants to the Hamlets to bring in Presentments...	: 3 :	
To Warrants to the Hamlets for Collectors of Land Tax to bring their last quarterly payments	: 3 :	
To Coronors Warrants and Jurors Fees on the death of —— Ashton ...	: 2 :	4
To Horsehire to Rochdale with the Assize Presentment 2'- Clerks for Writing it 1'- High Constables with it 1 - Deputy's Expences thither & back 1 6	: 5 :	6
To the High-Constables Warrant for repair of Brokenbank and publick Bridges, the Governor's Salary, and for repairing the House of Correction at Manchester	36 : 18 :	8
To Belman three Cries on account of Streetwalkers	: 3 :	
To Mr Joseph Chippindall's Bill for Law	7 : 5 :	2

15th	To Coal to the Guardhouse	: 11 :	5½
March 18th	To Coal to the Guardhouse	: 4 :	4
	To Carting Ditto	: 1 :	
22d	To John Millard for Locks and Keys to the Dungeon &c	1 : 6 :	
25th	To sundry Expences attending Prisoners at the Royal Oak[1] in High-street	: 11 :	7
	To Coal for the Guard	: 6 :	
	To James Brown's Bill of Work done at the Exchange[2] in the Market-place	2 : 2 :	6½
	To Thomas Hough's Bill of Iron Work	: 5 :	5
26.	Warrants to the Hamlets for Overseers of the Poor to Acc'	: 3 :	

[1] This inn has, I think, occurred before in these Accounts.

[2] See p. 53, note 4. Here it is noticeable that it is described as "the Exchange in the Market place," to distinguish it from "the Exchange in King Street." (See p. 169, note 4).

28.	To three Horses 6/9 Expences, Turnpike, and baiting, dining &c 4/4 a Messenger 1/6, carrying Tom Tim-perley before Justice Townley	: 12 : 7
	To Robert Hilton for detaining and maintaining Prisoners	: 13 :
	To William Walkers Bill for Soldiers Benches in the Guardhouse	: 14 :
	To Jo. Harrop[1] for printing work about the Assize of Bread[2]	1 : 9 : 6
	To d° Advertisements about Shop-breakers	1 : 6 : 6
March 28	To Mr Danl Whittaker's Balance of his Account	4 : 17 : 5½
	To James Oldham going to Middle-ton with Ben: Thorp under Warrant	: 1 : 6
	To Ralp[h] Ryder attending the Engines	: 10 : 6
April 4	To Belman six publick Cries agt Lift-ing,[3] throwing at Cocks,[4] driving Girths[5] in the Streets &c	: 9 :
	To William Chorlton mending the Engine Waterbuckets	2 : 2 : 7
	To fetching William Moors a Felon from Woolverhampton	5 : 17 : 2
14.	To High Constables Warrant for Governor's Wages	: 10 :
May 2.	To Warrants to the Hamlets noticing the payment of Landtax and Window Duty	: 3 :
	To d° for calling out the Militia ...	: 3 :
	To d° to make new Militia Lists ...	: 3 :
	To d° for Assessors of Landtax &c ...	: 3 :
May 10.	To Thomas Davenport for paper and ruling Books for Window peepers[6]...	: 6 : 10½
	To Commissioners Clerk for Warrants and Blanks	: 10 : 6
13.	To an Inquisition on the Death of Jas Shore	: 2 : 4

---

[1] See p. 73, note 2.   [2] See p. 169, note 3.
[3] See p. 68, note 1.   [4] See p. 66, note 1.
[5] I am informed that "girths" may possibly mean "hoops," which makes this sentence clear.
[6] This slang expression has occurred before. (See p. 82, note 2.)

	To one Hanglock[1] for the Dungeon	: 8
June 2.	To Expences of two Messengers fetching Thomas Timperley from Winwick 16ˢ. 6ᵈ and Wages of one Messenger 5/-	1 : 1 : 6
6.	To an Inquisition on a person unknown	: 2 : 4
8.	To John Edwards' Expences on sundry prisoners at the House o' Correction	: 7 : 11
9.	To John Rishton, Expences at sundry times about Constables Business ...	: 4 : 6
	To a Note of Coals to the Guardhouse	1 : 9 : 2
	To relieving 170 Trampers[2] since Janry last	3 : 14 : 6
	To High Constables Warrant for conveying Vagrants and Forces, for Coroners Orders, Relief of Prisoners &c	25 : : 6
	Warrants to the Hamlets for their proportion thereof	: 3 :
23.	To a Block for repairing the Engine Buckets upon	: : 6
June 24.	To Diners 1ˢ Turnpike and bating at Middleton 3ˢ- Bating at Bury 3ˢ Returnˢ back to Middleton at the Request of Justice Harbord and attending Edmᵈ Cooper[3] all night there 4 6, Breakfasting at Bury 3 1. Three Horses from Manchester to Middleton 4 6. Three to Bury and back to Middleton 4 6. Three Horses from Middleton to Bury 3ˢ. from whence Cooper went forward to Lancaster	1 : 6 : 7

[1] A "hang lock" was probably a padlock. It occurs in the first volume of the *Constables' Accounts*. (See list of curious words.)

[2] See p. 119, note 2.

[3] Edmund Cooper, of Middleton, about whom so many payments are here recorded, was convicted at the autumn Assizes, at Lancaster, "of returning from Transportation and was ordered to his former sentence."

25.	To two men following a Gang of Cheats on horseback by a Warrant into Cheshire, indorsing the War[t] 1[s] Bailiffs and Assistants at Stockport 3 – baiting dining and Turnpike 3 4 Conveying Robert Walker one of the Gang to Justice Bayley [1] at Withington 2/2 Two Messengers 5/–	: 14 : 6
	To Music, drinking the Royal Healths at His Majesty's Birthday [2] 15[s] To the Ringers 10 6. To Six Troops of Dragoons [3] firing 63/–	4 : 4 : 6
	To cleansing Steps at Salfordbridge	: 2 :
29.	To passing Alice Taylor and Child to Ashton more than County Allowance	: 2 : 8
	To removing the Baggage of two Troops of Dragoons [3] to Knutsford more than allowed	: 15 :
	To Coal to the Guardhouse by James Taylor at twice	: 6 : 6
	To making a Cap for Richard Dixon [4] the new elected Beadle	: 1 : 8
July 1.	To passing Ann White and her Child to Burton in Westmoreland more than the County Allowance	: 13 : 3
2.	To Belfield about Thomas Timperley and about Selby's Children; Horsehire and Turnpike 2 6 all night 2 9 ...	: 5 : 3
	To Coroners Warrants and Jurors Fees an Inquisition upon John Dunkerley	: 2 : 4
10.	To Justice Harbord's concerning Bill Bill [sic] Ogden two Horses 2 6 Expences 1 7	: 4 : 1

---

[1] See p. 105, note 1.

[2] This was an annual festivity in the town. (See previous Accounts.)

[3] In the *Manchester Mercury* of April 26th this year it is stated that on Friday last "a party of Lord Ancram's Dragoons arrived here ; and on Monday the last Division of General Mostyn's Dragoons march'd from hence for Worcester." And on May 10th it is announced, "last week the Remainder of the Marquis of Lothian's Regiment of Dragoons, arrived here." It may be noted that the title of Earl of Ancrum had become merged in that of the Marquis of Lothian.

[4] Mr. John Oldham had been elected Beadle at the Court Leet held on the 14th Oct., 1767, but Richard Dixon was now appointed in his place, probably on account of the death of the former.

	To a pair of Shoes for the Beadle... ...	: 5 : 6
	To four Soldiers apprehending and detaining Richard Mills on Suspicion of Felony	: 6 :
	To three Men watching at the Request of Mr Byrom upon a Report of Felons lurking thereabouts	: 3 :
	To William Bennets Smith Bill repairing Engines[1]	: 11 : 5
18.	To Thomas Radford's Bill for Brass and Foundery Work dn[1]	1 : 19 : 2
21.	To Mr Harbord's Clerk for Business about a felonious Rape	1 : 19 :
	To him for Business touching Edmd Cooper,[2] returning from Transportation	: 17 :
23.	To James Brown for Carpentry Work at the Exchange, and for Watch-bills[3]	: 13 : 7
24.	To waiting on Justice Harbord on a special Request, touching a Gang of suspected Highwaymen, all night ...	: 3 : 6
26.	To High Constable's Warrant for Repair to Public Bridges	16 : 8 : 7
	To John Milward for Ironwork at Dungeon and Guard Room	: 5 : 10
	To Mr North's Bill for Beadles Cloth &c[4]	8 : 18 :
	To the Expences Laying the Ley ...	8 : 11 : 6
	To Paper ruling and writing the Leybook	1 : 7 :
30.	To John Holden, a Slater's Bill repairing the Dungeon	: 9 : 3
Augt 2.	To Expences sending men and Horses to Rochdale at the Request of the King of Denmark,[5] more than he allowed	: 19 : 8

---

[1] See page 87, note 1.   [2] See page 179, note 3.   [3] See page 31, note 4.
[4] This is an unusually heavy amount for the Beadle's clothes. Perhaps the new Beadle required to be well set up in starting on his new career. (See page 88, note 2.)
[5] This was Christian VI., King of Denmark, who had succeeded his father, Frederick V., in January, 1766. On the 1st October in that year he married the Princess Caroline Matilda, of England, sister to the King, George III., and in August this year—1768—he came to England on a visit.

	To the Governor of the House of Correction, for Repairs in the Exchange[1] at the Request of the Justices of Peace, and for sustaining Prisoners in the House	1 : 11 : 9
	To Thomas Hough for Nails at the Exchange[1]	: 3 : 9
4.	To Edmund Wrigley's Bill at the Engines[2]	1 : 10 :
	To Wages paid the Engine Men for eleven Months	6 : 18 :
5.	To Paper, ruling, writing and copying twice the Duplicates of the Militia of Manchester...	3 : 3 :
6.	To an Inquision over a Child	: 2 : 4
10.	To drawing the Assize Presentment, and Fees to the High Constables Clerks	: 2 :
20.	To Robert Nabb repairing the Dungeon	: 4 : 6
	To three Cart Load of Coal to the Guardhouse	: 15 : 9
	To the Ringers when his Danish Majesty was in Town[3]	1 : 1 :

[1] See p. 53, note 4.   [2] See p. 87, note 1.

[3] An account of the sudden and unexpected visit of the King of Denmark to Manchester, on Friday, the 2nd September, is given at considerable length in Harrop's *Manchester Mercury*. The King was attended with a retinue of about 50 persons, and he put up at the Bull's Head Inn, coming to the town from Rochdale. The Marquis of Lothian's Regiment of Dragoons, quartered in the town, were put under arms, but soon dismissed by his Majesty. The account continues :—

"After Breakfast, his Majesty very politely shewed himself at the window, and complaisantly bowed to a very brilliant Appearance of Ladies in the Neighbouring Houses. Soon after Edward Byrom, Esq., was introduced to his Majesty (by a Recommendation from Lord Morton, President of the Royal Society), to accompany him to view the Duke of Bridgwater's Canal and the Manufactories peculiar to this Town. Accordingly, about eleven, his Majesty (attended by his Nobles and several Gentlemen of the Town) was conducted to the Boats then in waiting for him ; the King went to the Head of the Canal, and then in smaller Boats to the Head of the Tunnel cut in the Rock (two miles under-ground), lighted all the way by Candles. His Majesty much admired the greatness of the Undertaking, expressed great Satisfaction at the Ingenuity and Facility with which the whole is conducted, and was pleased to give the Workmen a handsome Sum of Money. On his Return from Worsley, he then proceeded to the Warehouses here, where he was highly entertained, and much admired the Beauty and Elegance of the several Manufactories shewn to him, purchasing large Quantities of Velvet, Gold and Silver Shapes for Waistcoats and other Goods manufactured here."

He slept at the Bull's Head Inn that evening, refusing "the offer of a Ball," and left next morning, Saturday, about seven o'clock, for Buxton, Chatsworth, and Derby.

	To Isaac Clegg for New Water Buckets for the Use of the Engines[1]	18 : 17 :
	To Benjamin Taylor removing the King's Baggage &c[2]	2 : 14 : 10
	To a double Inquisition	: 4 :
Sep' 21.	To another Inquis[it]ion	: 2 : 4
22.	To a Load of Coal to the Guardhouse	: 5 : 1 ½
	To the Belman seven Cries	: 7 :
Octob. 7.	To a Load of Coal to the Guardhouse	: 5 :
	To Expences carrying a Man under Warrant to Bolton one Man and two Horses...	: 6 : 6
8.	To Coal again	: 5 :
9.	To Joseph Chippendall for Law ...	7 : 1 : 2
	To him for Interest of £129. 16. 6. Borrowed[3]	5 : 14 :
	To Benjamin Ashton turning a New Staff for the Burrough Reeve[4]... ...	: 3 :
	To William Hardwick for Silverwork for the same Staff[4]	3 : 4 : 7 ½
	To Market Lookers one Bill	3 : 10 :
	To D° another Bill	4 : 15 :
	To another d°	3 : 5 :
	To the Beadle in part of his Wages...	6 : 1 : 8
	To the Remainder of his Salary ...	3 : 18 : 4
	To the Deputy Constable one Year's Salary	30 : :
	To a Bill of Candles for the Guardhouse	5 : 12 : 8
	To Money paid by Constable Place...	: 4 :
1768.	To a Note of Sundries paid on the 15th of April last	6 : 13 : 5
October 9.	To the Belman a Cry about Militia...	: 1 :
	To Money repaid the Beadle	: 5 : 5
	To Expences at Ramshead[5] and Woolpack[5] about Prisoners	: 4 : 2

---

[1] See p. 87, note 1.   [2] See p. 182, note 3.   [3] See p. 171, and also p. 167, note 1.
[4] The Boroughreeve's staff has been once previously referred to, but this new one seems to have been very elaborately ornamented and finished.
[5] These two Manchester inns—the Ram's Head and the Wool Pack—are here named, I think, for the first time in these Accounts. The latter was a well-known inn in Deansgate—a black and white timber and plaster building, of which an illustration is given in James' *Views of Manchester*.

To one Year's Rent for the Engine-house in Tiblanc[1]	3 : 3 :
To James Hilton for extraordinary Trouble in collecting the Constable Ley	: 18 : 6
To Allen Vigors Bill for Law	7 : 2 : 2
[Total] ... ...£485 : 6 : 11

ℓ Receipts ℓ

1768.

Octob' 9.		
By remainder of last Years Ley ...	4 : 10 : 7
By the Hamlets their proportion of the Money Warrant 36 : 18 : 8 ...	24 : 12 : 5¼
By d° proportion of 0 : 18 : 4 ...	: 12 : 2½
By d° proportion of 0 : 10 : 0 ...	: 6 : 8
By d° proportion of 25 : 0 : 6 ...	16 : 13 : 8
By d° proportion of 16 : 8 : 7 ...	10 : 19 : 0½
By this Years Collection	310 : 15 : 8
By Balance owing	116 : 16 : 7¾
[Total]	485 : 6 : 11

Nov' 23rd 1768.

We the Jurors of the Court Leet now holden for the Manor of Manchester in the County of Lancaster have examined the foregoing Acc^ts of M^rs Jn° Whittaker & Mr Edwd Place and do allow the same.

(Signed)   JAMES HODSON
Thos Battersbee
Sam^ll Clowes Junr
Willm Bullock
John Markland Junr
Fran^s Mosley
Wm Newton
Benja: Bower
Joseph Tipping
Law^cr Gardner
Edward Holme.

---

[1] This gives us the situation of the Engine House, so often referred to.

[Constables' Accounts.]

[12th Oct., 1768, to 11th Oct., 1769.]

•••••••••••

𝕯ʳ Town of Manchester to Mʀ Jɴᵒ PARKER MOSLEY & Mʀ THOMAS STOTT, *Constables.*[1] [Elected 12th October, 1768.]

[𝕯isbursements]

1768		£	s	d
Octobʳ 9.	To the last Years Balance[2]	116	16	7¾
13.	To drawing a Presentment for the Quarter Sessions		2	
	To Mʳ Hindley's bill for Beadles Cloaths[3]	4	6	4
	To Jo: Shepley for Smithwork at the Pinfold		2	4
	To Thoˢ Hanson for Plastering work at Dungeon		3	4
	To Thoˢ Davenport for Bookbinding abᵗ Window tax		8	4
	To Ashley & Taylor for Glaziery at Exchange Windows	2	1	10
	To Taylor & Thompson removing Baggage to Nutsford [Knutsford] in April last[4]		15	
23.	To sundry Vagrants since the 9ᵗʰ June last	2	16	

---

[1] These two Constables were elected at the Court Leet held on the 12th October, 1768. (See *Court Leet Records,* vol. viij., p. 113.)

[2] See p. 184.

[3] See pp. 88, note 2 and 181 note 4. At the above court Mr. Richard Dixon was appointed Beadle.

[4] This would be for the baggage of General Mostyn's Dragoons, who then left the town for Worcester. (See p. 180, note 3.)

Novem' 11.	To Expences executing a Hue and Crie against Timothy Grett for Felony	: 7 : 6
	To a pair of Scarlet Hose for the former Beadle[1]	: 3 : 6
12.	To a High Constables Warrant repairing Ribble Bridge &c...	2 : 15 : 1
	To Buckley assisting the Enginemen often	: 5 :
	To Brick and Morter for repairing Dungeon	: 12 : 6
	To Will. Walker's bill for Carpentry at Dungeon	: 4 : 2
14.	To Thomas Hanson's bill for plastering there	: 7 :
	To Jere Ratcliff for Flags thither ...	: 13 : 8
	To Jo : Taylor for Lead and Plumbry there	1 : 4 : 4
	To John Shelmerdine's bill for Ale and Trouble attending and detaiñg Prisoners there	: 15 : 7
	To Beever and Shaw for Torches when a dangerous Fire broke out at the King's Head[2] in Deansgate	: 10 :
	To the Soldiers assisting to quench that Fire	1 : 11 : 6
	To Thomas Hanson Plasterwork at Dungeon	: 7 : 6
19.	To Thomas Hanson another Bill ...	: 3 : 4
24.	To Robert Nabb for Stone and Mason's Work at the Dungeon ...	2 : 1 : 6
	To half a Load of Straw to the Dungeon	: 5 : 6
25.	To William Walker for Timber to the Guardhouse	: 10 : 8
26.	To d° for Carpentry at Dungeon & Guardhouse	1 : 15 : 8
29.	To an Inquisition a Child dead at Infirmary	: 1 : 4
	To another Inquisition a Child burnt to Death	: 2 : 4

[1] See p. 185, note 3, and also p. 88, note 2.
[2] Here we have another Manchester inn referred to.

30.	To three Inquisitions over the Body of Nancy Lees[1] found drowned in the Infirmary Pool many Evidences examined, many more paid for attending, many Messages and great unavoidable Expences	2 : 2 :
	A Parcel of drunken Watchmen caused sundry Messengers and Errands to cost	: 1 :
Decem' 1.	To Jo. Taylor for Glaziery at Guardhouse	: 4 : 6½
	To Tho' Mee Brickwork at Guardhouse	: 3 : 2
	To d° repairing the Pinfold	: 4 : 10
	To more Straw for the Dungeon ...	: 5 : 6
3.	To Robert Nabb for letting in Irons at the Guardhouse	: 3 :
	To watching and apprehending two night Housebreakers near Scotland bridge	: 10 : 6
	To James Barton Trimming Beadles Cloaths[2]	1 : 17 : 5½
23.	To Matthew Falkner's Bill for Timber to the Dungeon	: 14 : 3
1769. Janry 1.	To a new Ladder for the Use of the Rogue's Post[3]	: 5 :
	To Belman sundry public Cries ...	: 7 : 6
2.	To Isaac Dicken's Wife's Inquisition	: 2 : 4
	To making the Beadle's Gown... ...	: 6 :
	To Edmund Wrigley's Bill mending the Engine...	: 14 :
7.	To extraordinary Expences this Winter about Soldiers	: 10 :
	To three pair of Stockings and dying for the Beadle[2]	: 9 :

---

[1] In the *Manchester Mercury* it is stated that on Friday, 18th November, an inquest was held on the body of Nancy Lees, "a young woman who was drowned on the Wednesday Evening before in the Pool of Water called the Daubholes, opposite to the Infirmary." As there was a suspicion she had been thrown into the water the inquest was adjourned to the 28th inst., when a verdict of wilful murder was returned.

[2] See p. 185, note 3, and also p. 88, note 2.

[3] See p. 84, note 1. The unfortunate persons who were whipped had to mount this ladder to reach the stage on which they were whipped in full view of the populace.

19.	To Expences Indicting William Travis for abusing Robert Wroe his Apprentice	: 6: 6
	To indicting Ann Heaton for keeping a Bawdy house	: 14 :
	To prosecuting Kenyon for misusing the late Constables in the Execution of their Office, and for making Riots[1]	1 : 18 : 10
	To Expences after a Felon to Burton upon Trent by Order of Sessions ...	1 : 10 : 6
	To Robert Bradley's Bill of Law prosecuting Seddon and Cooper[2] at Lancaster	11 : 13 : 10
20.	To two fair Copies of the militia Lists as usual	3 : 3 :
	The former Lists were likewise made out and two fair Copies made returned and refused...	3 : 3 :
26.	To a Vagabond Searchwarrant... ...	: 2 :
	To Surgeon Morton attending the Coroners Inquest and giving his Opinion as to the manner of the Death of Nancy Lees[3] drown'd in the Dawbholes	1 : 1 :
	To cleansing the Steps at Salford bridge, they being the Property of the Town for the Use of fetching Water from the River	: 2 :
	To detaining Joseph Kearsley all night, seized by a Gentleman in the night for assaulting him	: 2 : 6
	To an Inquisition a Man kill'd in Newton	: 1 : 4
	To maintaining three Soldiers all night	: 1 : 6

[The Remainder of this year's Accounts is missing.]

---

[1] At the Quarter Sessions in Manchester in January, 1769, " William White of Stretford and Thomas Haddock of Manchester, charged with assaulting the Constables of Manchester, were committed to Lancaster for six months, and to find sureties for their good behaviour for seven years."

[2] See p. 179, note 3.   [3] See p. 187, note 1.

[Constables' Accounts.]

[11th Oct., 1769, to 10th Oct., 1770.]

•••••••••••

[Mʀ SAMUEL CLOWES, junior, and Mʀ JOSEPH RYDER, *Constables.*[1]]

[Previous portion, including all the Disbursements, missing.]

[Receipts]

Contra ... ... Cʳ

1770.		£	s	d
By the Hamlets proportion of ... ... £ 2 : 15 : 0		1 : 16 : 8		
By dᵒ ... ... 47 : 4 : 6		31 : 9 : 8		
By dᵒ ... ... 6 : 8 : 10		4 : 5 : 10		
By dᵒ ... ... 8 : 5 : 8		5 : 10 : 5		
By the totall Collection from the Ley		315 : 2 : 10		
By balance owing to the Constables...		118 : 7 : 2		

[Total] ... ... 476 : 12 : 7

28ᵗʰ Novemʳ 1770. We the Jurors of the Court Leet holden for the Manor of Manchester in the County of Lancaster have examined the foregoing Accounts of Mʳ Samuel Clowes and Mʳ Joseph Ryder late Constables and do allow the same.

(Signed) Wᴹ ALLEN
JOHN HARGREAVE
JOHN HOLFORD
SAMUEL HIBBERT
JOSIAH KEARSLEY
ROBᵀ DANNETT
THOˢ BOARDMAN
WILLIAM HARDMAN
ARNOLD BIRCH
WALTER WILSON
JAMES HARRISON
JAMES DRURY

----

[1] These two Constables were elected at the Court Leet held on the 11th October, 1769. (See *Court Leet Records*, vol. viij., p. 120.)

[Constables' Accounts.]

[10th Oct., 1770, to 16th Oct., 1771.]

•••••••••••

Dr The Town of Manchester to Mr WM. BULLOCK & Mr
JOHN HEYWOOD, *Constables*.[1]

[Disbursements]

1770.

October 11th	To the last years balance[2]	118 : 7 : 2
	To William Bennets bill for repairing Engines	: 16 : 7½
	To searching in Manchester and Salford, and apprehending two Persons suspected of robbing a Man near Midleton	: 6 : 8
	To conveying them to Alkrington and back to Manchester house of Correction, horsehire, three Assistants and expences	: 13 :
	To Presentment drawing for the Sessions	: 1 :
13.	To James Grindrod for stonework at a small Engine house	: 6 : 10
15.	To Coals for the use of the Soldiers in the Guardhouse	: 5 : 1½
16.	To directing and sending 62 Hue & Cry warrants to various parts of England after two robbers	: 7 : 6
	To sending to Cocky Moor for Evidences against two Germans apprehended on suspicion of robbery, horse 1 6 Mess' 1' expences 1'/1d	: 3 : 7

[1] These two Constables were elected at the Court Leet held on the 10th October, 1770. (See *Court Leet Records*, vol. viij., p. 125.)
[2] See p. 180.

17.	To Postage of 62 Hue & Cry warrants paid Mr Willat	1 : 17 : 2
	To making enquiry in Newton in pursuance of an information after the two robbers	: 1 : 6
	To Clerk of the Peace for Business done this Sessions	: 13 : 6
	To discharging Fees paid him for Samuel Oldham a poor man of Manchester, who was committed to Lancaster	1 : 1 : 4
18.	To the Clerks for the warrants appointing new surveyors of the highways ...	: 4 :
	To John Gomersall for expences, Evidences attending there upon Towns Business during the Sessions	: 17 : 6
	To James Wild for maintaining a Dragoon[1] horse when he could not be quartered any where	: 12 :
	To a Messr from Skipton to Manchester, and from Manchr back to Skipton, about the robbers wanted by Hue & Cry	: 7 : 6
22.	To a Messr [Messenger] going to Chester for the Man who was robbed	: 10 : 6
	To another Messr to Burnley lanehead for two Witness's	: 13 : 8
	To going after the highwaymen on Information to Little Lever paid the Constable 1s/7d expences & horsehire all night at Bolton 5s/11d	: 7 : 6
	To an Assistant with a warrant to Hope[2]	: 1 :
	To John Jackson out 4 days in Yorkshire with Hue and Cry warrants, wages and keeping	: 18 : 6
	To James Hanson Do same road ...	: 18 : 6

[1] The dragoons here referred to were the first or Royal Regiment of Dragoons, which had succeeded the second regiment, or the Earl of Waldegrave's Dragoon Guards, which came into the town in April, 1769, with the intention of stopping there at least 12 months.

[2] Hope Hall, near Eccles, was the residence of Thomas Butterworth Bayley, Esq., a well-known and active local magistrate.

	To Samuel Greenlees, Eccles, Bolton, Chorley &c same business...	: 6 :
	To John Barlow Dᵒ Ratcliff, Bury, Blackburn &c	: 5 :
	To James Heys, Ashton, Mottram, Woodhead &c	: 5 :
	To Joshua Travis, Stockport, Cheadle, Altringham &c	: 5 :
27.	To a Load of Coals for Guardhouse	: 5 :
	To Belman's bill for one Cry	: 1 : 6
Novʳ 1.	To apprehending detaining keeping and conveying to Liverpool, two Marine vagabonds who were put to sea there	1 : 14 :
	To an Inquisition over Nicholas Bread-bury	: 2 : 4
2.	To expences conveying Ann Baxter from Manchester to Burton, more than the County allowance	1 : 1 :
7.	To James Bancroft, to leave unbuilt upon, his Land in Toad lane, to make the Kings highway more open ...	2 : 2 :
	To four Money Warts. [Warrants] to the Hamlets each 3ˢ	: 12 :
16.	To a Load of Coals for Guardhouse	: 5 : 5
	To Cash gave John Taylor to carry him to Richmond to see two men detained there, on suspicion of robbing him	2 : 2 :
	To a Messʳ to Burnley lanehead to bring the Mare back he rode on, paid for the mares keep 4ˢ Expences & wages 8ˢ	: 12 :
19.	To Wᵐ Walkers Bill for repairing Dungeon omited entry before ...	: 17 : 6
29.	To Candles bought for privy watch...	: 3
	To Warts [Warrants] to the Hamlets for Lists for Militia	: 3 :
Decʳ 1.	To an Inquisition over Thoˢ Gadman	: 2 : 4
4.	To Coals for the Guardhouse	: 5 : 2½
	To attending Partington a common Whore a night and a day, took by the privy watch	: 2 :

8.	To Tho' Mees bill repairing Guard-house	: 2 : 5
	To Coals again for Guardhouse ...	: 8 : 8½
20.	To John Oldham a Mess' from the Constables with a double horse to warrington all night there, to fetch two Felons on complaint of M' W'' Allen, expences 6/3 Mess two days 3' horsehire 5'...	: 14 : 3
22.	To Hope [1] on the same account horse and Turnpike	: 1 : 1
24.	To a special Watch attending and assisting all night long, when M' Siddalls house was blown down, nine mens wages	: 18 :
	To Joseph Whiteheads bill for repairing Engine Buckets	: 12 : 4
26.	To a quarters rent for the Guardhouse	: 12 : 6
	To Roger Jones for horsehire with John Taylor 25 days at 1' a day ...	1 : 5 :
	To apprehending, detaining a Man all night in Custody, for breaking windows	: 2 : 6
28.	To cleaning steps down to the river at Salfordbridge end	: 2 :
29.	To John Milward, for Locks and Keys about the Dungeon	: 4 :
	To Coals for the Guardhouse	: 7 : 3½
	To the Belman for a Cry	: 1 : 6
	To Tho' Townleys bill for building an Engine house in the Angel yard [2]	2 : 7 : 7
	To Four Men surveying the Town, to take the names of Militia men	4 : 4 :
	To John Moss upon an extraordinary watch	: 2 :
1771. Janry 10.	To the Beadle one quarters Salary ...	2 : 10 :
15.	To the Coroners Inquisition over a man found dead in Hulme	: 1 : 4
16.	To Coals to the Guardhouse	: 2 : 9

---

[1] See p. 191, note 2.

[2] This would appear to be a new Engine House which was to be erected in the yard of the Angel Inn in Market Street. The previous one was in Tib Lane. (See p. 184, note 1.)

		£ s. d.
	To a new Billet Book...	: : 3
21.	To charges impressing 12 baggage Carts to warrington &c [1]	: 12 :
	To Benj. Taylor with one Carts baggage to wigan [1]	: 15 :
	To Coals for the Guardhouse	: 2 : 3½
	To two distressed soldiers...	: 2 :
	To Ellen Askew for making information against makers of bad money, in and about the Almshouses	: 2 :
22	To drawing two fair Duplicates of the Militia Lists as usual	3 : 3 :
23.	To Coals for the Guardhouse	: 7 :
	To giving notice to the Publicans thro' the Town to provide for the 1st Party of Fuzileers [2] coming in... ...	: 2 :
24.	To d" the second Party coming in [2]...	: 2 :
28.	To an Inquisittion over Geo: Norris a soldier	: 2 : 4
Febry 2.	To Coals & candles for the Guardhouse	: 6 : 2
	To sundry expences prosecuting Stelfox [3] at Michm' and Janry Sessions last	3 : 3 : 6
	To Joseph Highams charges to Lancaster, and there, to give Evidence against Sara Stelfox [3] for receiving stolen goods from Orret [4] and Mather, who were both executed at Chester...	3 : 3 :
	To Deputy Kay the same Lent Assize, to give Evidence against Stelfox, [3] who was convicted	3 : 3 :
3.	To supporting soldiers in want of quarters	: 3 : 6

[1] This was when the Dragoons were leaving the town on being relieved by the Welsh Fusileers. (See next note.)

[2] The *Manchester Mercury* of Jan. 22, 1771, states: "Last week five Companies of the Royal Welch Fuzileers, commanded by General Boscawen, arrived here from the North, and the Remainder of the Regiment are expected here in a few Days. Yesterday [Jan. 21] 4 Troops of the first or Royal Regiment of Dragons, commanded by the Earl of Pembroke, marched from hence for Warrington and Wigan."

[3] At the March Assizes at Lancaster this year, Sarah Stelfox was convicted of receiving goods knowing them to have been stolen, and was ordered to be transported for fourteen years.

[4] Timothy Orrett, convicted of stealing goods at Stockport, was executed at Chester after the March Assizes there.

4.	To Coals for the Guardhouse	: 8 :	9
	To Candles for the Soldiers on Guard in Hanging ditch	: 3 :	1
	To Whitewashing the soldiers Hospitall [1]	: 2 :	
6.	To Titus Lees Note for superintending the watch	1 : 6 :	
	To Thomas Holt for 92 nights overlooking the watch	4 : 12 :	
	To Titus Lee for thirteen nights more	: 13 :	
9.	To Shovel, Tongs and Beesom, for Guardroom...	: 7 :	
10.	To an Inquisition over Mary Booth...	: 1 :	4
11.	To Coroners Inquisitions over Hilton, Longshaw & two Boys shudehill ...	: 9 :	4
12.	To three Persons attending John Townley & his wife under wart. [warrant]...	: 3 :	
13.	To Mr Alsop for expences of a privy watch	: 3 :	10
15.	To Coals for the Guardhouse	: 4 :	4
	To attendants before the Justices at Royal Oak [2]	: 3 :	7
19.	To Coals again for the Guard	: 3 :	9
	To an Inquisition over Jonas Wood at Lunatic Hospital [3]	: 2 :	4
20.	To conveying Phebe Dean a Vagrant to sourby [Sowerby]	7 :	
	To quenching the Fire at the Guardroom	: 5 :	3
20.	To a Bill of expences attending the apprehending three Waddingtons, and Samuel Lees, notorious housebreakers	4 : 4 :	9
22.	To Coals for the Guardroom	: 8 :	3
	To two Chimney sweeps assisting at the Fire at Guardh' [Guardhouse] ...	: 2 :	
23.	To Tho' Walker for watching	: 17 :	
	To John Townleys bill repairing Guardroom	1 : 7 :	7

[1] The Soldiers' Hospital has been referred to before. (See p. 93, note 1.)
[2] This Manchester inn has occurred before. (See p. 177, note 1.)
[3] The Lunatic Hospital had recently been erected, adjacent to the Infirmary.

	To Wm Walker for Carpentry work there	: 16 :	3
	To Benj. Oldham & Roger Jones, atting [attending] Waddingtons wives	: 6 :	6
	repaid John Taylor, a Constable Ley overcharged	: 2 :	8
26.	To executing a Wart. [Warrant] against John Morris to Hope attendance &c	: 3 :	
Mar 5.	To Coal for the Guardroom	: 10 :	2
	To support of Soldiers	: 4 :	
12.	To Tho' Walkers bill, attending Plowright under a wart [warrant]	: 11 :	
13.	To High Constables presentment at Bolton 2^s expences 1^s 9^d horsehire 2^s	: 5 :	9
14.	To Coals at the Guardhouse	: 9 :	8½
	To attendants Wittness's and expences, attending Jonas Woods inq^u	: 8 :	10
15.	To the Landlady at Wheatsheaf[1] in Hanging ditch, for the use of a room for the Fuzileers[2]	1 : 1 :	
	To Richard Dixon[3] a second quarters Salary	2 : 10 :	
22.	To Coals for the Guardroom	: 5 :	10
	To John Hopes bill for horsehire, on the Constables acct	1 : 11 :	
23.	To Saml Lees going to york, to get an Habeas Corpus to remove Timothy Orret[4] from Chester to Lancaster, to give evid[ence] against Sara Stelfox[5]	1 : 1 :	
26.	To Slaters bill, repairing Guardroom	: 17 :	0½
29.	To Guardhouse Coals	: 8 :	9
	To a quarters rent for Guardhouse ...	1 : 5 :	
April 5.	To Belmans bill for sundry Crys ...	: 4 :	6

---

[1] This inn has not, I think, occurred before.
[2] See p. 194, note 2.
[3] Richard Dixon was the Beadle.
[4] In the *Manchester Mercury* for Oct. 23, 1770, there is an account of Timothy Orrett's arrest in Cheshire for felony, after he had been discharged from the late Assizes at Lancaster. He was afterwards tried at Chester Assizes, convicted, and executed.
[5] See p. 194, note 3.

10	To attending W[m] Butterworth's[1] wife all night in private custody three persons		: 5 :	
	attending W[m] Butterworth[1] in like manner, two men with him two days and two nights		: 10 :	
	To three Men attending John Reed under a Bench wart [warrant]		: 3 :	
	To three Assistants to apprehend John Matley		: 3 :	
	To conveying Butterworth[1] to the house of Correction		: 1 :	
11.	To an Inquisition over Butterworth's[1] apprentice		: 2 :	4
13.	To Warts [Warrants] to the Hamlets for Militia to assemble		: 3 :	
	To D° for Lists of new Overseers ...		: 3 :	
	To a Man & a woman attending Butterworths family, whilst the Coroners Inquest sat		: 5 :	
	To a double Inquisition over Butterworth's apprent[ice][1]		: 2 :	8
	To a Justices warrant against him & his wife		: 3 :	
14.	To three Men to execute it		: 1 :	6
	To Chairmen twice, for a child to be Evidence		: 2 :	
	To three Persons, summoning many Evidences		: 3 :	
15.	To four Jurors attending two long days, when W[m] Butterworth[1] was found guilty of wilful Murder, and commited to Lanc[r]		: 10 :	
	To two Witness's attending same time		: 5 :	

---

[1] In the *Manchester Mercury* for April 16, 1771, there is the following paragraph:—
"Last Night the Coroner's Jury finish'd their Inquiry concerning the Death of Jemima Dixon, a poor girl lately bound Apprentice to one William Butterworth, a Check Weaver of this Town; when they brought in their Verdict, wilful Murder, against the Master by treating her with great Severity and Cruelty and refusing her necessary Sustenance. The Master was accordingly sent to Lancaster Castle to take his Trial at the next Assizes."
He was tried at the August Assizes, convicted, and sentenced to death, but was ultimately reprieved and transported.

To another Chair & Ale to the Men...	: 1 :	3
18. To Presentment drawing, for Quarter Sessions	: 1 :	
To James Rushworth to Chester, about Stelfox[1] wages 6ˢ expences 7ˢ/6ᵈ	: 13 :	6
To impressing 20 carriages for the Fuzileers[2]	1 :	
20. To Coals for the Guardhouse	: 3 :	6
To Clerk of the Peace for warrants this Sessions	: 3 :	
To him, Fees and other Business done this Sessions	1 : 13 :	
To Coals again for the Guard	: 6 :	8
23. To an Inquisition over James Hartley	: 2 :	4
24. To Holbrook of Midleton, expences of many persons at his house, about scotchman hiding his money	: 9 :	6
To four Bills of Indictment this Sessions	: 8 :	
To Cryer of the Court for swaring Witness's	: 6 :	6
To Jurors, Bailif Fees...	: 7 :	
To Witnesses attending the Trials one for keeping a Bawdy house, one for a misdemeanor, & two for a Felony	: 15 :	
To a High Constables warrant for County rates, and Governor of the house of Correction's wages	15 : 4 :	5
To conveying Eliz. Clarkson by Pass to Halifax, from whence she was brought back, the Pass being found there unlawful	: 13 :	8
To Paper, ruling and writing the Ley-book	1 : 10 :	
To conveying William Butterworth[3] to Lancaster under the Coroners Commitment, for Murdering his Apprentice	2 : 18 :	
To Waïts [Warrants] to the Hamlets, Overseers to Account	: 3 :	

---

[1] See p. 194, note 3.   [2] See p. 194, note 2.   [3] See p. 197, note 1.

	To James Barret for assisting the watch	: 1 : 6
24.	Paid John Gomersalls Bill for Meat & drink for Witness's attending the Publick Quarter Sessions three days	1 : 1 : 1½
	To Apprehending detaining and keeping all night, bringing before Justice, and conveying to house of Correct. Ann Mackenny for being a lewd woman	: 5 : 6
May 11.	To an Inquisition over Edward Dye	: 2 : 4
	To Warrants to the Hamlets for Assessors of Land Tax	: 3 :
	To a Load of Coals for the Guardhouse	: 6 : 5½
	To attending Matley a night & a day for breaking peace	: 2 : 6
	To Straw for the Dungeon	: 4 :
13.	To an Inquisition over Thomas Stafford	: 2 : 4
	To 22 new Window Leybooks[1] ...	: 11 :
	To binding them in Red	: 1 : 3
23.	To an Inquisition over Mary Appleton	: 1 : 4
	To 4 Thrave[2] more Straw to the Dungeon ... ... ·	: 4 :
June 3.	To sending sundry Messengers to give Invitation to the High Sherrif[3] and many Gentlemen, to drink the Royal Healths, being the añiver[s]ary of his Majestys birthday[4]	: 3 :
4.	To the Ringers on the same Occasion[4]	: :
	To Musicians same time 8 at 3ˢ each[4]	1 : 4 :
	To Militia Soldiers for Firing[4]	2 : 2 :
7.	To two Assistants conveying Thoˢ Davis to the house of Correc̃	: 1 :
13.	To an Inquisition over John Greenwood drowned	: 2 : 4

---

[1] That is, the books in which the names of those who had to pay the window tax and the respective amounts were entered.

[2] "Thrave," an old word meaning twenty-four sheaves of corn, or twelve of straw.

[3] The High Sheriff of Lancashire this year was Ashton Lever, of Alkrington, Esq.

[4] The birthday of King George III. (June 4th) was always the occasion of festivities in the town. (See previous Accounts.)

	To Ja⁺ Dawson for apprehending Wᵐ Ward & Margery his wife under Wart. [Warrant] for keeping a bad house & detaining & keeping him all night, and other trouble	4 :
13.	To Warrants to the Hamlets Collectors of Window Tax to make their payments	: 3 :
26.	To John Menton his wife & 2 children to Hull	: 2 :
	To Sundry Vagrants and Passengers relieved from the 11ᵗʰ of October last to this day	4 : 16 : 2
	To Straw for the use of the Soldiers in the Guard room	: 5 :
	To sundry Expences and Assistants attending the prosecution of Nield Devet and Ann Fox for Felony ...	: 11 :
28.	To Docter Drinkwater for examining the body and atting [attending] the Inquest of Jemima Dixon¹ Butterworths Apprentice	1 : 1 :
	To cleansing Steps at Salford Bridge	: 2 :
29.	To John Rawlinson for horschire twice to Rochdale to serve a Warrant there	: 4 :
	To John Shelmerdines² bill dated 23ᵈ of May last a house w[h]ere prisoners not proper for the Dungeon are usualy detained for Meat drink and lodging for them, and persons attending them for the then last 15 Months	4 : 6 : 11
July 6.	To Coals for the Guard in Hangingditch	: 2 : 6
	To the Belmans bill for five Crys ...	: 6 : 6
	To eating and Liquor for Edward Smith and Mⁿ Bolton from Burnley lanehead two Witnesses's attending the Sessions against a Felon apprehended by Hue and Cry having one horse with them 15ˢ/3ᵈ horsehire and their loss of time 14ˢ	1 : 9 : 3

---

¹ See p. 197, note 1.
² John Shelmerdine evidently kept one of the smaller inns in the town, but I am not certain which it was.

	To expences with Foot Serjeants setling their quarters	: 2 : 6
	Paid more to Edward Smith from Burnley lanehead	: 4 : 2
	Expences at Dangerous Corner[1] on a privy Watch	: 4 : 6
6.	To John Oldham and Thomas Walker two days and two nights in quest of two Waddingtons two housebreakers in the Month of February last... ...	1 : 8 : 8½
11th	To Guardhouse rent one quarter ...	1 : 5 :
	To Liquor to the Men who assisted in quenching the flames when Guardhouse was on Fire	: 5 :
	To carry James Connally an old Man into Ireland	: 4 : 6
12th	To Ann Duncan very ill to take her over into Ireland	: 4 :
	To Joseph Highams expences at Dangerous Corner[1] whilst attending the Sessions upon Stelfox's account...	: 7 : 9½
14th	Mary Rose and four children to York	: 4 :
	To a pair of Shoes for the Beadle by Jos. Whitehead	: 6 :
17th	To James Barret to execute a Summons of Justice Townleys at Ashton.	: 2 :
	To James Barret an extraordinary Watch	: 1 : 6
18.	To an Inquisition over Jonathan Amnet ·	: 1 : 4
20.	To James Dawsons bill for going into Cheshire after two theives and other trouble with prisoners	1 : : 2
22.	To detaining a Woman in Custody all night for fighting and raising a riot in Shudehill a woman attendant &c ...	: 2 : 6
24.	To presentment drawing to the Sessions	: 1 :
29.	To an Inquisition over Widow Ball...	: 2 : 4
	To John Gomersalls bill for Meat and drink to Witnesses attending these Sessions	: 18 : 11

---

[1] See p. 5, note 1.

To Eliz. Wolfenton for three days attending the Sessions to find a Bill against John Jones for keeping a Mastiff... ... ...   : 3 :

To Rich⁴ Wakefield on the same account ... ...   : 5 : 6

To Thoˢ Miller on the same occasion   : 4 :

29. To Wolfenton & Wakefield attending at Mʳ Jones Office ... ...   : 1 :

Augˢᵗ 1. To Edmund Wrigleys bill for repairing the Engines[1] ... ...   1 : 10 :

To Titus Lee for attending privy watch three nights ... ...   : 3 :

> On prosecuting John Matley[2] at Lancaster Assizes as being a common disturber of the peace in Manchester.

16ᵗʰ Two special Indictments ... 0 : 12 : 6
swearing in Court ... ... 0 : 2 : 6
Bailifs Fees... ... ... 0 : 4 : 0
James Knowles an Evidence six days away ...   3 : 3 : 0
Mʳ Humphreys attorney at Law dᵒ ... ...   4 : 4 : 0

———— –   8 : 6 :

> On prosecuting William Butterworth[3] for murdering Jemima Dixon an apprentice of his from Ackworth Hospital[4]

Conveying five Witnesses thither at 3ᵈ a mile each... ... ...   3 : 12 : 6

Meat drink and lodging upon the road ... ...   1 . 2 . 6

To three days Meat and drink at Lancaster ...   1 . 17 : 6

For lodging three nights there ... ...   0 : 10 : 0

To bringing the same Witnesses back ... ...   3 : 12 : 6

————

[1] See p. 87, note 1.

[2] I do not find any account of this John Matley in the notice of the August Assizes at Lancaster this year.

[3] See p. 197, note 1.   [4] See p. 207, note 2.

	keeping them upon the road back	1 : 0 : 0	
	To Edward Hartley for attending them to the Assizes and back again	2 : 12 : 6	
	To Ralph Worsley giving Evidence	1 : 1 : 0	
	To Ann Wood one of the Evidences for loss of time	0 : 10 : 6	
	To Mary Butterworth the same	0 : 10 : 6	
	To Deputy Kays horse-hire & Expences	3 : 13 : 6	
	To Incidentall expences during these prosecutions	0 : 13 : 6	20 : 16 : 6
17.	To the Ringers Judge in Town ...		: 10 : 6
19.	To Rich⁰ Dickenson attending a Man a day and a night for stealing a Watch		: 2 :
24.	To returning a Prisoner under Warrant to the Mayor of Wigan horse 3ˢ Turnpikes & Bating 1 6 ...		: 4 : 6
	To detaining John Hind[1] conveying him to Justice and to the House of Correction expences and Assistants ...		: 2 : 6
	To James Dawsons bill for assisting the watch		: 15 :
	To Eliz. Shepleys bill for smithwork repairing Dungeon		1 : 9 : 6
27.	To Wᵐ Walkers bill for Carpentry there		1 : 2 : 9
	To Thoˢ Shires for Masonry there ...		: 9 : 2½
	To the Engine Men for Ale		: 1 :
28.	To Surgeon John Drinkwaters bill for going to Lancasʳ there to give Evidence against Wᵐ Butterworth[2] for murdering the abovementioned Jemima Dixon		10 : : 4

---

[1] Hind was caught attempting to get into a warehouse near St. Ann's Square.
[2] See p. 197, note 1.

29.	To the Landlord at Kings Arms for Dragoon[1] Horses kept there waiting to be quartered by [Mr Thos Stott crossed through] when constab[le]... ...	: 12 : 6
Sepr 2.	To the Engine Mens bill for Eleven Months	11 : 11 :
4.	To the High Constables warrant repairing Ribchester and Ribble Bridges	7 : 4 : 5
6.	To an Inquisition over Edward Mass	: 2 : 4
14.	To an Inquisition over Martha Gaythorn	: 2 : 4
22.	To an Inquisition over Ann Newton[2]	: 2 : 4
	To Straw for the Dungeon	: 5 :
	To the Beadle of Salford[3] for serving a warrant in Salford	: 1 :
28.	To an Inquisition over George Baldwin	: 2 : 4
	To Warrants to the Hamlets for Alehouses to take Licences	: 3 :
	To D^o to return new Lists of Freeholders for Jurors	: 3 :
	To three dark Lanthorns for the watch	: 4 : 6
	To keeping Mary Wyley a Tramper[4] in distress 3 days	: 3 :
28.	apprehending and detaining John Shelmerdine a common drunkard and disturber of the peace and committment to the house of Correction ...	: 5 :
	To sundry expences at James Hodgkinsons upon Prisoners, attendants and Witnesses at Justices meetings since the 18th of May last	: 15 : 8
	To cleansing Steps at Milbrow one year	: 4 :

---

[1] The Royal Welsh Fusileers had left the town in March and April, and had been succeeded by the third regiment of Dragoons (not "Dragoon Guards"), commanded by the Earl of Albemarle.

[2] Ann Newton was killed by her sister's husband during a quarrel in the latter's house. (See also p. 205, note 2.)

[3] This is the first time the Salford Beadle has been mentioned in these Accounts.

[4] See p. 119, note 2.

To repaid Rich⁴ Dixon[1] for one Inquisition	: 1 : 4
d° for maintenance of prisoners in the dungeon	: 3 : 8
To Richard Dixons[1] bill for money advanced in the Constables business and extraordinary Messuages [*sic* for Messages] &c	2 : 1 : 5
To attending and keeping the Towns watch to their duty 25 several whole nights by Rich⁴ Dixon the Beadle ...	1 : 5 : 6
Octob 2. To an Inquisition over William Smith...	: 2 : 4
7. To an Inquisition over Joseph Taylor.	: 2 : 4
8. To John Shelmerdines bill on account of Prisoners being detained there ...	1 : 7 : 2
To three Assistants with the Deputy to apprehend Joseph Nutt[2] suspected of murdering his wives sister who was seized, and detained three days and three nights waiting for the Coroners Inquisition	: 9 :
To conveying him to Lancaster under the Coroners committment for Manslaughter upon the body of his said wives Sister[2]	2 : 18 :
To Rich⁴ Dixon the Beadle two quarters Salary	5 : :
To a Note of relief given to Passengers Beggars and Trampers[3] from the 27ᵗʰ of June last...	4 : 6 : 3
To several passengers by Mʳ Heywood	: 4 : 6
To an old Sailor	: 1 :

---

[1] Richard Dixon was the Beadle.

[2] The Coroner's Jury, according to the statement in the *Manchester Mercury* for Sept. 24th, brought in a verdict of manslaughter against Joseph Nutt, of Flixton, for causing the death of his wife's sister, Elizabeth [*sic*] Newton, a young woman, who died in the Infirmary from the injuries she had received at his hands. She came to Nutt's house, and finding there had been a quarrel between him and his wife, began to use "threatening and approbius words" against him, when he threw a piece of iron at her, which struck her on the head and fractured her skull. He was tried at the Spring Assizes at Lancaster, and being convicted of manslaughter, was burnt in the hand and ordered to be imprisoned for six months.

[3] See p. 119, note 2.

Octob 8.	To Tho' Barton for mending Constables Staffs	: 2 : 10
	To Thomas Walker and three others attending in the Market to prevent Regrating and Forestalling[1]	2 : 9 : 6
	To Postage of Letters paid by Mr Bullock	: 1 :
	To Mr Allsop at Bulshead[2] the totall of his four Notes	7 : 1 : 9
	To Mrs Cromptons Note of expences on the Anniversary of the Kings Birthday[3]	10 : 2 : 6
	To a Note of expences at Tho' Vauxs on privy Watch	: 7 : 9
	To a poor passenger by Mr Heywood	: 1 :
	To paper and writing the preparation of twenty two paper books for the service of the Assessors of the window Duty and binding the same	: 7 : 6
15.	James Hulme a Tramper[4]	: 1 :
	a Tramping Woman at Bul[s]head ...	: : 6
	To assistants attending Giles Aldred for Croftbreaking[5] and Richard Cresswell for buying Stolen Yarn all day seperate	: 2 : 6
	To Mr Norths bill for one year Clothing the Beadle	3 : 4 : 1½
	To Messrs Low & Bate two years Do...	9 : : 8
	To Deputy Kay one years Salary ...	30 : :

[Total] ... ... £409 : 15 : 3

---

[1] A "regrator" was a person who bought corn, &c., in any fair or market and sold it again at any fair or market within four miles of the one in which it was bought. A "forestaller" was one who bought up corn, &c., going to be sold in any fair or market, or before it came into the open market, with the view of enhancing the price of such corn, &c.

[2] The Bull's Head seems now to be carried on by Mr. Allsop in the place of Mr. Joseph Budworth. (See p. 119, note 4.)

[3] This was on June 4th. (See p. 199, note 4). Mrs. Crompton carried on Crompton's Coffee House after the death of her husband, James Crompton. (See p. 153, note 2.)

[4] See p. 119, note 2.

[5] Croft-breaking meant breaking into the crofts or meadows in which yarn was laid out to be bleached and stealing it. It was severely punished, and in this case both prisoners had seven years' transportation.

[**Receipts**]
                    Contra   ...   .   C^r

1771

By Cash received from Mr John Hague Misegatherer   131 : 17 :

By Mr Richard Scholes the other Misegatherer ... 175 : 2 : 8

By John Matley[1] prosecuted as a common disturb[er] ⎱   2 : 2 :
   of the Peace as a Fine ordered by Judge Gould ⎰

By the Trustees of Ackworth Hospitall[2] in part of ⎱
   the charges of prosecuting Wm Butterworth for ⎰ 5 : 5 :
   murdering an Apprentice Girl had from thence ⎰

By the Hamlets their proportion of £15 : 4 : 5 ...   10 : 3 :

By D^o proportion of ... ... 7 : 4 : 5 ...   4 : 16 : 3

By balance owing to these Constables ... ...   80 : 9 : 4

[Total] ... ... £409 : 15 : 3

October 30th 1771. We the Jurors of the Court Leet holden for the Manor of Manchester in the County of Lancaster have examined the foregoing Acc^t of Mr Wm Bullock & Mr John Heywood late Constables & do allow the same.

(*Signed*)   CHARLES FORD   WILL^M HOUGHTON
              THO^S STOTT   THO^S WHITTAKER
              BENJA: BOWER
              JOHN BELL
              SAM GOODIER
              J^{no} WHITTAKER
              SAM. WHITE
              FOLLIOTT POWELL
              ROB: HYDE
              JOHN TIPPING
              ARCH^D BELL
              RICH^D WITHINGTON

---

[1] See p. 202, note 2.

[2] The apprentice girl, Jemima Dixon, whose death had been caused by William Butterworth (see p. 197, note 1), had come to him from Ackworth Hospital. This was a Foundling Hospital at Ackworth, near Pontefract, in Yorkshire.

[Constables' Accounts.]

[16th Oct., 1771, to 14th Oct., 1772.]

••••••••••••

Ðr The Town of Manchester to Mᴿ BENJAMIN BOWER and Mᴿ JOHN BELL, *Constables.*[1]

[Disbursements]

1771.

Octob 16.	To the last years Balance[2]	80: 9: 4
17.	To drawing Presentment to Sessions as usual ... ... }	: 1 :
	On prosecuting John Jones's Traverse for keeping a Mastiff Dog	
	To Thoˢ Miller of Withington to give Evidence summons & serving 1/6 paid him for two days attendance 3ˢ... ... }	: 4 : 6
	To summoning Eliz. Wolfenton another Evidence 1ˢ paid her for two days attendance and meat & drink 3ˢ }	: 4 :
	To summoning Richᵈ Wakefield another Evidence 1ˢ his attendce two days 4ˢ... ... ... }	: 5 :
	On prosecuting Mary Newton and Ellen Thomas for Felony...	
	To Three Evidences Meat and drink two days ... ... }	: 4 :
	To two days wages for each	: 6 :
	To swearing Evidences in Court ...	: 1 : 6
	On prosecuting John Matley[3] as a common disturber of the Town ...	
	To summoning two Witnesses... ...	: 2 :

---

[1] These two Constables were elected at the Court Leet held on the 16th October, 1771. (See *Court Leet Records,* vol. viij., p. 136.)

[2] See p. 207.

[3] See p. 202, note 2.

To a Woman attending as Witness three days	: 3 :	
To Mr Arrowsmith's Man attending three days	: 4 :	6
To sundry expences attending this matter	: 2 :	6
On prosecuting John Johnson for stealing a Silver Watch out of a Warehouse near Churchyard		
To a Mess^r three times into Chetham to summon two Evidences who were very unwilling to attend	: 3 :	
To Summonses and summoning two Witnesses in Manchester	: 2 :	
17. To a Meeting at the Packhorse[1] Churchyardside to prepare Witness's	: 1 :	6
To the Clerk of the Peace altering the Indictment and adding fresh Witness's thereunto	: 4 :	
To swearing two of these Witnesses in Court	: 1 :	
To Bailliff of the Grand Jury	: 2 :	6
To Clerk of the Peace for two Bench Warrants agst Handly	: 8 :	
To the Cryer of the Court	: 5 :	6
To Deputy Kays dining and extra-ordinary expences attending Sessions three days	: 5 :	
To John Gomersall's Bill for Meat and drink during the three days Sessions	: 18 :	1
19. To a quarters rent for the Guardhouse	1 : 5 :	
To John Atkinson to Leeds	: :	6
To Rachel Bington to Carlisle	: :	6
To Jane Trotter to Whitehaven ...	: 1 :	
20. To John Birch and his Son to Ireland	: 1 :	
To Ann Wakes to Stockport	: 1 :	
To Joseph Hanson and his wife to Leeds	: 1 :	
To Peter Oldhams Son for his Assistance and attendance two days...	: 3 :	

---

[1] This Manchester inn has not, I think, occurred before in these Accounts.

	To employing three Persons to Apprehend one Oldham suspected of having stolen a Womans Cloak off her back and pursuing after him to Chadderton	: 3 :
20.	To Sarah Barrow & 4 children into Cheshire	: 2 :
	To Mary Shaw & her child to Stockport	: 1 :
	To Scotch Peggy for Lodging & Meat to Trampers[1]	: 3 : 6
Nov[r] 2[d]	To an High Constables Warrant for repairs of Bridges &c...	30 : 1 : 7
	To the Belman for three Crys	: 4 : 6
	To Susan Brown & her child to Ketleby	: 1 :
7.	To James Kentish to Dunstable ...	: : 6
	To John and Grace Ross to Perth in Scotland	: 1 :
	To Angush M[c]donald & his Wife to Scotland	: 1 :
	To an Inquisition W[m] Hunt drowned	: 1 : 4
	To Rob[t] M[c] Bend a blind Man with a Wife & 2 children	: 2 :
	To Roger Jones a special Errand to the Constables of Chetham and of Broughton	: 1 :
8.	To an Inquisition over a Man Killed at Bradford...	: 2 : 4
	To Augustine Tabre Wife & two children to Nottingham	: 1 :
	To keeping them all night	: 2 :
10.	To Susan Ablet to Daresbury extraordinary lame	: 2 :
	To Postage of sundry Letters	: 1 : 3
	To Notices to the Hamlets to pay their proportion of £30 . 1 . 7... ...	: 3 :
	To two Notices of Money to the Eleven Hamlets ommited last ye[r] ...	: 6 :
	To John Oldham attending Ann Buckley under a Bench Warrant a whole day 1[s] Expences 6[d]	: 1 : 6

---

[1] See p. 119, note 2.

	To two persons attending Tho' Travis a whole day waiting till Justice Bradshaw[1] could hear the complaint ...	:	2 :	
	To Mary Shore to Chesterfield waiting till a pass could be obtained	:	1 :	6
11.	Eliz: Collinge to Liverpoole	:	1 :	
	To Sara Peacock big with child to London	:	1 :	
	To Charles Holdaway to Bath	:	1 :	
	To Sara Traffles to her Husband at Fort St George	:	1 :	
13.	To Eliz: Bright & 4 children to Bingley Yorkshire	:	2 :	
	To Ralph Darcy to Scotland	:	:	6
	To Tho' Fowlers Bill for six p' of Stockings for the Beadle from time to time	1 :	2 :	4
	To an Inquisition over John Marshall 30th Octob. last	:	2 :	4
	To Roger Jones Bill for attending Felons sundry times	:	8 :	6
15.	To Tho' Pullen and his wife to Whitehaven	:	1 :	
	Susan Townley to Stockport	:	1 :	
16.	To Dan' Stock to Bentom	:	:	6
	To Tho' Salisbury to Carlisle	:	:	6
	To Tho' Perry his Wife and two children to Wrexham	:	1 :	6
	To Tho' Kelly to Greenwich Hospitall	:	1 :	
	To Ann Baguley committed to the House of Correction for stealing Loaves	:	3 :	
18.	To John Brown to London	:	:	6
	To Wm Beesley a discharged soldier to Leeds	:	1 :	
25.	To Ann Jones & 2 children to Pattrington	:	1 :	6
	Richd Stevenson & his Wife to Nantwich	:	1 :	
26.	Wm Garstang wife & 3 children to Harwich	:	1 :	6

[1] This was, I think, John Bradshaw, Esq.

	To John Gwyn an old Soldier to Whitehaven	: 1 :
27.	To Francis Worthington to Aston in Cheshire	: 1 :
	To Mary Smith & 2 children to Carlisle	: 1 : 6
	To Michael Mavroe to Carlisle... ...	: : 6
	To Marg' Fossell to Liverpoole ...	: 1 :
28.	To an Inquisition over Wm Greenhall	: 2 : 4
	To John Haworth Constables upon privy watch 19th of this Month 3' & to Assisstants 1' 6^d	: 4 : 6
	To keeping Tho' Kellow a Vagrant 3 days...	: 1 : 6
Decr 4.	To Mr Jones's Bill for Law	38 : 6 : 5
	To a Years Rent for the Engine House[1] in Tiblane due at Michaelmas last	3 : 3 :
6.	To Expences of a privy Watch... ...	: 3 : 6
	The Sign of the Mule[2] in Kingstreet was used as a Watch house during all last year where persons apprehended by the Watch were frequently detained till brought before a Justice of the Peace the Costs whereof was as under.	
	To one time 5' : 4^d another time 4' . 7^d again 2'	: 11 : 11
	To another time 3' : 11^d again 1'. 3^d and again 4 . 6	: 9 : 8
	To another time 3 . 4 . and again 6 . 2	: 9 : 6
	To Titus Lee superintending the Watch 47 nights betwixt the 6th day of February 1771 to the 15th of last November	2 : 7 :
	To Tho' Holt for superintending the Watch 60 nights ending at same time	3 : :
	To Ellen Reada [sic] attending the Sessions to give Evidence in a Felony	: 2 : 6
	To Edward Crane into Scotland ...	: 1 :

---

[1] See p. 184, note 1.
[2] This house is here mentioned for the first time.

To sundry other Passengers relieved
as follows viz

To John Wilson to London	: 1 :	
To Isaac Ballsall to Tiverton	: : 6	
To Isabell Fisher to Newport	: 1 :	
To William Cornwall & his wife to Liverpoole	: 1 :	
To Henry Dunblaine to Scotland ...	: : 6	
To John Condon to Shields	: 1 :	
To Sara Livistone to London	: : 6	
To John Shepherd to Scarbrough ...	: : 6	
To Susan Beauclerk to Perth	: : 6	
To Alex* Fletcher to Liverpoole ...	: 1 :	
To Jane Evans to Carlisle...	: 1 :	
To James Boyle to Liverpooll	: 1 :	
To an old Soldier going to Chester...	: 1 :	
To Mary Barns & her Daug* to Cockermouth	: 1 :	
To Ellen Dugdale to Burton	: : 6	
To Ann Ayres & her child to Berwick	: 1 :	
8.	To Thomas Ogden for superintending the watch six nights	: 6 :
11.	To Titus Lees Bill for watching and other assistance	: 12 :
	To Joseph Taylors Bill for Lead to the Dungeon	: 19 : 4
	To Joseph Thornhill's Note for work done at the Exchange by desire of the Justices at Quarter Sess	: 3 :
	To James Brown for Carpenters work there	: 10 : 1½
	To Thomas Whitlow for maintenance of Prisoners in the House of Correction	: 10 : 6
12.	Hanah Watson & her Son to Chatham	: 1 :
	To removing Thomas Kelly by Pass to Stockport he being sick & Lame more than the County allowance ...	: 2 : 2
	James Webster to London	: : 6
	James Henley to Lincoln he being lame	: 1 :
13.	To Robert Forsath and his wife to Durham	: 1 :

14.	To Mr Norths Bill for Cloth for Beadles Clothes	3 : 13 : 10½
	To Messrs Hindleys Notes for Trimming	1 : : 5
	To Thomas Jessop to Warrington ...	: : 6
	To Eliz: Holt & two children to Chester	: 1 :
	To Daniel Terry to Liverpoole... ...	: : 6
	To Ann Cardwell to Worcester ...	: : 6
16.	To James Knott to Shrewsbury ...	: : 6
	To John Wright very badly to Barnsley	: 1 : 6
19.	To Arthur Strode to Plymouth ...	: : 6
	To Mary Boyd to Flockton	: 1 :
	To Samuel Warrington to Beverley	: : 6
	To Richard Dixon the Beadle one quarters wage	2 : 10 :
21.	To a pair of Stockings for the Beadle	: 4 : 10
	To Patrick Goodman to Liverpoole...	: 1 :
	To Robert Cawthorn a wife & two sick children into Scotland	: 2 :
	To removing John Wright by Pass cost more than the County allowance he lying two days sick upon the road	: 5 :
23.	To John Thwaite to Weymouth ...	: : 6
	To Ann Nelson big [with child] into Westmoreland	: 1 :
	To Edward Butler to Craven	: : 6
	To Jane Gaskell with four children to Carlisle	: 1 :
24.	To Nicholas Loftus to Sheffield ...	: : 6
	To Ann Standring to London	: 1 :
	To John Morris to Plymouth	: : 6
	To Jos. Whiteheads Note for Beadles Shoes and repairing Engine Buckets	: 8 : 3
26	To James Royley wife & child to Liverpoole	: 1 :
	To Orme Wright to Carlisle	: : 6
	To returning two Warrants to Belfield¹ Horschire 2 . 6. Expences 1^s Mess^r wages 1^s	: 4 : 6

---

¹ Richard Townley, of Belfield, Esq., was an active Lancashire Magistrate at this time.

	To Susan Smith & Son to Woodhouse	:	1 :	
	To Robert Taylor & another Tramper[1]	:	1 :	6
	To Mary Bridge to Ratcliff	:	1 :	
27.	To Ann White & child to Halifax ...	:	1 :	
	To Robert Oates to Liverpoole... ...	:	:	6
	To Dolly Horner & her child to Wakefield	:	1 :	
	To Mary Mitchell to Leeds	:	:	6
	To Nancy Murry big [with child] to Doncaster	:	1 :	
	To Joseph Shoulton for cleaning Steps at Salford Bridge	:	2 :	
31.	To Grace Miller & 3 children to Poulton in Files [in the Fylde] ...	:	1 :	
	To Mary Smith & 2 children to Cocker	:	1 :	
	To Samuel Jackson lame to Wi[l]mslow	:	1 :	6
	To Thomas Williams to Wrexham ...	:	1 :	
1772.	To Samuel Laver an old Soldier ...	:	:	6
Janry 2.	To John M'Forleane & his wife to Scotland	:	1 :	
	To Ismael Bashaw to Constantinople[2]	:	1 :	
	To Robert Doggs to Sheffield	:	:	6
	To John Icome to Tuckenfield ...	:	:	6
	To James Powis to Winchester ...	:	:	6
3.	To Marg' Kempster to Liverpoole ...	:	:	6
	To a Soldiers wife & child to Ashton	:	1 :	
	To John Barlow to Leeds...	:	:	6
	To two Persons to apprehend Vivers under a Warrant for Embezelment who could not be found	:	2 :	
	To two Strollers[3] in the Street... ...	:	1 :	
	To maintaining & detaining Sam. Yates a day & a night in Custody for Theft	:	1 :	6
20.	To enquiring after Robert Buckley under a Wart. [Warrant] for Embezelment when he could not be found having five Persons to assist	:	3 :	

[1] See p. 119, note 2.
[2] This traveller was on a long journey to Constantinople.
[3] See p. 2, note 6, also p. 98, note 1.

To employing two Persons to assist the Deputy to apprehend Jonath. Pilling under a Warrant for destroying Game in Cheshire	: 2 :	
21. To expences on Sunday evening with the watch the night being very severe	: 1 :	
To Alexr Monroe to Radnor	: 1 :	6
To the Engine Men for extraordinary trouble...	: 2 :	6
To James Forrester to Marlbrough...	: 1 :	
To John Hughs ill to Wrexham ...	: 1 :	
To Ellen Ivanson to Sheffield	: 1 :	
To Joseph Wood to Lancaster ...	: :	6
To George Miles & his wife to Liverpoole	: 1 :	
To a lame Stranger	: 1 :	
To Luke Gibson to Yarmouth... ...	: :	6
To Ann Hurst & her child to Barnsley	: 1 :	
To George Metcalf to London ...	: 1 :	
21. To John Perry to Leeds with a sick Son	: 1 :	
To Isaac Wroe to Ireland...	: :	6
To Mary Lee to Macclesfield	: :	6
To John Corbet to Kendall	: 1 :	
To Joseph Taylor very lame to Hayfield	: 2 :	
To James Wilcox to London	:	6
To John Blanchard to Giberalter ...	:	6
To Richard Dixon for trouble ab{t} Sam. Yates...	:	6
23. To presentment to the Sessions ...	: 1 :	
To the Officers of the Sessions sundry fees	: 5 :	
To George Claytons Bill for Candles to the Guardhouse &c. during last year	2 : 3 : 7	
Jane Penketh to Carlisle	: :	6
To Thomas Vaun to Ireland	: :	6
25. To Sara Langdall to Worcester... ...	: :	6
To Thomas Greenwood wife & 2 children to Bradford in Yorkshire in great distress	: 2 :	
27. To Ann Floyd to Wem in Shropshire	: :	6
To Joseph Roberts to Shrewsbury ...	: :	6
To Mary Job to Nottingham	: :	6

	To removing William Thomas & his family by Pass to Sourby [Sowerby] cost more than the allowance	:	5 :	6
29.	To Jane Saunders to Newcastle ...	:	1 :	
	To James Smith & wife to Birmingham	:	1 :	
30.	To Charles Appleby to d"...	:	:	6
	To Thomas Horn & his wife to Reading	:	1 :	
	To James Savage a Stranger	:	1 :	
	To John Jones to Bishopscastle ...	:	1 :	
30.	To an Inquisition over William Hope [1]	:	1 :	4
	To detaining maintaining and attending John Ashworth kept in Custody twenty three days by the Justices order as by bill	4 :	7 :	10
Febry 2ᵈ	To John White an old Soldier... ...	:	1 :	
	To Anthony Thorp to Newcastle ...	:	:	6
	To Humphry Robinson to Warrington		:	6
5.	To expences of overlooking the Watch from the 11ᵗʰ Novʳ last to this present day	3 :	17 :	
	To Betty Waring a sick Stranger ...	:	1 :	
	To Luke Makin to Wotton	:	:	6
17.	To necessary attendance of Robert Buckley and his Son John under a Warrant for a breach of the Peace a whole day	:	2 :	
	To the expences of a privy watch this night	:	3 :	6
	To an Inquisition over John Clough [2]	:	2 :	4
	To an Inquisition over Esther Brabazon [3]	:	2 :	4
	To an Inquisition over Joshua Walker	:	2 :	4
18.	To the Beadles Note for Straw and cleaning the Dungeon	:	4 :	6
	To six Persons assisting the Privy watch	:	9 :	

[1] This boy, the son of James Hope of Bradford, near Manchester, was drowned in consequence of the ice on which he was sliding giving way under him.

[2] He was also drowned whilst sliding on the ice on the river Irwell.

[3] She is described in the *Manchester Mercury* as Esther Brabbarrow, wife of George Brabbarrow, of Manchester, dyer. She became insane and set fire to her clothes.

To William Andrew for Horsehire into Blackburn Parish to search after two Waddingtons Housebreakers ...	: 5 :	
To detaining and conveying before Justice and to the House of Correction Ann M^c kenny who was very troublesome and many assistants required having Assaulted the watch	: 5 :	
To Isabel Webster to Hereford ...	: 1 :	
18	To Wm Richardson for a new Truncheon and repairing several other Implements for the use of the night Watch...	: 19 : 6

To three Trampers[1] going home ... : 1 :
To John Dod for attending a prisoner broug[h]t from Heaton Norris under Justice Manwarings[2] Warrant two nights & one day ... ... : 4 : 6
To James Price to Tideswell ... ... : 1 :
To Eliz: Mason to Attercliff ... ... : : 6
19. To Thomas Wilson to Coventry ... : : 6
To Mary Jones to London ... ... : : 6
To Michael Groves & his wife to Cambridge ... ... : 1 :
To Mary Mitchell & two children to Beverley ... ... : 1 :
21. To Thomas Wilkinson to Gloucester : : 6
To Joseph Swinson to London... ... : : 6
To Mary Smith & three children to Huddersfield ... ... : 1 :
To Eliz: Tyre to Leeds ... ... : 6
To Walter Morgan & his wife into Wales ... ... : 1 :
22. To the High Constables Warrant for the County rate & the repair of Ratcliff Bridge... ... ... 15 : 16 : 6
To John Dods bill for attending Prisoners ... ... 2 : : 6

---

[1] See p. 119, note 2.

[2] This was Dr. Peter Mainwaring, a well-known doctor in the town, who was also in the commission of the peace. His name occurs in the account of the visit of the "rebels" to Manchester in 1745 (see p. 24, note 1).

	To drawing two fair Duplicates of Militia Lists.	3	3	
	To Susan Barns to Skipton			6
	To Rose Mure & two children to London		1	
	To Ellen Vare & two children to Newhaven		1	
	To Straw for the Dungeon		4	6
	To an insane Woman in the Street...			6
25.	To Mark Beswick to Liverpoole ...			6
	To James Greaves & his wife to Sheffield		1	
27.	To Eliz: Dennison very big [with child] to Preston		1	
March 2.	To John Lightboun to Huddersfield			6
	To Duncan McDonald and his wife...		1	
	To removing Susan Moor & her child to Stockport cost more than the County allowance		3	
5.	To an Inquisition over Joseph Youell[1]		2	4
	To the Belman for two crys		3	
7.	To three Persons to assist the watch 3' expences 1'. 6ᵈ.		4	6
	To detaining Maintaining and carrying before the Justice and to the House of Correct[ion] three lewd women apprehended by the watch ...		2	6
	To Martha Ralfin to Castleton... ...			6
	To Mary Davis & two children to Derby		1	
	To Ann Mason & two children to Flintshire		1	
	To Robert Nichols to Westmoreland			6
	To an Inquisition over Clough[2] ...		2	4
8.	To John Taylor & four children to the Isle of wight...		1	
	To a Warrant agᵗᵗ Wᵐ Townley for raising a Publick riot[3] in Yatestreet 3' Assistants to execute the Warrant 3'		6	

---

[1] Joseph Yeuell, a drawer, was killed whilst working in "the coal pits in Newton Lane, near this Town," owing to the fall of the roof.

[2] John, son of Joseph Clough, of Hunts Bank, joiner, between 8 and 9 years of age, was drowned whilst sliding on the ice on the river Irwell.

[3] There is no account of this riot in the local paper.

10.	To Mary Blun to Shropshire	:	1 :	
	To Daniel Mellor to Portsmouth ...	:	:	6
	To John Priest to d"	:	:	6
	To Ellen Knott & two children to Derby	:	1 :	
	To Warrants to the Hamlets for Militia Lists	:	3 :	
	To Betty Whitehead & 3 children to Sheffield	:	1 :	
	To detaining George Fletcher all night for drunkeness and disturbing the publick peace	:	2 :	7
	To other expences ab' Townley & Fletcher	:	3 :	
11.	To Eliz: Clayton & three children into Yorkshire	:	2 :	
	To Warrants to the Hamlets, Militia to exe[r]cise	:	3 :	
	To a summons Information & Warrant ags' Simeon Newton for Drunkeness & a breach of peace	:	3 :	6
	To Tho' Hartshorns bill for Ironwork at Exchange	:	13 :	
	To the Landlord at Blackamoreshead[1] expences of the privy watch and other Watchmen from time to time	:	13 :	11
14.	To Roger Jones for assisting the watch and attending prisoners sundry times	:	2 :	6
	To returning Militia Lists to the Deputy Leuten"	:	2 :	
	To Deputy Brown in advance for Business done for the Constables of Manchester...	:	2 :	
	To Sara Townley a Tramper[2]	:	:	10
	To M'" Mawson for three dark lant-horns	:	4 :	6
17.	To Thomas Walker att[e]nding Justices &c	:	2 :	
	To two discharged Marines	:	2 :	

---

[1] The name of this inn, the Blackamore's Head, has not, I think, occurred before.
[2] See p. 119, note 2.

		£	s	d
	To three Men most of last night to find a young Man that was lost ...	:	2 :	1
	To Charles Lestock to Gloucester ...	:	:	6
	To Wᵐ Wilson to Scotland poorly ...	:	1 :	
	To Joseph Thornhill for Nails to the Exchange, above	:	3 :	
	To James Brown for Carpentry at dⁿ above	:	10 :	1½
18.	To John Sheldon to Tottington ...	:	:	6
	To John Haworth for expences of privy watch &c	:	10 :	3
	To Jane Home & child to Cheadle...	:	1 :	
19.	To John Perry & Son to Sourby ...	:	1 :	
	To James Howard to Coventry... ...	:	:	6
21.	To Martha Beswick to Haslingden ...	:	:	6
	To Geo : MᶜDonald & Lad to Glascow	:	1 :	
24.	To Thoˢ Yates for the Hire of a Horse to Lancaster	:	10 :	6
25.	To Ann Smith & her child to York...	:	1 :	3
	To Edmᵈ Gaffer to Plymouth	:	:	6
27.	To Postage of a Letter & Warrant from Macclesfield		:	6
	To John Dod for watching four nights	:	3 :	
28.	To John Allenson & 4 children to Wittington	:	2 :	
	To Henry Waverham to Chester ...	:	:	6
30.	To the Belman's Note for two Crys	:	3 :	
	To William Eves to Winwick	:	1 :	
31.	To Daniel Hart to Hulton	:	1 :	
	To James Beverley to Whitby... ...	:	:	6
Aprl. 1ˢᵗ	To Mary Clough to Bolton	:	:	6
	To Mʳˢ Walker for damage done by the Fire at Guardhouse as by her Notes	2 :	2 :	0
	To Richard Dixon Beadle second quarters salary	2 :	10 :	
	To Mʳ Whitakers Bill for Law... ...	12 :	6 :	6
3.	To William Bevers to Driffield ...	:	:	6
	To Ann Stonthorpe to Carlisle ...	:	:	6
4.	To Ralph Buckley to Whitehaven ...	:	:	6
	To three more Vagabonds	:	2 :	
	To four persons executing a Hue & Cry Warrant	:	4 :	

6.	To two Strangers	1 :	
	To John Wrigley's bill repairing Guard-house	: 8 :	5
	To James Sutton removing Guard-house Benches	:	6
	To James Wilds Bill for Dale used at Bulhead Guardhouse when made new	: 16 :	6½
	To Mary Price & child to Newcastle	: 1 :	
10.	To James Ashworth lame to Rosen-dale	: 1 :	
	To Tho' Hage to Leeds	: :	6
11.	To Thomas Fowler for a pair of Stockings for beadle	: 3 :	8
	To Mary Hall & two children to Wrexham	: 1 :	
14.	To William Thompson to Scotland...	: :	6
	To a pair of Shoes for the Beadle ...	: 6 :	
	To two Men for conveying Joseph Crompton from Altringham to Manchester suspected of breaking Thomas Pickersgills Shop	: 10 :	
	To an Inquisition over James Smirk[1]	: 2 :	4
	To Ann Jepson & child to Wakefield	: 1 :	
15.	To John Atkinson to Kendall	: :	6
	To Robert Williams to Denbigh ...	: :	6
	To Ann Wilkinson to Leeds	: 1 :	
17.	To John Mayre to Bolton...	: :	6
	To a Load of Coals for the Guardhouse	: 8 :	8
	To Thomas Nevell to Clivegar... ...	: :	6
20.	To Eliz: Warren & child to Exeter	: :	6
	To John Connor to Edinburg[h] ...	: :	6
	To Peter Smart his wife & one child to Hull	: 1 :	
25.	To Marg' Black to Ireland	: :	6
	To John Oldham keeping a Man in Custody a whole day for breaking Windows	: 1 :	6
	To Tho' Hanson's Bill for Painting at Guardhous[e]	: 8 :	4

[1] In the *Manchester Mercury* for April 21st, 1772, it is stated that "on Tuesday last a boy of Widow Smirk's, about four Years old, was instantly killed by a Piece of Timber falling from off a Cart, on Shudehill."

	To Mary Worsley & chi[l]d to Notting-ham	:	1 :	
	To William Smith & wife to Bohun...	:	1 :	
28.	To Ellen Anderson & child to Leeds	:	1 :	
	To Martha Parker to Kendall	:	:	6
29.	To Mary Dilland to Ireland	:	1 :	
	To John Nixon to Walton le dale ...	:	:	6
	To John Ellison to Harwich	:	:	6
May 1st	To James Swymmer to York	:	:	6
	To Mary Brindley a lame woman to Nantwich	:	1 :	
	To Edward Plumpton to Ireland ..	:	:	6
	To Jane Martin & two children to London	:	1 :	
5.	To Thomas Ballard to Worcester ...	:	:	6
	To Isaac Dinnidy to Ireland	:	:	6
7.	To Ann Davenham to York	:	:	6
	To paper and writing the preparation of 22 Books for the service of the Assessors of the Window duty[1] ...	:	7 :	4
	To Warrants to the Hamlets for do...	:	3 :	
	To an Inquisition over Betty Sutton	:	1 :	4
9.	To Eliz: Ayres to Berwick	:	:	6
	To John Oldham for attending Fletcher a prisoner a whole day & going Errands when Window Assessors was appointed[1]	:	2 :	
	To William Morris into Flintshire ...		:	6
11.	To Marg't Williams to Wrexham ...		:	6
	To the High Constables Warrant for County rates the repair of Bridges Governors wages &c	36 :	8 :	6
	To Kath Davis & child to Salisbury...	:	1 :	
13.	To Mary Brown to Langard Fort ...	:	:	6
14.	To Mary Spencer & two children to Glassenbury	:	1 :	
	To Mary Murphy & Son to Fairham	:	1 :	
	To the Belmans Note for four Crys...	:	5 :	6
15.	To Sawny Mc Tork to Glascow ...	:	:	6
	To William Banks to Gloucester ...	:	:	6
16.	To an Inquisition over John Pendleton	:	2 :	4
	To William Ross to Leeds	:	:	6

---

[1] See p. 4, note 4.

		£	s	d
	To Rob‹ Ruckman & his wife to Stamford	:	1 :	
18.	To Phillip Yancall to Dublin	:	:	6
	To Ann Erwin to Leeds	:	:	6
	To Joseph Boak to Kendall	:	:	6
21.	To Jane Forsyth & two children to Kirklinton	:	1 :	
	To Mary Simmons to Aberdeen ...	:	1 :	
	To Jane Fletcher lame to Plymouth	:	1 :	
23.	To Jane Boswell into Lincolnshire ...	:	:	6
	To James Doyley to Coventry... ...	:	:	6
25.	To Eliz: Whitelock to York	:	:	6
28.	To James Hall to Northwich	:	:	6
29.	To Jane Tonson to Sheffield	:	:	6
	To Michael Harry to Hull	:	:	6
	To William Nunn to Hereford ...	:	:	6
June 3.	To expences with Quartermasters of Iniskillings[1] reg‹ at sundry times setling Quarters...	1 :	1 :	
	To the Expences of a special Watch with many Assistants...	:	14 :	6
	To Marg‹ Sutton to Lynn...	:		6
4.	To Robert Whaley wife & 3 children to Whitehaven	:	1 :	
	To David Padget to Wrexham... ...	:	:	6
5.	To an Inquisition over a woman drowned	:	2 :	4
	To Mary Kempster to Harding... ...	:	1 :	
	To Music it being the Anniversary of his Majestys Birthday[2]	1 :	4 :	
7.	To Ann Delaval to Dublin	:		6
	To Tho‹ Davenport for 22 Window Lay books and binding them in red Leather	:	9 :	9
	To Eliz: Shepley for Ironwork to the Guardhouse	:	7 :	6
	To James Davison to Denbigh... ...	:		6

[1] The *Manchester Mercury* of May 26th, 1772, has the following paragraph :—
"On Saturday last [May 23rd] Major-General Mackay reviewed the 6th or Inniskilling Regiment of Dragoons, now quartered in this Town, commanded by the Hon. General James Cholmondeley."

[2] This day, June 4th, was kept as an annual festival in the town. (See previous Accounts.)

9.	To James Johnson to Markethar-brough			6
15.	To Marg¹ Hippesley to Scotland ...	:	:	6
	To William Barlow for Horsehire to Liverpoole on the Constables Business		: 13 :	
	To Henry Bowden to Chapel le Frith	:	:	6
17.	To Mary Reaper to Worcester... ...	:	1 :	
	To John Bell to Hull	:	:	6
20.	To Jane Beckford to Oxford	:	:	6
	To William Loftus to York	:	:	6
22.	To William Griffith to Whitby... ...	:	:	6
	To enquiring in various parts of Manchester and the Neighbourhood after exchangers of bad money...		: 5 :	
	To a Mess⁴ to Rochdale upon that subject with a Warrant ag⁸ᵗ Abraham Baker		: 2 :	
	To apprehending and detaining a lewd woman two days and two nights found in a bad house kept by John Bond in Parsonage		: 6 :	
24.	To cleaning Steps at Salfordbridge...		: 2 :	
	To John Stott for Half a years rent for Guardroom and for Coals Candles and other things used there		3 : 9 : 8	
27.	To detaining & maintaining Long Ned¹ a common Gambler two days and two nights		: 2 : 6	
	To going with him to Justice Bayleys² of Hope two Persons as Assistants from whence he was committed and conveyed to the House of Correction at Manchester		: 3 : 4	
	To Thomas Benton to Gloucester ...			: 6
	To Lambert Blacklock to Chester ...			: 6
	To Luke Aston to Bolton			: 6
	To William Kirsey to Coventry... ...			: 6
28.	To two persons attending Hopping Sall³ one day and one night		: 2 :	

---

[1] Another instance of a local nickname. (See also p. 138, note 2.)

[2] This was Thomas Butterworth Bayley, of Hope Hall, near Eccles, Esq. (See p. 191, note 2.)

[3] Another nickname. (See p. 138, note 2.)

To a Mess' co[n]veying her to Hope[1] where she was convicted of Drunkeness...	: 1 :	
To two Persons attending Ann Mc kenny one night & one day wages 4' Meat & Liquor at a public House the Dungeon being full of men 2'... ...	: 6 :	
To Mary Benwell to Leicester	: : 6	
30. To William James to Carlisle	: : 6	
To Mary Finch & child to London...	: 1 :	
July 1st To three Persons apprehending Jonath: Pilling for Horsestealing and keeping him in the Dungeon till Witness's could be sent for	: 3 :	
To expences regulating Summer quarters of Dragoons[2] & Horses not gone to grass with Soldiers Officers & Landlords the matter being more troublesome than quartering 2 or 3 regiments	: 10 : 6	
To John Hulme to Bradford	: 6	
To Thomas Fowler for a pair of Stockings for Beadle...	: 3 : 8	
3. To Richard Dixon[3] for two quarters Salary	5 : :	
To him for Money advanced & for extraordinary Business	: 14 : 11½	
To Richard Dixon the Beadle for superintending the nightly watch thirty six nights betwixt 7th Febry and 19th of June	1 : 16 :	
To him for other extraordinary Business	: 6 : 8	
To the Sexton of the old Church for taking up the Body of Eliz: Sutton[4] by vertue of the Coroners waรt [warrant]	: 2 : 6	

---

[1] See p. 191, note 2.   [2] See p. 204, note 1.

[3] Richard Dixon was the Beadle.

[4] The case of Elizabeth Sutton is thus given in the *Manchester Mercury* of May 12th :—

"On Wednesday [May 6th] an Inquisition was taken by the Coroner, on View of the Body of Elizabeth Sutton, a poor Woman in Salford, who was reported to have been murdered in a most barbarous and unheard of Manner by her Husband, when it appeared on the clearest Evidence that she died of the Venereal Disease and not of

	To two Blind Men in the Street ...	: 2 :	
7.	To Mary Bentham to Warrington ...	: : 6	
	To David Thomas to Liverpoole ...	: : 6	
10.	To Joseph Johnson & his wife to Congleton	: 1 :	
	To a Mess' to Dunham about Jonath: Pilling under a Warrant for killing Game	: 2 :	
	To detaining the Man at Manchester upon this acct [account]	: 1 :	
	To Mary Griffiths a Tramper[1]	: 1 :	
11.	To Archibald Boyd to Sunderland ...	: : 6	
	To Joseph Heywood to Burnley ...	: : 6	
	To Richard Dixon the Beadle half the value of his Cap & Gown[2] he having wore them half a year	2 :	
14.	To Eliz: Bertles to Carlisle	: 6	
	To James Seddon for Taylors work for the Beadle	: 10 :	
	To apprehending 5 Shakers[3] on Sunday last 24 Persons 6ᵈ each for Assistants	: 12 :	
	To John Moss for expences on this and other such like sundry times ...	: 6 : 8	
	To John Atkins & wife to Kendall	: 1 :	

any Violence as had been reported. But one Mr. Croysor, an Apothecary in this Town having (or pretending to have) examined the Body and taken upon him, in very peremptory Terms, to contradict the above Facts, the Coroner caused the Body to be accurately examined on Saturday last, by Mr. Burchall, Mr. White, Mr. Edward Hall and other Gentlemen of the Profession in Mr. Croysor's Presence, when these Gentlemen unanimously declared it as their Opinion, that the Death of the deceased was occasioned by the Venereal Disease and not by any Violence from her Husband, or any other Person."

In the following number of the *Mercury* there was printed a long letter from Mr. John Drinkwater, the surgeon called in to attend her, giving the whole history of the case and an account of the cause of death, and his opinion is backed up by that of the other doctors whose names are given in the above paragraph. The body would appear to have been buried and then exhumed for further examination. Mr. Chippindall was the coroner.

[1] See p. 119, note 2.
[2] See p. 88, note 2.
[3] This is an interesting entry relating to the "Shakers," a so-called religious sect, at this time coming into notoriety by the eccentricity of their behaviour. The founders of this sect were John Lees of Manchester and his daughter Ann, who are subsequently referred to in this year's Accounts.

	To the day after attending them all day when two was committed to the House of Correction four Persons each 1 6 conveying them 1ˢ	7 :
	To Ale for 24 Persons about apprehending the Shakers[1]	: 5 : 6
	To maintaining and detaining a Stroller[2] a day & a night before she could be brought before the Justices... ...	: 1 : 6
15.	To Marg[t] Robinson to Holywell ...	: 6
	To M[rs] Hulme for drink when the Shakers[1] was brought before the Justice...	: 1 : 2
	To her for Meat & drink for John Twiss wife and children whilst a Pass could be obtained	: 2 :
	To a bill of expences at the Hare & hounds[3] about the goods which Rich[d] Glover[4] or his Son at [sic for had] stolen	: 3 : 10
18.	To Eliz: Bradley to Litchfield	: 6
	To Edmund Wrigleys Bill for repairing Engines	1 : 5 :
	To John Dod for attending two Prisoners at two several times	: 2 : 6
21.	To John Steell to Holt	: : 6
	To Mary Yellet & child to Whitehaven	: 1 :
	To pursuing Persons suspected of Breaking M[r] Pickersgills Shop on the 9th & 10th of April last when it was necessary that Miss Pickersgill should be one of the Mess[rs] who could not go without a Chaise at the Royal Oak[5] 1ˢ Turnpike 1ˢ at Stockport all night 12ˢ Turnpike from Stockp[t] 1ˢ	: 15 :

---

[1] See p. 227, note 3.

[2] See p. 130, note 3.

[3] This Manchester inn has not, I think, occurred before.

[4] On the 16th July, Richard Glover was committed to the House of Correction by Dr. Mainwaring, "strongly suspected of having broke into the Houses of M[r] Charles Radcliffe, M[r] William Preston and M[r] Francis Clay, of this Town and stealing thereout several Sorts of Goods, wearing Apparel &c. to a considerable Value." He was tried at the ensuing Quarter Sessions in the town, and sentenced to seven years' transportation.

[5] This inn has been before referred to. (See p. 195, note 2.)

To dining at the Royal Oak[1] 1' Stretford Turnppike [sic] 1' another 4ᵈ Bating at Buckley hill 2 - 2 at High Leigh 4' Fees for a Warrant 1' all night at Altringham 11' Turnpike back 8ᵈ...	1: 1: 2	
To James Hodgkinson for the Hire of a Chaise from Manchester to Stockport	: 10: 6	
To dᵒ from Manchester to High Leigh	1: 2: 6	
To James Brown & his lame wife to Liverpoole	: 1:	
To an Inquisition over Lydia Jackson[2]	: 2: 4	
To Richard Shepherd for att[e]nding Richᵈ Glover[3] and endeavouring to apprehend the Son	: 4:	
To presentments drawing to this and last April Sessions	: 2:	
To Expences and Evidences attending the prosecution of Long Ned[4] for leaving his family when he was sentenced to six Months Imprisonment and [to] be twice whip't	: 10: 6	
To the Jurors Baillif on prosecuting John Lees and his Daughter Ann[5] ...	: 1: 6	
To the Cryers Fees	: 2: 6	
To four Women Witness's att[e]nding each three days	: 12:	
To four Men Witness's att[e]nding each same time	: 18:	
To Meat & drink for each at 6ᵈ a day	: 12:	
To other Expences amongst them during the Sessions when both received sentence of commitment[6]...	: 7:	

(23.)

---

[1] See p. 195, note 2.

[2] This child had fallen "into a tub of scalding Wort and was immediately Suffocated."

[3] See p. 228, note 4.

[4] Another instance of the common use of nicknames at this time. (See p. 138, note 2.)

[5] These were the founders of the sect of the Shakers. (See p. 227, note 3). At the ensuing Quarter Sessions, John Lees and Ann Stanley were sentenced, for an assault, to be imprisoned for one month.

[6] See previous note.

To two old Soldiers	2 :	
To expences upon eight Persons at-t[e]nding as Evidences ag[st] Rich[d] Glover[1] for Housebreaking during the three days Sessions	: 12 :	
To the Deputys Expences during the three days Sessions	: 7 : 6	
To John Oldham for attending Sessions 3 days	: 4 : 6	
To Jonathan Butterworth following James Glover through Cheshire & to Newcastle in Staffordshire as a common Housebreaker in Manchester	1 : 1 :	
To Mary Smith big [with child] to Durham	: 1 :	

27.	To an Inquisition over John Steell ...	: 2 : 4
	To John Brown to Moulton	: : 6
	To Makepeace Horrox[2] a Reward for aiding in apprehending Richard Glover[1] and attending the prosecution of him at Sessions	1 : 1 :
	To Charles Haworth & two others for the same	1 : 11 : 6
30.	To Betty Broadbent to Grange ...	: 6
	To John Denton to Armley	: 6
	To Paper ruling and writing the Ley book	1 : 10 :
	To four Men for delivering out printed Bills 1500 about Two Horses killed near S[t] Pauls	: 4 :
	To a Bill of expences at the Mule[3] when Justice Mainwaring[4] attended to examine the Shakers[5]	: 2 : 7½
Aug 3.	To Mary Williams and child to Holy-well	: 1 :
	To a special Inquisition held at Eccles when the four Manchester Jurors had 1 . 6 each	: 6 :

[1] See p. 228, note 4.
[2] This is a curious combination of names to meet with at this time.
[3] This Manchester inn has occurred before. (See p. 212, note 2.)
[4] See p. 218, note 2.
[5] See p. 227, note 3, and also p. 229, note 5.

	To expences there	1 : 6
	To detaining Thomas Morris two days and two nights, a Felon	
	To Patrick Blake & two children to Halifax	: 1 :
	To enquiring after, Summoning and examining many Witness about Henry Markland suspected of killing two Horses near S¹ Pauls...	: 6 :
5.	To Jane Brown to Warbutton	: : 6
	To Lewis Earle to Bristoll	: : 6
7.	To Marg¹ Forrester to Durham ...	: 1 :
	To Mark Colley to Reading	: : 6
10.	To Mary Heys and two children to Chester	: 1 :
13.	To Eliz: Clifton to Coventry	: 6
	To James Morrison & wife to Newcastle	: 1 :
	To Daniel Kasey & wife to Glascow	: 1 :
15.	To James Smith to York	: : 6
	To Eliz: Dowden to Warrington ...	: : 6
	To Ann Hawkins & child to Liverpoole	: 1 :
17.	To Mary Birtles to Lincoln	: : 6
20.	To James Lester & two children to Northampton	: 1 :
	To Thomas Lomax for Watching two nights to Apprehend James Glover...	: 2 : 6
	To conveying James Welsh¹ under the Coroners commitment to Lancaster for Manslaughter by killing Alex¹ Shepherd	2 : 2 :
24.	To Eliz: France to Kendall	: : 6
	To Sara Roberts & child to Wem ...	: 1 :
	To Dan¹ Mᶜintosh lame to Newcastle	: 1 :
26.	To Jane Watson to Liverpoole ...	: : 6
	To William Hall wife & two children to Leeds	: 1 :
27.	To Peter Barnet to Liverpoole... ...	: 6

---

¹ This relates, I think, to the paragraph in the *Mercury* of August 18th, to the effect that two journeymen hat makers in Long Milngate having quarrelled, one struck the other "an unlucky Blow which Killed him on the Spot."

	To John Gaddis & his daughter into Scotland	1 :
	To detaining Thomas Morris two days and two nights a Felon ommitted entry before	: 2 :
	To four men surveying the Town to make preparation for the Militia Lists each one Guinea...	4 : 4 :
	To Tho' Harpurs Bill for delivering Handbills	: 2 :
29.	To an Inquisition over John Gregory	: 1 : 4
Sep' 9.	To an Inquisition over a Person unknown	: 1 : 4
	To Postage of Hue & Cry Warrants upon several Burglarys having been committed in the Town	: 3 :
	To two Persons going from House to House to warn Alehousekeepers to take Licences	: 4 :
	To an old Soldier	: 1 :
	To John Shelmerdine and his wife going to Lancaster Assizes to give Evidence against Henry Markland[1] for Horsekilling	2 : 14 :
	To Ann Gadman going to Lancaster and maintaining her there	2 : 2 :
	To bringing her back to Manchester	: 10 : 6
	To John Brown the same...	2 : 12 : 6
	To a Horse Messenger from Lancaster to Preston all night there with an Habeas Corpus for James Chantler...	: 10 : 6
	To the Governor of the House of Correction at Preston bringing him to Lancaster and taking him back... ...	1 :
	To James Heydock for a double Horse to Lancaster	: 15 :
	To James Kay an Evidence on the same account	2 : 12 : 6
	To James Chantler from Preston to Lancaster to give Evidence	: 10 : 6

[1] Henry Markland was tried at these Assizes charged with killing a mare and wounding another the property of John Brown, of Manchester, but was acquitted.

	To Deputy Kays Journey to Lancaster on the same Occasion	2 :	12 :	6
	To a Bill at the White Hart in Lancaster for Hostler Servants and Beds and other Extraordinaries for five Evidences there		: 13 :	
17.	To Robert Duxbury and Deputy Kay sent Express to Liverpoole in a Chaise about the Villains who had committed several Burglarys[1] in Manches[r] at Salford waiting of Robert Duxbury and the Chaise		1 :	
	To two Turnpikes to Warrington ...		: 2 :	
	To all night at Warrington four Men & four Horses		: 15 :	6
18.	To Breakfasting at Prescot &c... ...		: 4 :	
	To enquiring at Lowhill about the Robbers[2]		: 2 :	
	at Liverpoole		: 8 :	4
	To Turnpike betwixt Liverpoole & Prescot		: 1 :	
	at Prescot bating		: 4 :	
	To supping at Warrington & double feed for the horses		: 7 :	8
	To Hostlers at Liverpoole Prescot & Warrington		: 3 :	
	To Turnpikes from Warrington ...		: 2 :	
	To Baillifs & Assistants at Lowhill & Liverpoole		: 2 :	
	To Post Chaise and Post Boys[3] ...	2 :	18 :	
22.	To James Hodgkinson for meat & drink for prisoners Evidences and Persons attending the Justices from 23 Sep[r] 1771, to July 30th 1772 ...	1 :	11 :	6
23.	To Benj Taylors Bill for carting Baggage to Warrington		: 18 :	
23.	To five Passengers		: 3 :	6

[1] These burglaries are referred to in the *Mercury* of September 15th, the dwelling houses of Mr. William Williams and Mr. Robert Duxbury having been broken open and plate and money stolen; and also two horses out of the stable at the Cock in Market Street Lane.

[2] All these entries relate to the attempts to capture the men engaged in the recent burglaries in the town. (See previous note.)

To sundry Persons overlooking the watch from 5ᵗʰ Febry to this day ...	1 : 18 :	6
To Sarah Edwards to Derby	: :	6
To Eliz: Wilson to Ireland	: :	6
To an Inquisition over John Kenyon	: 2 :	4
To Mary Townley to Knutsford ...	: :	6
To Ann Ashworth & child to Lyn ...	: 1 :	
To Edmund Barker to Halifax ...	: :	6
To James Murray to Hull...	: :	6
To John Blumley to Sourby	: :	6
To Ellen Bateson to Chatham	: :	6
To Ann Smith to York	: :	6
To Susan Fitzpatrick & child to Ireland	: 1 :	
To Jane Smith & 3 children to Sheffield	: 1 :	
To Samuel Brewster to Liverpoole ...	: :	6
To Ann Kidson & 2 children to Doncaster	: 1 :	
To Ann Mathew to Coventry	:	6
To John Turner for Coals to the Guardhouse	: 8 :	8
To the Belman for five publick Crys...	: 8 :	6
To him for another Cry	: 1 :	
25. To an Inquisition over Thomas Files	: 2 :	4
28. To keeping three Lewd women two nights and two days when they was committed to the House of Correction	: 3 :	
To Charles Higgins to Ireland... ...	:	6
28. To George Kinder for rent of a Music room for Iniskillings Dragoons [1] ...	5 : 10 :	
To Messengers with Advertisements to seven different Towns after Persons Suspected of committing several Burglarys in Manchester [2]	: 10 :	6
To Widow Scholfield sundry expences with Soldiers, Prisoners, and Evidences upon the Coroners Inquisition over the body of Alexʳ Shepherd [3] ...	: 10 :	10

---

[1] See p. 224, note 1.   [2] See p. 233, note 1.   [3] See p. 231, note 1.

	To precepts to the Hamlets for new Surveyors of Highways	: 3 :
	To expences and attendance upon Ann Mc Kenny and others all night at the Regulus¹ at Shudehill	: 8 : 10
Octob 3.	To pressing Carriages for three Troops of Iniskillings Dragoons² out of the Country	: 3 :
	To Noticing the Hamlets to take Ale Licences	: 3 :
	To d° for their proportion of £15.16.6	: 3 :
	To d° for their proportion of £36. 8.6	: 3 :
	To d° for d° of £27.14.6	: 3 :
	To expences upon a Warrant with a pie Woman	: 1 : 6
	To three Browns by Pass	: 1 :
	To Eliz: Carty to Newcastle	: 1 : 6
	To Mary Hunt to Thorn	: : 6
	To Jane Smith a Tramper³	: 1 :
	To executing Hue & Cry after Henry Williams...	: 3 :
	To Geo: Clayton for a Hang Lock⁴ to the Dungeon	: 1 : 6
	To Widow Shepley for Ironwork when the Shakers³ was apprehended	: 2 : 6
3.	To the Constables and Baillifs employed in and about Rochdale to apprehend Abr[a]m Barker suspected of Coining Money	: 10 : 6
	To sundry persons and expences Quelling a Mob who were beginning to pull down the House of John Townley a Skaker⁵	: 5 : 6
	To an Inquisition over Peter Clough	: 2 : 4
10.	To John Stotts Bill for matters relating to the Guardhouse	: 16 : 2
	To delivering Bills about Burglary⁶...	: 1 : 6

---

¹ If this is the name of an inn at Shudehill it is a very curious one.

² It would appear from this entry that the Inniskilling Dragoons had left or were leaving the town, but I do not find any reference to this in the local paper.

³ See p. 119, note 2.

⁴ A "hang lock" would appear to have been a padlock. (See p. 179, note 1.)

⁵ See p. 227, note 3.   ⁶ See p. 233, note 1.

	To James Chantler in full for his Attendance at the Assizes to give Evidence ag^{st} Markland [1]	1 : 1 :
12.	To John Barber the Beadle for cleansing the Dungeon and maintaining prisoners whilst in his Custody	: 10 :
	To thirteen several Trampers [2] since the 1st of this Instant...	: 9 : 6
	To Mr Chippendall for Int. of £63.10.7 being the remainder of the principal Sum borrowed from him upon bond and owing at the beginning of this year...	2 : 10 : 9
	To John Gomersall for Meat and drink to Evidences and other persons attending Cons^t Business last April and July Sessions	: 15 :
	To Widow Shelmerdine at the Sun for receiving and maintaiñg Prisoners &c	2 : 18 : 3
	To the Governor of the House of Correc̄t, Fees & maint̄g Prisoners ...	2 : 7 :
12.	To the Engine Mens Bill for Eleven Months	11 : 11 : 5½
	To the Soldiers and the Militia Firing upon the Kings birthday last [3]	4 : 14 : 6
	To Mrs Cromptons Bill on the same day [4]	16 : 12 : 6
	To her other Bill when the Constable Ley was laid	6 : 6 : 4
	To five Men a day searching for a childs body drowned in the River Irwell	: 10 : 6
	To a High Constables warrant for rebuilding Eye Plat Bridge &c... ...	27 : 14 : 6

---

[1] See p. 232, note 1.   [2] See p. 119, note 2.

[3] There seems to have been a very special celebration of the King's birthday (June 4th) this year, judging by the amount of money spent both on the soldiers and at the Crompton Coffee House.

[4] Mrs. Crompton now kept the Crompton Coffee House (see p. 153, note 2), her bushand being dead.

To Mr Tunnadine an Attorney at Law for his trouble of perusing Copying and seeing proper deeds executed to preserve a foot road or passage from St Anns Church through the Exchange [1] to King " [street]...	5 : 5 :
To sundry small Articles by Constable Bell	: 6 : 6
To Deputy Kay one years Salary ...	30 :
To Thos Marsden a yrs rent for the Engine House	3 : 3 :
To Thomas Towlers Bill for Beadles Stockings	: 6 : 9
To Mr Jones Bill for Law...	11 : 17 : 6
To Mr Whitakers Bill for the same ...	15 : 10 : 2
To Surgeon Drinkwaters [2] Bill attending at the request of the Coroner the body of Alex^r Shepherd [3] when the Jury charged James Welsh with Manslaughter thereupon	1 : 1 :
To his Journey and attendance at Lancaster to give Evidences at the Assizes upon the same occasion ...	6 : 12 :
To Titus Leigh for watching and other Business done for the Constables ...	1 : 11 :
Octob. 12. To Joseph Harrops [4] Bill for printing Work	2 : 13 : 6
To Thos Walker for Business done for the Const[ables] &c.	: 10 :
To James Dawson for the same ...	: 19 : 5
To John Whipp for Cat with nine tails [5]	: 4 : 4
To Mr Chippendall in full for Law Business	36 : 4 : 9

---

[1] See p. 169, note 4. It would be interesting to see these deeds, so as to get to the history of this old building. The passage still exists leading from St. Ann's Church to King Street, and is now an important thoroughfare.

[2] Mr. John Drinkwater was the surgeon whose verdict in the case of Elizabeth Sutton had been called in question (see p. 226, note 4), and for which he obtained a verdict with damages against Mr. Croysor at the autumn Lancaster Assizes.

[3] See p. 231, note 1.

[4] See p. 73, note 2.

[5] This instrument, for use on the unfortunate people condemned to be whipped, has been previously referred to. (See p. 64, note 2.)

To John Prescotts[1] Bill for printing work ... ... } 4 : 2 : 6

To Interest paid M' Joseph Chippendall for £129 . 16 . 6 borrowed upon Bond as setled 9ᵗʰ Nov' 1767. amounting in the whole to

£32 . 14 . 0

To him Int in part 9ᵗʰ Octob. 1768 ... ... } 5 . 14 . 0

To dᵒ 29 Sep' 1769 5 . 4 . 0
To dᵒ 29 Sep' 1770 6 . 12 . 3
To dᵒ . this day ... 2 . 10 . 9
To him more in full of all Interest ... ... } 12 . 13 . 0 12 . 13 .

[Total]... ... ... £589 : 4 : 10½

˻Receipts˼

Contra ... ... Cʳ

1772.

Octob 12. By Cash received from the last years Ley ... ... } 4 : 7 : 6

By the Hamlets proportion of
£30 . 1 . 7 } 20 : 1 :

By dᵒ... ... ... £15 . 16 . 6 10 : 11 :
By dᵒ... ... ... £36 . 8 . 6 24 : 5 : 8
By dᵒ... ... ... £27 . 14 . 6 18 : 9 : 8

By the Misegatherers from this years Tax ... ... } 303 : 18 : 6

By Money allowed by the Judge on the prosecution of James Welsh[2] for Manslaughter ... ... } 5 :

By balance owing to the Constables... 202 : 11 : 6½

[Total] ... ... £589 : 4 : 10½

---

[1] Mr. John Prescott was the printer of Prescott's *Manchester Journal*, the first number of which appeared on the 23rd March, 1771.

[2] See p. 231, note 1.

Decr 10th 1772.[1] We the Jurors of the Court Leet holden for the Manor of Manchester in the County of Lancaster have examined the foregoing Acc^{ts} of Mr Benj^a Brown & Mr John Bell (late Constables) & do allow the same.

(Signed)   EDW^D BYROM

JAMES HODSON

THO^s CHADWICK

EDWARD TOMKINSON

J^{NO} HEYWOOD

SAMUEL HIBBERT

JAMES COOKE

HEN^Y BARTON

JOHN TIPPING

JOHN WRIGHT

LAW^{CE} BROCK

THO^s TIPPING

WILLIAM CRANE

[1] As appears by the *Court Leet Records* (vol. viij. pp. 147-8), on the adjournment of the Court Leet to this date, they met at the house of Mrs. Margaret Jackson at the Windmill Tavern, the first occasion they had visited that inn.

[Constables' Accounts.]

[14th Oct., 1772, to 13th Oct., 1773.]

●●●●●●●●●●●

𝔇r The Town of Manchester to MR JAMES CLOUGH & MR SAML GOODIER, *Constables.*[1]

[Disbursements]

1772.

Octob 13.	To last Years Balance[2]	202 : 11 :	6½
	To drawing Presentment to Sessions as usual	: 1 :	
	To George Walker wife & two children to Canterbury	: 1 :	6
	To Peggy Smith poorly to Edinburgh	: 1 :	
17.	To John Birch to Chester...	: :	6
	To Richard Dickenson att[e]nding Robinson[3] three days & one night charged with Sodomy!	: 4 :	6
	John Cotrell with the same Person three days	: 3 :	6
	To Lodging Robinson[3] two nights in Custody	: 2 :	
	To Meat & drink for him during that time	: 2 :	
	To Jonath: Butterworth att[e]nding a Prisoner 1 day & 1 night	: 2 :	
	attending James Welsh[4] under Suspicion of Man Slaughter	: 2 :	

---

[1] These two Constables were elected at the Court Leet held on the 14th October, 1772. (See *Court Leet Records*, vol. viij. p. 143.)

[2] See p. 238.

[3] As stated in the *Manchester Mercury* for Oct. 20th, 1772—

"One Robinson was [at the Quarter Sessions then held in the town] found guilty of attempting to commit a detestable Crime, and ordered to stand in the Pillory three Times and to be imprisoned twelve Months."

See p. 236, note 1.

Jane Gratton a Vagrant to Hulmes Chapel...		6
To three Men three days running up and down the Country in search of Wellings Johnson & Boardman under Justices Warrant for breaking Esq' Haworth's Fences at 2:6 a day & a night each Man	1 : 2 : 6	
To Walter Wilson for repairing the Towns Wiegh beam	: 1 : 6	
19. To a Lock & Key for the use of the Dungeon	: 1 : 2	
To repairs making good the breaches at Lees's in Toadlane in order to apprehend a gang of Shakers[1] lock't up there	: 5 : 2	
To dickenson for watching two nights and attending a Thief to Hope[2] ...	: 2 : 6	
20. To John Welsh & wife to Kilkenny...	: 1 :	
To Job Grimshaw to Colne	: : 6	
To two Men one day & one night att[e]nding Wm Makin for a breach of Beace [sic for Peace] when he was commited & conveying him to Prison	: 4 :	
20. To the like apprehending and detaining James Lees[1] whilst he could find Sureties	: 2 :	
To apprehending 8 Persons and att[e]nding them all day & all night for destraining a Cow under false pretences with Assistants	: 10 :	
25. To apprehending in the Exchange a Gang of Imposters one of whom was a woman pretending to be of super natural Strenght having with them a set of dancing Dogs with several Assi[s]tants...	: 3 :	
To detaining these people in the Prison house a day & a night and for attendance & Meat & drink there ...	: 5 : 4	

[1] See p. 227, note 2.
[2] Hope Hall, near Eccles, was the seat of Thomas Butterworth Bayley, Esq., an active local magistrate at this time.

To High Constables warrant rebuilding Ratcliff Bridge & Governors wages of the House of Correct[ion]	15 : 13 : 10
To Warrants to the Eleven Hamlets for their proportion	: 3 :
To a Mess' with a Warrant to Stretford Davy Hulme & Barton ag'' John Taylor for breach of the peace upon complaint of Councellor Dawson ...	: 1 : 6
To a second Mess' upon the same occasion	: 1 :
To three person[s] upon privy Watch with the Deputy Cons[table]	: 3 :
To four Evidences att[e]nding last Sessions against Robinson[1] who was found guilty of Sodomy and sentenced to be pillor'd each Man 3 6	: 14 :
To Fees to the Clerk of the Peace for orders ab' Vagrants and soldiers Baggage	: 4 :
To Deputy Kays unavoidable expences attending the Sessions	: 5 : 6
25. To two Trampers[2] going to Ireland ...	: 1 :
To Eliz: Bilton & child to Warrington	: : 6
To Anthony Goolden to Liverpoole	: : 6
27. To several Assistants to apprehend Sam' Barret & John Kent for buying stolen yarn when they were caught and detained all night	: 3 :
To James Hughs & his wife to Wolverhampton	: 1 :
To Ann Bancroft to York...	: 6
30. To Charles Sandiford giving Evidence at Lancaster upon the trial of James Welsh[3] in a case of Manslaughter upon the body of Alex' Shepherd ...	: 17 :
Joseph Gorst to Farnley	: : 6
To Edw[d] Briggs to Newcastle under lyne	: : 6

---

[1] See p. 240, note 3. [2] See p. 119, note 2. [3] See p. 231, note 1.

Nov' 3.	To detaining Cath. Campbell all night to be examind ab' Shopbreaking for Prisonroom 1' two attendants that night & the day following 3' the like for another woman who turned Evidence, when Campbell was committed 4'	: 8 :	
	To Jane Jackson to Carlisle	: : 6	
	To Philip Harley & wife to Leeds ...	: 1 :	
	To Sam' Burton to Lincolnshire ...	: : 6	
5.	To attendance upon Jane Weatherhog & Jane Ferguson both informed ag'' by Campbell for receiving stolen goods when they were bound over to the Sessions	: 3 :	
	To maintenance of Campbell Weatherhog & Ferguson whilst in Custody...	: 6 :	
	To Catherine Stanley to Pomfret ...	: 6	
7.	The Justices ordered Campbell to be took out of the House of Correction and detained in Custody 2 days & 1 night waiting to find Sureties it cost with att[e]ndants	: 6 : 7	
	To Richard Dickenson overlooking the watch 4 nights	: 4 :	
	To him for attending Campbell & others of that Gang	: 4 : 6	
	To Edw'd Finch & child to Liverpoole	: 1 :	
	To John Atkinson to Kendall	: : 6	
	To John Collins to Ireland	: : 6	
9.	To a special watch last Saturday all night the streets abounding with disorderley persons 4 Men each 1' the like again last night 4 Men each 6'd...	: 6 :	
	To Tho' Dyan & wife to London	: : 6	
	To W'm Rox to the Isle of Wight ...	: : 6	
	To Jane Scott lame to Northumberland	: 1 :	
	To an old Soldier up[on] his Tramp	: 1 :	
	To expences with Q'Masters setling & regulating Three Troops of Dragoons for one Month	: 2 : 6	
10.	Hanah Morton & her child to Carlisle	: 1 : 6	

To Eliz: M⁰ Load to Scotland	: 6	

To Eliz: M° Load to Scotland		: 6	
To Warrants to the Eleven Hamlets for Militia Lists		: 3 :	
To the like to fix up direction Posts on the Highway[1]		: 3 :	
To four Travellors going to Germany		: 4 :	
11. To apprehending and keeping in Custody two days & one night under Justice Bayleys[2] waīt [warrant] for stealing Great Coats out of Gentlemens Lobbys James Chorlton & others paid to Assisstants...		: 4 :	
To detaiñg James Chorlton in the Prison house with 3 others two days & one night with Meat & drink there		: 5 : 6	
To three old Soldiers		: 2 :	
To Richard Penn to Exeter		: : 6	
To Mary London to Hull...		: : 6	
12. To two Persons att[e]nding Charles Edmondson one day under suspicion of Felony		: 2 :	
To Meat & drink for all three, one day		: 2 : 6	
To two Assistants conveying Chorlton to Justice Bayley[2] at Hope & bringing him back to the House of Correction		: 3 :	
To superintending the watch six last nights		: 6 :	
To Robert Barlow to Newcastle ...		: : 6	
15. To a special watch this night 4 Persons		: 3 : 6	
To fresh Painting the Deputy Constables Truncheon[3] and putting the arms[4] thereon		: 10 : 6	
To an old Soldier going to Chelsea...		: 1 :	
To Margt Ralph & her daugt to Staffordshire		: 1 :	
18. To an Inquisition over Wm Read Warts [warrants] to the Hamlets 1ˢ Jurors Fees 1ˢ 4ᵈ		: 2 : 4	

---

[1] This is the first reference in these Accounts to the fixing of public signposts.
[2] See p. 225, note 2.
[3] The Deputy-Constable's truncheon has been mentioned before.
[4] This is the first instance of any arms being painted on the truncheons, and one would be interested to know what arms the town of Manchester then used.

	To Mary Merphew & child to Scotland		: 6
	To John Whip for Leather for Beadles Caps & a new Cat o'nine tails[1]... ...	: 6 : 4	
20.	To Peter Oxberry to London	:	: 6
	To a sick Sailor going home	: 1 : 6	
21.	To Henry Bingley to Carlisle	:	: 6
	To Kath. Liverstone & 2 children to Liverpoole	: 1 :	
25.	To Hanah Moor to Wiggan	:	: 6
26.	To Jonath: Fellows & his wife to Liverpoole	: 1 :	
	To John Ellis to Liverpoole		: 6
27.	To a special watch from the evening to five next Morning on account of a Warehouse being broke open six Men	: 6 :	
	To Mary Jackson to Neston	:	: 6
	To Ann Hunter & 3 children to Liverpoole	: 1 :	
29.	To an old Soldier to Whitehaven ...	: 1 :	
Decr 2.	To Oliver Hoyley to Lancaster ...	:	: 6
	To Wm Hall and his wife to Northwich	: 1 :	
	To Margt Blacket to Shrewsbury ...	:	: 6
5.	To Duncan Campbell wife & child to London	: 1 :	
	To Nicholas Collier & his wife to Liverpoole	: 1 :	
	To Eliz: Preston to Ayre in Scotland	:	: 6
	To Jonathan Butterworths Bill for Business done	: 5 :	
6.	To three Trampers[2] to Ireland... ...	: 1 :	
7.	To Robert Shone to Chester	:	: 6
	To Martha McCales to Edinburg ...	:	: 6
	To five Persons clearing the Streets of Manchester it being suspected the Town was full of Theives & Pickpockets	: 5 :	
10.	Two old Soldiers going to Chelsea Hospitall	: 2 :	

---

[1] A "cat o' nine tails" was supplied to the authorities a short time previously. (See p. 237, note 5.)

[2] See p. 119, note 2.

	To Titus Leigh & Wm Blerkeley superintending the watch the last Ten nights 3/6 being collected from the Inhabitants who did not attend ...	: 6 : 6		
14.	To Jane Cole & two children to Stafford	: 1 :		
	To Samuel Butterworth assisting to execute several Justices Warrants in different Townships on many various occasions as by his receipt	: 16 :		
24	To an old Man & his wife into Scotland	: 1		
24.	To cleansing Salford Steps as usual	: 2 :		
	To cleansing Steps at Milbrow three years omitted entring	: 12 :		
	To making Beadles Cap and gown 9' Neb[1] for Cap 1'	: 10 :		
	To a Warrant by a Mess^r to the Constable of Withington	: 1 :		
	To an old Soldier to Coventry... ...	: 1 :		
	To John Stott rent for Guardhouse & for two Loads of Coals...	2 : 1 : 3		
29.	To a new Engine Rope	: 6 :		
1773 Janry 4.	To a Mess^r to Hope[2] with a Warrant & attending there	: 1 :		
	To James Chandley in full for giving Evidence at Lan^r ags^t Henry Markland[3] for stabbing Horses...	: 10 : 6		
11.	To sundry Strollers[4] turned out of Town and relieved from 7th of last Month to this day	: 15 : 6		
	To Mary Permenter & 2 children to Stockport	: 1 :		
	To four quire of Paper for Billets during this year	: 3 :		
13.	To Joseph Cusworth & wife to Liverpoole	: 1 :		
	To William Iland to Kendall	: : 6		
14.	To William Ridde & his wife to Leeds	: 1 :		
	To half a Load of Straw for Dungeon	: 7 :		

---

[1] Query, meaning the peak of the beadle's cap.
[2] See p. 191, note 2.   [3] See p. 232, note 1.   [4] See p. 130, note 3.

16.	To an old Soldier in distress	:	1	:
	To Marg' Campbell & young child to Whitehaven	:	1	:
	To Isaac Evans to Leicester	:	:	6
	To three Men stroling the Streets in search of Vagabonds & apprehending them 3' another day 2'	:	5	:
17.	To Ann Backhouse to Sourby	:	:	6
	To Alex' Hulme to Wrexham	:	:	6
	To Titus Leigh superintending the watch 15 nights	:	15	:
18.	To Mary Davis & 2 children to Chester	:	1	:
	To a distresst Seaman	:	1	:
18.	To four Men surveying the Town in order to make new Militia Lists 21' each Man as usual	4 :	4	:
	To writing out a fair List thereof ...	1 :	11	6
	And also writing a Duplicate	1 :	11	6
20.	To John Taylor & four children to Montgomery	:	1	6
	To Oil for the Engines	:	2	6
	To Alex' Halley to Aberdeen	:	:	6
22.	To Dinah Wilding to Whitehaven ...	:	:	6
	To John Dew to Plymouth	:	:	6
23.	To an Inquisition over John Gee ...	:	2	4
24.	To an Inquisition over Mary Wright	:	1	4
	To George Davis to St Asaph in Wales	:	:	6
26.	To John Pettys & his wife to Halifax	:	1	:
27.	To a Coroners Inquisition over Tho' Sudworth	:	2	4
	To Ann Hague to Tideswell	:	:	6
	To James Carter assisting the Deputy Const to apprehd the thieves that broke M' Duxburys house & stole his Plate[1]	:	2	6
	To maintenance of a Horse kept by Ralph Worsley at sundry times for the use of the Constables business ...	:	18	4
	To an old soldier & his wife in great distress...	:	1	6

[1] See p. 233, note 1.

30.	To Luke Jackson & 2 children to Warrington...	: 1
	To Fanny Scholfield for prison room 36 nights at 1' each night for Prisoners at seperate times held in custody there during the last four months	1 : 16 :
	To meat & drink 36 nights & 36 mornings	: 18 :
	To Thomas Heskin to Lancaster ...	: 6
30.	To John Oldham jun' superintending the Watch	: 1 :
Febry 1.	To Phebe Leith to Northumberland	: 6
	To Mary Bale & her young child to same place	: 1 :
3.	To James Croft to Chester	: : 6
	To Biddey Edwards sick to Huntington	: 1 :
5.	To Samuel Prestwich to Scotland ...	: : 6
	To Susan White & two children to Glascow	: 1 :
	To Jane Collier to Liverpoole	: 1 :
10.	To James Lumb to Tadcaster	: : 6
	To Mary Richards & child to York...	: 1 :
13.	To Coroners Inquisition over Alice Thorpe	: 2 :
	To Mark Butler to Stafford	: : 6
15.	To John Jackson to Ulverstone ...	: : 6
	To three Men to Ireland	: 1 :
	To John Gawcoger [Gawkroger] to Halifax	: : 6
16.	To Ralph Withington to Osset... ...	: 6
17.	To James Brierley all night Prisoner at Sun [1]	: 1 :
	To Mary Vesty to Sheffield	: : 6
	To William Howard to Liverpoole...	: : 6
	To a Load of Coals for soldiers Guard-room	: 8 : 8
20.	To Isabell Gilpin to London	: : 6
	To Eliz. Ratcliff & two children to London	: 1 :
	To Robert Barton attending the watch two nights	: 2 :

[1] This Manchester inn has occurred before. (See p. 173, note 3.)

	To William Falkner to Warrington...	:	6	
23.	To Belman for two crys ag.t throwing at Cocks[1]	: 3 :		
25.	To John Bradley to Thetford	:	6	
	To spent upon the Watch after a long nights fatigue	: 1 :		
26.	To James Bateson & wife to Norwich	: 1 :		
	To Ann Pool & child to London ...	: 1 :		
26.	To three men assisting the Deputy to clear the Streets of Vagabonds... ...	: 3 :		
27.	To Sarah Ponton to Knighton... ...	:	:	6
	To John Newby to Scotland	: 1 :		
	To Jonath: Gillet to Liverpoole ...	:	:	6
Mar 1.	To Inquisition over Jacob Butterworth[2] Jurors Fees 2.s warrants to the Hamlets 1.s...	: 3 :		
2.	To Pickering one night superintending the watch and John Oldham another...	: 2 :		
	To Daniel Martin to Gradwell	:	6	
	To expences examining sundry Persons apprehended by the watch & took to the Blackmoreshead[3]	: 3 : 4		
	To Jonath. Butterworth assisting ab.t a warrant	: 1 :		
3.	To John Moss to Derby	:	:	6
	To Eliz.: Smith a stranger going home	: 1 :		
	To Beadles new Stockings 4:6, new Shoes 6.s	: 10 : 6		
	To Richard Dickenson superintending the watch	: 3 :		
5.	To Joseph Wood to Liverpoole ...	:	:	6
	To Eliz: Stacey & child to Liverpoole	: 1 :		
	To detaining a Man in Custody all night on suspicion of uttering False money Prison room 1.s a man attending him 1.s : 6.d Meat for both 1.s	: 3 : 6		

---

[1] See p. 66, note 1.

[2] The *Manchester Mercury* of March 16th states that "on Tuesday last [March 9th] the Coroner's Jury finished their Inquiry touching the Death of Jacob Butterworth, a poor Boy who died in our Infirmary, a few Days before." He was an apprentice to a shoemaker in Ashton-under-Lyne, where he had received such severe and cruel treatment that the Jury returned a verdict of wilful murder against his master, John Brierley.

[3] The "Blackamoor's Head," one of the inns in the town, has been mentioned before. (See p. 220, note 1.)

6	To Thomas Harpur with the Deputy Constable endeavouring to clearing the Streets	1 :	
	To William Sedgwick very poorley to London	1 :	
	To Susan Connell to Altringham ...	: 6	
9.	To Richard Topping w[i]fe & 5 children to Lancaster	: 1 :	
10.	To delivering presentments at Bolton Horschire 2 6 Turnpikes & dining 2ˢ High Constables Clerk for present- ments 1ˢ	: 5 : 6	
11.	To Eliz: Duncan to Carlisle	: : 6	
	To Thomas Vaun to Kendall	: : 6	
12.	To an Inquisition over Robert Humphrys	: 2 : 4	
	To Mary Herberts to York	: 6	
	To Mary Heald & child to Warring- ton	: 1 :	
15.	To Mary Dean & two children to Gosworth	: 1 :	
	To Margᵗ Mᶜ Leane to Scotland ...	: 6	
16.	To Eliz. Murry & child to Dum- fries	: : 6	
19.	To John Pickford at the Ramshead[1] Salfordbridge Note for eating & Liquor to sundry Prisoners in Dung[eon] ...	: 18 : 5	
	To Sarah Savill into Kent	: : 6	
	To Isaac Monroe to Liverpoole ...	: : 6	
20.	To Wᵐ Pickering superintending the watch 5 nights	: 5 :	
	To James Holt dⁿ three nights... ...	: 3 :	
	To Grace King & daughter to Liver- poole	: 1 :	
	To John Tetlow to Rochdale	: 1 :	
22.	To an old Soldier & his wife	: 1 : 6	
	To Mary Davids to Holywell	: : 6	
23.	To detaining a Man all night known by the name of Rake, Prison room 1ˢ Meat & drink 1ˢ wages of an att[e]ndant 1ˢ	: 3 :	

---

[1] The "Ramshead" has occurred before. (See p. 163, note 5.)

	To expences detaining Mary Isher-wood all night & one day on suspicion of Felony 1. 3. Prisonroom 1ˢ wages of a Man one day att[e]nding her 1ˢ...	: 3 :	3	
26.	To Mary Jones & two children to Nantwich	: 1 :		
26.	To James Stubbs to Chelsea		: 6	
27.	To Margᵗ Kershaw to Altringham ...		: 6	
	To a Coroners Inquisition over John Bowden	: 2 :	4	
	To Abigal Smith to Halifax		: 6	
	To James Dawson for assisting the Misegather[er]s to Collect the Con-stables Tax	: 10 :	6	
	To Paper ruling and writing the Leybook	1 : 10 :		
31.	To Eleanor Cadogan to Ireland ...		: : 6	
Aprl 1.	To an Inquisition over James Allsworth	: 3 :		
	To Archibald Campbell to Whitehaven		: : 6	
	To Mary Mills & two children to Liverpoole	: 1 :		
5.	To Luke Martin & his wife to Ply-mouth	: 1 :		
6.	To Mary Johnson to Coventry... ...		: 6	
7.	To Edmund Wrigleys bill for repair-ing the Engines[1]	1 : 13 :		
	To William Bennet for Ironwork about dᵒ	: 14 :	1	
	To attending 7 Persons in Custody one whole day at the Sun[2] who were apprehended and driven out of Town as Strollers[3]	: 3		
9.	To James Gatley to Rib Chester ...		: 6	
	To supertnding [sic] the watch 10 nights	: 10 :		
10.	To Frank Byers to Loughbrough ...		: 6	
12.	To an Inquisition a Man drowned at Barton cost...	: 2 :		
	To Robert Mᶜ Quay to Colchester ...	: : 6		
	To Eliz : Broadbent to Ireland... ...	: 1 :		

[1] See p. 87, note 1.
[2] The Sun Inn has been mentioned before. (See p. 248, note 1.)
[3] See p. 130, note 3.

	Description	£	s	d
	To three Assistants attending the Constables upon a privy watch... ...	:	3	:
13.	To Eliz: Pike & 2 children to Derby	:	1	:
13.	To Beadle John Barber two quarters wages	5	:	:
	To cleaning Dungeon twice & Meat to Prisoners there	:	4	6
	To backing a warrant at Stockport 1ˢ and Messʳ executing it there 1 :6 ...	:	2	6
	To John Barber for overlooking the watch twelve long nights	:	12	:
	To Eliz: Crow to Berwick	:	:	6
14.	To Nancy Moors to Derby	:	:	6
	To Ann Roberts & 2 children to Sheffield	:	1	:
	To Michael Sherry to Liverpoole ...		:	6
	To Henry Fitzsimon to London ...		:	6
	To expences detaining Samuel Ashton by order of four Justices thirteen days and thirteen nights in Custody intended as an Evidence against several Persons whom he charged with having diminished the Kings Coin.			
	and uttering the same ziv. [*sic*] Samˡ Ashton himself 13 Breakfasts at 3ᵈ 3ˢ . 3ᵈ 13 dinners at 6ᵈ each 6ˢ . 6ᵈ 13 Suppers at 3ᵈ 3ˢ . 3ᵈ & one Quart of Ale each day at 4ᵈ a Quart 4ˢ . 4ᵈ...	: 17	:	4
	the like for William Pickering one of the attendants	: 17	:	4
	the like for Oldham another attendant	: 17	:	4
	To Prison room during this mans confinement	:	8	:
	To Pickering for his attendance during this time	:	13	:
	To Oldham & others for their attendance	:	13	:
16.	To Warrants to the Eleven Hamlets Overseers to accᵗ	:	3	:
	To George Fowler to London	:	:	6
	To Thomas Sample to London ...	:	:	6

16.	To John Milwards Note for Locks and Pikel[1] for the use of the Dungeon ...	: 3 : 10
17.	To Impressing 8 Carts by virtue of Justices Warts [Warrants] to convey the Kings Baggage out of Manches'	: 8 :
18.	To James Dixon to Preston	: 6
	To John Hosier to Whitehaven ...	: 6
19.	To Ellen Lawson & her Sister to Lancaster	: 1 :
20.	To given Sam¹ Ashton by the Justices order for his openness in declaring against Money Clippers & Money Coiners	1 : 1 :
	To Kath. Barret & child to Whitehaven	: 1 :
	To Ellen Thomas & two children to Whitehaven	: 1 :
21.	To expences giving Personal notice to the Alehous[e] keepers to prepare provisions for the Dragoons[2] coming 3' several meetings with the Q'Mastrs thereupon 7.6.	: 10 : 6
	To a Stranger in great distress... ...	: 2 :
22.	To John Dargin & wife to London...	: 1 :
	To expences summoning thirty two Militia Men and attending them and their substitutes being near Sixty in number the greatest part of a day waiting to be swore in before the Deputy Lieuť and the Justices... ...	1 : : 1
	To Warrants to the Hamlets Militia to come to arms...	: 3 :
	To John Stott for Rent Coals Candles & repairs of the Gaurdroom [sic] as by his Note...	2 : 10 : 3
	To William Mason & wife to Fort George	: 1 :
	To John Turner to Berwick	: : 6
23.	To Ann Johnson to Berwick	: : 6

[1] "Pikel" is a well-known local word for pitchfork.

[2] In the *Mercury* for May 18th, 1773, is a paragraph that "The 3ʳᵈ Regiment of Dragoon Guards, quartered in this Town were reviewed in Castle-Field by Major General Mackay."

		£	s	d
	To Mary Low & daug' to Warrington	:	1 :	
25.	To John Dinlup to Newcastle	:	:	6
	To Eliz: Bond to Coventry	:	1 :	
27.	To Ann Ramsbottom to Blackburn...	:	:	9
	To Sarah Briscow & two children to Essex	:	1 :	
28.	To Ralph New to Stratford		:	6
	To William Harris to Oxford		:	6
	To presentment drawing for Sessions omitted in Janry	:	1 :	
	To drawing for this Sessions	:	1 :	
	To Deputys expences attending this Sessions	:	5 :	
30.	To Marg' Cowell to Sourby	:	:	6
	To John Jackson to Feversham ...	:	:	6
	To Ellis Sprecklestone to Sheffield...	:	:	6
May 4.	To Eliz: Butcher to Westham... ...	:	1 :	
	To Mary Burn & child to London ...	:	1 :	
8.	To John Todd wife & two children to Chester	:	1 :	
	To Betty Barnet to Winwick	:	:	6
	To Ann Brown to Hampshire	:	:	6
10.	To John Haynes to London	:	:	6
	To Bellmans Note for three Crys ...	:	5 :	
13.	To John Ellison & wife to Liverpoole	:	1 :	
	To Martha Henrys to Holywell ...	:	:	6
	To four Travellors to Ireland	:	2 :	6
	To Sarah Langley & her child to Plymouth	:	1 :	
15.	To James Kanady to Liverpoole ...		:	6
	To Edward Heap to Barnard Castle		:	8
18.	To Jeoffrey Tomkins to Chester ...		:	6
19.	To William Sampson to Nottingham		:	6
22.	To Thomas Hartshorn for Ironwork at the Exhañg [Exchange][1] for the use of the Quarter Sessions	3 :	12 :	2
	To Hanah Stracey & two children to Mansfield	:	1 :	
	To Coroners Inquisition over Samuel Mellor...	:	2 :	4

[1] See p. 53, note 4.

23.	To a second Inquisition open [*sic* for upon] the same occasion	: 2 : 4
	To Joseph Blythe to Newark	: : 6
	To Sarah Lambert a soldiers wife & 2 children to London	: 1 :
25.	To Mary Pratt to Chester...	: 1 :
	To enquiring several days & nights after a set of Persons suspected to sell stolen Cloth they were seven in a gang and at last two were apprehended & kept in Custody all night but discharged for want of full Evidences ...	: 5 : 6
	To Deputy Kay waiting upon Colonell Townley[1] at Belfield concerning Persons Who were suspected of Coining and uttering false Money Horsehire 3ˢ Turnpike & Bating 1ˢ the like to a Messˢ summoning Ashton to Belfield there to be examined touching the same Money 4ˢ to two Persons attending Ashton at the Old Coffeehouse were he was examined before two Justices two several days 3ˢ	: 11 :
27.	To Deputy Kay carrying Ellen Birch under Wart. [Warrant] to Belfield there to be bound over to the Assizes Horsehire double 4ˢ bating the Horse & two Persons dining 2ˢ 6ᵈ	: 6 : 6
28.	To returning Frank Wrigley under Warrant to Justice Lever Horsehire 2ˢ Bating & Turnpike 7ᵈ	: 2 : 7
	To Eliz: Robinson & three children to Blackburn	: 1 : 6
28.	To the High Constables warrant for the County Rates rebuilding Tootell & Tonge Bridges & wages of the Governor of the House of Correction at Manchester	62 : 17 : 3
	To David Frazer & his wife to Kingsgate	: 6

---

[1] This was Richard Townley, Esq., of Belfield, near Rochdale, a well-known agriculturist and magistrate.

	To Susan Evans to Warrington ...	: 6
29.	To Betty Rushworth to Midleton ...	: 6
	To Belman crying about a Mad Dog	1 : 6
	To Warrants to the Hamlets for Assessors of Window duty	: 3 :
	To Thirty two Notices to Persons to appear before the Commissioners in order to be appointed Assessors[1] ...	: 5 : 4
	To expences attending them all After-noon at the Dangerous Corner[2] before the Commissioners	: 2 : 8
	To 24 Window Ley Books pd to Tho' Davenport for Paper & ruling	: 9 :
	To writing the preparation of the same Books for the Assessors ap-pointed	: 4 :
	To binding the Window Ley Books in red Leather	: 1 : 6
	To Phillips & Greenway for Ribbons werewith to dress the Bridle[3] for scold-ing Women	: 1 : 9
30.	To William Cooper an old Soldier ...	: 1 :
	To searching with Assistants to appre-hend Long Ned...	: 1 : 2
	To Ann Lees a shaker[4] apprended for disturbing the Congregation in the old Church detaining her in the Prison room two days 2' maintaining her with meat & drink and her at-tendant 2. 3. wages 2'	: 6 : 3
June 1"	To John France to Liverpoole... ...	: : 6
	To Martha Taylor to Derby	: : 6

---

[1] That is, assessors of the Window Tax. (See p. 82, note 2.)

[2] See p. 5, note 1.

[3] This is the first time there has been any reference to the "Bridle" for Scolding Women in this volume, and the second time it has been mentioned in the *Constables' Accounts*. An account of it will be found in Volume ij, p. 59, note 5. I do not know why it should have been necessary to dress it with ribbons on this occasion.

[4] See p. 227, note 2. The report of the July Quarter Sessions held in the town states that "John Townley, John Jackson, Betty Lees and Ann Lees (Shakers) for going into Christ Church, in Manchester, and there wilfully and contemptuously in the Time of Divine Service disturbing the Congregation then assembled at Morning Prayer in the said Church, were severally fined Twenty Pounds each."

[June] 1st	To apprehending Edward Edwards otherwise Long Ned[1] under Justice Bowers Warrant on suspicion of committing a Robbery on the Highway detaining him at the Sign of the Sun[2] two days and two nights in Custody of two Assistants in the mean time waiting upon Justice Bower who drew his commitment for Lancaster but for some particular reasons sent him in Custody to Justice Watson[3] at Stockport who again returned him back to the Constables of Manchester, Prison room during this time 2s Meat & drink for Long Ned[1] his two att[e]ndants & the Person who complained against him during the said two days and two nights 11s 6d...	: 13 : 6
3.	To conveying him to Stockport a second time from whence he was committed to Chester Castle were the two Mess[rs] staid with him all night this cost 6s 6d Jonath: Butterworth attending him two days at Manchester 3s...	: 9 : 6
	To Richard Dickenson and another seeking Evidences against Long Ned[1] attending him and other Errands ...	: 5 :
	To Long Neds[1] Committment... ...	: 4 :
	To Mary Gibborn & two children to Beverley	: 1 :
	To a Mess[r] [Messenger] with Long Ned[1] to Chester wages and expences	: 14 : 3
	To Ann Lewis to Dartmouth with a young child	: 1 :
	To Thomas Harpur superintending the watch 3 nights	: 3 :
	To Ann Mc Coy to London	: : 6

---

[1] See p. 229, note 4.

[2] This inn has occurred several times before. (See p. 248, note 1, and also p. 251, note 2.)

[3] This was the Rev. John Watson, M.A., F.S.A., the well-known rector of Stockport.

3.	To apprehending and detaining James Goodin on suspicion of selling stolen raw Silk in Custody two days & one night Meat & drink for him & his attendant 3 : 8. Prison room at Pack-horse[1] 1ˢ Attendants wages 2 days & one night 3ˢ	: 7 : 8
	To conveying him to Stockport there to be examined w[h]ere he enlisted to be a Soldier, Messʳ & expences... ...	: 2 : 6
	To apprehending two women for stealing Printed [goods] & detaining them in the Dungeon all night with their maintenance the day following when the[y] were discharged because the Prosecutors would not give Evid[ence]	: 1 : 6
6.	To Mary Holme to Wolverhampton	: : 6
	To William Green & wife to Carlisle ...	: 1 :
	To Alexander Mackintoss to Glascow	: : 6
7.	To an old Soldier to Liverpoole ...	: 1 :
	To two Messʳˢ sent to apprehend a Man[2] for Clipp[ing] & coining [going] into Tormorden Rochdale & the Edge of Yorkshire	: 8 :
9.	To Andrew Reynolds to Barnesley ...	: : 6
	To James Vaun to Whitehaven ...	: : 6
12.	To Mary Edwards & her daugʳ to Derby	: 1 :
	To detaining Martin Southern a day & a night for a breach of the Peace agᵗ his wife & family Prison room 1ˢ Maintenance	: 2 :

---

[1] This inn has occurred before. (See p. 209, note 1.)

[2] A few weeks later the *Manchester Mercury* of July 13th has the following paragraph :—

"We are glad to inform our Readers, that on Wednesday last, one J. Milner, was apprehended near Bingley in Yorkshire, by Virtue of a Warrant from Col. Townley [of Belfield] and brought before him the next Day. He, for some Time denied the Charge of clipping Money which was proved against him ; but when his Mittimus was drawing, his Resolution failed him. He then confessed, very candidly, the Crime he was charged with, and afterwards made some very material Discoveries against some very notorious Offenders, against whom Warrants were immediately issued, and 'tis hoped they will soon be apprehended, and also brought to exemplary Punishment."

[June] 12.	To Mary Smalley & child to Liverpoole	:	1 :	
13.	To an old Soldier	:	1 :	
15.	To Mary Hornby to Huddersfield ...	:	:	6
	To Joseph Bowls to Northampton ...	:	:	6
	To Richard Bryan & wife to Liverpoole	:	1 :	
17.	To Ann Davis & child to York ...	:	:	6
	To Katharine Wadsworth going to Ireland	:	:	6
18.	To Eliz: Brant & four children to Kilverstone...	:	1 :	6
20.	To Jane Mc Quay to Liverpoole ...		:	6
	To Saml Ashton for further trouble abt Coiners as by his receipt		: 10 :	6
	To two Persons to Warrington to bring back three Men for Picking a Gentlewomans Pocket in the Market Place in Manchester cost	1 :		
	To detaining John Buckley & another Lad suspected to be of the same Gang one night and one day Prison room 2s Meat & drink 1s. 2d an attendant one day 1s	: 4 :	2	
21.	To Marjery Macclesfield to Montross		:	6
	To Ann Scholfield & three children to Halifax	:	1 :	
	To Prison room for Ann Chapels Son two nights apprehended as an idle disorderly Person	:	2 :	
23.	To the Chairmen[1] for carrying home Math. Higginson rashly and dangerously wounded by Martin Southern	:	1 :	
	To Prison room five nights 5s meat & drink five days 6.6 detaining Martin Southern by order of the Justices waiting to see w[h]ether Math: Higginson could recover his Wound or not	: 11 :	6	
	To a man attending him all the while	:	5 :	
24.	To James Morgan & his wife to Walterstone	1 :		

---

[1] This has reference to the sedan chairs, which were at this time in common use. They were carried on long poles, borne on the shoulders of two men called "chairmen."

	To an old Soldier with his wife to Scotland	:	1 :	
	To cleaning Salford steps as ususual [sic]	:	2 :	
25.	To Charles Mᶜ Leane to Glascow ...	:	:	6
	To Ann Steuart & three children to Glascow	:	1 :	
	To Thoˢ Baron assisting abᵗ a Warrant	:	:	6
27.	To Joseph Armiger to Durham ...	:	:	6
	To an old Soldier going to Chelsea ...	:	1 :	
29.	To an Inq̃ over Geo. Wood who strangled himself	:	2 :	4
	To Geo : Walker wife & two children to Bawtree	:	1 :	
	To detaining one Worrall at the Sun¹ three nights for Prison room 3ˢ for meat & drink 2 . 6	:	5 :	6
	To William Baguley to Plumpton in the Fild [Fylde]	:	:	6
	To Cath : Carter & two children to Liverpoole	:	1 :	
July 2.	To John Wray to Runcorn	:	:	6
	To three Strollers² at Poorhouse door	:	1 :	6
	To John Dod overlooking the watch one night	:	1 :	
3.	To Charles Flower to Port Patrick ...	:	:	6
	To David Britton to Hereford	:	1 :	
	To an Inq̃ over Joseph Blakely ...	:	2 :	
	To committing two Lewd women cost	:	4 :	6
	To Archibald Williams to Hull	:	:	6
4.	To Eliz : Wroe & child to Leek ...	:	1 :	
	To drink for the Engine Men as encour[a]gement	:	1 :	6
	To apprehending & detaining under Justice Heskeths wart [warrant] James Clark for Bastardy till a Messʳ could be found to convey him before Just[ice] Hesketh at Preston	:	4 :	8
4.	To John Oldham conveying the before named James Clark to Preston expences himself & the Prisoner thither & himself back 8 : 6 wages three days 4 : 6	:	13 :	

---

¹ See p. 257, note 2.   ² See p. 130, note 3.

		£	s	d
6.	To three Strangers to York	:	1	:
	To apprehending & detaining John Hyde on suspicion of Felony Prison room 1ˢ maintenance 8ᵈ an Attendant one day 1ˢ.6ᵈ when he got Bail ...	:	3	: 2
	To John Clark and his wife to Carlisle	:	1	:
	To Ann Robinson to Rochdale ...	:	:	6
7.	To William Berkeley overlooking the watch 1 night	:	1	
	To James Oldham for Business done at various times on the Constables account	:	6	:
	To John Dod going to Justice Watson[1] at Stockport about Long Ned[2] Ben. Thorp & Charles Clayton three notorious Thieves & robbers backing warrant & expences 3ˢ wages one day 1ˢ.6ᵈ	:	4	: 6
	and again to Knutsford & other parts of Cheshire to apprehend Ben. Thorpe for Highway robbery Expences 5ˢ wages two days 3ˢ	:	8	
	To Ellen Lutwidge & two children to Liverpoole	:	1	:
	To thirty two Militia Men[3] each 1ˢ at the time they was swore in	1	: 12	:
	To Corbet Onslow & his wife to Swansey	:	1	:
	To Thomas Johnson to Orford ...	:	:	6
8.	To a Soldier with a wife & four children in distress	:	2	: 6
10.	To Sarah Chetham & child to Chester	:	1	:
	To Janet Hely to Liverpoole	:	:	6

[1] See p. 257, note 3.   [2] See p. 257.
[3] In the *Manchester Mercury* for July 6th, 1773, is the following paragraph :—

"Yesterday [July 5th] the whole of the Royal Lancashire Militia, in this Town, commanded by the Right Hon. Lord Stanley, were disembodied; they were publickly reviewed on Thursday last, and went through the whole of their Manœuvres and Firings with great Credit to the Assiduity and Instruction of their Officers, and to the entire Satisfaction of a great Number of Gentlemen, who came from all Parts of the Neighbourhood upon the Occasion ; in the Evening was a grand and elegant Ball, given by the Officers to the Ladies and Gentlemen of the Town, and last Night another grand and elegant one was given by his Lordship."

		£ s. d.
	To Mary Shelmerdine & two children to Stockport	: 1 :
[July] 12.	Edwd Bell & wife to Luton	: 1 :
	To Mary Birkhamshire detaining all night appreh. by the Watch Prison room 1ʳ expences 9ᵈ	: 1 : 9
	To Ben. Oldham assisting about a Warrant	: : 6
	To Tho' Herd to Lincoln...	: : 6
13.	To an old Soldier going to Berwick...	: 1 :
15.	To Jane Laithwaite to Altringham ...	: : 6
	To Jane Brown & three children to Landric	: 1 :
	To putting up a new pair of Steps at the end of Milbrow Bridge the old ones being quite worn away the care and property of which always belonged to the Constables of Manchester as under	
	To Richard Greenwood Bricksetter 29 days work	2 : 8 : 4
	To Chris Mohun Mason 11½ days ...	1 : 3 :
	To John Wrigley Carpenter 2 days...	: 3 : 8
	To 3500 Bricks at 10ʳ a Thousand ...	1 : 15 :
	To 10 Lds of Lime 1 . 6 & 5 Lds of Sand at 1 . 4	1 : 1 : 8
	To 34 feet of solid Stone at 6ᵈ a foot	: 17 :
	To Flaggs for Steps and Landings ...	1 : 9 : 9
	To Carting the said Flaggs	: 1 :
	To 20½ P^d of Iron Cramps at 4ᵈ and 40℔ of Lead at 2ᵈ	: 13 : 6
	To Boards & nails 4ʳ . 10ᵈ . drink for the workmen 10ʳ . 1ᵈ	: 14 : 11
	To Labouring work by Paul Barns 11 days at 1ʳ. 4ᵈ a day	: 14 : 8
	To Thomas Lee a Lad 11 days at 8ᵈ a day	: 7 : 4
	To keeping a Woman in Custody till she could be sent to Whitehaven ...	: 1 : 6
17.	To John Holt to Bridgenorth	: : 6
	To three men in the night endeavouring to appreh[en]d John Buck for an a[s]sault	: 1 : 6

		£	s	d
	To Susan Bradley & child to Coventry	:	1 :	
18.	To Sarah Mather to Glocester... ...	:	:	6
	To Eliz: Smith & lad to Carlisle ...	:	1 :	
	To a Blind Stranger	:	:	6
	To Wm Barlow for Horschire on sundry occasions on the Constables account	:	12 :	
	To apprehending under warrant Ann M^c kenny keeping her in Custody till she could be brought to Justice and conveying her to the House of Correction	:	3 :	
20.	To a Sailor going to Liverpoole ...	:	1 :	
	To detaining James Widows two days & 1 night in custody for leaveing his wife and children chargeable meat & drink 1 . 6 . an attendant one day 1^s. 6^d	:	3 :	
	To John Pemberton in Custody for violently assaulting his Neighbour. Prison room 1^s two Men attending him 8 hours the following day till the Justice could be seen 2^s meat &c. 1^s	:	4 :	
	To fetching a man under Justice Booths wart [warrant] from Chowbent	:	3 :	
22.	To drawing Presentment to Sessions	:	1 :	
	To the discharge of a man in Yatestreet by approbation of the Court	:	5 :	
	To the Clerk of the Peace sundry Fees for Sessions business	:	10 :	6
	To four Men for attending the Sessions doors three at [sic] days at the request of the Justices upon the Bench	1 :	4 :	
	To Mary Swift to Kingsale	:	:	6
	To Peter Smith wife & child to Case Horton	:	1 :	
	To John Swinburn to Hull	:	:	6
23.	To a pair of Shoes for Beadle	:	5 :	9
	To apprehending John Buck under Warrant for attempting to commit a Rape upon the body of Aimy Miflin who was bound over to the Sessions	:	3 :	
	To Warrants to the Hamlets for Presentments	:	3 :	

To John Gillet wife & 2 children to Barnsley	: 1 :	
[July] 23. To maintaining Rob' Taylor 1 night & 1 day in Custody for leaving his family when he was ordered to be whip't ...	: 1 : 6
To maintaining a man all night in the Dungeon for Croftbreaking [1]	: 6
To Archibald Williams to Hull... ...	: 6
To Warrants to the Hamlets to pay High Constables warts [warrants] ...	: 3 :
To a second course the other being Countermanded and day changed ...	: 3 :
26. To Ann Ward with a lame arm to Wiggan	: 1 :
To John Oldhams Bill conveying Ben. Thorpe to Lancas' for Highway robbery	2 : 14 :
To Tho' Shepherd drawing the Commitment and two Renognizances [sic] to give Evidence at Chester	: 6 :
Four Trampers [2] going to Ireland ...	: 1 : 6
To Francis Burling & a sick wife to London	: 1 :
27. To maintaining a woman & two children at Sun [3] till they could be removed by Pass having no w[h]erc else to be at	: 3 : 6
To a Copy of a Conviction against Joseph Bates for fraudulently carrying his goods away to prevent making distress 1' serving him therewith 6'...	: 1 : 6
To detaining Rich[d] Coe a night & a day for feloniously taking a Watch out of John Browns Shop when he was committed to the House of Correction	: 3 :
To William Cawthorn to Ireland ...	: 6
To three sets of Warrants to the Eleven Hamlets for their proportion of three several High Constables Warts [Warrants]	: 9 :

---

[1] See p. 206, note 5.   [2] See p. 119, note 2.
[3] This inn has been several times mentioned before. (See pp. 248, 251, and 257.)

28.	To Robert Hunter wife & child to Glascow		: 1 :	
	To Thomas Bell to Exeter		: 6	
28.	To apprehending John Pemerton as a Madman for disturbing the Congregation in the old Church & detaining him till the Justices meeting when he was ordered to the Poorhouse and there chained fast, Prison room meat and attendants wages...		: 8 : 8	
	To a soldier discharged going home...		: 1 :	
	To Beadle Barber[1] one Quarters Wages...		2 : 10 :	
	To him for Meat for Susan Newton whilst in Prison		: 1 :	
	To going twice with two Warrants to Justice Lever[2]		: 2 :	
	To attending Ann Lees[3] two whole nights		: 3 :	
	To Superintending the watch three long nights...		: 3 :	
	To cleansing the Dungeon twice ...		: 2 :	
	To Straw for the Dungeon		: 3 : 6	
	To removing Ann Peyan & two children by Pass to Sourby cost more than the County allowance		: 6 : 2	
	To Isaac Speller for Whitehaven ...		: 6	
29.	To Belman crying Carriers Warehouse broke		: 2 :	
	To Ann Brunt to Lancaster		: 6	
	To William Smith an old man to Chelsea		: 1 :	
30.	To Roger Dawson to Whitehaven ...		: : 6	
	To Belman for one Cry		: 1 : 6	
Aug" 2.	To Betty Blag to London...		: : 6	
	To Jane Heward & 2 children to Carlisle		: 1 :	
3.	To Ellen Hostler to York...		: 6	
	To John Dale to Liverpoole		: 6	

[1] Mr. John Barber was at this time the Beadle.
[2] This was Ashton Lever, of Alkrington, Esq., who was High Sheriff of Lancashire in 1771.
[3] See p. 227. note 3, and also p. 256, note 4.

To three Men attending George Lees for stealing Soldiers Linnen	: 3 :	
[Aug.] 5. To Kath Caves to Ireland	: 6	
To several assistants with the Deputy to apprehend John Needham raging Mad in the streets	: 2 :	
To a Mess' to Stockport to bring his father to give Evidence of his Sons setlement before the Justices	: 1 : 6	
To a Mess' the day after, he rufusing to come with the first when he shewed his Sons Setlem' at Bollinfee	: 1 : 6	
Paid on the Fathers account & for his Examination	: 2 : 6	
To a Mess' to Bollinfee to desire the Officers to fetch the Madman away two days wages 3' Expences 2'... ...	: 5 :	
To Prison room for this man five days & five nights	: 5 :	
To two Men attending him five days & five nights he being very troublesome & was at last sent to the Lunatic Hospitall [1] at 2. 6 a day and night ...	. : 12 : 6	
To Meat & drink at the Sun [2] during this time	: 6 :	
To David Griffith to Ruabon	: : 6	
6. To Robert Bolf to Castleton	: : 6	
To Sarah Garner & 2 children to Newcastle	: 1 :	
To a Stranger going to Dublin ...	: 1 :	
To two Persons all night endeavouring to apprehend a Man under Warrant for an Asault	: 1 : 6	
To Warrants to the Hamlets for Ale-licences	: 3 :	
To a Mess' to Legh to fetch an order from the Clerk of the Peace for removing Geo: Denton to Crigglestone	: 3 :	
To maintaining him three days whilst Sessions order could be obtained ...	: 1 : 6	

[1] See p. 195, note 3.
[2] This inn has been frequently mentioned before. (See p. 204.)

8.	To keeping a Soldier whilst the Land-lord could be forced to provide for him according to his Billet	:	1 :	6
	Hanah Penny & her child to Leeds	:	1 :	
8.	To Robert Young to Sheffield... ...	:	:	6
	To John Birch & two children to Whitehaven	:	1 :	
	To four Men assisting to apprehend James Makin for Rioting & conveying him to Prison	:	2 :	
10.	To William Roberts to Salop	:	:	6
	To Susan Garner & 2 children to Liverpoole	:	1 :	
	To Andrew Dewhurst to Preston ...	:	:	6
11.	To Coroners Inquisition over John Boardman[1]	:	2 :	
	To a meeting of fourteen Serjeants Militia & Regulars to setle the Billets of both in May last cost in expences	:	9 :	2
	To a Renognizance [sic] of James Gleaddill agᵗ Long Ned[2]	:	4 :	
12.	To Ann Moors to Birmingham ...	:	:	6
	To John Holt & wife to Birmingham	:	1 :	
14.	To John White to Liverpoole... ...	:	:	6
	To James Brown to Liverpoole ...	:	:	6
	To Chris. Watts to Penistone	:	:	6
	To Thoˢ Barton to superintending the watch 2 nights	:	2 :	
	To Joseph Whitehead for Beadles Shoes	:	5 :	9
	To him for repairing Engine Buckets	:	4 :	
	To Prison room for James Scholes in Custody for breaking windows 1ˢ meat & drink 1 day 8ᵈ	:	1 :	8
17.	To Daniel Robinson & wife to Liver-poole	:	1 :	
	To repaid two Inquisitions to James Carter	:	4 :	

[1] The *Manchester Mercury* of August 17th states that "On Tuesday [August 10th] a Youth about 18 Years of Age, Son of Charles Boardman, Wheelwright, in Salford, was drowned by bathing in the River Irwell."

[2] See p. 229, note 4.

To an Inquisition over Abram Walmesley	: 2 : 4
To Tho' Newton to Halifax	: : 6
To John Tetlow to London	: : 6

[Aug.] 18. To returning Presentment at Rochdale 1ˢ for dinner 1ˢ Bating the Horse Turnpike & extraordinaries 1ˢ . 7ᵈ. Horsehire 3ˢ … … … … …   : 6 : 7

To High Constables Warrant for repairs of Ribble Bridge &c … …   1 : 7 : 7

To another of money expended on account of the House of Correction at Manchester … … … … …   3 : 4 : 3

19. To apprehending & detaining in the Dungeon all night for notorious Drunkeness … … … … …   : 1 :

To Martha Sedley & two children to Chester … … … … … …   : 1 :

To an Assistant two days giving Personal Notice & taking a List of Alehousekeepers to apply for Licences   : 3 :

20. To James Bosley wife & two children to Ireland … … … … … …   : 1 :

To the Beadle of Salford[1] asisting abᵗ a warrant … … … … … …   : 1 :

To Peter Watson to Newcastle …   : : 6

21. To Margᵗ Sayer to Wolverhampton … … … … … …   : : 6

To conveying William Watmough & his wife under Wart [Warrant] for Coinage two men attending them at Manchʳ 2ˢ their Dinners with Extraordinaries at Rochdale 2ˢ dinners &c of two Assistants 2ˢ bating two Horses & turnpikes twice, being obliged to wait at Belfield till night 2ˢ 9ᵈ Horsehire one Horse single 4ˢ another double 5ˢ   : 17 : 9

To Wages of two Assistants … …   : 5 :

25. To Thomas Gleave to Liegh … …   : : 6

To Jacob Phillips wife & child to Hull… … … … … … … …   : 1 :

---

[1] The Salford Beadle has been once before referred to. (See p. 204, note 3.)

	To returning a man under Justice Levers[1] warrant to Alkrington with two Assistants	:	3	:
25.	To an old Soldier	:	1	:
	To detaining Charles Barns Apprentice all night in the Prison room at Sun[2] cost	:	1	: 3
28.	To Sarah Morrell & child to London	:	1	:
	To Kath Higson to Liverpoole ...	:	:	6
30.	To Thomas Hulmes wife all night in the Dungeon attending her at Packhorse[3] near a day & searching her house for stolen Cloths...	:	2	:
	To Marg[t] Carrey to Dublin	:	:	6
	To Bridget Kenny to Dublin	:	:	6
	To Fanny Scholfields receipt for one years rent of an Ammunition room for the Militia	3	3	:
Sep[r] 1.	To Ann Dillon & child to Liverpoole	:	1	:
	To Ann Brown to Colne	:	:	6
2.	To Betty Barns to Burnley	:	:	6
3.	To Mary Moffet to Berkshire	:	:	6
	To Sarah Atkinson near blind to Royden	:	1	:
4.	To George Brown an old Soldier ...	:	1	:
	To James Gleaddill in part of the Prosecution of Long Ned[4] and Ben. Thorpe at Chester Assizes by the special request of several Justices in Manchester...	5	5	:
	To the Loosing of a Silver Watch which was necessary as a point of Evidence to be produced at the Assizes which Watch had been before pawned by some of the Gang	1	5	:
	To Timothy Ogden to Lewes	:	:	6

---

[1] See p. 265, note 2.

[2] There have been several previous references to the Sun Inn, and from this entry it would seem as if there was a "prison room" there where prisoners were taken from time to time, perhaps when the Dungeon was full.

[3] This Manchester inn has been mentioned once or twice before. There seems to have been a "prison room" there too.

[4] See p. 237.

[Sept.] 7.	To Two Assistants to apprehend Mary Brown and Mary Mason for picking a Mans Pocket	: 2 :
8.	To Edward Morris wife & child to Dumfries	: 1 :
	To John Wrenshaw to Market Har-brough	: 6
	To Cornelius Rich to Bath	: : 6
	To two Assistants to appreh. Wm Ratclif with the Deputy, cost many nights trouble 2ˢ conveying him to Hope[1] & back to the House of Correction 1ˢ	: 3 :
9.	To William Yates & wife to Stafford	: 1 :
	To Jane Webster to Garstang	: : 6
	To Dolly Horner & child to Wakefield	: 1 :
11.	To Wid: Shepley for three new Watch Bills[2] repairing a Engine & putting Pikes[3] upon the Pinfold ...	: 10 :
	To Edwᵈ Miffin to Londonderry ...	: : 6
13.	To Patrick Rook to Ireland	: : 6
	To returning a Warrant of Sʳ John Fieldens[4] to Hope[1]	: 1 :
	To a Messʳ to Bury to summon Wᵐ Booth to give Evid agˢᵗ Thoˢ Charles before Justice Lever[5] at Alkrington...	: 1 :
	To Deputy Kay with Thoˢ Charles under Wart [Warrant] to Justice Levers[5] Horsehire 1 . 6 . waiting a long while & Bating at Midleton 1ˢ...	: 2 : 6
14.	To Coroners Inquisitions over Thoˢ Roscoe & another two Jurys 4ˢ War-rants to the Hamlets 1ˢ	: 5 :
	To Mathew Walston & wife into Kent	: 1 :

---

[1] See p. 191, note 2.   [2] See p. 31, note 4.
[3] Or rather, I should think, "Spikes."
[4] Sir John Fielding was a well-known personage at this time, being the chief of the old London police force. About this period he began to advertise for criminals in the provincial papers, and extracts from "Sir John Fieldings Hue and Cry," dated from the "Public Office, Bow Street, London," are to be found regularly every week in the *Manchester Mercury* and other papers.
[5] See p. 265, note 2.

	To Tho' Harpur for clearing the Streets of strollers &c	: 3 :
17.	To an old Soldier & his family going into Scotland	: 1 :
18.	To Thomas Smith wife & child to Helmesley	1 :
	To Mary Brenks to Cumberland ...	: 6
19.	To Joseph Roberts & wife to Liver-poole	: 1 :

[Carried forward]   ... ...£414 : 18 :

[The remainder of this Year's Accounts is missing.]

[Constables' Accounts.]

[13th Oct., 1773, to 12th Oct., 1774.]

••••••••••••

[**Dr** The Town of Manchester to MR. THOMAS MARRIOTT and MR. RICHARD LEIGH,[1] *Constables.*]

[**Disbursements**]

[The first portion of these Accounts is missing.]

1774.		£	s	d
Janry 24.	Brought over	254 :	5 :	2
	To costs of detaining attending & maintaining a Gang of Housebreakers who had alarmed the whole Town very much			
	Eliz: Hunt wife of Edw[d] Hunt for receiving and vending stolen Goods prison room 4 nights 4ˢ meat &c for her & a man attending her 5ˢ Wages of attendant 4 days 4ˢ		: 13 :	
	To James Taylors wife another of the same Gang kept in Custody at the Sun[2] 1 day & 1 night cost		: 3 :	6
	When she was removed to her husband at Packhorse[3] to be further examined & both were detained 5 days & 5 nights whilst Edw[d] Hunt was sought for up & down the Country...			
	Meat & drink for them two, 5 days...		: 10 :	
	prison room 5 nights...		: 5 :	
	two attendants Wages during the whole time...		: 10 :	

---

[1] These two Constables were elected at the Court Leet held on the 13th Oct., 1773. (See *Court Leet Records*, vol viij., p. 151.)
[2] See p. 269, note 2.   [3] See p. 258, note 1.

		£	s	d
	Meat for the attendants	:	5 :	
27.	To Eliz. Brown to Derby	:	:	6
	To a meeting of the Q'masters to regulate the Billets	:	3 :	
	To attending upon Glover a most notorious Theif for which he afterwards suffered death, a whole day & night in preparing to convey him to Lancaster Castle	:	3 :	6
	To Joseph Taylor wife & 2 children to Bewdley	:	1 :	
28.	To Jane Robinson to Carlisle		:	6
31.	To a Jurors Inquisition over John Walwork	:	3 :	
	To John Beckham & wife to Norwich	:	1 :	
	To Rich⁴ Dickenson assisting the Deputy to discover whether a Man had been killed in Ashley Lane or not when he lost a day	:	1 :	6
31.	To several Men searching Deans House & a Pit in Strangeways park where Pewter Brass a Gun Hams & other stolen goods were found concealed	:	4 :	
Febry 1ˢᵗ	To James Dawson for his assistance upon sundry occasions & detaining Prisoners in his House	:	8 :	
	To Kath. Day to London		:	6
	To James Ridge to Midleton		:	6
	To Tho' Harpur & two others assisting the Deputy to clear the Town of Vagabonds	:	3 :	
	To materials & Workmens wages preparing a room for the amunition belonging to the Dragoons as by Tho' Hansons Bill	1 :	6 :	11
	To six Men searching the River in Ashley Lane to find the Body of a Man supposed to be drowned there ...	:	6 :	
3.	To Frances Brereton to Leeds	:	:	6
	To three discharged Soldiers going home	:	1 :	6

		£	s	d
	To Jack Oldham a Messuage to Rochdale on the Constables Business ...		: 2 :	
	To two Men sent into Swinton to make Enquiry after Edwd Hunt were it was thought he lay to secrete himself		: 3 :	
	To Jonath Butterworth & Tho' Beavers to many Towns & places in Cheshire were the[y] heard of and pursued Hunt but could not apprehend him expences 21'. 3^d. Wages 4 days each 12'	1 :	13 :	3
4.	To Sarah Phillips & child to Chester		:	: 6
	To Robt Brown wife & 2 children to Plymouth		: 1 :	
	To Harpur & Shepley attending Pearson · and Mather for stealing Cheese out of a Shop in High-street & conveying them before Justices		: 2 :	
6.	To Harpur & another assisting Beadle to clear the Streets of Ballad singers[1] &c		: 2 :	
	To Ann Davis & two children to Plymouth		: 1 :	
	To Thomas Harpur returning a Warrant to Justice Watson[2] at Stockport		: 2 :	
	To an extraordinary attendant upon Glover who was suspected of breaking out of the House of Correction two nights		: 2 :	
	To the Clerks for his Committment to Lancas^r		: 4 :	
	To them for a Warrant agst Shaw for an asault		: 3 :	
	To Summons & summoning two Loiterers		: 2 :	
	To a sick Sailor going to Liverpoole		: 1 : 6	

---

[1] This is the first reference to ballad singers in this volume of Accounts.

[2] See p. 257, note 3.

		£	s	d
[Feb.] 9.	To three Cheshire Constables seeking after and apprehending Edward Hunt[1] there, their expences with him to Manchester, at Manchester and back again cost	2 :	1 :	3
	To a reward of Five Guineas offerd for the taking of Hunt,[1] which was claimed and paid to these three Cheshire Constables	5 :	5 :	
	To Jonath. Butterworth & another Man attending Hunt[1] 3 days whilst under examination and afterwards committed to Lancaster		: 9 :	
	To him for two Messuages [sic for Messages] to the Constables of Droylesden to come to the Justices at Manchester		: 3 :	
	To Robert Prestwage to Ashton ...	:	:	0
9.	To a Mess[r] fetching an Evidence from Stretford to be examined ab[t] Hunt[1]		1 :	
	To another Mess[r] to Hope[2] upon the same Business		: 1 :	
	To Sarah Moreton & 3 children to Macclesfield		: 1 :	
	To detaining James Dean[3] another of the Gang of Housebreakers 5 days & 5 nights with a Man to attend him the whole time cost in Meat drink & prison room	1 :	5 :	6
	To 5 days wages of the attendant ...		: 7 :	6
	To a deaf & dumb Man		: 1 :	
	To summoning M[r] Kirk in order to prove his keeping a Tipplinghouse that Dragoons might be quartered upon him paid to Evidences and for summons		: 3 :	

---

[1] There are several references to this Edward Hunt, who seems to have been a somewhat notorious offender. He is mentioned in the account of the March Assizes at Lancaster, and he seems to have been charged with breaking into the shop of Mr. Stevenson, a brazier in the town, but to have been acquitted chiefly on the information of James Dane, who was subsequently tried and convicted of wilful and corrupt perjury.

[2] See p. 191, note 2.

[3] This is probably the man mentioned in note 1.

		£	s	d
	To Wm Greenhalgh another Mess^r 4 days after Hunt & others of the same Gang wages		: 6 :	
[Feb.] 11	To Roger Ryon wife & 4 children to Ireland		: 2 :	
	To Marg^t Newsam & child to Skipton		: 1 :	
12.	To High Constables Warrant for repair of the House of Correction[1] & other necessarys there	2 :	:	6
	To Warrants to the Hamlets for their proportion		: 3 :	
	To Andrew Quiod to Ireland		:	: 6
	To Eliz: Mayres to Leek		:	: 6
	To Jonath. Butterworth twice to Stockport to apprehend a Man under a Warrant there Wages 2 . 6. backing Warrant 1^s expences both days 2^s...		: 5 :	6
	To Horschire to Hope[2] to get Hunts commitment to Lancaster...		: 1 :	6
14.	To Eliz: Hartley & two children to Liverpoole		: 1 :	
	To apprehending two Lads for stealing Keys out of Warehouse doors[3] detaining them 3 days whilst under examination when they was order'd to be sent to the Places of their setlement Meat for both 3 days 4.6 prison room 3 nights 3^s		: 7 :	6
	To three Men clearing the Town of Strollers[4]		: 3 :	
	To an old Soldier & his Wife		: 1 :	
	To Eliz. Ripton to Chesterfield... ...		:	: 6

---

[1] In last year's Accounts (see p. 268) there is an entry of repairs to the House of Correction, and it was entirely rebuilt in 1775. (See *postea.*)

[2] See p. 191, note 2.

[3] In the *Manchester Mercury* for Jan. 25th, 1774, is the following :—

"A CAUTION. Several evil disposed Persons having made a Practice of stealing the Keys from the front Doors of many Houses in this Town, either with an intent to sell them or for a worse Purpose, it would be prudent in all Persons to hang their Keys in some convenient Place, out of the reach of such strolling Vagrants as infest our Streets."

[4] See p. 130, note 3.

		£	s	d
	To Ann Kenny a common lewd woman apprehended by the Watch prison room 1ˢ an attendant till she could be took before the Justice 1 6 when she was committed		2	6
19.	To John Robinson wife & 2 children to Bristoll		1	
	To Robert Miller to Glascow			6
	To Edward Hartley for Horschire to Lancaster		18	6
	To the Belman for crying a Gang of Shoplifters who were thereby discovered		1	6
	To two foot Messengers pursueing these Persons who were overtaken in a Chaise at top of Blackstone Edge Messengers were obliged to Hire two Horses at 4ˢ at Littlebrough		4	
	Messⁿ brought these Thieves back to Manchʳ in the Chaise for which was paid to Mills of Littlebrough 22ˢ Expences upon the road 4ˢ . 4ᵈ	1	6	4
	To attendants and expences at the Packhorse[1] & Sun[2] till they could be comitted being 3 days		13	
	To Prison room at each House 3 days & nights		6	
21.	To Timothy Richards to Liverpoole			6
	To John Whip for a new nine corded Whip[3]		2	3
23.	To Sarah Marryon & six children to Liverpoole		2	
	To Supper & breakfast Dawson in the Dungeon			6
	To prison room & meat Mary Holt confined 1 day & 1 night for abusing the Officers...		2	
	To returning Wheeler under a Warrant to Justice Watson[4] at Stockport for killing Game unlawfully		2	

---

[1] See p. 269, note 3. [2] See p. 269, note 2.
[3] This is a fresh description of the cat-o' nine-tails.
[4] See p. 257, note 3.

		£	s	d
25.	To Joseph Dewhurst to Islington ...	:	:	6
	To detaining a Woman having raised a Mob & a riot in the Streets		:	6
	To loss by sale of light Money out of Cash received on the Constables account	:	4 :	6
	To Tho⁵ Walingford to Exeter ...		:	6
	To Mary James & two children to Wrexham	:	1 :	
26.	To Belman for five Crys on the Constables acct...	:	6 :	6
	To Grace Swan to Carlisle	:	:	6
	To an old soldier to Chelsea	:	1 :	
28	To Ann Pettys & 3 children to Liverpoole	:	1 :	
29.	To James Bowker to Ashton		:	6
	To William Eves to Winwick		:	6
	To 4 Men driving Vagabonds Balladsingers[1] & strollers out of the Town...	:	4 :	
March 2.	To Mary Jones & two children to Whistonstone ... ·	:	1 :	
	To John Gleny to Scotland	:	:	6
4.	To Sara Gosling to Norbury	:	:	6
	To John Fowley very old to Ireland	:	1 :	
5.	To apprehending and detain[in]g James Butterw[or]th for stealing Meat out of peoples Carts keeping him till he could be examined cost 2ˢ. 6ᵈ prison room 3 nights 3ˢ pᵈ an attendant 2ˢ...	:	7 :	6
5.	To James Chubs to Oxford	:	:	6
6.	To detaining John Yates & Samˡ Mullineaux two Strangers found by the Watch lying on the Shambles Boards till they could be examined...	:	2 :	6
7.	To Ann Rice & 3 children to Denbigh	:	1 :	
	To Jⁿ Brown to Liverstone	:	:	6
	To John Rawlinson for Horschire to Lancaster with an Evidence agsᵗ Markland[2] for killing Horses in the night time	:	12 :	

Ballad singers have been once before referred to. (See p. 274, note 1.)
[2] See p. 232, note 1.

		£	s	d
8.	To apprehending Welsh and Shepley for attempting to rob a Woman in Redbank keeping them in Custody cost	:	3 :	6
11.	To Mary Lister to Farnworth	:	:	6
	To conveying Wm Bird a sick passenger to Stockport cost more than County allowance	:	2 :	4
	To Ann Ainsworth to Burnley... ...	:	:	6
12.	To Warrants to the Hamlets for Assize presentm"	:	3 :	
	To two men assisting the Deputy to clear the Streets of strolers[1] this day	:	2 :	
	To George Homsell & wife to Ramsgate	:	1 :	
	To Peter Stevens to Stony Stratford	:	:	6
14.	To Eliz. Par to Warrington	:	:	6
	To Wm Mortimer to Bradford	":	:	6
	To Marg^t Smith to Liverpoole ...	:	:	6
15.	To Ann Davis sick into Yorkshire ...	:	:	6
	To Betty Burnley & 1 child to Haworth	:	1 :	
17.	To Warrants to the Hamlets Militia to attend their exercise	:	3 :	
	To Joshua Iron to Braintree	:	:	6
18.	To delivering presentment for the Assizes	:	2 :	
	To James Royley & 4 children to Liverpoole	:	1 :	6
	To Danl Mason & his Wife to Isle of Wight	:	1 :	
20.	To Wm Kelly wife & 4 children to Ipswick	:	1 :	
	To Warrants to the Hamlets to call Overseers of the Poor to account ...	:	3 :	
	To David Jones to Wellspoole... ...	:	:	6
	To Ann & Mary Wood two Sisters to Prescott	:	1 :	
23.	To Ann Fishwick & two young children to Derby	:	1 :	
24.	To loss of three light Guineas sold this day	:	5 :	

---

[1] See p. 130, note 3.

	£	s	d
To Eliz: Bibby to Malden	:	:	6
To Mary Hammon to Rumsey ...	:	:	6
To Four Evidences to Lancaster Assizes on the prosecution of Hunt[1] & Dean for House and Shop breaking three of these Evidences could neither walk to Lancaster nor ride on Horseback therefore was obliged to Hire Chaises			
At Bolton breakfasting 3'. 5ᵈ Turnpikes 1 . 6 Chaisehire 15' Chaise Boys 2'	1 :	1 :	11
Bating at Chorley 3' Turnpike 1' Chaise 15' Boys 2'	1 :	1 :	
Dining at Preston 4'. 8ᵈ Chaisehire & Boys 15 . 9	1 :	:	5
all night at Garstang 11'. 3ᵈ . Chaisehire & Boys 15 . 9	1 :	7 :	
at Lancaster Chaisehire & to the Boys		: 16 :	
To Richard Ardern one of the Evidences six days from home & for Meat & drink upon the road and at Lancaster	1 :	1 :	
To Mr Mills at Lancaster towards carrying on this prosecution		: 6 :	6
To Baillifs Fees 3' 6ᵈ Gave Hunt for walking to Lancaster to save Horsehire when first committed 5'		: 8 :	6
[March] 24. To Fees and other Incidental Charges in consequence of Indicting Dean[2] for Perjury		: 16 :	5
To Boots Servants and Beds for four persons		: 14 :	6
To Meat & drink at Lancaster four Persons four days & four nights cost	3 :	16 :	7
To Robt Stevenson for his trouble attending these Assizes six days ...		: 10 :	6
To Isaac Gatley the same		: 10 :	6
To Deputy Kay for all his trouble and attendance in this prosecution ...	1 :	1 :	

[1] See p. 275, note 1.　　　[2] See p. 275, note 3.

		£	s	d
	Bating at Garstang coming back 3ˢ turnp[i]ke 1ˢ Chaischire & Boys 15ˢ.9ᵈ		:19	9
	at Preston all night three Persons 8ˢ . 1ᵈ Chaise hire & Boys 16ˢ	1	:4	1
	Breakfasting at Chorley 2.3. The last Turnpike 1ˢ this Turnpike 1ˢ Chaise-hire & drivers 14.6		:18	9
	Dining at Bolton three Persons ...	:	5	3
	Turnpikes 1ˢ Chaischire 15ˢ Drivers 2ˢ		:18	
	Chaischire to Manchester 15ˢ two turnpikes 1.6		:16	6
	Two Lads for driving		: 2	
	To Hostlers at the end of Twelve stages going & coming 6ᵈ each ...		: 6	
	To Mary Carr & child to Prestbury...		: 1	
28.	To Thomas Barton att[e]nding a prisoner 1 night...		: 1	
	To Samˡ Belchier wife & 2 children to Bocking		: 1	
	To Alexʳ Swinton to Plymouth ...		:	6
29.	To Mary Ward to Lilford...		:	6
	To Margᵗ Cameron to Carlisle... ...		:	6
29.	To a Sailor lame of one arm going to Hull		: 1	
30.	To detaining a Soldier all night for raising a riot cost		: 1	6
	To several persons superintending the night watch[1] from the 24ᵗʰ Novʳ last to this day £6 . 7 . 0. towards which the Inhabitants paid £1 . 16 . 6 which being deducted from the former leaves	4	:10	6
April 1ˢᵗ	To Wᵐ Houlse & wife to Ireland ...		: 1	
	To Jane Harding to Doncaster... ...		:	6
2.	To a Coroners Inquisition over Thoˢ Ryder		: 3	
	To Mary Burton & 2 sick children to Lancasʳ		: 1	
4.	To Eliz. Mᶜ Lullum to Edinburg ...		:	6

---

[1] A "winter watch" was, at each Michaelmas Court Leet, ordered to be kept from the date of that Court to the 25th March following, but the expense of this has not been entered in the Constables' Accounts. The "night watch" for the 24th November referred to in the text was probably a special and extra one.

		£	s	d
	To John Bullcock w[i]fe & child to Leek		: 1 :	
	To Coroners Inquisition over Ann Lidgate		: 3 :	
[April] 5.	To Peter Giles & wife to Bedding-ton			: 6
	To committing two Women Inhabi-tants of the Almshouses fighting there cost		: 4 :	6
	To Jane Tyne to Dewsbury		:	: 6
7.	To Marg¹ Grimshaw to Warrington...		:	: 6
8.	To Eliz : Gill to Warrington		:	: 6
	To M' Josiah Birch Money that he advanced for building a small Engine House ¹	3	: 16 :	8½
	To Mary Jackson to Bewdley		:	: 6
10.	To a Coroners Inquisition over Peter Wood ²		: 3 :	
	To Mary Calwood & child to Black-burn		:	: 6
	To John Withers to Newcastle... ...		:	: 6
	To five Men searching Salford river to find the Body of Ann Lidgate drowned there		: 5 :	
11.	To Kath Dupont & two children to London		: 1 :	
11.	To apprehending & detaining a woman all night for picking Pockets prison room 1' Meat &c 1' attendants wage 1'.6 when she was examined and committed		: 3 :	6
14.	To Hanah M⁰ Leod to Liverpoole ...			: 6
	To James Bedworth to Newcastle very lame		: 1 :	
15.	To Ann Lewis to Hull		:	: 6
	To a new pair of Handcuffs		: 4 :	
	To John Dowell wife & 2 children to Sterling		: 1 :	

¹ A new engine house was referred to as being erected in the yard of the Angel Inn. (See p. 193, note 2.)

² This was probably one of the two men referred to in the *Manchester Mercury* as having been accidentally drowned in the Irwell, at Salford Bridge, whilst bringing back a carriage to their master, Mr. Alsop, of the Bull's Head Inn.

		£	s	d
16.	To several Messengers to various Townships to impress Carts for the removal of six Troops Baggage[1] ...	:	6	:
	To returning a Warrant to Justice Whitehead[2] at Bolton Horse 3ʳ Turn-pike bating Horse and for Dinner 1 . 10½	:	4	10½
	To Jacob Miles to Stafford	:	:	6
	To Peter Johnson to Liverpoole ...	:	:	6
	To searching for apprehending detaining & keeping Yorkshire Moll Dolly Stokes Rusholm Bett Ann Ward & Ann Bishop five notorious lewd Woman drunkards & theives till they could be examined before the Justices 1 day & 1 night cost	:	5	6
	To assistants conveying them to Hope[3] and back to the House of Correction 3ʳ prison room 1ˢ	:	4	:
17.	To prison room for Thomas Files confined by order of the Officers for being drunk	:	1	:
	To Mary Lee to Brimingham [sic] ...	:	:	6
	To a dumb Man leaving the Town ...	:	1	:
18.	To Jere Hunter wife & child to Scarbrough...	:	1	:
	To apprehending Aimy Ashley & others being common Pickpockets detaiñg them in Custody all night 1ˢ & a Warrant 3ˢ	:	4	:
20.	To conveying by Pass Jane Buersell to Sourby cost more than the County allowance	:	3	2
24.	To attending a Man a day & night u[n]der a Warrant upon complaint of the Silkweavers 2ˢ prison room 1ˢ he was afterwards Indicted	:	3	:
	To Stranger in the Streets in distress	:	1	:

---

[1] This was probably the baggage of the outgoing soldiers, for on May 3rd it is stated that "on Tuesday and Wednesday last [April 26th and 27th] arrived here the 7th Regiment of Dragoons, commanded by General Howard who are to take up their Quarters here." A few weeks later they were reviewed in Castle Field.

[2] See p. 172, note 4.   [3] See p. 191, note 2.

		£	s	d
[April] 25.	To Esther Higgin & 2 children to Dover		: 1 :	
	To presentment drawing to the Sessions		: 1 :	
	To two committments for two Lads who had been stealing Shoes & other Articles		: 4 :	
	To prison room 3 nights whilst under examin[a]tion		: 3 :	
	To Meat for both during this time ...		: 3 :	6
	To Mary Massey att[e]nding as an Evidence ags' Taylor[1] & his wife for Housebreaking when they were both transported 3 days		: 4 :	6
	To James Isherwood & Thomas Metcalf other two Evidences on the same prosecution each 3 days att[e]nding Sessions 9' allowed them for expences 1,6...		: 10 :	6
	To Evidences attending Sessions ags' Shepherd & Tillotson[2] when both was transported for stealin[g] goods out of several persons Shops in Manch'			
	To Jonath. Butterworth 3 days ...		: 4 :	6
	To Thomas Jackson another Evidence 3 days...		: 4 :	6
	To Thomas Beavers another 3 days...		: 4 :	6
	To four Barkeepers attending Sessions 3 days at the request of the Justices each 6'	1 :	4 :	
25.	To Fees to the Clerk of the Court of Q' Sessions		: 4':	6
	To Deputy Kays dining & unavoidable expences attending these Sessions ...		: 5 :	
	To Thomas Beavers Bill for Wages to various parts of the Country on Constables Business		: 13 :	

---

[1] In the account of the Quarter Sessions in the town in April, 1774, it is stated that "James and Ann Taylor for stealing Goods out of the Shop of Robert Stevenson of Manchester," had been sentenced to seven years' transportation.

[2] At the same Sessions, "Miles Tillotson and Ann Whitaker for stealing Muslin out of the Shop of M' Heron of Manchester" had seven years' transportation, but I do not find any mention of any one named Shepherd convicted at these Sessions.

		£	s	d
27.	To Ann Mills to Ashburn	:	:	6
	To two Men clearing the Streets of Strolers[1]	:	2	:
	To Eliz. Edwards to Ox[t]on... ...		:	6
	To Wm Fish to Plumbton into the Fild		:	6
29.	To Charles Heys to Newcastle ...		:	6
	To Mary Bates to Warrington... ...		:	6
30.	To keeping Thomas Lees in Custody for Croft breaking[2] whilst examinations could be took & a commitment to Lancaster made cost 3 . 4 . an attendants wages for being with him. 1 . 6.	:	4	: 10
	To Jane Sedridge & two children to Gildersome...	:	1	:
	To cleaning Dungeon & Straw ...	:	2	:
	To a permit Pass for Thomas Srimple to London	:	2	:
May 2^d	To Joseph Bolt & his wife to Exam [sic]	:	1	:
	To Eliz. Pince to St Johns Bristoll ...	:	:	6
3.	To the Belmans Note for Ten Crys...	: 12	:	6
	To Thos Walkers Note for work done for Constab.	:	2	: 10
	To John Pearson to Liverpoole ...	:	:	6
	To Mary Blackman to London ...	:	:	6
	To Thos Harpur for sundry assistances	:	1	: 6
4.	To David Stocks a blind Man to Liverpoole	:	1	:
	To Robt Stevenson towards the loss of his Goods by his Shop being broke	:	5	:
	To Martha Davis to Worcester ...	:	:	6
	To James Dawson at White Lyon[3] for receiving prisoners & Meat & drink for them there	:	5	: 1
5.	To Mary Bradshaw to Halifax... ...		:	6
	To Eliz : Creamer & a young child to Hull	:	1	:
7.	To Warrants to the Hamlets for Assessors of Landtax & Window Duty	:	3	:
	To Math Cameron to Margate... ...	:	:	6

---

[1] See p. 130, note 3.   [2] See p. 206, note 5.
[3] This Manchester inn has not, I think, occurred before.

		£	s	d
To Horsehire to Chorley 4 . 6 another Horse to Irlam 3' on the Constables account		:	7 :	6
To a Horse to Lancaster with a prisoner under committment thither		:	17 :	4
To Mary Strickland to Grange ...		:	:	6
[May] 9. To conveying Wm Wellings under Warrant to Justice Levers[1] for an assault...		:	2 :	6
To thirty two Notices to persons to appear before the Commissioners to be appointed Assessors of Window Tax		:	5 :	4
12. To expences attending them all afternoon at [Dangerous] Corner[2]		:	2 :	
To 24 Window Ley Books paid Tho' Davenport for Paper & ruling... ...		:	9 :	
To writing the preparations of the same Books for the Assessors appointed		:	4 :	
To Tho' Davenport binding them in red		:	1 :	6
To Coroners Inquisition over James Beswick		:	3 :	
To Kath Murray to Scotland		:	:	6
To Meat for two people in the Dungeon		:	1 :	
To George Gordon to London ...		:	:	6
To searching a many Houses in Manch' and Salford to find a parcel of stolen Yarn and smalwares cost in assistants		:	2 :	
To detaining Ryder & her Son upon whom the goods was found in Custody 1 day & 1 night prison room 1' Meat &c. 1. 6 an attendant 1' when after examination they was sent under Wart. [Warrant] to Wigan		:	3 :	6
12. To Horsehire conveying them to Wigan 5' expences thither of three Persons & Mess' back 5' Mess'' wages two days away 3'...		:	13 :	

[1] See p. 265, note 2.
[2] Where they were sworn in before the Magistrates. (See p. 5, note 1.)

		£	s	d
	To apprehendg Toft Shelmerdine & Booth under Warrant keeping them in Custody a whole day till the Justice could be seen cost	:	3 :	6
13.	To Ellen Fulton to Newcastle	:	:	6
	To Dolly Grimes & child to Scotland	:	:	6
	To detaining Mary Houghden a night walker apprehended by the Watch till she could be examined by the Justices two nights room 2ˢ Meat 1ˢ Committment to House of Correction 2ˢ... ...	:	5 :	
	To two Vagrants with a Pass	:	1 :	
	To Meat drink & attendants conveying a notorious Whore know by the name of Wryneck to Prison	:	1 :	6
16.	To James Mᶜ Lolland to Hull		:	6
	To Henry Bentley to Liverpoole ...		:	6
	To three Men following three several persons who came from Huddersfield and had stole Goods out of many Shops in this Town		: 3 :	
	To Sall Travis in Custody all night for a breach of the Peace prison room 1ˢ Supper & breakfˢ 6ᵈ	:	1 :	6
17.	To Mary Mags bigbelly'd to Bristoll		:	6
	To Zachary Illington to Newberry...		:	6
	To a Man delivering & putting up advertisements agsᵗ Persons shewing Stallions in the Streets	:	2 :	6
	To an old Soldier upon his March ...	:	1 :	
18.	To Mary Whittle to Clivitshire ...	:	:	6
18.	To Thoˢ Henrys wife & 4 children to Norwich	:	1 :	6
19.	To Sarah Robertson to Coldstream...	:	:	6
	To attending John Matley under a Bench Warrant till he could be bound over cost in prison room attendants wages & Meat	:	3 :	3
	To assistants in apprehending Thoˢ Welsh for rioting in the night time keeping him in Custody till he was commited cost 1 . 6 Commitment 2ˢ	:	3 :	6

		£	s	d
[May] 20.	To detaining Scott & his wife for keeping a Bawdyhouse in Sugarlane prison room two nights 2ˢ Meat two days 2ˢ conveying them to the House of Correction 1ˢ		: 5 :	
	To Robᵗ Dormer to Dover		:	6
	To detaining two Whores at Sun [1] & two at Packhors[e] [1] till they could be examined & committed having made great disturbance in Highstreet prison room at both Houses two nights 4ˢ Meat 3ˢ		: 7 :	
21.	To detaining Stones for pilfering many little things he being young was discharged after being in prison two nights cost		: 2 :	
	To taking a Madman into Custody who had been breaking the Windows of Jⁿ Haworth Esqʳ paid an assistant 1ˢ keeping him till he could be sent to Blackley the place of his settlement cost 2ˢ . 6ᵈ		: 3 :	6
	To expences with the Serjeants of the Militia [2] in fixing the Billets of the regiment		: 2 :	2
26.	To Patrick Jones wife & child to Ireland		: 1 :	
	To Cristian Serjeant & Lad to Liverpoole		: 1 :	
26.	To Martha Hill to Scotland		: :	6
	To expences detaining Welsh for breaking a Womans room door down		: 1 :	2
28.	To an Inquisition over one Hall ...		: 3 :	
	To a Gang of Strangers going into Scotland		: 3 :	6
	To conveying Peter Clark by pass to Liverpoole cost more than the County allowance		: 2 :	9

---

[1] These two inns are generally mentioned together, and a room seems to have been reserved in each in which prisoners could be kept a short time. (See p. 269, note 2, and note 3.)

[2] On May 31st it was announced in the *Mercury*, "Yesterday the whole Battalion of the Royal Lancashire Militia, were embodied here, in order to be exercised and trained for twenty-eight Days."

		£	s	d
	To Martha Holden & a young child to Sheffield		: 1 :	
	To the rent of a Guard room 27 days for the use of the Dragoons		: 8 :	6
30.	To an assistant in apprehend[ing] 3 Whores		: 1 :	
	To Paper ruling & writing the Constable Ley	1 : 10 :		
June 2.	To Mary Shipping to Carlisle		: :	6
	To Ann Nelson & two children to Carlford		: 1 :	
	To the High Constables Warrant for County rates repair of Bridges rebuilding the House of Correction at Manchester[1] Governors Salary &c ...	86 : 18 :		
	To Deputy Kays expences in paying the Warrant	1 : 10		
•	To Warrants to the Hamlets for their proportion of the above Warrant ...		: 3 :	
3.	To Francis Hatton to Westham ...		:	6
4.	To the Engine Mens Bill for Eleven Months & Buckets mending	11 : 13 :		6
	To Isaac Green to Wolverhampton...		:	6
	To John Kerr to Whitehaven		:	6
	To Meat for Moll Wells & Alice Horrocks both in the Dungeon a day & a night		: 1 :	6
	To seven Musicians it being the aniversary of his Majestys Birthday[2]	1 : 1 :		
	To the Soldiers firing upon the same occasion there being 10 Companys in Town[2]	5 : 5 :		
4.	To the High Constables premium of a Bill in paying a money Warrant ...		: 3 :	6
5.	To detaining Tho' Pearson a pilfering Lad in Custody 2 nights prison room 2' Meat for him 1 . 6 then he was enlisted with Cap't Allen		: 3 :	6

[1] The House of Correction in Hunt's Bank appears to have been restored this year.
[2] This was an annual festival in the town. No doubt the Dragoons and the Lancashire Militia made up the "10 Companys" referred to in the text.

		£	s	d
[June] 7.	To Giles Vane & 2 children to Strat- ford	:	1 :	
	To Assan Ackmet a Turk to London	:	1 :	
10.	To Tho⁴ Stafford to Ludlow	:	:	6
	To the Belmans Bill for seven Crys	:	10 :	
	To three Men with the Deputy & Beadle clearing the Town of disorderly persons	:	3 :	
11.	To Sam¹ Sowdan to Longnor	:	:	6
	To Betty Royley to Ormskirk	:	:	6
	To Henry Hicks wife & 2 children to Leeds	:	1 :	
	To Tho⁴ Harpur for a Messuage [Mess- age] to the Constab[le] of Openshaw	:	1 :	
	To returning a Man under Warrant to Justice Lever¹ at Alkrington Wages of Mess⁴ 1⁴. 6ᵈ Bating 4ᵈ	:	1 :	10
	To clearing & repairing the Steps at Milbrow the Rock & Wall having fallen upon them by the Floods & made them impassable took two Men three days in clearing Rubbish at 1 . 6 a day	:	9 :	
13.	To Grace Charles to Glascow	:	:	6
	To Clayton Wildick & a deserter kept in Custody all night at the request of the Justices till the matter could be further heard attendants maintenance and prison room cost	:	7 :	
14.	To Eliz. Johnson to Liverpoole ...	:	:	6
	To Jonath. Bell to Whitehaven ...	:	:	6
17.	To George Porney to Scotland ...	:	:	6
	To Kath Osburn to Scotland	:	:	6
18.	To an Inquisition over Joseph Sandi- ford	:	3 :	
	To fifteen Assistants to the Deputy in assisting to suppress many Gangs of Militia Soldiers & many other Per- sons perpetualy assembled as common Gamblers on the six days as well as on the Lords day in and about Walkers Croft	:	15 :	

¹ See p. 265, note 2.

		£	s	d
	To a Sailor in great distress	:	1 :	
20.	To James Rowland to Dorchester ...	:	:	6
	To Abr[a]m Pilling assisting in apprehending two Whores & conveying them to Dungeon	:	1 :	6
	To James Russell to London	:	:	6
	To apprehending four Men under special Warrant for breaking Windows in the night & detaining them till they could be examined by the Justice cost in attendants wages &c	:	2 :	8
21.	To a Coroners Inquisition over James Jones	:	3 :	
	To Ruth Martin with a lame leg to Lancaster	:	1 :	
	To detaining Tho' Kirk in Custody for violently assaulting his wife & putting her in fear of her life prison room two nights 2' Meat 1 . 6	:	3 :	6
23.	To conveying Hana Aikin by Pass to Stockport & another to Liverpoole cost above County allowance	:	4 :	6
	To John Smith to Gisburn	:	:	6
24.	To John Jess to Plymouth	:	:	6
	To cleaning Steps at Salford Bridge	:	2 :	
	To the same at Milbrow as usual ...	:	2 :	
24.	To John Smethurst to Hull	:	:	6
26.	To Coroners Inquisition over Charles White 6 Jurors 3' Warts [Warrants] to the Hamlets 1'	:	4 :	
	To Tho' Davenport binding a 2ᵈ set Window books	:	1 :	
	To Nehemiah Kemp for his trouble in finding a bad woman from Northwich & turning her out of Town ...	:	2 :	
	To two Men for killing a Mad Dog in Hanging ditch as a reward at the request of the Just[ice]s there being a many loose in & ab' the Town... ...	:	5 :	
	To assistants Apprehending Tho' Huberd and conveying him to the House of Correction for a breach of the Peace	:	2 :	

		£	s	d
	To Sara Maddock to Warrington ...	:	:	6
28.	To fresh Straw for the Dungeon ...	:	1 :	6
	To Marg^t Willis & two children to Glascow	:	1 :	
	To John Suthern to London		:	6
29.	To prison room for two Women under Wart [Warrant] for fighting till they could get Bail 1^s an attendant waiting a whole day 1^s. 6^d	:	2 :	6
	Sarah Ward & 3 children to Birmingham	:	1 :	
	To Money given as relief to sundry sick prisoners	:	3 :	6
July 1.	To Philip Tellis wife & 3 children to Ireland	:	1 :	
	To Martha Kitts to Dunstaple... ...	:	:	6
2.	To two Men clearing the streets of strolers	:	2 :	
	To repairs at the Exchange as by James Browns Bill	:	5 :	3
	To Duncan Baton to London		:	6
	To a permit for John Denton going to Exeter	:	2 :	
2.	To Thomas Harpur for sundry assistances in serving Warrants & other things belonginge to the Constableship	:	6 :	
4.	To Thomas Wood to Cockram ...		:	6
	To Thos Davis losst one arm & his wife to Dumfries	:	1 :	
5.	To Jane Walton to Coventry	:	:	6
6.	To Mary Tarning to Doncaster ...	:	:	6
9.	To Thomas King to Carlisle	:	:	6
	To Saml Kirk wife & 3 children to Liecester	:	1 :	
	To Michael Wilson to Durham ...	:	:	6
	To Horsehire a Horse double^2 to Lancaster	:	18 :	8
	To two Journeys to Lancaster with single Horses	1 :	4 :	
	To a single Horse twice to Bolton returning Warrants to Justice Whitehead^1	:	5 :	

---

^{1} See p. 172, note 4. ^{2} See p. 29, note 1.

		£	s	d
	To another Horse to Alkrington with a Warrant to Justice Lever[1]		2	
12.	To detaining Mary Brown two days and two nights in Custody under a Bench Warrant prison room 2ˢ Meat two days 1 . 8 . an attendant 1 . 6 ...		5	2
	To Eleanor Houlse & child to Portsmouth			6
13.	To prison room for a Woman found drunk by the Officers in their walk...		1	
	To Mary Holiday to London		·	6
	To Miles Fleetwood to Brindle... ...			6
16.	To Law. Petit to London...			6
	To one years rent for a room for the Dragoons[2] to lay their Powder in due 23ᵈ April last	3	3	
	To one years rent for an amunition room for the use of the Militia[3] ...	3	3	
	To Mary Lawrinson to Newcastle ...			6
18.	To Thoˢ Burwick wife & 5 children to Scotland		2	
	To Joseph Taylors Bill for Glasing work done at the Exchange & for new Sash weights	3	12	6
	To him for Lead to the Dungeon ...		2	
20.	To three Men assisting to quell a riot in the Market Place		1	6
22.	To Wᵐ Mᶜ Grigger to Edinburg ...			6
	To Walter Mᶜ Kinsey to Edinburg...			6
	To drawing presentment to Sessions		1	
	To James Sutton attending Sessions two days to give Evidence agsᵗ Scott & his wife for keeping a Bawdy House		3	
	To Jonathan Butterworth three days on the same prosecution		4	6
	To sundry Fees to the Clerk of the Peace Cryer of the Court & Jurors Bailif		10	
	To Witness's wages & Meat & drink attending this Sessions on prosecution of a Man for holding an unlawfull Auction		8	

[1] See p. 265, note 2.   [2] See p. 283, note 1.   [3] See p. 288, note 2.

		£	s	d
	To four Barkeepers attending Sessions three days as usual	1	4	
	To Deputy Kays expences attending Sessions		4	
25.	To Francis Rose & wife to Stafford...		1	
	To Marg¹ Hodgen & 2 children to Walsall		1	
	To two two [sic] Men for killing a Mad Dog by recommendation of the Justices		5	
	To William Mason to Stockport ...			6
July 26.	To Tho' Hartley a Lame Man to obtain a Wart [Warrant] against several Persons for breaking his Shop		2	
	To William Dowlar to Whitehaven...			6
	To expences with six Quartermasters regulating & fixing Billets for a whole Regiment of Dragoons¹		7	6
	To assistants to apprehend Eliz: Shoemaker for stealing a parcel of Yarn of Wᵐ Pilling cost		1	6
	To detaining her one day & one night in Custody prison room 1ˢ Meat 10ᵈ		1	10
	To an Sailor going to Hull		1	
28.	To returning a Warrant to Bolton ...		2	
	To Ann Portis to Blackburn			6
30.	To Wᵐ Kelly to Scotland...			6
	To maintaining Marg¹ Massey a Vagrant till a pass could be obtained		2	2
	To three Men with the Deputy clearing the Streets & lodging Houses of Vagabonds & Beggars		3	
	To Thomas Loxham expences of the Constables & their Assistants at several privy search[e]s and with the Watchmen	1	11	9
Aug. 1ˢᵗ	To detaining Sall Travis two days and two nights for being a common street walker prison room 2ˢ Meat 1.2. an attendant 1.6		4	8
	To Alice Wood & 4 children to Halifax		1	

¹ See p. 283, note 1

		£	s	d
	To Wm Tomkins & Moses Pointon for conveying a Felon to Altringham ...		: 5 :	
2.	To William Till to Warwick		:	6
	To Joseph Elliott to Cambridge ...		:	6
5.	To Eliz: Stanton to Wigan		:	6
	To Assistants in apprehending a Man under Wart [Warrant] in Deansgate being obliged to keep watch most part of a night		: 1 : 10	
8.	To inevitable expences in apprehending John Smith als Rake & 4 Lewd woman for breaking open the Shop of Wm Hill & stealing thereout a parcel of Stockings when one woman was discharged the rest committed to Lancaster		: 5 :	
	To prison room for Rake 4 nights 4' Meat & drk [drink] 4 days 5' an attendants wage 4 days 4'...		: 13 :	
	To Meat & drink for the four women and their attendants 4 days		: 14 : 6	
	To prison room for them 4' To a Man attending these four women 4 days 4'...		: 8 :	
	To turnpikes on the road to Lancaster Castle these four Persons in a Cart ...		: 3 :	
	To Martha Low & two children to Lym		: 1 :	
9.	To a Coronors Inquisition over Cuthbert Topping		: 3 :	
11.	To Richard Thompson to Derby ...		:	6
	To Eliz: Hughs & 3 children to S' Asaph		: 1 :	
	To Vagrants before the Justices at Hodgkinsons		: 2 :	
	To conveying one of these Vagrants to Burton in Westmoreland cost more than the Justices allowance		: 10 :	
	To Warrants to the Hamlets to bring in presentments to the Assizes		: 3 :	
12.	To Thomas Irvin to Burnley		:	6
	To Richd Dickenson for sundry Messuages [Messages] and assistance on the Constables account		: 4 :	

		£	s	d
	To a permit Pass for Cath. Booth to Grimsall		: 2 :	
	To Wm Hough very old to Winwick...		: 1 :	
[Aug.] 13.	To Jonath. Butterworth for running several Messuages [Messages] to different Townships of the Constables Business		: 7 :	6
15.	To a Coroners Inquisition over John Wrigley[1]		: 3 :	
	To Susan Thomas to Nantwich ...		: ·	6
	To John Sheilds & his wife to Ireland		: 1 :	
	To Prison room two nights for John Cristian apprehended & kept in Custody on suspicion of Forgery ...		: 2 :	
	To Meat & drink for two days... ...		: 2 :	
	To a Man to attend him two days & two nights		: 3 :	
	To the Justices committing him to prison and conveying him thither cost		: 3 :	
	To Eliz: Walton & 4 children to Ware		: 1 :	
17.	To John Smart & his wife to Wallisey		: :	6
	To apprehending maintaining & conveying to Lancaster Castle James Dean[2] for returning back from Transportation cost more than the County allowance		: 14 :	4
	To two Men with the Beadle clearing the streets		: 2 :	
	To Shepley for assisting the Watch two nights		: 2 :	
18.	To Danl Frazer wife & 3 children to Scotland		: 1 :	

[1] As stated in the local newspaper of August 16th, "Yesterday one Wrigley was killed by a Press falling on him at a Calendar House in Back Square."

[2] James Dean has been previously referred to. (See p. 275, note 1.) The account of his recapture is given in the *Manchester Mercury* of August 23rd, as follows :—

"On Wednesday about 10 o'Clock at Night, James Dean, who was sentenced to be transported for seven Years the last Lent Assizes, for wilful and corrupt Perjury in the Trial of Edmund Hunt, charged with robbing the Shop of Robert Stevenson, Brazier, in this Town, whereby Hunt was acquitted was seized in Long Miln-gate, after a very resolute Resistance, at his House, where he was regaling himself over a Pitcher of Ale and Bread and Cheese, he is strongly suspected of committing the above Burglaries [mentioned in previous paragraphs] and was yesterday committed to Lancaster."

		£	s	d
	To Marg^t Lee to Liverpoole	:	:	6
20.	To Thomas Parsons to Matton ...	:	:	6
	To assistants holding Dean[1] in Custody from the time of his apprehension till his commitment could be made to Lancaster	:	5	8
	To Meat & drink for Alice Haworth kept in the Dungeon from Saturday night to Monday	:	1	:
23.	To John Hinchman to Spalding ...	:	:	6
	To Marg^t Kensey to Aberdeen ...	:	:	6
	To James Fletcher expences when Constables Tax was laid	9	4	:
25.	To Coroners Inquisition over Ann Walmesly	:	3	:
	To the same over a person in Salford	:	2	:
	To Sarah Warren & child to Wells...	:	:	6
	To Jane Rathbone to London	:	:	6
	To fetching a Man from Litlebrough to be an Evidence before Just. Manwaring[2] in a case of Felony	:	2	8
27.	To an old Soldier & his wife	:	1	:
	To a place for the Dragoons[3] to lay their Baggage in till store rooms could be found for them	:	3	:
	To Paper for Billets used during this year	:	4	:
	To Susan Mc Grey to Liverpoole ...	:	:	6
28.	To James Haworth to Heaton after Hunt	:	1	6
	To returning a Man under Warrant to Justice Lever[4] cost	:	2	:
	To two Persons assisting the Deputy to make distress upon 20 Quakers[5] for refusing to pay their small Tythes ...	:	5	6
30.	To detaining Mary Cook an accomplice of Deans 1 night & 1 day till she could be examined	:	2	:
	To Francis Pritchard wife & 3 children in great distress going to Scarbrough	:	2	:

---

[1] See p. 296, note 2.   [2] See p. 218, note 2.
[3] See p. 283, note 1.   [4] See p. 265, note 2.
[5] This is the first reference to the Quakers in this volume of Accounts.

		£	s	d
Sep' 1"	To conveying a Woman & her Son to Sourby cost more than the County allowance		: 3 :	6
	To Ruth Milliger to Liverpoole ...		:	6
Sep' 1.	To Richd Dickenson for assisting in serving three Warrants		: 2 :	
3.	To Judith Kershaw to Preston... ...		: :	6
	To High Constables Warrant for repair of common and Publick Bridges	36 :	18 :	5
	To Warrants to the Hamlets their proportion thereof		: 3 :	
5.	To Dolly Haynes & two children to Stratford...		: 1 :	
	To Postage of Letters on account of the Constableship during this year ...		: 5 :	
	To four Trampers[1] going into Ireland		: 1 :	6
	To detaining a woman[2] in Custody all night for Imbezleing Yarn prison room 1' two Men conveying her to Hope[3] 1 . 6		: 2 :	6
7.	To Hanah Oxbury to London... ...		: :	6
	To John Hoyle w[i]fe & 4 children to Wakefield		: 1 .	6
	To Tho' Harpurs Note for attending Prisoners & going sundry Messuages [Messages] both in Town & County		: 12 :	
9.	To Sam' Lord to Sheffield		:	6
	To John Fidler to Isle of Ely		:	6
13.	To M' Bower for a Laced Hat[4] for the Beadle	1 :	7 :	
	To Warrants to the Hamlets Alehousekeepers to take Licences		: 3 :	
	To Marg' Lucas to Liverpoole ...		:	6

---

[1] See p. 119, note 2.

[2] This is probably the woman mentioned in the following paragraph in the *Manchester Mercury*, Sept. 6th, 1774 :—

"The same day Friday [Sept 2] Rebecca Mee, of Manchester, Single Woman, was convicted before Mr. Bayley, of embezzling and purloining three Pounds Weight of combed Wool, the Property of Mr. Ottiwell Kershaw, and was committed to the House of Correction, to be kept to hard Labour for 14 Days and to be once publickly whipped at the Market-place in Manchester."

[3] See p. 191, note 2.

[4] The gorgeous apparel of the Beadle was evidently still kept up. (See also p. 88, note 2.)

		£	s	d
14.	To Warrants to the Hamlets for Freeholders Lists		: 3 :	
	To an assistant two days giving Personal Notice to Alehousekeepers to take Licences		: 3 :	
	To Alice Bell to Penrith		:	6
	To Joseph Bagshaw wife & two children to Derby		: 1 :	
16.	To impressing six Carts to Warrington & Wigan		: 6 :	
16.	To Nancy Ayres to Hull		:	6
17.	To three Persons with the Deputy clearing the Streets of Strolers[1] & vagabonds		: 3 :	
18.	To Ann Downs & 3 children to Cumberland		: 1 :	
	To an old woman to Walton le dale		: :	6
	To Warrants to the Hamlets for surveyors of the Highways to be appointed		: 3 :	
22.	To delivering the Surveyors List ...		: 1 :	
	To drawing Surveyors List & copy for the Justices		: 2 :	
	To Judith Nadin to Litchfield... ...		:	6
23.	To Mr Wright & Prestons Bill for making Beadles Clothes & Trimming[2]	1	: 17 :	3
	To Wm Ogden & blind wife to Todmorden		: 1 :	
24.	To Susan Herries to Derby		:	6
	To a Messr to Sr Thos Egertons[3] abt a Man having stopt his Carriage upon the Highway		: 1 :	
27.	To keeping the Man in Custody 1 day & 1 night prison room 1s Meat & drink 1s		: 2 :	
	To two Men conveying him under Warrant to Belfield[4] cost		: 4 :	
Octob 1st	To four pair of Money scales & weights requested by the Justices At the Quarter Sessions to be sent for	6	: 6 :	

---

[1] See p. 130, note 3.   [2] See p. 298, note 4.
[3] This was Sir Thomas Egerton, of Heaton, Bart.
[4] See p. 255, note 1.

		£	s	d
	from the Mint that the Publick might know how to adjust their private Weights and Scales cost			
	To Miriam Mathews to Prescott ...	:	:	6
	To Maintaining & keeping Robert Marshall a sturdy Vagabond till he could be conveyed by Pass to Kendall cost more than the allowance	:	6 :	
Oct 1ˢᵗ	To John Barber for whipping a Vagabond by Justice Bayleys[1] warrant ...	:	2 :	6
	To Dennis Lloyd to Pensance... ...	:	:	6
4.	To detaining Darbyshire for Felony under a Bench Warrant prison room 1ˢ Meat 1ˢ	:	2 :	
	To Eliz: Bobine to Burton	:	:	6
	To a permit for Leonard Davis & his wife to Holywell 2ˢ relief given them 1ˢ...	:	3 :	
7.	To the Belmans Bill for 5 Crys ...	:	7 :	6
	To Eliz: Hulme to Lancaster	:	:	6
	To Mary Mitchell to Chelsea	:	:	6
8.	To Alexʳ Laman to Glascow	:	:	6
	To Jane Abbot & 2 children to Daresbury	:	1 :	
9.	To John White to Halifax	:	:	6
	To one years Salary to the Deputy Constable[2]	30 :	:	
	To one years Wages to the Beadle[2]	10 :	:	
	To superintending the Watch for Twenty nights last past by Thoˢ Harpur & others	1 :	:	
	To Thoˢ Stockport for removing the Baggage of one Troop of Dragoons[3] to Wiggan but on the road was commanded to return back		:	9 :
	To Mʳ Chippendales Bill for Law before the Justices & at Sessions's ...	22 : 15 :		6
	To Mʳ Whitaker an Attorney for the last Business	8 : 4 :		

[1] See p. 191, note 2.

[2] Mr. John Kay still continued Deputy Constable, the Beadle being Mr. John Carter. (See *Court Leet Records*, vol. viij, p. 155.)

[3] See p. 283, note 1.

	£	s	d
To Mr Jones Bill for Law...	4	3	
To Mr Charles Hindley for Cloth for Beadles Clothes[1]	1	14	4
To Thomas Fowler for Beadles Stockings[1]		13	8
To Joseph Whitehead for 3 pr. of Shoes for Beadle		17	3
To him for 1 pr. for a Man going to Lancaster for an Evidence ags^t Hunt & Dean[2]		5	9
To John Prescott³ for Printing work & advertising	2	12	
To Thos Harpur for assistances in serving Warrants & precepts upon sundry occasions		9	6
To loss by six light Guineas received on this acc^t...		8	
To Thomas Marsden one years rent for Engine House in Tiblane[4]... ...	3	3	
To Wm Darbyshire for an Engine standing in Highstreet		10	
To John Carter the Beadle for superintending the nightly watch 10 nights		10	
To him for cleaning Dungeon & for Meat & drink to prisoners confined there during this year		16	6
To him for other extraordinary attendance upon prisoners & going sundry Messuages [Messages] out of Town...		9	6
To Mr Chippendale 18th Janry 1774 attending & advising the Defendants on their being served with Writs and respecting the cause of Action & taking their directions to take Care of and defend such Action betwixt Mr Marriott the Constable & John Upton⁵		6	8
Warrant to defend 1^s Filing common Bail 7^s. 2^d		8	2

---

[1] See p. 298, note 4.   [2] See p. 296, note 2.
[3] See p. 238, note 1.   [4] See p. 184, note 1.
[5] I do not find any mention of this trial in the local paper, nor is it referred to in the *Court Leet Records*. The various items in the bill of Mr. Joseph Chippendall, the lawyer, are here set out at full length.

	£	s	d
attending Mr Marriott & Mr Orme at the Kings head in Salford and consulting and advising touching their defence & taking their directions to retain Mr Lee and Mr Davenport¹ ...		: 6 :	8
Writing Letter to agent to retain Mr Lee & Mr Davenport			
Retainer to Mr Lee his Clerk & attending him	1	: 10 :	2
The like to Mr Davenport his Clerk & attending him...	1	: 10 :	2
Searching several times for Declaration		: 3 :	4
Paid for Declaration Duty & Warrant		: 2 :	11
Copy thereof received from Agent ...		: 2 :	4
Summons for time to plead Copy Service & att[e]nding thereon		: 7 :	4
Order Copy & Service & Copy sent		: 5 :	
Second Summons for further time att[e]nding & Order		: 12 :	4
Third Summons for further time att[e]nding & Order		: 12 :	4
26th Janry Attending this day & the greatest part of several other Days & reducing into Writing very particularly the Evidence of 13 Witnesses stating the whole of the Transaction from beginning to end in order to be laid before a special Pleader to advise of the proper Plea on behalf of the Defendants	2	: 2 :	
Close Copy thereof to send to London		: 16 :	8
Postage to London		: 3 :	
Drawing the Pleas	2	: :	
To Mr Warren to peruse & se[t]tle & advise on the Defendants case... ...		: 10 :	6
Attending him therewith & many times thereon		: 10 :	6
Copy Plea received from Agent ...		: 13 :	4
Attending Mr Davenport with Declaration Plea & Proofs for him to advise & se[t]tle the same		: 6 :	8

---

¹ This was Thomas Davenport, Esq.—a well-known barrister at this time, and living, I think, in York—afterwards knighted. (See *East Cheshire*, vol. ij., p. 413.)

	£	s	d
Fee him with the same	2 :	2 :	
Attending Mr Davenport several times afterw[ar]ds & conferring with him upon the Pleas & the nature of the Proofs to be made by the Defendants when he gave his Opinion in writing & advised the General Issue only ...		: 13 :	4
Copy of the Opinion received... ...		: 1 :	8
Drawing Plea of General Issue Ingrossing Duty & Copy received ...		: 4 :	4
Paid for the Issue duty & entring Plea		: 5 :	3
Copy received with Notice of Tryal...		: 5 :	
Three Supenas 27ˢ Term Fee Letters & Postage 10ˢ	1 :	17 :	
Making several Observations upon the Defend[an]ts Plea & the nature of their Proofs & writing thereon to Mr Davenport at York		: 6 :	8
Fee Mr Davenport advising on this Occasion 21ˢ his Clerk 2 . 6	1 .	3 .	6
Attending the Parties & taking further Instructions for Brief		: 6 :	8
Drawing the same with Observations 11 Sheets	3 :	13 :	4
Three Copies thereof 11 Sheets each	5 :	15 :	6
Twelve Supena Tickets 12ˢ Service thereof 24ˢ	1 :	16 :	
Paid Dr Mainwaring[1] with his Subpena	3 :	3 :	
Miss Small 21ˢ Miss Denman 21ˢ ...	2 :	2 :	
Sarah Barton 21ˢ Mrˢ Budworth 21ˢ...	2 :	2 :	
Mrˢ Patten 21ˢ Mrˢ Feilden 21ˢ... ...	2 :	2 :	
Edwᵈ Morley 10ˢ 6ᵈ John Speakman 22ˢ	1 :	12 :	6
Mr Cresswell 21ˢ Thomas Boddington 21ˢ	2 :	2 :	
Mr Ned Kenyon	1 :	1 :	
paid John Speakman more at Lancaster	1 :	3 :	
paid Mr Cresswell more at Manchester	1 :	16 :	

---

[1] See p. 218, note 2.

	£	s	d
Special Journey to Lancaster to attend the Tryal of this cause out five days	5 :	5 :	
Expences at Lancaster myself & Servant	2 :	12 :	6
Chaisehire & expences myself & Mrs Feilden upon the road going & coming back being lame of the Gout & not able to go on Horseback	7 :	17 :	6
Mr Milnes Journey as a Witness in this cause out 5 days	5 :	5 :	
Horsehire & expences	2 :	12 :	6
Attending the Martial [sic for Marshall] to see how the Plaintif had entered his Record		6 :	8
Fee Mr Lee with his Brief 5.5.0 his Clerk 2 6	5 :	7 :	6
Attending him therewith		6 :	8
The like to Mr Davenport his Clerk & att[e]nding him	5 :	14 :	2
Several Attendances upon Mr Lee & Mr Davenport in order to fix a time for a Consultation		6 :	8
Fee Mr Lee upon the Consultation 42^s his Clerk 7 6	2 :	9 :	6
The like to Mr Davenport 42^s his Clerk 7 6	2 :	9 :	6
Attending the Court upon such Consultation and explaining the D.fendants case & consulting thereon		10 :	6
Assize Fee & attending Court when the Cause shou'd have been tried but it was referred by rule of Court to Mr Greaves of Culcheth	1 :	6 :	8
paid the Court Fees on the part of the Defendant	2 :	3 :	
Letters Postage Porterage & Messengers in this Busin[e]ss	2 :	2 :	
paid my Agent for a Copy of the rule of Court & Postage		4 :	10
Journey to Culcheth to see Mr Greaves about this Business & to inform him how the Matter stood & to leave him a Brief & Horsehire	1 :	1 :	

	£	s	d
Attending Mr Greaves at his Sisters in Churchstreet & advising him upon this Business when he fixed Friday the 20th May to hear the Evidence at the Colledge		: 6 :	8
Attending Mr Greaves all this day at the Colledge & examining Witnesses on both sides	1 :	1 :	
My Clerks attendance at the same Place		[torn off]	
Mr Milnes attendance at the same Place to be examined as a Witness in this		[torn off]	
paid expences at the Bulshead ...		[torn off]	
Attending the Witnesses before the day fixed to give them Notice of the Meeting when Mrs Budworth Mrs Feilden & Mrs Patten desired Copies of their Examinations previous to the Meeting		: 10 :	6
Making such fair Copys & my Clerks attendance upon them with the same		: 10 :	
paid Mr Ridgway for one part of the Award		: 10 :	6
Drawing & Engrossing general Release from Upton to Mr Marriott & the other Defendants & Clerks Attendance to have got same executed by Upton being from home it was left at his House		: 10 :	6
For all our extraordinary Trouble in this Cause in searching the Books to state the Law respecting the Office & Duty of Constable & for inumerable attendances on the Parties & Witnesses not before charged	5 :	5 :	
Mr Marriotts Charges of taking Witnesses to and from Lancaster	24 :	14 :	3
Mr John Orms Charge of D^o	12 :	8 :	2
To Joseph Harrops[1] Note for Printing work	2 :	1 :	

[1] See p. 73. note 2.

To Mʳ Benj: Bower Interest of £200 } £ s d
borrowed to support this account ...   10 :   :
Deputy Kay last year paid to the
Town on the Constables account
Two Pound Twelve Shillings & six-
pence more than he actualy received
upon . . . [torn off] . . . that
Mʳ Wᵐ Steell one of the Mise . . .   2 : 12 : 6
[torn off] . . have paid the same
Sum on his . . . [torn off] . . .
account to James Dawson the Col-
lector . . . [torn off] . . . refused
to do ... ...

                                        ————

                  [Total] ... ... £786 : 14 : 11

[Receipts]

1774.
Octob 9.   Contra ... ... Cʳ

By Cash received from the last years } £   s   D
Tax ... ... { 11 : 8 : 5
By more Cash received from the {
same ... ... }   7 : 14 : 6
By the Hamlets pro- } £7 . 17 . 3   5 : 4 :
portion of ... ...)
By Dᵒ ... ...   2 : 0 : 6   1 : 7 :
By Dᵒ ... ...   86 : 18 : 0   57 : 18 : 8
By Dᵒ ... ...   36 : 18 : 5   24 : 12 : 3
By the Misegather[er]s from this Years } 425 : 5 : 6
Tax ... ...)
By balance owing to the Con- {
stables... ... ...)   :   :
By more Cash received from James {
Dawson out of last years Tax ... ...)   4 : 15 :
By balance owing to the Con- } 248 : 9 : 7
stables... ... ...)

                      ————

               [Total] ... ...£786 : 14 : 11

Dec' 14. 1774. We the Jurors of the Court Leet, holden for the Manor of Manchester in the County of Lancaster, have examined the foregoing Acc" of M' Tho: Marriott & M' Richd Leigh (late Constables) & do allow the Same.

(Signed)   SAM^{LL} CLOWES
BENJAMIN BOWER
JOHN TIPPING
RICH^D FARRER
JOHN WILSON
THO^S BAYLEY
FOLLIOTT POWELL
W^M NEWTON
J^{NO} HILL
FRA^S TOMLINSON
SAM GOODIER
EDW^D RISHTON
GEO BRAMALL
SAM HARRIS

[Constables' Accounts.]

[12th Oct., 1774. to 11th Oct.. 1775.]

•••••••••••

𝕯ʳ The Town of Manchester to Mᴿ ADAM OLDHAM & Mᴿ ED: HUDSON, *Constables.*[1]

[𝕯isbursements]

1774.

Octo. 13.	To last year's Ballance[2]	248:	9:	7
	Paid presentment to Quarter session	:	1 :	
	To Judith Davies to Chester	:	:	6
	To Kitty Mᶜ Donald to Edinburgh...	:	:	6
	To James Mᶜ Donald & Wife to Dublin	:	1 :	
14.	To Mʳˢ Vaux expences of privy Watch...		:10:	6
	To Searching a House in order to find Goods Stolen from Mʳ Black-more		: 2:	6
	To detaining a Lad apprehended in Smithy door for picking pockets, 3 days in Custody		: 6:	
16.	To James Halliwell, apprehended upon Suspicion of Coining money, kept in Custody all night, the next day took before the Justices, and con-veyed from thence under Mittimus to the House of Correction		:12:	
18.	To apprehending Glover, and Taylor for breaking Daniel Walker's Shop, and Stealing printed Handkercheifs &c		: 6:	

---

[1] These two Constables were elected at the Court Leet held on the 12th Oct., 1774. (See *Court Leet Records*, vol. viij,, p. 159.)

[2] See p. 306.

Date	Description	£	s	d
	To James Cowley, Sarah Cook, & Jos: West, by pass		1	6
19.	To Conveying Mellor & that Gang before Mr Bayley at Hope,[1] and all four Back to the House of Correction		5	
	To their Maintenance 2 Nights & days, and assistance making Search and enquiry after Pearson, Suspected of Stealing a Silver Cup from Fletcher's Tavern	1	2	
19.	To William Osborn, to Liverpool ...			6
	To Elizabeth Jones to Bacup			6
	To Jonathan Butterworth, attending sessions		6	
	To John Barber, attending Do		6	
21.	To John Orford to Sheffield			6
22.	To Ellen Tilney & 2 Children to Warrington		1	
	To Sarah Mathews to Liverpool ...			6
	To John Hodgkinson to Devon ...			6
24.	To Elizabeth Powell & 2 Children to Dover		1	
26.	To Peter Vaux to Chelsea...			6
	To Martha Davies & Child to London			6
27.	To Agnus Moor to Burton			6
	To Attending Hyde a painter under a Warrant for Inhumanly abusing two Women		2	
28.	To Benjamin Marlar attending sessions three Days against Wm Ogden for Felony		3	
	To William Ryder to Bollington ...			6
29.	To Aggy Barton to Liverpool			6
	To Ann M'intosh & 3 Children to Inverness		1	6
	To Cornelius Sulivan to Dublin ...			6
31.	To Rebecca Gardner to Lynn			6
	To John Mc Cowl & Wife to Glasgow		1	
Nov' 1.	Edward Ambross & Wife to London		1	
2.	Joseph Bostock to Liverpool			6

[1] See p. 191, note 2.

	To Jurors over an Inquisition over Warren	1	:	4
[Nov.] 3.	To James Foster & Wife to Richmond	: 1	:	
4.	To Jurors of an Inquisition over Becket	: 1	:	4
	To James Martin to Swansea	:	:	6
	To assistance Driving a Gang of Beggars out of Town	: 1	:	6
5.	To Ann Kennedy & Child to Maidstone	:	:	6
5.	To Jonathan Craig to Barnsley... ...	:	:	6
	To Catherine Golding & 2 Children to Whitehaven	: 1	:	
7.	To Morris Down, to Pool...	:	:	6
	To Bridget Barnet to London... ...	: 1	:	
11.	To William Mc Gray & Wife to Barwick	: 1	:	
12.	Samuel Morris to Sheffield	:	:	6
14.	To Kitt Cassado to Liverpool	:	:	6
	To William Ward & 3 Children to Norfolk	: 1	:	
	To John Wallis to Derby	:	:	6
16.	To Ellen Lisle to Nottingham... ...	:	:	6
18.	To John Dooley to Glasgow	:	:	6
	To Thomas Thompson to Bulwell ...	: 1	:	
	To Jurors of an Inquisition over Wood	: 1	:	4
19.	To Jane Ferguson to Scotland... ...	:	:	6
	To John Leigh to Tewksbury	:	:	6
21.	To Jonathan Butterworth for assistance &c	: 5	:	6
	To Do to Belfield, with Pearson & Oldham	: 3	:	
	To Jane Gray & Child to York... ...	: 1	:	
	To Daniel Hart to Liverpool	:	:	6
	To Ellen Mc Far to Whichchurch ...	:	:	6
24	To Thomas Munday to Bath	:	:	6
	To Jonathan Butterworth, in full ...	: 4	:	
	To Maria Cload to Carlisle	:	:	6
26.	To Elizabeth Twine to Richmond ...	:	:	6
27.	To Joseph Bitty to Carlisle	:	:	6
30.	To Joseph Clough, attending Halliwell a day and a night	: 2	:	
30.	To George Wooders to Aberdeen ...	:	:	6
	To James Green to Liverpool	:	:	6

		£	s	d
	To Duncan Mc Fardsy & Wife to Warrington	:	1 :	
Dec' 1.	To Thomas Charles to Cambridge ...	:	:	6
3.	To Jonathan Diggles attending Dewhurst a Felon	:	1 :	6
	To William Nugent to Ireland		:	6
	To John Loop to Woolwich		:	6
5.	To Mary Meuse & 2 Children to Leicester	:	1 :	
7.	To Henry Yates to Ribchester ...	:	:	6
8.	To Alexander Wilson to Lancaster...	:	:	6
9.	To Thomas Harper assisting on the Watch...	1 :	1 :	
10.	To Richard Payne to Northwich ...	:	:	6
	To Anthony Seddon to Reading ...	:	:	6
	To assistance clearing the Streets of Ballad Singers [1] ...	:	2 :	
11.	To Jane Gaskell to Carlisle	:	:	6
13.	To Jane Widows to Dover	:	:	6
15.	To John Evans to Liverpool	:	:	6
16.	To Alexander Allen to Leigh	:	:	6
17.	To Jane Wilks to Lancaster	:	:	6
	To Jonathan Butterworth for assistance	1 :	3 :	6
21.	To John Dod & John Walker to Liverpool ...	:	1 :	
22.	To Jonathan Butterworth, Again ...	:	13 :	7
	To Mary Cowley to Winwick	:	:	6
23.	To Joseph Spencer & Wife to Ely ...	:	1 :	
	To Betty Broome to Cornwall	:	:	6
26.	To Joel Dobson, to Scarborough ...	:	:	6
27.	To cleaning the Steps at Salford Bridge	:	2 :	
28.	To Mary Ford to Chatham	:	:	6
	To Ralph Alstead to Devon	:	:	6
	To William Lloyd to Flint	:	:	6
	To Thomas Woodstock to Beverley	:	:	6
	To John Cooke to Preston	:	:	6
31.	To Ann Bentley & 2 Children to Bury ...	:	1 :	
	To Samuel Jackson, opening Widows Locks To find Stolen goods	:	1 :	
1775.				
Jan' 2.	Simon Frazer to Ludlow	:	:	6

---

[1] See p. 278, note 1.

1775	To Arthur Butters to Liverpool ...	: : 6
[Jan.] 3.	To Ann Kennedy & 2 Children to Bristol...	: 1 :
	To Jane Gordon to Carlisle	: 6
	To Jeffery Bow to Fokenham	: 6
6.	To John Wilkinson Wife & Child to Hull	: 1 :
	To Mary Hays & Sarah Huntley to Chester	: 1 :
	To the Jurors & other Expences attending two Inquisitions over the Body of Marg[t] Howard[1] who was killed at Dob Lane, by Phineas Makin &c	: 10 : 6
9.	To 4 Ship wrecked Sailors to Hull ...	: 2 :
	To Sarah Jenkins & 5 Children to Hull	: 1 :
10.	To James Randolph & Wife to Salop	: 1 :
11.	To James Holden to Liverpool... ...	: : 6
12.	To James Robinson to Nantwich ...	: : 6
	To Ellen Barret & 3 Children to Skipton	: 1 :
14.	To Joseph Vest to Yarmouth	: : 6
16.	To John Ellison to Liverpool	: : 6
17.	To John Darrison to Glasgow	: : 6
19.	To Esther Smith to Bradford	: : 6
20.	To Sarah Hutchinson to Liverpool...	: : 6

[1] The account of this horrid murder is set out at some length in the *Manchester Mercury* of Jan. 3rd, 1775, as follows :—

"On Saturday Night last [Dec. 31st, 1774], as Martha Howard, an Huxter, at Failsworth, near this Town, was returning Home, she was attacked by a Man betwixt Newton Heath and Failsworth Turnpike, who treated her with much brutality and insolence, but a Carter accidentally coming up she took refuge in his Cart ; soon after the Man being joined by three more they threatened to serve the Carter in the same Manner they intended to do by the Woman, if he did not turn her out ; he, being intimidated, left her to their Fury, and she was found in the Morning by her own Son, in a Ditch, most cruelly and barbarously Murdered. The Villain who first assaulted her (and who was known by the Carter) when he got Home appearing all bloody and being charged by his Wife with Murdering somebody, packed up what Clothes were at Hand, made off, and has not been heard of since. The Coroners Inquest sat all Yesterday [Jan. 2nd] upon the Body, but as many Witnesses were to be examined it was adjourned to this Day."

In the next week's paper there is this paragraph :—

"On Wednesday Morning was committed to the Castle of Lancaster, Phineas Makin, on a violent Suspicion of having committed a Rape and Murder upon the Body of Martha Howard, a Widow, at Dod Lane End near this Town, as mentioned in our last."

		£	s	d
23.	To Isaac Holt to London...			6
	To loss by 6 light Guineas Sold by the direction of the Late Constable, Mr Marriot		7	2
	To John Connor to Dunfries			6
25.	To Thomas Reddish for Attendance at the sessions		4	6
	To Dº going to the Hamletts with Warrants		1	
26.	To Jonathan Diggles going with Carter two Days to form a Billet List... ...		2	
	To Extra Expence Settling Kirks Billet of Dragoons [1]		4	6
27.	To Richard Sidney to Lancaster ...			6
28.	To John Thomas to Hull...			6
	To Mary White & 2 Children to Winchester		1	
	To William Golightly to Liverpool...			6
30.	To John Jones to Montgomery ...			6
	To Mr Christopher's Bill, when waiting to do Business with Prisoners, at Mr Booths[2]...		19	3
Febr 3.	To Jonathan Butterworth's Bill ...	1	4	
	To George Williams to Portsmouth...			6
	To John Roberts, Wife, & Child to Kendall		1	
4.	To Amy Jackson to Liverpool... ...			6
	To paper, ruling, & writing a Complete Militia list	1	1	
6.	To John Watson to Dublin			6
	To Jurors at Inquisition over James Gorse		2	
8.	To Phillip Dooley to Nottingham ...			6
	To Thomas Spencer to Liverpool ...			6
9.	To James Smith to Leigh...			6
10.	To Mary Fitzgerrald to Ireland ...			6
11.	To Susanna Connor to Halifax ...			6
	To James Bayley to Worcester ...			6

[1] I do not find any reference in the local paper to Col. Kirk's regiment of Dragoons coming into the town. Later on, however, there is an account of "the Earl of Pembrooks Dragoons quartered here" being reviewed on May 29th.

[2] This was John Gore Booth, Esq., an active magistrate, living in Salford.

			£	s	d
[Feb.] 13.	To Margaret Hammond & 2 Children to Burton		:	1 :	
	To John Sharpe to Bristol		:	:	6
	To Mary Hewit to Rugby...		:	:	6
16.	To Thomas Digges to Inveness ...		:	:	6
18.	To Thomas Reddish for Sundry Messages		:	1 :	
	To Kitty Johnson to Bristol		:	:	6
	To Ann Rimmer to Liverpool... ...		:	1 :	
	To Eliza Redford to Framlingham ...		:	:	6
	To Loss by conveying Margt Hay to Burton		:	6 :	6
	To Ann Sky & a Blind Man		:	1 :	
	To Martha Brown & 3 Children ...		:	2 :	
	To Mary Robinson to Warrington ...		:	:	6
	To Mary Hargreaves to Nottingham		:	:	6
	To a Messenger to the Hamlets for the Constables to Bring their Assize presentments		:	3 :	
22.	Martha Brown to Chester...		:	:	6
	To Ann Hargrave to Warrington ...		:	:	6
	To 2 Women to Nottingham, both Ill		:	1 :	
23.	To Mary Allicot to Newark		:	:	6
	To Beadle whipping two Vagrants ...		:	2 :	
	To Joseph Crispe to Worcester... ...		:	:	6
	To William Gammon to Liverpool ...		:	:	6
24.	To Alice Brunet to London		:	1 :	
	To Charles Idea to Liverpool		:	1 :	
	To John Lumley to London		:	:	7
25.	To James Haydock to Edgworth ...		:	1 :	
	To 3 assistants clearing the Streets of Vagrants		:	3 :	
	To Ellen Bedlow & 3 Children to Salop		:	1 :	
Mar 1.	To Isabel Septon to Whitehaven ...		:	:	6
	To Frances Harrison to Headon ...		:	:	6
	To William Garstang & 3 Children to York		:	1 :	
	To Mathew White. Wife & 4 Children to Yarmouth		:	1 :	
	To Thomas Johnson to the Greenland Fishery		:	1 :	
3.	To Sarah Friender & Child to Liverpool		:	1 :	

	To Ellen Rogers to Aberdeen... ...	:	:	6
	To John Fox to Salop	:	:	6
	To James Smith to Ely	:	:	6
	To Charles Murphy to Dᵒ	:[1]:		
	To Isabel Mᶜ queen to Inverness ...	:	:	6
	To Dolly Grimes & Child to Liverpool	:	:	6
11.	To Milly Young to London	:	:	6
	To Betty Powell to Preston	:	:	6
	To a Soldier to Scotland	:	:	6
	To Joseph Clowes to Leek	:	:	6
11.	To High Constables Warrant for County Rate, rebuilding the House of Correction[1] &c	102 : 10 : 2		
	To making Beadles Cloak...	: 9 :		
14.	To Betty Smith to Liverpool	:	:	6
	To Nicholas Duckworth to Exon ...	:	:	6
	To Mary Spencer, Chappel le frith...	:	:	6
17.	To Ellen Kitts to Bristol	:	:	6
	To Hannah Mellor to Kendall... ...	:	:	6
	To Barrow Clough & 3 Children ...	: 2 :		6
18.	To Margaret Mᶜ quire to Barwick ...	: 1 :		
	To a Passenger to Columbine in Ireland	:	:	6
	To Gold Weights	: 8 :		
	To Thomas Harpur	: 4 :		
	To William Ogden & Wife to Littleborough	: 1 :		
	To Ann Pilling & Child to Hull ...	:	:	6
	To Mary Reynolds to Stockton ...	:	:	6
	To John Silver to London...	:	:	6
	To Molly Rawlinson to Warrington...	:	:	6
	To Ann Taylor to Hull	:	:	6
19.	To John Dickenson. Wife & Child to Burton	: 1 :		

---

[1] Although the House of Correction had been repaired a year or two ago (see pp. 276 and 289), it must have been almost entirely rebuilt this year, judging from the amount spent upon it. From an advertisement in the *Manchester Mercury* it would appear that some of the prisoners took the opportunity of making their escape from the building whilst it was being rebuilt. The advertisement is headed as follows :—

"Escaped from the House of Correction, in Manchester, on Thursday Evening, the 23d of February, 1775, by the help of Ladders, which were obliged to be used in the Rebuilding of the said Prison, and supposed to be assisted by some Workmen there."
The names and descriptions of the three escaped prisoners are given, and five guineas reward is offered by Mr. Whitlow, the Keeper or Governor of the said prison.

21.	To Jurors viewing the Body of Wm Hulme	: 2 :		
22.	To John Roberts & Wife to Sheffield	: 1 :		
	To Ann Hay to Liverpool	:	:	6
	To Mary Baker to Coventry	:	:	6
	To Ann Jackson to York...	:	1 :	9
23.	To John Robinson to Glasgow...	:	:	9
25.	To Sarah Paulden & 2 Children to Leeds ...	: 3 :	6	
27.	To Sarah Smith to Hull, Hannah Hope to Salop	: 1 :	6	
	To a Woman p pass ...	:	:	6
29.	To William Pellet to Liverpool	: . 1 :		
30.	To Jurors attending Inquest	: 1 : 10		
	To Betty Ward & 4 Children to Burnley	: 1 :	6	
	To assize presentments	: 2 :	6	
30.	To writing Warrants to the Hamlets and Messengers with them agreeable to Six different Rolls from the High Constables at 3/- Each	: 18 :		
April 5.	To Thomas Stopford to London	: 1 :	6	
6.	To Peter Barnes to Newcastle ...	:	:	6
	To William Speakman to Sheffield...	: 1 :		
	To Ben. Oldham for assistance...	: 2 :		
7.	To Frances Aubecca to Wimslow	:	:	6
	To Ann Mc Claud to Liverpool	:	:	6
	To Sarah Woodward & 2 Children to Warrington...	: 1 :		
	To Ann Firth & Rosamond Bower to Doncaster ...	: 1 :		
11.	To Cleaning the Dungeon	: 1 :		
	To Mary Charles by a pass	: 1 :		
	To Postage of a Letter	:	:	6
	To a Vagrant	: 1 :	6	
14.	To James Higgin & Patrick Collin to Ireland	: 1 :		
	To Thomas Sugden attending sessions in Octo^r	: 1 :	6	
	To Mr Hunt for writing on the Engine doors	1 : 1 :		
	To Jos. Whitehead for Beadles Shoes	: 5 :	9	

To James Oldham to Stockport & other Errands	3 : 6
To Belman's receipt for Public Cries	: 6 :
To John Stotts Bill with prisoners to Rochdale	: 15 : 6
To Richard Dickenson for assistance	: 5 :
To Thomas Gelder for Errands ...	: 3 :
To Mr Hope's for Horse Hire... ...	: 4 :
To Christopher Moon for work at the Steps at Mill Row Bridge...	: 11 : 4
18. To Dickinson & others for assisting at the Riot	: 3 :
20. To Spent at Billeting the soldiers ...	: 1 : 3
To a Vagrant to Stockport	: 1 : 6
To Richd Greenough for Work at Mill Row Bridge	: 8 : 10
20. To Ann Gumersall for meat & drink for Evidences	: 8 : 10
To Titus Leigh's Bill going to Lancaster	1 : 7 :
To Fanny Scolfield for Rent for powder Room	4 : 4 :
To Do for Do for the Militia powder	2 : 2 :
To Do for the Maintenance of Prisoners	1 : 9 : 8
To Mr Shelmerdines Bill for Do ...	2 : 18 : 2
To Wrigley kept in Custody some time afterwards Convey'd to Alkrington,[1] and bound over	: 7 : 1
To John Edwards Bill for maintenance of Prisoners...	: 8 : 6
To Thomas Harpers Bill Watching & Clearing the Streets &c	: 17 : 6
21. To 2 Ruled Books	: 1 : 6
To Paper for Billets	: : 10
To 2 Men clearing the Streets	: 3 :
To Betty Williamson & 2 Children to Liverpool	: 1 : 6
22. To Butterworth 2 days going round the Town	: 3 :

---

[1] Alkrington was the residence of Ashton Lever, Esq. (See p 265, note 2.)

23.	To apprehending & detaining a Boy found in Mr Cotes's Cellar, all day & all Night	: 2 : 6
	To Jane Carter to Leeds, very Lame	: 1 :
24.	To John Brown & 2 Children by a foot Pass from Dr Mainwaring [1] to Glasgow	: 2 : 6
25.	To Michael Bent, Wife & Child to Sheffield	: 1 : 6
	To attending and detaining 2 Men & a Woman two days and a Night, on Suspicion of Felony	: 5 : 6
26.	To prison Room, meat & Drink for 4 Men under Dr Mainwaring's [1] Warrant for a Riot, discharged for want of Evidence	: 9 : 6
	To two Women Confined one day and one Night, by Mr Booth, [2] discharged & sent out of Town	: 3 : 10
	To Jacob Hartley & 2 Sons to Derby	: 1 : 6
27.	To Pasting up Notices of the Militia	: 1 :
	To Mary Lancaster pass'd to Chorley, Supper and Lodging by Dr Mainwaring's [1] order	: 2 : 4
	To Betty Brown confined from Saturday to Monday for a Riot, discharged by Mr Booth [2]	: 4 : 4½
28.	Benjamin Johnson, Wife & 5 Children to Worcester, very Ill and Lame ...	: 3 : 6
30.	To James Lenton a Stroler confined 2 days and one Night discharged by the Church Wardens...	: 2 : 6
May 2.	To Betty Haddock ordered from the sessions into Confinement, Two days & one Night	: 2 : 6
3.	To James Greenhill, Wife & 3 Children to Gainsbro'	: 2 : 6
4.	To Sending Coroners Warrants to Broughton &c and Spent on the Inquest at Ardwick	: 3 : 6
	To Edward Thompson & Wife to Newcastle	: 1 :

---

[1] See p. 218, note 2.   [2] See p. 313, note 2.

5.	To Sending Coroners warrants to Pendleton &c and attending the Inquest at White Lion [1] Deansgate ...	: 3 :	6
	To 2 Men bringing the Child from Hulme to the Bone House [2] in the old Church yard	: 2 :	
	To John Carter for Sundrys	: 5 :	6
6.	To William Heywood & 2 Sons by a foot pass from Mr Booth [3] to Ormskirk	: 2 :	6
	To John Davies and Wife to Chester	: 1 :	
8.	To William Wilson & John Andrews to Morpeth...	: 2 :	
9.	To 4 Vagrants kept in Custody all day and all Night, then removed by a foot pass from Mr Booth [3]...	: 11 :	
10.	To Cleaning the Dungeon, fresh Straw &c	: 5 :	
	To James Howard, Wife & Child to Dublin	: 1 :	6
	To Thomas Harpur clearing the Streets...	: 3 :	6
	To Sarah Halliwell Confined 3 days & 2 Nights, By Dr Mainwaring, [4] whipped & discharged	: 4 :	6
14.	To a poor Woman at Scotch Peggy's	: 5 :	
	To Gold Weights	: 1 :	3
17.	To Sarah Edmunds & 2 Children till I could have an Answer from Stafford her husbands Supposed Place of Settlement 5 days & ½	: 5 :	
19.	To Sending Coroners Warrants to Ardwick &c and attending the Inquest at the Oak [5]...	: 3 :	6
	To Paid Hodgkinson for a Man and a Horse Two Nights & a day by Mr Mainwarings [4] order	: 4 :	9
20.	To Hester Bradshaw & Child to York	: 1 :	

---

[1] This Manchester inn has not, I think, occurred before.

[2] The "bone house" in the Churchyard seems to have been occasionally used as a mortuary. In the second volume of these Accounts a building called "the lodge," in the Churchyard, seems to have been used for that purpose. (See vol. ij., pp. 5, 10, 58.)

[3] See p. 313, note 2.   [4] See p. 218, note 2.

[5] The name of an inn in Ardwick is here given.

21.	To John Jackson & Edwd Wills confined one day and one Night by Mr Booth,[1] Whipped and discharged ...	3 :
	To the Beadle for whipping 3 Vagrants	: 6 :
24.	To Betty Haddock confined 3 days & 3 Nights, removed to the Lock Hospital[2]	: 6 :
26.	To Sarah Halliwell one day & Night, removed to Rochdale by an Order ...	: 1 : 6
	To Hannah Johnson and two Children to Derby	: 1 : 6
27.	To J. Guest, R Mills, & S. Thompson, old soldiers to Chester	: 1 : 6
	To James Berry & Mary Foster for Rioting in the Streets, Berry confined in the Dungeon, Foster at the Packhorse[3] 2 days & Nights by Dr Mainwarings[4] orders	: 4 : 6
29.	To Betty Thompson and 4 Children to Retford	: 2 : 6·
30.	To Ellen Davies and 2 Children to Hull	: 1 : 6
	To James Grant & Wife to Chester...	: 1 :
June 1.	To John Fitzmaurice & Child to Ireland	: 1 :
	To Wm Garstang, Wife, and 3 Children to Chelsea	: 2 : 6
2.	To Sarah Boo, to Whitehaven... ...	: : 6
	To J. Mc Donald, Wife & 2 Children to Scotland...	: 2 :
	To Elizabeth Craddock to Birmingham	: : 6
	To Robt Runcurn to London	: : 6
3.	To James Foster and Wife to Chester	: 1 :
	To Wm Wilson, T. Powell, J. Graham, H. Johnson, to Chester	: 2 :

---

[1] See p. 313, note 2.

[2] This is the first time the Lock Hospital in Manchester has been mentioned. It had only recently been erected.

[3] The Packhorse Inn, which has been mentioned before. seems to have had a room for the custody of prisoners. (See p. 288, note 1.)

[4] See p. 218, note 2.

[June] 5.	To Betty Waters & 2 Children by a foot pass from D[r] Mainwaring[1] to Derby	:	2 :	6
	To Postage of a letter		:	6
	To Ann Watson by pass from M[r] Bradshaw[2] to London	:	1 :	6
	To John Jackson & Edw[d] Thompson to Chester	:	1 :	
	To Richard Sykes & John Richardson to Chester	:	1 :	
	To Nancy Williamson to Leicester...	:	:	6
	To the High Constables Warrant for the County Rate, rebuilding the House of Correction[3] &c...	52 :	15 :	10
	To Cash paid the Engine Men ...	12 :	14 :	
7.	To Arthur James, Wife & 3 Children to Prescott	:	1 :	6
9.	To Elizabeth Morris & Child to Holliwell	:	1 :	
	To James Raymur & Wife to Halifax	:	1 :	
10.	To Geo. Johnson & Betty Craddock confined one day & one Night for a Riot discharged by M[r] Bradshaw[2] ...	:	2 :	6
12.	To Margaret Ramsbotham confined two Days & Nights for Robbing her Lodgings, Whipped 2 - & sent out of town 3 6	:	5 :	6
14.	John Smith & 3 Children to Leeds...	:	2 :	
16.	Henry Jones & Wife to London ...	:	1 :	
	To Eliza Wass & 4 Children to London	:	2 :	
18.	To James Stuart to Scotland, very old	:	1 :	
20.	To Arthur Macloss, Sent by order to Liverpool	:	2 :	
22.	To Soldiers fireing on Kings Birth day[4]	3 :	3 :	
	To Music playing on D[o][4]...	1 :	4 :	
22nd	To the Ringers on the Kings Birth day[4]	:	5 :	
	To Betty Hyron & 3 Children to Nottingham By a foot pass from M[r] Bradshaw[2]	:	3 :	6

---

[1] See p. 218, note 2.   [2] See p. 211, note 1.   [3] See p. 315, note 1.
[4] These payments were for the usual rejoicings on June 4th, the King's birthday.

24.	To pasting up Advertisements about Gunpowder	: 1 :
	To cleaning the Dungeon & Fresh Straw &c	: 5 :
27.	To Bartholemew Hunter & Wife to London	: 1 :
	To Jonathan Graham, Wife & 3 Children to Carlisle	: 2 :
	To a Turk	: 1 :
28.	To Ben. Oldham going to Withington	: 1 :
30.	To John Shaw an old Soldier very lame to Chester	: 1 :
	To releived Achmet a Turk	: 1 :
July 1.	To John Roberts & William King to Whitehaven	: 1 :
	To James Newton Confined 3 days & 3 Nights for abusing his Wife	: 6 : 9
3.	To Sarah Bradshaw & Child by foot pass from Dr Mainwaring[1] to Scarboro'	: 2 : 6
4.	To Sending Coroners Warrants to Pendleton &c and attending at the Dog in Salford	: 3 : 6
	To Ann Mc Kenna & her Companion at the Sun	: 3 :
	To Betty James & 2 Children to Chesterfield	: 1 : 6
5.	To the Porters playing the Engines...	: 3 :
6.	To three Men attending the Deputy 3 Nights in Parading the Town when st Ann's Wall was So much Damaged &c	: 9 :
	To Thomas Wilson & Son to Carlisle	: 1 :
7.	To Mary Bradbury & Child by foot pass from Dr Mainwaring[1] to Rotherham	: 2 : 6
	To conveying two Men to Middleton under a Warrant from Col. Townley,[2] Cost	: 5 :
8.	To Expences at Fletcher's Tavern[3]...	8 : 16 :

---

[1] See p. 218, note 2.   [2] See p. 255, note 1.
[3] This inn has not, I think, occurred before.

	To writing the Ley book &c	1	7	
	To Edw⁴ Johnson, Wife, & 2 Children to Hull		2	
10.	To a Lock for the Engine door... ...		6	6
	To Butterworth 3 Month's Salary ...	2	10	
	To Betty Jones to Denbigh			6
12.	To Edmund Newton & Wᵐ Wright to Chester		1	
	To Horse Hire to Didsbury & Heaton Norris, after Thomas Birtles for a Rape		3	6
	To Sending money warrants to the Hamlets		3	
13.	To James Fletcher a Felon confined two days & two nights till he could find Bail, afterwards Committed to the House of Correction		4	6
	To Mary Smith & 2 Children to Liverpool		1	6
16.	To Elizabeth Greenlees releived & sent out of Town by Dr Mainwarings¹ order		2	
	To James Seddon & Wife to Warrington		1	
19.	To Mary Jacob & 4 Children to Liverpool		2	6
20.	To Daniel Austiss & Wife by a foot pass from Mr Bradshaw to Cambridge		2	6
22.	To Sending Summons's from Dr Mainwaring, to Heaton Norris, Audenshaw, Ashton & Chorlton Row		3	
	To 4 Evidences at sessions		2	
	To James Weaver & Wife to Lynn...		1	
24.	To Ann Shepherd & Child to Sheffield		1	
	To Eliz. Maclean to Carlisle, very Ill		1	
24.	To Andrew Cameron, Wife & 2 Children by a foot pass from Mr Bayley,² to Edinburgh		3	

¹ See p. 218, note 2.   ² See p. 225, note 2.

26.	To the Witnesses against Wolstenhome & Wife [1]	: 5 : 3
	To attending their being Pilloried [1] ...	: 1 :
	To two Vagrants to Liverpool	: 1 : 6
28.	To Betty Lecky & 2 Children to Morpeth	: 1 : 6
	To Cleaning the Dungeon & Fresh Straw &c	: 5 :
29.	To Sending Coroners warrants to Broughton &c, and attending the Inquest at the Flying Horse [2]	: 3 : 6
	To Horse Hire & other Expences taking four Bailiffs under Warrant from Col: Townley [3] to Belfield ...	1 : 0 : 6
	The Deputy & Beadles Horses, & Expences attending them &c	: 10 : 9
30.	To James Lambert & Wife to Kendall	: 1 :
	To Wm Jones & Edwd Inis 2 old Soldiers to Liverpool...	: 2 :
Aug^st 1.	To James Williamson, Wife & 3 Children to Bristol	: 2 : 6
2.	To the Beadles Staff	: 12 : 6
	To Thomas Dixon to York	: 1 :
4.	To Sending Summon's to Blakeley, Droylsden &c	: 2 :
6.	To Sending D° to Ashton...	: 2 :
	To a Man by pass to London	: 1 :
	To D° to Durham	: 1 :
	To D° to Cumberland ...	: 1 :
8.	To Elizabeth Delaney & 5 Children to Ireland	: 2 : 6
9.	To Benjamin Talbot	: 1 :
	To Robt Murray Wife & Child... ...	: 1 : 6
11.	To going to Bolton with a Man & Woman under Warrant from Mr Rasbotham, [4] detained all night	: 4 :

[1] In the account of the July Quarter Sessions given in the *Mercury*, it is stated that "Lawrence Wolstenholme, Labourer, and Margaret his Wife for Keeping a common Bawdy House, stood in the Pillory the same day [July 20th] from Twelve to One and then passed to the lower End of Pilkington their Place of Settlement."

[2] This inn occurs here for the first time.

[3] See p. 255, note 1.

[4] This was Dorning Rasbotham, of Bolton, Esq.

	To Rich⁴ Cartlidge, Wife & 2 Children to Hull	: 2 :		
14.	To Rob¹ Johnson to Worcester ...	:	: 6	
	To Catherine Wright, & 3 Children to Coventry	: 2 :		
16.	To a Lock for Lower Dungeon Door	: 1 :		
	To Sending Coroners Warrants & Jury at Crown¹ Milgate	: 3 : 6		
17	To cleaning Salford Bridge Steps ...	: 2 :		
19.	To James Greenhill & Wife to Litchfield	: 1 :		
	To Cha' Davies & 2 Children to Wales	: 1 : 6		
21.	To Sending a Woman to Middleton sessions	: 2 :		
	To Eliza. White & 3 Children to Beverley	: 2 :		
	To two pair of Shoes for the Beadle	: 12 :		
22.	To a poor Woman in Distress	:	: 6	
	To Horse Hire & Expences to Rochdale to deliver in assize presentments	: 6 :		
23.	To going to Altringham after Birtles	: 2 : 6		
	To Thomas Watson, Wife & 2 Children to Northampton...	: 1 : 6		
25.	To John Richards & Wife to Hereford	: 1 :		
31.	To the Dragoons² going to Liverpool	: 2 : 6		
	To a Woman to Whitehaven	: 1 :		
	To Several Messengers on the Constables Business	: 1 : 6		
	To Mr North for Beadles Gown & Cap³	2 : 14 :		
	To Loss on Light Gold	: 6 : 0½		
Sept. 2.	To Martha Rowbotham & 2 sons to Ashton...	: 1 :		
	To Cleaning the Dungeon & fresh Straw &c	: 5 :		
4.	To Jonathan Marvel, Wife & 3 Children to York	: 2 :		
6.	To Edw⁴ Whitehead & Cha' Delane to Halifax	: 2 :		

¹ This inn occurs here for the first time, I think.

² These were the Earl of Pembroke's Dragoons. (See p. 313, note 1.) There was a riot at Liverpool at this time, in which a number of sailors were concerned.

³ See p. 88, note 2.

7.	To Sending Alex[r] Watson to Lancaster Horse Hire à 5[d] p Mile 1 . 3 . 4. Wages & keep 1 . 1 . 0	2 : 4 : 4
12.	To Christopher Heywood & son to Ashburn	: 1 :
15.	To taking Nan M[c] Kenna to the Dungeon	: 1 : 6
	To a poor Woman to London... ...	: 1 :
	To paid for a Baggage Cart to Liverpool	: 9 : 3
18.	To John Davies to Wrexham	: 1 :
	To Ann Fallows to Whitehaven ...	: 1 :
19.	To Betty Johnson & Elizabeth Jones for taking Care of Eliza. Heywood's Child, by Order of D[r] Mainwaring[1]...	: 3 :
	To sending to Oldham to overseer concerning D[o]	: 2 :
	To Conveying Eliza. Heywood to the House of Correction	: 1 :
20.	To W[m] Williams & 2 Children to Wrexham	: 1 :
	To John Dutton & Wife to Nanptwich	: 1 :
23.	To M[rs] Hope for prisoners in the Dungeon &c	: 9 : 3½
26.	To Edward Poor and Wife to Nottingham	: 1 :
30.	To relcived Mary Hargon & 3 Children, while I wrote to Leeds, after that to York, to know their place of Settlement, being 8 days at 1/6 p Day, by order of M[r] Bayley,[2] & D[r] Mainwaring,[1] afterwards Sent to York by an order from the two Justices	: 12 :
Octo[r] 2.	To Mary Jackson & 2 Children to Burnley	: 2 :
3.	To Sending Coroners Warrants to Pendleton &c and attending the Inquest at the Dog in Salford	: 3 : 6
5.	To the Belman for three public Cries	: 6 :

[1] See p. 218, note 2. [2] See p. 225, note 2.

7.	To Mr Prescott[1] for Books paper, Quills & Ink &c...	: 11 : 9
	To Ann Moorehouse to Wakefield ...	: : 6
9.	To Peter Madan, Wife, & 2 children to Creol in Scotland, his Wife Ill, Stayed here two days by Mr Bradshaw's order	: 3 :
10.	To Jonathan Butterworth's Salary in full	2 : 10 :
	To Sarah Morton & Child, to Wigan	: 1 :
	To Straw for the Dungeon	: 9 : 8
	To the Man who Saved the Gunpowder in Toad Lane	: 5 :
	To a Vagrant	: 1 :
	To William Darbyshire for rent for Engine House	1 :
	To Benj. Tyldsley for assisting at 3 Privy Watches	: 5 :
	To Lowe, Bate & Co for trimming for Beadles Gown & Cap	1 : 14 : 3
	To Mr Bower, one Years Interest on 200£	10 : 0 :
	To Thomas Radford for Engine pipes & hooping the Constables Staffs ...	: 13 :
10.	To John Whip for Leather for Beadles Cap	: 2 : 6
	To D^o for two whips with 9 tails for the Beadles	: 4 : 9
	To John Prescott[1] for Printing... ...	1 : 19 : 6
	To Thos Fowler for Stockings for Beadle 73 . 74 . 75	1 : 5 :
	To M^m Crompton for the Kings Birth day &c. &c[2]	16 : 17 :
	To George Clayton for a new pair of Butter Scales and repairing others ...	2 : 7 :
	To Mr Alsops[3] 3 Bills for Expences on different Occasions	7 : 9 : 9
	To James Carter for a Journey to Lancaster, Bound over under a Subpoena by Justice Booth,[4] to give	4 : 5 : 6

[1] See p. 238, note 1.
[2] This seems an unusually large outlay on the King's birthday, &c.
[3] Mr. Richard Alsop was the proprietor of the Bull's Head Inn at this time.
[4] See p. 313, note 2.

Evidence against James Dean[1] returned from Transportation, 10 days at 7/6 Horse Hire 10/6		
To James Kay, for a Journey to Lancaster, Bound over under a Subpœna, by Justice Booth,[2] to give Evidence against James Dean,[1] returned from Transportation, 10 days à 7/6 Horse Hire 10/6	4 : 5 : 6	
To Straw for Dungeon had in 1774...	: 7 : 8	
To Mrs Milward for Locks and other Work done at the Dungeon	: 8 : 7	
To Thomas Marsden for rent for the Engine House	3 : 3 :	
To James Dawson Numbering the Militia &c	1 : 3 : 8	
To Joseph Harrop[3] for Printing ...	2 : 2 :	
To Geo: Astley, for meat and Drink for four Evidences	: 8 : 4	
To Ralph Miller, for Iron Stantions for a Lock up House, done by order of the Late Deputy Kay[4]...	: 10 : 2	
10. To Mr Benjamin Bower, in part of 200£ owing to him by the Constables	100 : 0 :	
To Edmund Wrigley for work done at the Engine	1 : 12 :	
To the Late Deputy Kay's[4] Salary for 6 Months	15 : 0 :	
To Deputy Wilford's[5] D° for 6 Months	15 : 0 :	

[1] See p. 296, note 2.   [2] See p. 313, note 2.   [3] See p. 73, note 2.

[4] Mr. John Kay had held the office of Deputy-Constable for many years. At the Court Leet held on the 3rd March, 1775, there is the following entry *(Court Leet Records,* vol. viij., p. 165).

"We the Jurors aforesaid do appoint Mr William Henry Wilford Deputy Constable in the place of Mr John Kay who is now incapable of serving that Office any longer And power is hereby given to the Constables of this Town to remove the said William Henry Wilford from the said Office at their Will and Pleasure."

In the *Manchester Mercury* for May 9th, 1775, the following paragraphs occur :—

"On Wednesday Night [May 3rd] died, after a lingering Illness Mr John Kay, who for upwards of twenty seven Years discharged the important but troublesome Office of Deputy Constable of this Town, with Credit to himself and Advantage to the Public."

"On Wednesday last [May 3rd] was sworn in at the Court Leet Mr Wilford, Deputy Constable in the room of the late Mr John Kay."

[5] See previous note.

To Mr Peters for our Government ...   1 : 1 :
To John Carters[1] Salary in full   ...   10 : 0 :

[Total]...   ...£711 : 18 : 2½

[Receipts]

1775.   P Contra ...   .   C^r

	By Cash from the old Ley Book ...	33 : 11 : 5
Ap. 19.	By the Hamlets Proportion of 102 : 10 : 2	77 . 0 : 3
May 26.	By the Hamlets Proportion of 52 : 15 : 10	34 : 12 : 4
	By Cash from the Ley Book	333 : 18 : 6
	By Cash from the County	9 : 8 : 6
	By Ballance Owing to the Constables	223 : 7 : 2½

By Cash in the Ley Book yet uncol-
lected, 187:4:1 which when Collected,
will leave a Ballance due to the late
Constables of 36 : 3 : 1½ ...   .

£711 : 18 : 2½

Decr 20th 1775. We the Jurors of the Court Leet, holden for the Manor of Manchester, in the County Palatine of Lancaster, have Examined the foregoing Accounts of Mr Adam Oldham, and Mr Edward Hudson, (Late Constables) and do allow the Same.

(Signed)   DAN^L WHITTAKER
JOHN BROOME
WILL^M HOUGHTON
NATHAN HYDE
THO^S STARKIE
FALK^R PHILLIPS
W^M SANFORD
THO^S WALKER Junr
THO^S STOTT
LAW^{CE} GARDNER
EDM^D BATTERSBEE
WILL^M BULLOCK
SAMUEL HIBBERT

[1] Mr. John Carter was the Beadle.

[Constables' Accounts.]

[11th Oct., 1775, to 16th Oct., 1776.]

•••••••••••

𝔇ͬ The Town of Manchester to Mͬ BENJ͙ͯ L. WINTER & Mͬ THO͙ˢ CHADWICK,[1] *Constables.*

[Disbursements]

1775.	By the last years Ballance[2]	223: 7: 2½	
Octor 11.	To the Ringers	: 16:	
	John Cole & Wife to Durham... ...	: 1 :	
12.	To a Messenger to Ashton with Summons's...	: 2:	
	To Dᵒ to Rochdale	: 2:	
13.	Walter Roberts, Wife, & 3 Children to Ludlow	: 2: 6 .	
	Ellen Christie & 2 Children to Glasgow	: 1: 6	
16.	To a Load of Coals to the Guard Room	: 10: 3	
	To 3 lb of Candles 1/7½, Fender 1/6, 2 Baskets 1/- Brooms 4½	: 4: 6	
	Elizabeth Clayton & Child to Leek	: 1:	
	Ann Johnston to Edinburgh	: 1:	
17.	James Hampson, & John Williams confined two days and two nights, by order of Col.Townley,[3] upon Suspicion of Felony	: 8:	
18.	To a Doz.Candles for the Guard Room	: 6: 4	
19.	To Cleaning the dungeon after the Flood, half a load of Straw &c ...	: 6: 6	
	To a Coroners Inquest at the Flying Horse[4]...	: 3: 6	
20.	To Dᵒ a[t] Royal Oak[5] ...	: 3: 6	

[1] These two Constables were elected at the Court Leet held on the 11th October, 1775. (See *Court Leet Records*, vol. viij., p. 167.)

[2] See p. 329.   [3] See p. 255, note 1.

[4] This inn has, I think, occurred before.

[5] There are references to this inn on pp. 177 and 195.

		£	s.	d.
	Sarah Davies & 2 Children to Flint...	:	1:	6
	Henry Wilson and Wife to Derby ..	:	2:	6
21.	To A Riddle for the Guard Room ...	:	2:	
	To a Shovel & pair of Tongs D⁰ ...	:	4:	10
	To Hanging Lock[1] and three Keys for the Dungeon	:	4:	
22.	To 6 pair of Handcuffs, a! 6' -... ...	1:	16:	
	To two Women Confined at Pack-horse[2] till they Could be Sent by a pass	:	4:	6
23.	Ann Payne to London	:	1:	
	Margarett Carr, & 3 Children to Hull	:	2:	
	Ann Johnson & 2 Children to Birmingham	:	1:	6
24.	To the Bell man crying Down horns &c	:	1:	6
25.	To a Coroners Inquest at the Dog, Salford	:	3:	6
	Mary Mills & 2 Children to Carlisle...	:	1:	6
	Mary Griffith & 3 Children to Wrexham	:	2:	
	Eliz. Cash and 4 Children to Birmingham	:	2:	6
26.	Robert Cramp, Wife & 2 Children to Liverpool	:	2:	
	John Campbell & Wife to Borougstowness with permitt pass...	:	3:	
	To a Pair of Scarlett Stockings for Jonathan[3]	:	5:	6
	To a Pair of Shoes D⁰	:	5:	9
	To D⁰ for Carter[3]... ...	:	5:	9
	To a pair of Stockings for D⁰	:	4:	6
27.	Relcived Tho' Ogden found in the streets, Dying	:	2:	6
	Mary Morris & Child to Northampton	:	1:	
	Susan Johnson & 2 Children, very Ill, to Loughboro'	:	2:	
	Mary Smart & 3 Children to Clerkenwell...	:	2:	6

---

[1] A "hanglock," or padlock, is referred to on pp. 179 and 235.

[2] See p. 209, note 1.

[3] Jonathan Butterworth was the new Beadle elected at the Court Leet held on the 11th Oct., 1775 (see *Court Leet Records*, vol. viij., p. 171), whilst John Carter had been Beadle in the previous year.

	John Lambert, Wife, and 2 Children to Hull		: 2 :	
28.	Paid Money Warrant to Mr Jones ...	54 : 19 :		
	A Coroners Inquest at the Half Moon[1] Deansgate		: 3 :	6
	Ann Gosling & 2 Children & Abby Coulshaw & Child to Leeds		: 3 :	
	Michael Shephard to Sheffield... ...		: 1 :	
	To 2 strollers confined at the sun[2] ...		: 2 :	6
	To Mary Dempster confined at the Packhorse		: 1 :	3
29.	Alice Houghton, & Mary Bradshaw to Middlewich		: 1 :	
	Edwd Ellis & Child to North Wales...		: 1 :	
	John Hampson, Wife, & 3 Children to Wayley		: 2 :	6
30.	A Coroners Inquest at the George,[3] Ardwick		: 3 :	6
	Mary Langton & 2 Children to Settle		: 2 :	
30.	Susan Turner & Child Bristol		: 1 :	
	Ellen Pollit to Hull		: 1 :	
	Margaret Wilson & 2 Children to Edinburgh		: 1 :	6
	John Downs & 3 Children to Penzance		: 2 :	
31.	John Watson & Wife to Yarmouth...		: 1 :	6
	To 9 Cords for a Whip[4]		: 1 :	6
	To a New Whip[4]		: 2 :	6
	To Leather for the Beadle's Cap ...		: 2 :	6
Novr 1.	Edmund Wrigley, confined for buying Guides &c		: 11 :	6
	John Lees Do upon Suspicion of Felony		: 1 :	6
	To my Bill of Charges, Sending John Rogers to Lancaster & going to prosecute	7 : 5 : 4		
2.	To a Load of Coals to the Guard Room		: 12 :	
	To 1½ Doz Candles Do		: 9 :	6

[1] This inn is mentioned here, I think, for the first time.
[2] See p. 269, note 2.
[3] This inn in Ardwick occurs here, I think, for the first time.
[4] These are references to the "cat o' nine tails," used for flogging persons sentenced to be whipped.

	Sending to Stockport to apprehend Wm Hudson &c	:	4:	6
	Elizabeth Gray, & 2 Children to Derby	:	1:	6
	Mary Humphreys & 3 Children to Chester	:	2:	
	Ann Roby, & 4 Children to Morpeth	:	3:	
3.	Geo: Walker, Wife & 4 Children to Liverpool	:	3:	
	Ann Rosthern & Child to Nottingham	:	1:	
	Sarah Westall & 3 Children to Burton	:	2:	
	Esther Higgings & 2 Children to London	:	1:	6
	John Wright, Wife, & Child, & Mary Harrison & Child to Hull ...	:	2:	6
	Expences taking two Men under a Warrant to Mr Rasbotham[1]	:	3:	6
4.	To the Bellman crying Down Bonfires &c twice	:	4:	
	Mary Trainer & Eliza. Johnson & Child to Hadfield	:	1:	6
	Hannah Thompson & 4 Children to Burnley	:	2:	6
4.	A Coroners Inquest at the House of Correction	:	3:	6
	Mary Grant & Child to Portsmouth...	:	1:	
	Margaret Barry & 3 Children to Liverpool	:	2:	
	Betty Fildes, confined at the Sun,[2] 2 days & 2 Nights...	:	3:	
5.	John Jones confined 3 days at the Packhorse,[3] passed	:	3:	6
	Widow Holt & Child to Prescott ...	:	1:	
	Jane Wright to Hull...	:	1:	
	John Brown & Wife to Worcester ...	:	1:	
	Mary Williams & 3 Children to Grantham	:	2:	
	Ann Volumes & 2 Children, Eliz. Waring & 3 children to Hull	:	3:	6
	Jane Dane to Witney	:	1:	

---

[1] See p. 324, note 4.   [2] See p. 269, note 2.   [3] See p. 269, note 3.

[Nov.] 6.	To paid Barns for Ducking Stool[1] ...	4: 0:	
	To —— Bennet for Iron Work for D[o][1]	1:11:	1
	To 4 Men confined for a Riot at the Packhorse[2] 2 Days and discharged by D[r] Mainwaring[3]...	: 8:	6
7.	Mary Dawson confined for Reeling Short Yarn two Days & 3 Nights at the Sun,[4] by M[r] Livesey	: 7:	
	A Coroners Inquest at the George[5] at Ardwick	: 3:	6
	Mary Musters & 4 Children to Mansfield	: 2:	6
	Sarah Dewhurst & Child to Preston	: 1:	
8.	Francis Mills & 2 Children to Wellingboro'	: 1:	6
	Jane Price & Hannah Eaton to Yarmouth	: 1:	6
9.	Six Women of the Town confined two Nights and Sent to the House of Correction	:12:	9
10.	John Gibson & 2 Children by a permit pass...	: 3:	
	Two Girls confined a Day & a Night at the Sun,[4] for Stealing Silk from a poor Weaver, Sent to prison	: 4:	6
11.	To Cleaning the Dungeon & fresh Straw	: 5:	
	Joseph Adshead & Wife to Newcastle	: 1:	
11.	Hannah Walker & 3 Children to Halifax	: 2:	

[1] The DUCKING STOOL, as it was now called, instead of the much older and more correct form, "Cucking Stool," has been referred to in both the previous volumes of the *Constables' Accounts* (see vol. j., p. 57, note 3, and vol. ij., p. 64, note 2), as well as in the *Court Leet Records*. It was a punishment provided for scolding women and women of ill repute, as well as for women bakers and brewers who sold bread or beer contrary to the provisions regulating their sale. The culprit was securely fastened in a chair or stool, placed at the end of a long pole or otherwise suspended over a pool of water, into which she was ducked from time to time. Hence its more modern title. An entirely new "ducking stool" was evidently now made, and it was used in the Daub Holes, two large sheets of water in front of the Infirmary. A drawing is extant of a woman being "ducked" in this water, under the superintendence of the Beadle in his large hat and official costume, and in the presence of many spectators.

[2] See p. 269, note 3. [3] See p. 218, note 2.
[4] See p. 269, note 2. [5] See p. 332, note 3.

	Martha Leach & Eliz. Ashton confined two Days, Sent to prison	: 5 : 9
	Three People at the Packhorse[1] all night, going by pass	: 3 :
12.	A Coroners Inquest at the Royal Oak[2]	: 3 : 6
	Ann Chadwick & Child to Littleboro'	: 1 :
	Martha Jackson & Child, Ann Willings and Two Children to Hull ...	: 2 : 6
	Paid for 6 Lanthorns	: 12 :
13.	Two Men & 3 Women for a Riot in Toad lane Confined by Dr Mainwarings[3] orders & Sent to prison	: 5 : 6
	Samuel Pool & Wife to Rotherham	: 1 :
	Alice Hampson to Burnley	: 1 :
	Ann Worrall & 2 Children to Macclesfield	: 1 : 6
	William Garstang, Wife, & 4 Children to York	: 3 :
15.	James Morris & Wife to Cowley ...	: 1 :
	Geo. Paterson, Confined by order of Dr Mainwaring[3] 3 Days & afterwards passed to Scotland	: 4 : 9
	Paid for Shoes & Stockings for Do ...	: 4 : 8
17.	Mary Wilson & 2 Children to Sheffield	: 1 : 6
	Ann Power & Child to Worksop ...	: 1 :
18.	Paid Prescott[4] printing 500 Bills Mr Morris's Robbery	: 4 : 6
	Delivering Do & pasting up	: 2 : 6
	Paid Mr Jones High Constables Warrant	30 : 7 :
	Sarah Moor & 5 Children to Leicester	: 3 :
	James Berry Confined two days & Sent [to] prison	: 3 : 6
19.	Paid for 8 Watch Bills[5]	: 16 :
	To 3 Men going with us 4 Nights upon the Watch	: 12 :
22.	Jane Morrison & 2 Children to Edinburgh, were obliged to Stay here 3 days, one of the Children being Ill...	: 5 : 6

---

[1] See p. 269, note 3.   [2] This inn has been referred to before.
[3] See p. 218, note 2.   [4] See p. 238, note 1.   [5] See p. 31, note 4.

	Nails &c for the Change & Lock for Guard Room door	: 2 : 6
	A Girl Confined two days upon Suspicion of Stealing Silver Spoons from Lady Edgertons[1]	: 3 :
25.	A Coroners Inquest at the Dog in Salford	: 3 : 6
27.	Sending a man, his Wife & Eight Children in a Cart to Spotland here all night	: 10 : 6
	Mary Jones & 2 Children to Monmouth	: 1 : 6
28.	William Lockart, Wife & 2 Children to Dumfries	: 2 : 6
	Sarah Singleton & Child to Derby ...	: 1 :
	Eliz. Thompson, & Mary White & Child to Beverley	: 2 : 6
29.	Ryeneck[2] confined two days at the Sun,[3] and Sent to Middleton	: 3 : 10
	William Whitefoot, Wife, and two Children to London	: 2 :
	Alex[r] Murray & 2 Children to Fife	: 2 :
	Mary Middleton & 3 Children to Shrewsbury	: 2 :
30.	To the Bellman Crying Down Copper coin 3 times	: 4 : 6
	To Prescott[4] advertising D[o]	: 4 :
Dec[r] 1.	Five Lads Confined for breaking Windows and other Disorders, 2 Days at the Sun,[3] and afterwards Sent to prison	: 7 : 6
	Paid three Men two days Wages on Acc[t] of D[o]	: 12 :
	D[o] their Law Charges &c	: 10 :
	Margarett Williamson & 2 Children to Coln	: 2 :
	John Dodd, Wife & 3 Children to Ulverston	: 2 : 6

[1] This was Lady Egerton, the wife of Sir Thomas Grey Egerton, of Heaton, near Manchester. (See p. 299, note 3.)

[2] This was probably a local nickname.

[3] See p. 269, note 2.   [4] See p. 238, note 1.

[Dec.] 2.	Hannah Hope & Child to Wakefield	: 1 :	
	3 Girls confined two Nights at the Packhorse[1]	: 8 :	6
3ᵈ	Mary Davidson & Ann Laggit to Dundee	: 1 :	6
	Barbara Smith & 2 Children to Richmond	: 1 :	6
4.	Expences taking four People to Mildrow [? Milnrow] sessions under a Warrant from Col: Townley,[2] Horse Hire &c	: 13 :	6
	Margᵗ Mᶜ Murdoch & 2 Children to Edinburgh	: 1 :	6
5.	A Coroners Inquest at the Falcon,[3] Milgate	: 3 :	6
	Thomas Chadwick for assaulting his Wife & Sister at the Packhorse[1] from Sat. to Monday, Sent to prison ...	5 :	
	Jane Stowar, & Eliz. Jones to Ludlow	1 :	
6.	Nan Kenna, Moll Foster & Mal. Leach at the Sun Two Days, Sent to Prison	: 6 :	
	Thomas Craddock & Wife to Pennistone	: 1 :	
7.	To a Load of Coals for the Guard Room	: 12 :	
	To a Doz Candles Dᵒ	: 6 :	4
9.	Mary Dawson & 3 Children to Scarboro'	: 2 :	
	William Stevenson, Wife & Child to Salisbury	: 2 :	
10.	Lewis Quin & 3 Children, by Mʳ Bradshaw's Permit to Little Wootton	: 4 :	
11.	To Mʳ Wright, Making the Beadles Cloaths	1 : 17 :	2
	To Sedden making Gown & Cap ...	: 9 :	
.	Mathias Daziel, Wife & 7 Children at the Packhorse till they could be passed	: 12 :	6
	Simeon Wilson & Wife to Darlington	: 1 :	

---

[1] See p. 269, note 3.   [2] See p. 255, note 1.
[3] This inn has not, I think, occurred before.

[Dec.] 13. Cleaning the Dungeon & fresh Straw &c	5 :	
To three Men upon the Watch 2 Nights...	: 6 :	
Edw⁴ Coppock & Wife to Grantham	: 1 :	
14. To five Riotous persons confined at the Sun 2 Days	: 9 :	1
Sarah Goodwin & 3 Children to Ashburn	: 2 :	
15. Mᵣ Pidiock, and 4 Other Vagrants at the Packhorse Two days, Sent to prison	: 7 :	9
16. Sending two Men to Bolton, under a Warrant	: 3 :	
Eliza : & Martha Howard to Liverpool	: 1 :	
John Shore, for abusing a Child, confined 3 days, Sent to prison ...	: 4 :	6
John Hudson for Robbing a Sick box, and a Woman For reeling Short Yarn confined 2 Days by yᵉ Justices order	: 5 :	9
18. Mary Lomax & 4 Children to Westbury	: 2 :	6
20. John Nuttall, upon Suspicion of returning from Transportation, confined 3 Days, for further Examination &c	: 6 :	6
22. Sent the said John Nuttall to Lancaster &c Cost	2 : 4 :	6
James Thompson & Wife to Wellington	: 1 :	
Ann Green & 3 Children to Birkhemsted	: 2 :	
24. John Eaton for breaking out of Chester Castle, confined 5 Days, Sent to Chester	: 12 :	3
26. Mary Merryman & 2 Children to Dudley	: 1 :	6
Paid Mʳ Alsops Bill for Privy Watch	1 : 9 :	6
To Prescott[1] advertising disturbing the Town	: 3 :	6
To Dᵒ a Robbery at Colsshill ...	: 3 :	6

See p. 238, note 1.

	To D° Printing 500 Bills, delivering &c.	: 6 :
27.	Martha Davies & 5 Children to S' Asaph	: 3 :
	To a Coroners Inquest at the Oak, Jury Sat twice	: 5 : 6
29.	Jane Powell & Eliza. Watson to Leeds	: 1 :
	Charlotte Armstrong & Child to Tarporley	: 1 :
30.	John Hamilton & Wm Cunliffe, Confined by order of Col: Townley[1] for Felony 4 days, Sent to prison	: 18 : 10
31.	Ellen Howard & 3 Children to Bridport	: 2 : 6
1776. Jany 1.	To a 7 Inch Lock & 2 Keys Engine Door at Mr Birches	: 6 :
	To a pair of Scarlett stockings the Beadle[2]	: 5 : 6
	To Whitehead two pair of Shoes D°...	: 12 :
2nd	Ann Simmons & 2 Children to Whitehaven	: 1 : 6
	Mary Sutton & Child to Derby ...	: 1 :
	Caleb Jones Wife & 3 Children to Mansfield	: 2 :
	To Joseph Shulton Cleaning the Bridge Steps	: 4 :
3.	Marriane Gregory & Child to Oswestry	: 1 :
4.	John Carter a pair of Stockings ...	: 4 : 6
	James Johnson & Phillip Farrar, confined two days for Rioting in Withy Grove, Enlisted	: 4 : 9
5.	To a Coroners Inquest at Royal Oak	: 3 : 6
	Ann Mason to Whitby	: 1 :
	Martha Lees & 5 Children to London releived by Order of Dr Mainwaring[3] with	: 5 :
	Sarah Johnson & 2 Children to Coventry	: 1 : 6
	John Wilson and Wife to Newcastle	: 1 :

---

[1] See p. 255, note 1.   [2] See p. 88, note 2.   [3] See p. 218, note 2.

	Owen Williams Wife & 2 Sons to Anglesea	: 2 : 6
[Jan.] 6.	Mary Metheringham & 2 Children to Boston...	: 2 :
	Permitt Pass for Dº	: 2 :
	Margaret Carr & 3 Children to Hull...	: 2 :
7.	Ann Coggill, & Jane Allen to Ireland	: 2 :
	John Bradley & Child to Liverpool...	: 1 :
	Ann Dorricott to Wellington	: 1 :
8.	Mary Walton & 2 Children to Newcastle	: 1 : 6
	Eliza. Buchannan & 2 Children to Edinburg	: 1 : 6
	Eliza. Falconer to Folkstone	: 1 :
	Two new Keys to the Dungeon Door	: 7 :
	M. Parker & 2 Children to Blakburn	: 2 :
9	Three pair of Dble Handcuffs 6 6 ...	: 19 : 6
12.	24 Baskets Coals to the Guard Room	: 12 :
14.	Ann Shepherd & Child to Liverpool	: 1 : 6
	Janes [sic] Harris to Kendall	: 1 :
	Susan Nield & 3 Children to Edinburgh	: 2 : 6
15.	To a Doz Candles Guard Room ...	: 6 : 4
	To 2 Small Keys Lower Dungeon ...	: 1 :
	Eliza Douglas & Child to Hull ...	: 1 : 6
	Francis Smith, Wife & Child to Wallingford	: 2 :
	Eliza. Ridgworth to Derby	: 1 :
16.	To 21 Ruled Books for Numbering the Militia à 1/3	1 : 6 : 3
	To Writing two Duplicate lists of Dº	2 : 2 :
	To two qʳ ruled folio's for Dº	: 4 :
	To James Carter, John Humphreys, & James Dawson, For Surveying the Town for Dº	6 : 6 :
	To liquor at the White Bear¹ & Royal Oak, by order of the Justices when the Militia was Balloting	2 : 3 : 4
17.	Nicholas Wilson & Child to York ...	: 1 : 6
	Martha Jones & Jane Davies to Flint	: 2 :

¹ This Manchester inn is here mentioned, I think, for the first time.

19.	John Thomas & 2 Children to Brecknock	:	2	:
20.	Cleaning Dungeon, Fresh Straw &c	:	5	:
	Mathew White, wife & 4 Children to Grimsby	:	3	:
	Ann Hewit to Prescott	:	1	:
21.	Mary Lloyd & 5 Children to Denbigh	: 3 : 6		
	Sending to Stockport to get a Warrant Backed	:	2	:
	The Clerks fees for Dº	:	1	:
	To Ale for 2 Men who were assisting the Watch	: 1 : 6		
	John Stott & 5 others confined for breaking Windows and other disorders 2 Days, Sent to prison	:	12	:
23.	Paid Mʳ Alsop's[1] Bill for privy Watch	: 15 : 4		
	Amelia Greenwood & 2 Children to Warwick	: 1 : 6		
24.	Thoˢ Thornally Confined 3 Days at the Sun[2]	: 4 : 6		
24.	John Castleton, Wife & Child to Norfolk	: 1 : 6		
27.	Edwᵈ Mollyneux to Brighthelmstone	:	1	:
	Sending a Man, his Wife & 7 Childⁿ to Mottram...	: 10 : 6		
	To Maintenance One Night	: 3 : 9		
28.	To a Hanging for Star Chamber[3] at Packhorse	: : 10		
	To two Stock locks & 2 Staples Dungeon Lower Door	: 3 : 4		
29.	To painting Lamp posts in Church Yard	:	5	:
	John Barker & Wife to Chester ...	:	1	:
	Betty Williams & Child to Mold ...	: 1 : 6		
Febʸ 1.	William Gordon & James Anderson to Glasgow	:	2	:
	Margaret Dennison to Liverpool ...	:	1	:
	Elizabeth Bolsover to Hull	:	1	:

[1] See p. 327, note 3.

[2] See p. 269, note 2.

[3] This is a curious entry, referring to the "Star Chamber" at the Packhorse Inn, in Manchester. At this inn, as at the Sun Inn, there was a room or rooms in which prisoners were temporarily confined. (See p. 269, notes 2 and 3.)

[Feb.] 2.	Mary Rigby & 2 Children to Ormskirk	: 1 :	6
	Ann Wild to Ashby de la Zouch ...	: 1 :	
3.	Rachel Scott, begging in the streets confined as a Lunatic 5 Days at the Sun[1] by the Justices's order	: 10 :	6
	Shift, Petticoat, & Shoes for D° ...	: 5 :	10
5.	John Duke to Newcastle	: 1 :	
	W[m] English, Wife, & 2 Children to Perth	: 2 :	6
7.	Susannah Hilliard, to Worcester ...	: 1 :	
18.	Mathew Happess, Wife & 3 Children to Suffolk, Ill	: 3 :	6
	Permitt pass for D°	: 2 :	
	John Woodward, Wife and two Children to Canterbury	: 2 :	6
12.	John Higginbotham, Confined by M[r] Bradshaw,[2] 2 days	: 3 :	
	Charles Donnelly to Ely	: 1 :	
	Esther Grimshaw to Garstang	: 1 :	
13.	Peter Unwin & Wife to Warwick ...	: 1 :	6
	John Stephens to Compton	: 1 :	
15.	John Gibson confined at the Pack-horse[3] two nights For abusing his Wife	: 3 :	6
	Sarah Lee to Coventry	: 1 :	
	John Vernor to Gloucester	: 1 :	
17.	Rich[d] Wild, Wife & 3 Children to Liverpool	: 2 :	6
	John Walker Confined one night, Sent to Prison	: 1 :	6
18.	Ann Balsover to Cork	: 1 :	
	To the Bellman, crying down throwing at Cocks[4] twice	: 3 :	
19.	William Davies & Wife to Plymouth	: 1 :	
	John Finney to Carlisle	: 1 :	
20.	To Window Stanchens at the Sun[5] (Strait)	: 14 :	4½
	To D° (Piked) ...	1 : 1 :	8
	Holdfasts, fixing & Nails	: 2 :	6

[1] See p. 269, note 2.   [2] See p. 211, note 1.
[3] See p. 341, note 3.   [4] See p. 66, note 1.
[5] These were evidently to guard the windows in the room or rooms at the Sun Inn, where the prisoners were confined. (See p. 269, note 2.)

	To Window Stanchens at the Pack-horse[1] (Piked)	: 18 :	9
	To Holdfasts & Fixing	: 1 :	6
	Locks & Keys for Star Chamber[2] Doors	: 2 :	6
23.	Letitia Heap & Ann Cooley to Edinburgh	: 2 :	
	John Thompson, Wife & 2 Children to Whitehaven	: 2 :	6
	Mary Moor to York	: 1 :	
24.	Paid Money Warrant to M[r] Jones ...	6 : 8 :	10
26.	William Morton & Wife to Stockport, permit pass...	: 3 :	
28.	To confinement of 8 Girls from Sat: to Monday at the Sun,[3] & 7 Men the same time at Packhorse[4]	1 : 5 :	6
	To three Men Assisting in apprehending the above	: 6 :	
	To the Beadle Whipping Six of the most Abandoned[5]	: 12 :	
28.	Coroners Inquest at the Blue Boar[6]...	: 3 :	6
	Cleaning the Dungeon & Fresh Straw	: 5 :	
Mar 1.	John Unsford Confined two nights ...	: 2 :	6
2.	Ellen Hayes to Birmingham & Permit pass	: 3 :	
3.	Benj. Wood Wife & 2 Children to Lincoln	: 2 :	
5.	A Woman Confined for abusing her Child	: 2 :	6
	Ann Woolner & 3 Children to Doncaster	: 2 :	
6.	Joseph Hulme Confined one Night, Sent to prison	: 1 :	6
7.	Margaret Butterworth to Oldham ...	: 1 :	
	John Brown & Wife to Cumberland	: 1 :	6
	Elizabeth Walker to Aire...	: 1 :	
8.	John Wood & Wife to Dumbar ...	: 1 :	6
	Thomas & Edw[d] Cartwell to Lincoln	: 1 :	6

---

[1] These were for the same purpose as those at the Sun Inn. (See p. 342, note 5.)
[2] See p. 341, note 3.   [3] See p. 269, note 2.   [4] See p. 269, note 3.
[5] This is the largest number of women recorded as being whipped at any one time.
[6] This inn is here named for the first time.

[March] 9.	Sarah Dungannon & 4 Children to Sutton St Edmunds	: 2 :	6
11.	A Load of Coals to the Guard Room	: 10 :	
	A doz of Candles to Dº	: 6 :	4
13.	Jane Petty to Liverpool	: 1 :	
	Jane Leveck to Tideswell...	: 1 :	
14.	Richd Walthy, Wife & Child to Horsley Green	: 1 :	6
	Mary Bolton to Burnley	: 1 :	
15.	James Edwards & Wife to Carnarvon	: 1 :	6
	John Jones & 2 Children to Hollywell	: 1 :	6
16.	Ann Worrall & 2 more Girls Confined 2 Days...	: 7 :	6
17.	Anna Creed & Child to Liverpool ...	: 1 :	6
	To the Bellman Crying Dragoons[1] coming in	: 2 :	
	Two lads confined upon Suspicion of Felony 2 days	: 5 :	6
	Conveying them to Liverpool	: 11 :	9
19.	Eliz. Murphey & 3 Children to Ireland	: 2 :	
	A Lad from Sheffield, enlisted, but being an Apprentice Capt. Horsfall gave him up, confined two days ...	: 3 :	6
	To 3 Silver Caps, engraving & fixing to Small Truncheons[2]	2 : 0 :	9
	To Painting Dⁿ Arms &c[2]	1 : 10 :	6
20.	Delivering assize presentments Horse hire &c	: 5 :	6
21.	John Silver, Wife & 3 Children to Canterbury...	: 2 :	6
22.	A Coroners Inquest at Flying Horse[3]	: 3 :	6
	To 2 Men bringing a Child from Dolefield[4] Found Dead there, Liquor & other expences	: 5 :	6

---

[1] In the *Mercury* for March 19th it is stated that "Yesterday the first Division of ne Earl of Pembroke's Regiment of Dragoons, marched from hence and this Day the second Division marches for the South." It is not stated what regiment supplied their place in the town.

[2] These three truncheons, mounted in silver and embellished with the arms of the town, were probably the official insignia of the Boroughreeve and the two Constables.

[3] This inn has been mentioned before. (See p. 330, note 4.)

[4] It is stated in the *Mercury* of March 26th that on "Thursday morning last [March 21] a new born Male Child was found wrapped in a Woollen Apron, near the River Side at the bottom of Dolefield in this Town."

23.	To Mr Bew for Opening the Child &c	1 :	1 :	
	Margaret Smith confined upon Suspicion of the Said Murder, till the Coroner was Satisfied	:	6 :	6
25.	To Jury Summoned Again	:	3 :	6
	Ann Wharton to Wolverhampton ...	:	1 :	
26.	Margaret Williams & 3 Sons to Hereford	:	2 :	
	Ann Worrall, Confined under a Warrant	:	1 :	6
	Nan Kenna, Poll Foster & 2 More Whores at the Packhorse 2 Days for Cutting Barkleys Nose &c	:	10 :	
27.	Paid Mrs Scholfield Rent for Powder Room	4 :	4 :	
28.	D^o Prescott[1] advertising Contributions	:	6 :	6
	D^o D^o 500 Bills Lamps Broke & Delivering	:	6 :	
	D^o advertising Counterfeit Copper twice	:	8 :	
30.	Thos Meadowcroft & Saml Briscoe Sent under a Warrant to Mr Rasbotham[2]	:	3 :	6
Ap 2.	John Clark, Wife & 2 Children to London	:	2 :	6
3.	Esther Siggars to Newbury	:	1 :	
4.	Mary Pearson to Reading...	:	1 :	
6.	John Wood, Wife & Child to Rudson Yorkshire	:	2 :	
	Richard Thompson Wife & Child to York	:	2 :	
	Expences taking Henry Jordan, Wife to Hope[3] & Bringing them from thence to Prison...	:	7 :	6
	D^o Again there for further Examination	:	6 :	
8.	Cleaning the Dungeon, Fresh Straw &c	:	5 :	
10.	A Load of Coals to the Guard House	:	9 :	6
	1 Doz Candles to D^o...	:	6 :	4

---

[1] See p. 238, note 1.   [2] See p. 324, note 4.   [3] See p. 225, note 2.

12.	A Coroners Inquest at the Sawyers Arms[1]...	: 3 :	6
13.	The Jury Sat Again ...	: 2 :	
14.	Ann Marshall & 2 Children to Durham	: 2 :	
	William Guest to Dudley...	: 1 :	
16.	Mary Harrington & 6 Children to Ireland	: 4 :	
	Jane Downes to Bridport ...	: 1 :	
17.	John Burgess, Wife & Child to New-castle ...	: 2 :	
	James Brown & 2 Children to Carlisle	: 1 :	6
19.	To 3 Men 4 Nights upon Privy Watch	: 12 :	
	Martha Connor & Child to Ireland...	: 1 :	6
20.	Elizabeth Thompson to Dartmouth	: 1 :	
	Mary Downs to Biddeford ...	: 1 :	
24.	To 4 Men attending the Quarter sessions twice 3 days Each time a¹ 1 – p Day each ...	1 : 4 :	
24.	Lucy Fenton & 2 Children to Bristol	: 1 :	6
	Esther Casson, Jane White & 3 Children to Lynn ...	: 2 :	6
	To Cha* Wheeler[2] printing 500 Bills of a Burglory ad [sic] Coventry 4/6. Prescott[3] advertising twice 7/-...	: 11 :	6
25.	Elizabeth Gelmer & Child to Derby...	: 1 :	6
	Permitt Pass for D⁰ ...	: 2 :	
27.	Esther Bowbine to Westham ...	: 1 :	
	John Doronton to Holywell ...	: 1 :	
	Peter Brown to Petersfield ...	: 1 :	
28.	To Sending 2 Men under a Warrant to Col Townley[4]...	: 5 :	6
	Sue Clogger & 3 More Girls confined 2 days Committed ...	: 7 :	6
29.	James Graham, Wife & 5 Children to Cupar ...	: 3 :	6
	To the Bellman Crying lifting[5] Down twice ...	: 4 :	
May 1.	Ellen O'Casey to Ireland ...	: 1 :	
	Margaret Woods to Astenfield...	: 1 :	

[1] This inn is here mentioned for the first time.

[2] This is the first time the name of Charles Wheeler as a letterpress printer in the town, has occurred.

[3] See p. 238, note 1.   [4] See p. 255, note 1.   See p. 68, note 1.

3.	Mary Brock & 2 Children to Maccles-field	: 1 : 6
	To Lodging, Victuals &c 3 poor men	: 2 : 6
4.	To a Burns Justice[1] & a Complete parish officer[1] by order of Mr Bayley...	1 : 7 : 6
6.	Do a Sword & pair of Pistolls[2] by order of Do...	: 16 : 6
8.	James Berry & 2 other Men confined for Rioting...	: 4 : 6
	To the Bellman Crying Dragoons[3] coming in	: 2 :
10.	Mary Pickup to Rosendale	: 1 :
	John Nicholls, Wife & Child to Rotherham	: 1 : 6
12.	Sarah Lawson to Ireland	: 1 :
	Mary Hartston & 3 Children to Ireland	: 2 : 6
	A Coroners Inquest at Coach & Horses[4]	: 3 : 6
13.	Hannah Simmons & 2 Sons to Canterbury...	: 1 : 6
	Susan Nailor to Warrington	: 1 :
14.	To Bread, Cheese, & Ale for Dungeon had at Sundry times	: 7 : 10
	To Cleaning Do & Straw	: 5 :
16.	Bellman Crying Watering the Streets	: 2 :
18.	John Royle confined 3 Days by Dr Griffith...	: 3 : 9
20.	Six Girls confined at the Sun & Pack-horse, taken by ye Watch	: 10 : 6
21.	Mary Brown confined upon Suspicion of Felony by Dr Mainwaring, till she could be Examined	: 7 :
	To Cash to Jonathan Butterworth[5] to give Evidence agst Jordan at the Old Bailey...	4 : 14 : 6

---

[1] These were two well-known law books, probably purchased for the use of the town on the order of Thomas Butterworth Bayley, Esq., one of the local magistrates.

[2] It is not easy to understand by whom these should be required or by whom worn.

[3] The *Mercury* of April 30th announces that " Yesterday the first Division of the Royal Scotch Grey Dragoons arrived here from the North ; and this Day the Remainder are to come in, to be quartered here."

[4] This inn occurs here, I think, for the first time.

[5] Jonathan Butterworth was the Beadle.

23.	Judith Price & 3 Children to Ruthin	: 2 :	
	John Darbyshire confined by Mr Orme	: 2 :	6
24.	Martha Mee to Scotland	: 1 :	
	Mary Clewley & 2 Children to Church Stretton	: 2 :	
	Permitt pass for Dº	: 2 :	
27.	A Man Confined in the dungeon one Night and Then removed to the Sun	: 2 :	6
	Martha Marshall & Child to Barwick	: 1 :	6
	Hannah Robinson to York	: 1 :	
	Eliz. Bolsover to Chirk	: 1 :	
29.	William Broadhead & Wife to Lancaster	: 2 :	
	Lucy Freer to Ashburn	: 1 :	
30.	Jane & Martha Green to Bingley ...	: 2 :	
	To Thomas Guilder for Lighting a Lamp at the Corner of Marsden Street, Several Nights	: 5 :	
	A Coroner's Inquest at the Dog & Partridge[1] Milgate	: 3 :	6
June 3.	To Mr Jones a High Constables Warrant	63 : 14 :	8
	To the Beadles each a pair of Shoes	: 12 :	
	To Dº a pair of Stockings ...	: 8 :	
6.	To a Coroner's Inquest at the Dog Salford	: 3 :	6
	To the Bellman Crying Militia... ...	: 1 :	6
	Mary Harrop & 4 Children to Warrington	: 2 :	6
	Thomas Percival & Robert Moody to Hereford	: 2 :	
9.	James Berry & Sue Clogger confined one day	: 2 :	6
	Hannah Roberts to Bishopscastle ...	: 1 :	
13.	A Coroner's Inquest at the Royal Oak	: 3 :	6
	Cleaning the Dungeon & Fresh Straw	: 5 :	
	Richd Wilson, Wife & 2 Children to Maidstone	: 2 :	6
14.	Elizabeth Rogers & 2 Children to York	: 2 :	

---

[1] Yet another Manchester inn not mentioned before.

16.	To three Men two Nights upon the privy Watch	: 6 :	
17.	John Coop Wife & 2 Children to Walton	: 2 : 6	
18.	Hannah Taylor & 4 Children to Middlewich	: 2 : 6	
	To 5 Girls confined two Nights & Committed	: 11 : 6	
20.	To paid more than the County Allowance to Burton	: 7 : 9	
21.	Edward Watson and Wife to Birmingham	: 1 : 6	
	Paid Mr Alsop's[1] Bill when laying the Constable Ley	9 : 0 : 4	
	To a Ruled Book for Constable Ley	: 2 :	
	To Writing the Ley Book	1 : 11 : 6	
24.	Two Women to Wirksworth	: 2 :	
27.	Jane Howard & 2 Children to Ireland	: 1 : 6	
	Thomas Davis & Wife to Beaumauris	: 1 : 6	
30.	Three People Confined at the Sun two nights & passed	: 7 : 6	
July 2.	Thomas Godfrey & son to Newcastle	: 1 :	
3.	Peter Johnston & 2 Children to Greenock	: 1 : 6	
	Eleanor Green to Harboro'	: 1 :	
4.	William Garstang & 4 Children to Hull	: 2 :	
6.	A Coroner's Inquest at the Royal Oak	: 3 : 6	
7.	Eliza Gilmore & 2 Children to Marlboro' by order of the Justices	: 6 :	
10.	James McCullock & Wife to Aberdeen	: 1 : 6	
	Patrick Ramsey & 2 Children to Dundee	: 1 : 6	
12.	Mary Pownall & 3 Children to Gosport	: 2 :	
	Paid for Ale &c at the Sun	: 1 :	
14.	To 12 Window Surveyor's Books ruled à 1 8	1 : :	
16.	Mary Powell & 2 Children to Worcester	: 1 :	
	A Coroner's Inquest at the Griffin[2] at Broughton	: 3 : 6	

---

[1] See p. 341, note 1.   [2] This inn has not been previously mentioned.

18.	Dᵒ　　　　at the Royal Oak	:	3 :	6
19.	Betty Watkinson to Derby　... ...	:	1 :	
23.	Margᵗ Millet & 5 More Girls Confined all night Committed	:	6 :	3
27.	Cleaning the Dungeon & Fresh Straw	:	5 :	
Augᵗ 2.	Robert Davidson & Wife to Wrexham	:	1 :	6
4.	To Two Surgeons Examining a Girl Suspected to have Murdered her Child	1 :	1 :	
10.	A Coroners Inquest at the Royal Oak	:	3 :	6
15.	Going to Bolton to Deliver in assize presentments　...	:	5 :	6
16.	Patrick Murphy and James O'Connor to Ireland	:	2 :	
	Susan Clogger confined 2 Days at the Sun　...	:	4 :	
	Benjᵃ Cooper　Dᵒ at Packhorse ...	:	4 :	
19.	A Coroners Inquest at the Yew tree[1] Collyhurst	:	3 :	6
20.	To the Engine Men in full　... ...	15 :	3 :	
22.	James Martin & Son to Nottingham	:	1 :	6
23.	Edwᵈ Robinson, Wife & Child to Oxford　...	:	1 :	6
26.	Thomas Brown to Dunchurch	:	1 :	
28.	Emanuel Robinson to Morpeth　...	:	1 :	
Sepᵗ 1.	Margᵗ Edwards & Child to Wrexham	:	1 :	
2.	Two Women confined by order of Dr Griffith	:	3 :	4
4.	Jane Coe & 2 Children to Blackburn	:	1 :	6
[? Aug.] 30.	To Mr Jones for High Constables Warrant　...	74 :	3 :	5
Sepʳ 7.	William Greaves & Wife to Chesterfield　...	:	2 :	
8.	A Coroner's Inquest at the Dangerous Corner[2]　...	:	3 :	6
11.	To three Men two Nights upon the Watch	:	6 :	
	To Repairing the Exchange	3 :	3 :	
18.	To Writing three Duplicates of Freeholders &c	1 :	11 :	6
	To 3 Men two days at the Quarter sessions　...	:	6 :	

[1] This inn occurs here for the first time.　　[2] See p. 5, note 1.

		£	s	d
	Ink, Pens, & Paper for the sessions Room	:	2 :	6
19.	Bellman Crying Dragoons coming up from Grass	:	2 :	
21.	A Coroners Inquest at the Horse Shoe Pendleton	:	3 :	6
27.	To the Bellman Crying cleaning the streets	:	1 :	6
28.	Going to Mildrow [? Milnrow] sessions with a Warrant from Col. Townley,[1] & taking a Man there	:	5 :	6
Octo. 1.	Bellman crying, Walking the fair[2] ...	:	2 :	
	Edwd Edwards, Wife & 3 Children to Denbigh	:	2 :	6
2.	John Darbyshire & Son to West-minster	:	1 :	6
3.	Women to Liverpool by permitt pass from Dr Mainwaring & Dr Griffith, ordered	:	6 :	
4.	Cleaning the Dungeon &c	:	5 :	
5.	To Jonathan Foster for privy Watch	:	19 :	6
	Four Women Confined by the Watch	:	5 :	6
	To Mr Jones for High Constables Warrant	2 :	2 :	1
7.	To two pair of Shoes the Beadles ...	:	12 :	
	To two pair of Stockings D^o... ...	:	8 :	6
8.	To Quills, Ink, Paper, &c for Billets	:	7 :	9
	To Postage of Letters	:	6 :	10
	To the Music on the Kings Birth Day[3]	1 :	4 :	
11.	To Jonathan Butterworth's[4] Salary in full	10 :	0 :	
	To John Carter's,[5] D^o in full... ...	10 :	0 :	

---

[1] See p. 255, note 1.

[2] This is the first time the Acres Fair has been mentioned in these Accounts.

[3] The celebration of the King's Birthday, June 4th, this year is thus recorded in the *Manchester Mercury* of June 11th:—

"Tuesday [June 4th] being the Anniversary of his Majestys Birth-day, when he entered into the 39th Year of his Age, was observed here with Ringing of Bells at intervals during the Day. At five o'Clock in the Afternoon a Party of the Royal Lancashire Militia were drawn up at the Top of Deansgate, and fired three Volleys in Honour of the Day. The Evening concluded with a brilliant Assembly."

[4] Jonathan Butterworth was the Beadle.

[5] John Carter was the late Beadle.

	To Deputy Wilford's,[1] Salary in full...	30: 0:
28.	To M⁽ʳ⁾ Crompton for Entertainments[2]...	16:14:
Nov⁽ʳ⁾ 9.	To Edmund Wrigley repairing the Engines[3]	3:10:
Dec⁽ʳ⁾ 16.	To Tho⁽ˢ⁾ Marsden for Rent for Engine House	3: 3:
	To M⁽ʳ⁾ Bower a year's Interest on £100	5: :
	To D⁰ for Beadle's Hatt	1: 7:
	To Conveying Vagrants at Sundry times	19:13:
24.	To Lowe Bate & C⁰	8: 1:
28.	To M⁽ʳ⁾ Milne in full for Law Charges	18: 4: 8
	To M⁽ʳˢ⁾ Milward...	: 9: 6
Jan⁽ʸ⁾ 24.	Omitted John Castleton Wife & Child to Norfolk	: 1:

[Total] £750:13: 5

1776.	rec⁽ᵈ⁾ from Hamlets their 2/3 of the Bridge warrants & Salary of the Governor of the House of Correction & his Expences one 54.19.0 one D⁰ 30.7.0		
	Bradford	1. 6. 9½ ...	0:17: 4½
	Blakeley	4.18. 9½ ...	2:14: 4½
	Crumpsall	3:12: 8½ ...	1:18: 4½
	Gorton	4: 9: 1½ ...	2: 8: 6½
	Hulme...	1:12: 8½ ...	1: 1: 4½
	Drylesden	3:12: 8½ ...	1:18: 4½
	Harpur Hey ...	1: 6: 9½ ...	:17: 4
	Newton	6: 0: 3½ ...	3: 4: 1½
	Failsworth	4: 9: 1½ ...	2: 8: 6½
	Openshaw	2: 7: 6½ ...	1: 7: 9½
	Ardwick	2: 7: 6½ ...	1: 7: 9½
	Manch⁽ʳ⁾	18:14:10½ ...	10: 3: 0
		54:19: 0	30: 7: 0

---

[1] Mr. W. H. Wilford was the Deputy-Constable. (See p. 328, note 4.)

[2] These "entertainments" probably included the festivities on the occasion of the King's birthday. (See p. 351, note 3.)

[3] See p. 87, note 1.

[Receipts

P. Contra... ... ... Cʳ

1776.

			£ : s : d
	By Cash from the Old Ley book ...	108 : 17 : 6
Octoʳ 28.	By Dᵒ from the Hamlets	36 : 4 : 1½
Nov. 19.	By Dᵒ from Dᵒ	20 : 4 :
May 30.	By Dᵒ from Dᵒ	41 : 1 : 7½
Augᵗ 12.	By Dᵒ from Dᵒ	55 : 1 : 2
	By Cash from the Ley Book	305 : 0 :
	By Dᵒ from the County...	22 : 9 : 6
	By Ballance Owing the Constables ...	161 : 15 : 6

[Total]... ... ...£750 : 13 : 5

Deceʳ 28ᵗʰ 1776. We the Jurors of the Court Leet, holden for the Manor of Manchester, in the County Palatine of Lancaster, have Examined the foregoing Accᵗˢ of Mʳ Benjⁿ L. Winter, and Mʳ Thomas Chadwick (late Constables) and do allow the Same.

[*Not Signed.*]

[End of this Volume of the Accounts.]

APPENDIX No. I.

THE TRIAL OF MR. WILLIAM FOWDEN (ONE OF THE TWO CONSTABLES OF MANCHESTER IN 1745-6) AT LANCASTER IN 1747, FOR HIGH TREASON.

IN the Accounts for the year Oct., 1745, to Oct., 1746, there are several entries marked in the original volume with red ink, which, as explained on pp. 21-23, related to money paid on behalf of the "rebels," when Prince Charles Edward, the "Young Pretender," with his army, was in Manchester. These entries were subsequently brought up at the trial of Mr. William Fowden (one of the two Constables for that year) at Lancaster in 1747, for high treason, when he was honourably acquitted, it being proved that he acted as he did under compulsion and not willingly.

I am not aware that any account of this trial is to be found in *Whitworth's Manchester Magazine* (the only newspaper then published in the town) for that year,[1] so that the following curious broadside, now preserved in the Free Library, seems worthy of being here reprinted. It is obviously hurriedly drawn up and still more hurriedly printed, but in spite of the political bias displayed, it gives an interesting account of what took place, of which there is little or no other record. I have added a few explanatory words in square brackets:—

A Full and True

Account

of the

Whole Tryal, &c.

Of the Manchester Constables for high Treson before

m' Baron Reynolds at the Castle of Lancaster on

munday the 13th Day of April 1747.

Also

Of the Riot which was comitted in a Market street lane of

Manchester aforesaid upon there comming to go home.

That the town of Manchester is a most notoryous Place there is none but Jacobits and Prisbitterians will offer to dispute; the rebbles in there progres to Darby and back agen had so infeckted it with disafection that no Execvtions prossecutions imprisenments Whippings and the like of its Inhabitents have been able to cure

---

[1] The incomplete set of Whitworth's newspaper in the Free Library is deficient of the very number in which the trial would be noticed, if at all.

them of there romish Shupersticions and idollatrees. This wicked
town is said to be guverned by a depity [*sic* for Boroughreeve][1] and
2 Constables who were all 3 of them sent vp to London and so to
Lancaster Jale by means of some worthy Persens who were desirous
of Pease and Quiet, and [of securing] the libberty and Propperty of
their Neigbors, for high Treson, and Notwithstanding 2 of them
found means to get them Selves descharged by bribeing as is suposed
one M*r* Muckinfield [? Robert Dukinfield, Esq.] to give them a
good carricter, yet the other [M*r* William Fowden] together with
M*r* Theoculus Ogden of Oldam were both [of] them by the vigillence
of his magisties Justices and others of the Coran [Quorum] after a
long and tedious Confinement tried for there Lives, and very narroly
escaped for want of Evidence it hapning unfortvnatly that Thomas
Dex the Cheef [witness] of [*sic* for against] them an honest
Drummer both for his magistie and the Pretender and so a
propper witnes [of] what was done by the rebbles Behavier, for want of
better Instructions perjured him Self most Shamfully in open
Court, and the Rest not comming vp to what was hoped for being
but mean Persens of no Capasity the country being so disafeckted
that Nobody of any carricter would appeer agenst them. And so
the Jvry finding that what they had been gilty of was by meer force
and Compultion without going from the barr immediatly Ackwitted
them, and the Judge being a persen of two mild a Dispositian for
these Tempestious times declared that he never knew a more Un-
christian Prossecution.

Now as they were comming to go home to there own Houses
being attended by several of there Frends a horsback an Offiser of
his Magistics army being in the [Market] street lane leading to the
Constables House and heering a rioutous Shouting for joy among
the townspeeple that they were comen of [*sic* for home] drew his
Sword and said that he would kill the first Man that should stur any
further and made a push at several persens and wounded some of
them whereupon one of them assalted him violently by force in the
middle of the said [Market] street lane and laid him on one side
upon his Back whereupon the Company went forwerd and All was
Quiet. only the Officer lost his las't [laced] Hat and the Silver hilt
of his Sword which whether it was found agen or not will appear
when this horrid Insult upon a Gentleman in the Execvtion of his
Offis comes to be inquired into.

Finis.

---

[1] It is, however, possible that this may be intended for the two Constables and the
Deputy-Constable.

APPENDIX No. II.

CONTRIBUTIONS FROM THE GENTRY AND MERCHANTS OF MANCHESTER AND SALFORD TO PUT DOWN RIOTS, &c., IN 1749.

THE following document has a special interest for this volume of Accounts, which contains so many references to food riots and other disturbances in Manchester and the neighbourhood. By it all the principal inhabitants of Manchester and Salford agreed to contribute towards a fund, by means of which those persons who incited and encouraged such riots and disturbances might be punished. The names of the contributors to this fund are appended, and supply a list of the chief inhabitants of the two towns in the middle of the last century. The original document is in my possession, and it has never been printed before :—

Whereas many great Riots Tumults and disorders have of late arisen and been committed by some evil disposed persons within the Townships of Manchester and Salford to the great disturbance of the peace of the said Townships and to the great terror and danger of the Inhabitants thereof

And Whereas such Offenders are greatly encouraged in their wicked and disorderly practices by the impunity they too often meet with occasioned partly by the poverty and inability of the more imediate Sufferers to prosecute and bring to justice such Offenders and partly by the Connivance if not the encouragement of those whose duty it is to restrain and suppress such disorderly practices

Now know all men by these presents that for the better and more effectual puting a stop to such Riots Disorders and abuses and for restoring the peace quiet and security of the said Townships and the Inhabitants thereof We whose names are hereunder written being Inhabitants or Landowners of the said Townships of Manchester and Salford do promise and agree to pay upon demand into the hands of Sir Thomas Grey Egerton Barronet Edward Greaves Esquire John Houghton Esquire John Dickenson Robert Livesay Otho Cook Joseph Bancroft Roger Sedgewick and James Massey

Gentlemen or some of them the several and respective sums set over against our names for the better carrying on and supporting such prosecutions as aforesaid in manner hereafter mentioned

𝕬𝖓𝖉 we do hereby authorize and impower them the said Sʳ Thomas Grey Egerton Edward Greaves John Houghton John Dickenson Robᵗ Livesay Otho Cook Jo: Bancroft Roger Sedgewick and James Massey or any five or more of them from time to time as there shall be occasion by with and out of the moneys so subscribed or so much thereof as shall be necessary to prosecute criminally as Councel shall advise all such person or persons as they shall from time to time upon enquiry or Information find or have reason to believe have been or hereafter shall be guilty of any Riots Tumults disorders or abuses in prejudice or disturbance of the peace of the said Townships or of the Inhabitants thereof And for that purpose to demand and receive from us the several Subscribers hereto the several sums so respectively subscribed or so much thereof as shall from time to time be necessary for the carrying on and maintaining such prosecutions rateably and proportionably according to the several sums by us respectively subscribed

𝕴𝖓 𝖂𝖎𝖙𝖓𝖊𝖘𝖘 whereof we have hereunto set our hands this third day of May in the year of our Lord one thousand seven hundred and forty nine [1749].

(Signed)

Edward Byrom	... 15 . 15 . 0	John Robinson	... 10 . 10 . 0
John Lees ...	... 10 . 10 . 0	James Wroe ...	... 10 . 10 . 0
Rob: Booth ...	... 10 . 10 . 0	Benj. Makin ...	... 10 . 10 . 0
Edwᵈ Greaves...	... 10 . 10 . 0	J. Cooke	... 10 . 10 . 0
Robᵗ Livesey ...	... 10 . 10 . 0	Henry Hindley	... 10 . 10 . 0
John Dickenson	... 10 . 10 . 0	John Gatliff ...	... 10 . 10 . 0
James Liptrott	... 10 . 10 . 0	James Chadwick	... 10 . 10 . 0
Otho Cooke ...	... 10 . 10 . 0	Thomas Taylor	... 10 . 10 . 0
J. Greaves ...	... 10 . 10 . 0	Edwᵈ Markland	... 10 . 10 . 0
Wᵐ Starkie ...	... 10 . 10 . 0	Robᵗ Ayrton ...	... 10 . 10 . 0
Joseph Bancroft	... 10 . 10 . 0	Tho: White ...	... 10 . 10 . 0
Tho : Parrott ...	... 10 . 10 . 0	Richard Hall ...	... 10 . 10 . 0
Robert Gartside	... 10 . 10 . 0	James Wroe ...	... 10 . 10 . 0
Jnᵒ Fletcher ...	... 10 . 10 . 0	Samˡ Goodier ...	... 10 . 10 . 0
Charles Downes	... 10 . 10 . 0	John Bell ...	... 10 . 10 . 0
Chaˢ Newdigate	... 10 . 10 . 0	Lawrance Taylor	... 10 : 10 : 0
Edwᵈ Borron & Cᵒ ...	... 10 . 10 . 0	Richard Barton	... 10 . 10 . 0
Thoˢ Phillips ...	... 10 . 10 . 0	Joseph Heywood	... 10 . 10 . 0

Ja' Bateman ...	... 10.10.0	Sam' Riding ...	... 10.10.0
John Broome...	... 10.10.0	Wm Harrison ...	... 10.10.0
Jn° Hawkswell	... 10.10.0	James Greatrex	... 10.10.0
Jam' Blinkhorn	... 10.10.0	Tho' Barlow ...	... 10.10.0
Avery Jebb ...	... 10.10.0	Will Barlow ...	... 10.10.0
John Clough ...	... 10.10.0	Cha' Bramell Junr ...	10.10.0
Sam' Edgley ...	... 10.10.0	Rob' Barlow ...	... 10.10.0
Tho: Green ...	... 10.10.0	Sam' Hall ...	... 10.10.0
Jn° Heywood ...	... 10.10.0	Richd Gorton ...	... 10.10.0
Tho: Boardman	... 10.10.0	John Upton ...	10:10.0
Richd Holme ...	... 10.10.0	Tho: Dunnington ...	10.10.0
James Clough...	... 10.10.0	Hugh Holt ...	... 10.10.0
Thomas Holme	... 10.10.0	Walker & Taylor ...	10.10.0
Tho' Stott ...	... 10.10.0	Jos^h Boardman	... 10.10.0
Rand' Woolmer	... 10.10.0	Richard Assheton ...	10.10.0
Daniel Woolmer	... 10.10.0	Adam Bankes...	... 10.10.0
James Edge ...	... 10.10.0	Thomas Moss...	... 10.10.0
Goodwin Oates	... 10.10.0	Wm Shrigley ...	... 10.10.0
J° Bullock ...	... 10.10.0	John Clayton ...	... 10.10.0
Ra: Woolmer...	... 10.10.0	Tho' Aynscough ...	10.10.0
Ja' Horton ...	... 10.10.0	Ashton Lever...	... 10.10.0
John Cotgreave	... 10.10.0	Wm White ...	... 10.10.0
Miles Bower Junr	.. 10.10.0	William Thackeray..	10.10.0
Tho' Grey Egerton...	10.10.0	John Hardman	... 10.10.0
Rob' Feilden ...	... 10.10.0	Tho' Arrowsmith ...	10.10.0
R. Sedgwick ...	... 10.10.0	Dan' Whittaker & Co.	10.10.0
Jam' Marsden...	... 10.10.0	James Massey...	... 10.10.0
Sam' Walker ...	... 10.10.0	R. Davenport...	... 10.10.0
Kenrick Price...	... 10.10.0	Ja' Berwick ...	... 10.10.0
Josiah Nichols	... 10.10.0	Jona° Patten ...	... 10.10.0
John Wilson ...	... 10.10.0		

APPENDIX No. III.

The Riot in Manchester on June 7th and 8th, 1757.

THE first riot which attained any serious dimensions, and which is mentioned in the foregoing Accounts, took place on June 7th and 8th, 1757. It will be found referred to on p. 100. The following account of what then happened is taken from Harrop's *Manchester Mercury* of June 7th to June 14th, 1757, and seems to be a trustworthy and accurate account of what actually took place. It is an interesting narrative, and gives a vivid picture of the way in which the riot was effectually stopped—for the time at any rate.

It was alleged at the time that Messrs. Bramall and Hatfield, millers, whose shops had been broken into, had been deceiving the public by mixing beans and whiting with their flour. This they indignantly denied in a long statement addressed to the High Sheriff, James Bayley, Esq., of Withington, which was printed in the *Manchester Mercury* of June 21st, 1757. It is, however, too long to be reprinted here.

"MANCHESTER JUNE 13 1757

"*The following Account of the late Riot here, will we hope, be acceptable to our Readers, as it is collected with the greatest Impartiality.*

"On Tuesday last [June 7th], two Women cheapening some Potatoes in the Market, and the Seller asking what they thought an unreasonable Price, they, without further Ceremony, overturned their Sacks, and scatter'd the Potatoes abroad, which the Boys and Women near, seized and carried away.

"Encouraged by this, and joined by more Rabble, they directed their Way to the Meal-House, which they entered, and began to Plunder, but by the Resistance of the Owners of the Meal, and the Magistrates of the Town, assisted by the principal Inhabitants, they were drove away, except a few who were made Prisoners in the Meal-House, the Doors whereof were secured.—A Part of the dispersed Rioters, joined by some others near Ardwick-Green, stopped a Cart coming to Market, and plundered it of eight Loads of Meal.

"The Magistrates discharged their Prisoners out of the Meal-House, after two Hours Confinement, with Admonitions to retire peaceably to their respective Homes; instead of observing which Advice, they re-assembled, grew more numerous and insolent, broke the Windows and into the Shop of one Bramhall, a Corn-factor and Corn-Chandler at Hide's-Cross, carried off his Bread, &c. and abused his Wife, who was forced to fly to avoid worse Usage.— The Officers of the Town seized two Women, who they had but just before discharged from the Meal-House, and imprisoned them in the Dungeon, on Salford-Bridge. The Rioters continued together and meeting with no Opposition they marched to the Dungeon, and with large Forging Hammers, broke down Part of the Wall, threw the Door into the River, and carried off the two Women in Triumph.

"Flushed with their Success, and having tasted the Sweets of Plunder, they directed their Course to the Warehouse of the same Bramhall, situate in Toad-lane, broke it open, and began to carry away Grain, Flower [sic for Flour], Meal, Cheese, and here continued plundering.

"The Magistrates and principal Inhabitants of the Town immediately assembled, and came to a Resolution to repel Force by Force, armed themselves with stout Sticks, directed their Servants to be in Readiness, and a Number moved down to the Toad-lane, and in a few Minutes dispersed the Mob, and by their Vigilance and Activity, secured the Peace of the Town all that Night.

"This being Market-Day, and the Traders and Market People chiefly returning Home about eight or nine o'Clock, when the Mob was the most outrageous, an Account of it was soon circulated through the Country, and very possibly with Additions; for on Wednesday Morning [June 8th] some Colliers at Clifton, (about four Miles to the N.W. in the Road to Bolton) assembled and came forwards to join the Rioters.—About nine an Account was receiv'd of their coming, and Fame multiplied their Numbers.

"The Town was greatly alarmed, and while a Force was collecting to oppose them, a Party slipped over Salford Bridge, and through the Hanging-Ditch. What young Gentlemen and Tradesmen were assembled, immediately pursued them, and five or six of the nimblest out-stripping the others, came up with the Colliers at Shude-hill, took two Prisoners, (who were handsomely drubbed and turned out again) and fairly drove off the rest, who fled towards Oldham and Ashton.

"Apprehensive least these escaping should Influence the Oldham Colliers, Persons on Horseback were dispatched, who soon returned, with an Account, that by the prudent Conduct of Thomas Percival, and Edward Gregge, Esq" all Danger from that Quarter was prevented.

"About three o' Clock, James Bayley, Esq ; our worthy High Sheriff, came into Town from his Country Seat, attended by fifty of his Tenants, Neighbours and Friends, well armed.—He was receiv'd at the Cross with loud Acclamations.—In about an Hour after his Arrival, he on Horse-back, preceded by a Vanguard of three or four Hundred armed with stout Sticks, immediately followed by sixty Gentlemen armed with Muskets and Swords, and in the Rear by eleven or twelve Hundred, armed promiscuously with Guns, Swords, and Clubs, traversed all the principal Streets in and Avenues to the Town ; and stopping in several Parts of the Town, in a very concise elegant Manner, at each Place explained the Inconveniences that must necessarily arise to the Poor from Tumults, with proper Observations on the Dangers consequent.

"This done they disbanded, and at a Meeting in the Evening, a Resolution was taken to appoint a Number of Special Constables.

"On Thursday Morning [June 9th] they were appointed, and thirty of them on Friday Morning [June 10th] mounted Guard, well armed.   Centinels were fixed at all the Entrances into the Town, and regularly relieved every two Hours.   This Guard was continued, and effectually preserved the Peace of the Town till the Arrival of my Lord Albemarle's Dragoons, who came here last Night [June 12th], and this Morning relieved it.

"The Management of the Defence of the Town has been wholly under the Direction of the HIGH SHERIFF, in which he has shown uncommon Resolution and Judgment.   The Magistrates have properly exercised their Authority, and the Gentlemen in and out of Trade, assembled for this Defence, have given Proofs of a Conduct which will always entitle them to the grateful Acknowledgments of all those who have any Property in, or wish well to the Peace of the Town of Manchester."

APPENDIX No. IV.

THE GREAT RIOT IN MANCHESTER ON THE 15TH NOVEMBER, 1757, GENERALLY KNOWN AS "THE SHUDE-HILL FIGHT."

SOME five months after the riot described in the last few pages (Appendix No. III.), a far more serious one occurred on Tuesday, the 15th Nov., 1757. An account of the events prior to this disturbance was given in the *Manchester Mercury* of Nov. 8th to Nov. 15th, 1757, but the more full account, which no doubt appeared in the following week's paper, is unfortunately now not available, owing to the second sheet of that paper having been torn out of the bound volume of the *Mercury* for that year, in the set preserved in the Chetham Library. By this theft on the part of some unprincipled individual, who has had access to these unique volumes in that library, the description of an interesting episode in the past history of Manchester seemed to be entirely lost. I have, however, been fortunate enough to meet with a very full and accurate account of this riot, which is contained in *Whitworth's Manchester Advertiser and Weekly Magazine* for Nov. 15th to Nov. 22nd, 1757,[1] the most complete set of this paper now known having recently been acquired by the Free Library.[2] This account by being here reprinted will be preserved to posterity, should any similar accident happen to this newspaper. Whitworth's paper was the rival of Harrop's, but, unlike the latter, no complete set is now known to be preserved anywhere, only a few volumes and a few single examples of that paper being now available.

"MANCHESTER, *November* 21 [1757].

"The late Riots and Disturbances within the Town of Manchester, having been the Subject of much Conversation, the Publick may depend upon the following Account to be as authentick and impartial as can be collected.

---

[1] A copy of this paper for this very week has also fortunately been preserved by being bound up with two or three nearly complete volumes of *Adam's Weekly Courant*, printed at Chester, and until I knew of the incomplete set of *Whitworth's Manchester Advertiser*, now in the Free Library, Manchester, I considered this copy as unique, and I had the narrative given in the text transcribed, so that it should not be lost. See p. 101, note 1.

[2] This is the set formerly in the possession of the late James Crossley, Esq., F.S.A., and referred to in Harland's *Manchester Collectanea* (Cheth. Soc.), vol. ij., p. 106.

"On Saturday the 12ᵗʰ Instant, several Persons from the Town and Neighbourhood of Ashton-under-Line, armed with Clubs and Sticks, came in a riotous Manner to the Town of Manchester, and advanc'd to the Meal-House, at the top of Market-street-Lane, which occasion'd a great Hurry and Tumult. The High Sheriff,[1] and a considerable Number of the Gentlemen of the Town, being apprized of their coming, assembled in St. Ann's Square, and gave Orders to the Lieutenant of the Invalids[2] to draw up his Men, and march them towards the Meal-House, that they might be at Hand, to prevent or suppress any Disturbances; the High Sheriff and several Gentlemen, advanc'd with the Invalids, and coming up to several of the Rioters, they offered to seize them; but the Rioters making Resistance, several Blows ensued; however the Scuffle soon ended, and 12 or 14 of the Rioters were seized; the rest either went off, or dropping their Sticks retir'd among the Crowd; the Prisoners were conducted by the Invalids to the Dungeon, and there secur'd, but were all discharg'd in the Evening, on finding Securities, who entered into Recognizances with them for their personal Appearance at the next Quarter-Sessions; except one Person, who could not procure Bail then; but on Monday Morning after he likewise found Securities, entered into the like Recognizance, and was thereupon also discharg'd. In the same Evening several of the Town's Mob paid a Visit to Travis Mill; but on firing a few Guns, loaded with small Shot, from the Mills, they immediately dispers'd. Reports were received on Sunday and Monday, that the Rioters were greatly dissatisfied with the Treatment they had met with, and intended another Visit with a greater Force; and the Names of several Gentlemen were mentioned, to whom they threatned Destruction; and on Monday [the 14th inst.] a considerable Body of 'em was collected in Ashton-under-Line, and in that Neighbourhood, where they forcibly took away Meal, Cheese, and other Provisions, from several Huxters, and committed many other Acts of Violence.

"On Tuesday, the Day following [15th November], they got together early in the Morning and proceeded in a very large Body to Clayton Mills, where they cut up Part of the Wear, broke the Mill-Stones and did a deal of Damage; and from thence they proceeded towards Manchester, arm'd with Sticks, Clubs, Pickaxes and other dangerous Weapons.

[1] The High Sheriff was James Bayley, of Withington, Esq., who had been so successful in putting a stop to the rioting in the previous June. (See p. 361.)

[2] The "Invalids" were a body of veteran troops, which seem to have been stationed in the town at this time, having probably been sent there from Liverpool.

"The High Sheriff, and many other Gentlemen of the Town, met in St. Ann's Square, where the Invalids were drawn up, and the Officers of several Recruiting Parties in the Town also attended, to advise and assist on the Occasion.

"Several Persons were sent out to observe the Motions of the Rioters, who brought Intelligence of their advancing towards the Town ; upon which it was judged best for the High Sheriff, and several of the Gentlemen, to go on Horseback and meet the Rioters, to know the Occasion, as well as to lay before 'em the Consequences of their proceeding in so illegal a Manner, and to pacify and dissuade 'em, if possible, from persisting therein.

"Accordingly the High Sheriff attended with several other Gentlemen went to meet the Rioters and to know their Demands. The Mob desir'd a Conference, which was granted, first to one single Person, and afterwards to a few of the Ring-Leaders, at a Distance from their main Body. They told the High Sheriff they insisted upon his giving his Bond that Oatmeal should be sold at 20s. and Potatoes at 4s. per Load, and Flower at five Farthings a Pound, for 12 Months to come. He told them it was impossible for him to oblige the Farmers to do any such Thing ; represented the bad Consequences of their Proceedings ; told them he had made it his Business to do the Poor all the Service in his Power, and shou'd be still glad to serve them as far as he legally cou'd. Incens'd by this Refusal, one of the Mob made a Stroke at him, with a Scyth fasten'd to a Pole, with this Expression, 'then G—— d—— you, you shall be the first to suffer,' whilst another endeavour'd to seize his Bridle ; but he had the good Fortune to escape unhurt.

"The other Gentlemen labour'd, by all the Arguments in their Power, to prevail upon the Rioters to return and desist from their Attempts ; but unhappily all their Efforts and Mediation, produced no better Effect, than seemingly to encourage and hasten the Approach of the Rioters ; upon which the Gentlemen retreated to the Top of Shude Hill, where the Invalids had marched and were drawn up, to prevent the Rioters from entering the Town, with several Gentlemen of the Town, who under the Direction of the High Sheriff had taken up Arms to preserve the Peace of the Town, as well as to protect their own Property.

"This Retreat of the Gentlemen was imputed to their Fear of the Rioters, and they received many Insults as they returned, from Numbers of the Inhabitants of Manchester, who attended in Crowds to observe what pass'd. Some Gentlemen of the Town, and one in Particular, continued their Applications and Intreaties to the Rioters for an Accomodation, and to prevent the impending

unhappy Consequences, till they advanced very near to the
Invalids, and even to the Points of their Bayonets, and had
stay'd longer than was consistent with their own Safety, but for
the great Calmness and Temper of the commanding Officer, who
was personally struck at, saw great Numbers of Stones and Brickbats flung amongst his Men, his Corporal kill'd, and several of his
Men bruis'd, and wounded, and one of the Mob got into his Ranks,
before he gave the Command to his Men to fire ; and he made 'em
present and level several Times before such Command was given,
to see if that last Extremety could be avoided. The commanding
Officer, having an Order sign'd by the Civil Magistrate, to justify
him in repelling Force by Force, finding that no other Means could
be of any avail, order'd his Men to fire, which was obey'd ; by
which two of the Rioters were kill'd on the Spot ; and also one
innocent Person, the Son of a reputable and substantial Farmer,
whom a fatal Curiosity had brought thither, and who stood in a Tree
near the Place where the Fray happen'd.

"A Number of Persons having lined the Hedge between this
Tree and the Invalids, and Stones and Brickbats being flung by
several of these Persons in great Quantities, many of the Invalids
fir'd at or over the Hedge, and it is suppos'd kill'd this unfortunate
young Man.

" Many Persons were also wounded and carried to the Infirmary,
of whom one is since dead, and another is in great Danger. But,
thro' the great Care and Skill that has attended this Charity, since
its Institution, the rest, its hop'd will recover ; tho' the Loss of the
Limbs of two of them will mark 'em as the unfortunate Examples
of this seditious and lawless Attempt.

"The Officers sent the Bellman about the Town, on Tuesday, long
before the Rioters came up, to desire the Inhabitants to keep in
their Houses for fear of any bad Consequences, and that the Innocent, whom Curiosity might draw together to be Spectators of what
pass'd, might not be involv'd in the same Danger with the Guilty ;
for in Mobs and Tumults its impossible to make a Distinction.

"Upon the Soldiers firing the Rioters retreated with great Pre-
cipitation ; but after it ceas'd they continued together and did not
totally disperse, but many of 'em join'd, as it is suppos'd, by
Numbers of the Inhabitants of Manchester, went down to Travis
Mill belonging to Messrs. Bramall and Hatfield, uncover'd Part of it,
and destroy'd the Stones and Tackles, plunder'd it of great Quantities
of Flour, burnt a great Quantity of Hay, gutted and damaged the
House, and pull'd down the Building belonging to Mr Hatfield,
which stood near the Mill.

"The Officers of the several recruiting Parties, seeing the Confusion things were in, offer'd to put their Men under Arms to assist the Lieutenant of the Invalids, in Case of Necessity, which was accepted by the Gentlemen of the Town; thereupon a new Guard was formed at the Bull's Head, which continued to be reliev'd regularly till Saturday, when Part of Col. Stewart's Regiment, with a great Quantity of Arms came to Town.

"In the Evening the Mob return'd to the Town of Manchester, and went to the Dungeon, but upon the coming up of a Party of Soldiers they retreated into Salford, whither a Serjeant was sent after them, to know what they wanted; which was to have one Prisoner that had been seiz'd and imprison'd there, released; and upon this being comply'd with, they promis'd to fling away their Clubs and Sticks; upon which the Prisoner was releas'd, and accordingly the Mob dispers'd and went off.

"An Express was sent away by the Gentlemen of the Town on Tuesday Night to the Secretary at War, with a Representation of what had happen'd, and to desire an additional millitary Force, which He was pleas'd to order; and in Consequence thereof a Troop of Sir Robert Rich's Dragoons are expected to arrive in Town Tomorrow [Nov. 22nd], who have Orders not only to protect the Town of Manchester, but also to suppress any Riots or Disturbances in the Neighbourhood, and to repel Force with Force whenever it may be found necessary.

"The Gentlemen of Manchester are determined to put the Laws in Execution as far as they can, against all Forestallers, Ingrossers, and Regraters of their Markets, and have publish'd an Advertisement to incourage Informations against Offenders of this kind, and will be very glad if any lawful Means they can make use of, will tend to reduce the Price of Corn, Meal, and other Provisions, and thereby afford the Poor all the Assistance in their Power; but they are equally determin'd to repell all violent Attempts to disturb the Peace and Quiet of the Town, and to put the Laws in Execution against all Persons who shall attempt to bring about by Force, what may be effected by a Course of Justice.

"The following Extracts out of Serjeant Hawkins's Pleas of the Crown, Chap. 17, Sect. 25. shew in what Light this Affair stands in the Eye of the Law, both with Regard to the unfortunate Persons who were engag'd in it, as well as the Authority by which it was repell'd and suppress'd; and there are many other Authorities to the same Purpose.

"'Those also who make an Insurrection in order to redress a public Grievance, whether it be a real or pretended one; and of

their own Authority attempt with Force to redress it, are said to
levy War against the King, altho' they have no direct Design against
his Person, inasmuch as they insolently invade his Prerogative, by
attempting to do that by private Authority, which he by public
Justice ought to do ; which manifestly tends to a downright
Rebellion; as where great Numbers by Force attempt to remove
certain Persons from the King, or to lay violent Hands on a Privy
Counsellor, or to revenge themselves against a Magistrate for
executing his Office, or to bring down the Price of Victuals, &c.'"

The rioting described in the above report excited much
apprehension in the town and neighbourhood, and was generally
known as "the Shude-hill Fight."[1] In Harrop's *Manchester
Mercury*, Nov. 22nd to Nov. 29th, 1757, it is stated that "on
Wednesday last [Nov. 23rd] a Troop of Sir Robert Rich's Regiment
of Dragoons from York; and on Friday [Nov. 25th] two Companies
of the Earl of Hume's Regiment of Foot from Derby, arrived here
in order to preserve the Peace and Quiet of the Town &c. The
same Day the Invalids quartered here marched from hence to
Liverpool."

In the next week's paper there is the following account of the
inquest held on the unfortunate people who had been killed :—

"On Tuesday and Wednesday last [Nov. 29th and 30th], the
Coroner's Inquest brought in their Verdicts, upon the Deaths of the
persons killed in the late Riots in this Town ; and with Respect to
the Corporal of the Invalids, found to be wilful Murder by Persons
unknown; and as to the others, who were engaged in the late Riots,
that they were killed thro' Necessity, in suppressing the Riots, and
preserving the peace, as well as the necessary Defence of the Persons
convened for that purpose ; and as to Mr. John Newton, the
unfortunate young Man in the Tree, that he was kill'd per infor-
tunium (thro' Accident) by a person unknown.

"Mr. James Greatrex the Younger, of this Town, was charg'd to
be the person who shot the young Man in the Tree, but the
Evidences who were examin'd against him, contradicted one another
very materially in several Circumstances, and it was proved, to the
full satisfaction of the Jury, who brought in their Verdict, That at
the Time of the Firing, Mr. Greatrex, the person charg'd, was not
either with the Invalids, or the Gentlemen who were arm'd and
drawn up at the Shude-hill, and that before the Firing, he went

---

[1] Mr. John Collier, generally known as "Tim Bobbin," printed an allegorical account
of this riot, which will be found in his works. It is entitled "Truth in a Mask or
Shude-Hill Fight : being a short Manchesterian Chronicle of the Present Times 1757."

home and dined there, at a great Distance from the place where the Firing was, and that he was met in going to and returning from Home, by persons of undoubted Character and Reputation, and that he never had any Fire Arms in his Hands after he left St. Ann's Square, about 11 o'Clock in the Forenoon, above two Hours before the Firing, which several Circumstances, with the Characters of the Witnesses, not only convinced the Jury, but also the Friends of the deceased, who attended the Inquest, that there was no Foundation to charge Mr. Greatrex as the Author of the young Man's Death."

An inaccurate account of this riot appears to have found its way into *Lloyd's Evening Post*, a well-known London paper of that period, and in the *Manchester Mercury*, 27th Dec., 1757, to Jan. 3rd, 1758, the queries[1] which had appeared in the London paper of Dec. 7th are severally answered in a long letter, signed R. R. and dated Manchester, Dec. 14th, 1757. As some of the facts there given are important, the chief portion of this reply is here reproduced.

" 1. It is an unquestionable Fact that the Corporal of the Invalids was killed, and several others knocked down with Stones, thrown by the Rioters, before a single Gun was fired ; and the Commanding Officer was personally attacked before he ordered his Men to fire.

" 2. Long before the Rioters approached the Town, the publick Crier was sent to Order the People to keep in their Houses, and the Sheriff himself desired the Rioters to disperse, informing them what would be the Consequence of their persisting : The Proclamation was ready to have been read, but the Rioters by attacking the Military, prevented the Observance of that necessary Form of Law.

" 3. The Coroner's Inquest answers this Query, to the Satisfaction of every impartial Person, that they were killed thro' Necessity in suppressing the Riots and preserving the Peace, as well as the necessary Defence of the Persons convened for that Purpose.

" 4. What is said to the first Query sufficiently proves the Falsity of this.

" 5. That the two Men killed were amongst the Rioters, and that one of them was a principal Ringleader is indisputable ; but supposing them innocent, what could be their Inducement to accompany the Rioters, when they saw an armed Force ready to receive them, who could not distinguish the innocent (if any such were amongst the Rioters) from the guilty ?

---

[1] These "queries" and the reply to them are not given in *Whitworth's Manchester Advertiser*, but in that paper for Jan. 9th, 1758, is a long statement by Messrs. Bramall and Hatfield as to the damage done to them, and indignantly repudiating the alleged adulteration of their flour. This also appears, I think, in the *Manchester Mercury*.

"6. His suggestion of the Corporal being killed by a Manchester Townsman, is as improbable as it is absolutely false ; as the few Gentlemen that were under Arms were stationed in the Rear of the Military, and the Corporal killed was in the Front Rank, so that consequently a Ball must pass thro' at least fourteen Ranks to kill him.   But what is still more convincing is, that the Soldier was knocked down before a Piece was fired, and some of his Brains seen upon the Stone that struck him.

" 8. Without doubt the Civil Magistrate was a competent judge of his own Authority in Cases of this Nature, and fully satisfied of the Legality, as well as Necessity of such Orders.

" 11. That the Rioters were invited into Town by some Towns-men of their own Party, and assured that they should only be fired at with Powder, is perhaps true ; but that any Gentleman, who was afterwards under Arms, gave them any such Encouragement, the Apologist is challenged to prove.

" 12. That the Order from L———d B———n was spurious is a most scandalous Assertion ; as it was publickly read to the Town's Gentlemen in the Coffee-house, and seen by many others.

" 13. Sergeant Hawkins's Opinion justifies the Steps taken to suppress the Riots—*Riots of all kinds, (he says) tend to downright Rebellion :* So in Course the Civil Magistrate must use all the Means in his Power to suppress them."

APPENDIX No. V.

THE RIOTING IN MANCHESTER ON JULY 12TH, 1762.

AFTER "the Shude-hill Fight" of Nov. 15th, 1757, described in Appendix No. IV., the town was apparently untroubled with any other cases of rioting or disturbances for nearly five years. But in the summer of 1762 another outbreak occurred, which, as it is alluded to in the foregoing Accounts (see page 138), seems to deserve notice here. It was not nearly so violent as the riots of 1757, but had it not been promptly checked it might have been very serious. The account here given is from Harrop's *Manchester Mercury* of July 20th, 1762 :—

"*Manchester, July* 17, 1762. On Monday last [July 12th] a great Number of disorderly Persons entered this Town, under Pretence of regulating the Prices of Grain, Flower, and Oatmeal, which had been lately very much advanced ; but instead of making any Application to the Chief, or other Magistrates for that Purpose, they avowed their Intentions to murder a considerable Dealer in Corn.—He escaped their Fury, but they instantly fell to Work, and plundered his Shop and Warehouse, of all the Grain, Flower, Beans, and Oatmeal, which they in a most odious Manner rendered unserviceable, except what was stolen and carried off ;—They robbed his House entirely of all the Furniture, and with Pick Axes, and other Instruments, which they brought in a Cart for that Purpose, destroyed the Window Frames, the Body of the House, and Part of the Front Wall, in the Course of which a Person lost his Life, by the Fall of Part of the Warehouse Furniture. Being now joined by a considerable Number of Women and Children, and a very few Townsmen, they attacked and plundered the Shop, Warehouse, and House of another Dealer in Corn, and destroyed the Window Frames there likewise. From the last Place they proceeded to the Houses and Shops of other Dealers in, and Retailers of Corn, broke into them, drank all their Liquors, and carried off[f] what Eatables they thought proper.

" Small parties of them patrolled through different Parts of the Town, and some compelled the Shopkeepers to give them Ribbands, others went into private Houses and demanded Liquors and Money, which they forced the Owners and Servants to give them. After these Outrages, the Rioters proceeded to some Mills in the Neighbourhood, which they broke into, and threw several Loads of Grain, Flower, and Meal, into the River, to render unserviceable what they could not carry away. It is computed that the Damage done on Monday by those Rioters, does not amount to less than * *One Thousand Pounds*, besides putting a total stop to all Kind of Business.

"In Consequence of Expresses dispatched to the Right Hon. the Secretary of War, and to the Commandants of the Militia quartered nearest this Place, a Corps of the Flintshire Militia arrived here [from Liverpool] on Tuesday [July 13th] in the Afternoon, and about Midnight another of the Cheshire Militia; since which, several of the Offenders have been taken up, and Information having been made against many others, Warrants are issued out for the apprehending them.

"As this is one of the most daring Insults upon the Police of a well ordered Government that has been remembered, every Method will be taken to bring the Offenders to Justice, that the Laws of this Realm have directed; and in order to enforce them, above 30 special Constables are already appointed and sworn."

The two following advertisements appeared in the same paper, and seem worthy of reproduction here :—

Manchester, July 16, 1762.

WHEREAS several Reports have been brought to us of *George Bramall*, of *Manchester*, having long made a Practice of buying Corn growing, and ingrossing Corn in an illegal Manner,

This is to give Notice,

That if any Person or Persons will appear before us, and give in such Evidence as shall enable us to convict the said *George Bramall*, of the said Practices, we will put the Laws strictly in Execution against him.

> JOHN BRADSHAW.
> JAMES BAYLEY.
> GEORGE LLOYD.

---

* "A great Part of this Damage will be recovered from the Hundred, so that the intent of the Rioters to distress the Individuals is mistaken."

Manchester, July 19, 1762.

WHEREAS it has been industriously reported, that I have frequently bought Corn standing, and ingrossed Corn unlawfully, whereby I have undeservedly sustained great Damages.

Therefore to satisfy the Publick whether I have or not been guilty of the above Practices, and to do myself Justice, I hereby offer a Reward of Five Pounds to any Person who can and will prove the same against me.

GEORGE BRAMALL.

APPENDIX No. VI.

LIST OF UNCOMMON, OBSOLETE, AND DIALECT WORDS TO BE FOUND IN THE PRECEDING PAGES.

As so much interest is now being taken in the scientific study of words and their meanings and employment in times gone by, it has been thought well to follow the course pursued in the case of the early volumes of the *Court Leet Records*, and to print here a list of the uncommon, obsolete, and dialect words to be found in the preceding pages. This list, we hope, will be found of service to many readers, and will save much time and trouble to those who may wish to consult these pages in the search of out-of-the-way words. The figure opposite each word shows the page on which it will be found, and in the case of most of the rarer words an explanation of their meaning (when it has been found possible to obtain it) will be found in the notes on the pages where the words occur.

374

INDEX.

—

Names of Persons are printed in ordinary type.
Names of Places are printed in *italics*.
References to Subjects, &c., of importance are printed in SMALL CAPITALS.

This Index contains the names of all persons mentioned in the Accounts and in the Appendices, but does not contain the names of places unless they are of importance or there is something of interest connected with them. Thus an entry, for example (p. 33), where Alexander Mordough had a pass from York to Liverpool, the man's name is indexed, but neither of the place-names.